TO HUNT A MOONBORN BEAST

The Lycanthrope Protection Agency
Book 1

CJ Ravenna

Editing by Carta's Editorial Services

Copy and line edit by Jennifer Smith

Proofreading by Lori Parks

Beta reading by Rare Bird Beta Reading

Cover designed by Danielle Doolittle | DoElle Designs | www.doelledesigns.com

First edition 2023

CONTENT WARNINGS

- On-page depictions and discussions of domestic violence

- Trauma recovery

- Graphic violence and gore

- Scenes of wolves hunting prey animals

- Prejudice and bigotry

- Mentions of past child abuse and torture that occurred off-page

I'd like to dedicate this book, this whole series, to my pack. Not just my family for their support, but every editor and beta reader who had a role in shaping this story. Thank you for all your support, feedback, and belief in my stories. Without you, this series wouldn't have been possible.

CHAPTER 1
BAD MAN

BAD MAN'S COMING.

The wolf trembled. The air was ripe with the stench of his own pitiful fear. Wide eyes strained, struggling to pierce the total darkness closing in on him.

With his loud voice that stinks of alcohol. With his belt that burns against my hide.

The floorboards squeaked beyond the pantry door. His heart raced faster than a hare on the run.

He's coming. He's coming. He's going to hurt me. He's going to kill me this time.

A growl rumbled from his throat, as loud as he could make it.

Have to fight. Have to kill. Don't hurt me. Don't hurt me.

The doorknob rattled. His tail curled between his legs. The smell of his own urine burned away the stale smell of dried, crusty blood. His blood.

"Max? Honey?"

The pale face of a woman peered in at him. Not Bad Man. Her smell was of sweat and salty tears, acidic with fear that made her blood pump fast. She was familiar. He knew her. He couldn't remember from where, but the sight of her made something warm bloom in his chest. Something comforting. Memories tugged at his mind. Her smiling face and warm arms around him. If only he could remember her...

"Max. Oh Goddess. You're feral. What did that monster do to you?" Wiping her eyes, she reached out to him. "It's okay now. I'm so sorry I couldn't find you sooner. We're leaving, I promise. He'll never hurt you again. Come here, baby. Come here, please."

The salty smell of her tears gave pause to his fury. Who was she talking to? Him?

No. She'll hit me. Hurt me. Make me bleed. I'm not Max. I'm Filthy Mutt. Like Bad Man says. A mongrel.

"Max. It's me. Don't you remember me at all?"

The door opened wider. Freedom. All he had to do was run. Go far away. He'd never be hurt again. The woman beckoned to him, but what for? To hold him, protect him?

No! No! She'll hold me down. Hurt me. Trap me.

She smiled, her eyes full of tears. Her smile spoke of love. He wanted to trust, wanted her to hold him and protect him, take him far away. She knelt and opened her arms. Waiting for him to come to her.

"I won't hurt you, baby. Please. Please, come here."

He took one step, then another, extending his snout toward her hand. Her fingers settled on his nose, gently stroking his fur. She would help him. He could trust her.

He came closer until he could smell her perfume. It was... familiar, somehow. It smelled like lunar flowers underneath a blue sky. Of safety and comfort. Home.

She motioned him toward the door, mouth trembling as she smiled. "That's it. Come on, Max. Let's go." She opened the door wider for him.

Mother. That was who she was. His mother. She'd never hurt him.

The tiles were cool beneath his paws. His mother touched his head, caressing between his ears. He closed his eyes. Hadn't she used to pet him this way? Even when he was... human. He was human. A man. That name she'd uttered was his. Max. That was right. He was Maxwell Gallagher.

He was nineteen, almost twenty. He lived in New York City. His stepdad was an asshole and his life was full of uncertainty and fear, but right now he was safe. He was loved. He was free.

Closing his eyes, he felt inside himself for the bond they shared, tattered but warm. He found it, beating along with his heart. He grasped it the way one might grab an anchor, let it pull him to shore, toward where the human in him dwelled.

"That's it, honey. Shift back. You can do it." She gasped. Gravel crunched in the driveway outside. Headlights splashed across the room. "He's coming! Max, hurry!"

Beneath her hand, his paw turned to fingers, then back to a paw. The shift wouldn't come. He was stuck. Their bond was frayed; it wasn't strong enough to bring him back. Frustration pulled a snarl from him. No! He had to shift back. He was Max. No, he was wolf... He was... What was he?

"Max, come on! You can do it. Please, please..." Her voice wavered and broke. "Find our bond. Find it and shift back!"

Max felt for the thread connecting them and grasped it tighter. His paws turned to hands, red fur rippling and receding over his arms. Almost there...

The door crashed open. A bulky shape filled the doorway. The relief in his mother's scent turned to fear, and she was knocked aside. A clawed hand clamped around the scruff of his neck, puncturing his skin. Max's paws buckled, and he collapsed against the tile.

"Richard! Get your hands off him!" His mother grabbed the man's arm.

That smell... of pungent cologne, of whiskey, of fiery anger and utter contempt. It curdled his insides, made him want to bare his fangs and bite and rip and tear and—

"Trying to run away, Maxie boy? I thought we had a connection!" Bad Man sneered. He hurled Max back into the pantry and slammed the door.

"Let him go!" His mother snarled, and then she cried in anguish. Her pained cries hurt his ears.

Max threw himself against the door, clawing frantically.

This wasn't supposed to happen. His mother was never meant to get hurt. He'd tried so hard to keep her safe. His heart sank when her cries turned to whimpers.

The knob rattled and the door opened. Max's snarling died to a whine in his throat. Bad Man had her by the throat, claws dimpling her skin. Blood matted her hair, claw marks ripping across the side of her face.

"Look at that, Maxie. She got hurt because of you. How awful. You really are nothing but trouble, aren't you?" He shoved her against the wall. She collapsed with a grunt.

The guilt had Max regressing back toward his animal instincts, the humanity in him slipping away. If she'd just stayed away, if he'd just been stronger...

The will to fight drained out of him. The wolf's feral mind sang to him, promising a sweet release from pain and guilt. He closed his eyes and the memory of his mother disappeared. He forgot his name. Why he was here.

With a whine, the wolf rolled onto his back and showed his belly in submission.

"Good mutt." Bad Man grunted, and he grabbed a chair nearby and shattered it against the floor. He wielded the chair leg and stepped into the pantry. "But don't think I'm falling for that shy, submissive act."

The chair leg flew toward his face, and blinding pain dragged the wolf into darkness.

HE WOKE TO THE smell of damp grass, raindrops heavy in his fur. He smelled him nearby, Bad Man. His paws and muzzle were bound with rope. He couldn't attack even if he wanted to.

Crickets chirped. The darkness of the countryside blinded him. Coyotes howled to the waxing gibbous moon. An engine rumbled, and headlights burned his eyes. A van rolled into the driveway, tires crunching over rocks. It was black, with curtains obscuring the windows.

One sniff sent a ripple of fear down his spine, making his fur bristle. The coppery scent of blood emanated from the van. From within, there came distressed cries and snarling.

The doors opened. The two men coming toward him looked human enough, but they weren't. Their eyes flashed in the dark, cruel smiles displaying pointed fangs. They were wolves wearing the forms of men. Werewolves.

Bad Man bared sharp white teeth. "Took your time, assholes."

"Traffic was a bitch," one of the men growled, his face hidden in shadow.

The wolf trembled as hostile eyes surveyed him.

"What's with his fur color? I ain't ever seen a werewolf with red fur like that."

Bad Man grinned as if he were proud of himself. "Oh, he's special, all right. I just know he is."

One of the shifters scoffed. "Oh yeah? He do anything 'special'?"

"Well, no," Bad Man snapped, squirming under the robed shifter's sneer. "But it's just like the stories! Red wolves have always been special. If I'd had more time with him, maybe I'd have proof."

The wolf shivered as the robed man bent close, breathing in deep and letting it out hard, hot and damp in his fur. He jumped as a cold hand lifted his paw, inspecting the pale scars that cleaved through his fur.

"This *thing*? Special? The hell are you on about? Looks like a filthy mutt with pretty fur. Throw it in the truck."

Bad Man grinned. "Hey, how's Stone doing these days? I haven't heard from him in a while. He must be busy cleaning the streets of hybrid trash. Tell him his pal Richie says hey, would you?"

"Yeah, man, whatever." One of the wolves grunted, grabbing hold of the wolf's bound paws.

"Special hybrid," the other muttered, choking on a laugh.

Bad Man bristled. "And hey, how'd he like those hybrids I sent his way?"

One of the werewolves shrugged. "Farley and the other kid? They were fine."

"Good, good. Now, if you'll excuse me, gentlemen, I've got a meddling mate to teach a lesson to." He cracked his knuckles and strode back inside.

Two sets of boots stopped in front of him. Hands fisted in his fur and lifted him, throwing him across a wide shoulder like a sack. He had a view of the interior of the van. There were three cages inside. Wide, terrified eyes gleamed at him in the dark. The stench of fear and blood-matted fur made him whimper.

The third cage was empty.

Someone. Anyone. Please. Please help me.

He tumbled into the cage, and it locked shut. The wolves whimpered in the dark, and his own voice joined theirs in a chorus of fear and despair. The car doors slammed. Darkness came for him again and this time he feared he'd never see the light again.

CHAPTER 2

CHILI AND CINNAMON

T UCKED BENEATH THE SHADOWS of the High Line that ran along Tenth Avenue, Gabriel Reyes reclined on his motorcycle, face concealed by a helmet and fingers tapping rhythmically against the metal of his bike. One hand lingered by his back pocket where his phone was, waiting for the call that had brought him out into the late hours of this warm June night.

With the exception of a few joggers getting in a late run and a few dog walkers, the streets were quiet. Dogs trotted past with their owners. One dog, a fat little pug, stopped and stared. The pug growled and barked but with one low growl from Gabe, the pug darted ahead of its owner.

The phone vibrated in his pocket and Gabe jumped to turn down the Latin pop music blaring from the speakers in his helmet. He took off the helmet and cradled it under his arm as he yanked his phone to his ear. "Ben? What's up?" Gabe yawned into the back of his fist.

Ben's usually gruff voice softened when he laughed. "Fallin' asleep, huh?"

"At ten thirty at night in this heat? No way, Viejo."

Any humor in Ben's voice was gone. "Well, wake on up. I got sights on them."

Adrenaline kicked Gabe awake. "Where?" He swung one leg across his motorbike.

"They're running along the river on Eleventh Avenue. There are police after them, so get on them—fast. They're shifted, and we all know how some cops feel about that."

The engine roared to life underneath him. "Shit." The last thing he needed was a quarrel with the police. They had no tact when it came to werewolves. He sped off toward Eleventh Avenue and flew around the corner, bumping over cobblestones as he neared the Hudson River highway. Distant sirens howled in the night. He growled. "Better leave those poor kids alone!"

He wove between speeding cars, ignoring their angry honks, and over the smell of exhaust fumes, he caught a whiff of fur matted with dirt and leaves. They couldn't be more than a mile ahead of him. Over the wind in his ears and the howl of the engines, distant screams urged him to speed up. Ahead of him was the bike path, and on the Hudson River walkway, people ran past throwing looks over their shoulders.

He was close.

Beneath the streetlamps on the walkway, two shapes hurtled along the waterfront. Eyes flashed, fangs gleamed, and moonlight rippled in dense fur. Gabe glanced at the bike path and seeing no incoming bikes, he lurched off the road and soared across the bike path. He left his bike lying on the walkway and ran, the world a blur around him as his eyes locked on his targets.

People tore past him screaming, though the wolves weren't attacking anyone. The smell of their fear was tangible, and they ran with their tails tucked, keeping to the shadows and darting away from any humans who ran by. If they were feral, at least they weren't aggressive.

The wolves ran beneath the metal awning attached to a riverfront winery. The crowd cut Gabe off, bumping into him as they hurtled past. Gabe pounced, latching onto the metal awning and pulling himself on top. Feet clanking over the metal as he ran, Gabe leaped down and landed before the wolves. They startled.

One of the two, a young female, bared her fangs. She stood protectively before the other wolf. Her sibling, perhaps? Their eyes were human shades of blue and green rather than a wolfish yellow. Thank the goddess. They were in control of their shift, not feral.

Gabe removed his helmet and it clattered to the floor. He looked them in the eyes and scented the air, smelling their fear. "Easy there, kids." He raised both hands and knelt. "I'm not gonna hurt you."

The female sniffed the air and, scenting his wolf, lowered her guard and took one tentative step toward him.

"Can you understand me?"

The wolves regarded him, still wary. Scared, but not feral. The female had a notch in her ear, and one of the male's ears was floppy. Gabe smiled, recognizing them at once. It was as he'd hoped; they were the missing twins. "Are your parents Jenny and Elizabeth?"

The female whined, tail wagging. Her brother's ears flew straight up.

"They've been looking for you all day. I'm Gabriel Reyes of the Lycanthrope Protection Agency. Your moms hired me to find you."

In a blink, the female shifted to a young girl covered in gray fur, her face partially human. "They left us!"

Gabe laughed and shook his head. "No way. They've been worried sick."

"It was his fault." She patted her brother's furry head. "He wandered off, and they didn't see."

"And you were a good sister and went after him. They'll be proud of you." Sirens cut off nearby. Gabe sighed, turning toward the highway as two officers marched over the bike path and came toward them. Oh boy...

"These your kids?" a stern-faced, mustached officer asked. "Anyone ever tell you shifting in public's illegal?"

Gabe bit back a growl. So, he was one of *those* officers. Plenty of police were on good terms with werewolves, but occasionally Gabe dealt with schoolyard bullies wearing badges. "No, Officer." He forced a smile. "Just some lost kids."

The officer leaned around him, squinting at the kids. "They gone omega?"

Anger rolled through Gabe at the outdated term. "No, Officer, they're not *feral*. Just frightened. They need to go home."

"Really now? 'Cause there's been an incident up the street in that old warehouse. Bodies ripped to pieces. These kids got nothing to do with that?"

Fury brought Gabe's fangs out. Just because wolves were feral didn't mean they were dangerous. Many were only scared and reacting the way any animal might toward a perceived threat, some with shyness and fearfulness, others with aggression to protect themselves.

But not all humans were understanding. Some simply wanted to see a monster where there was none, and Gabe wouldn't have some bigoted human mistreating innocent kids because of who they were.

"They're children, Officer," Gabe said, forcing as much patience into his voice as he could, "not wild animals. They're scared, and when werekids get stressed, they shift. It happens."

The officer in the back reached for his taser at the sight of Gabe's fangs. "They sure looked like animals a moment ago." The officer came closer with his partner.

The sister grabbed her brother's scruff and pulled him close, her small trembling hand gripping onto Gabe's leg.

"Evening, Officers." Gabe's head turned at Ben's deep voice and he huffed his relief.

Ben Stroud crossed the bike path, moonlight reflecting on his bald head, biker boots clumping as he walked with easy purpose toward them.

"Alpha Stroud!" The officer's eyes went wide, and he dipped his head in greeting. "Didn't know you were here."

Ben grimaced beneath a bushy brown beard streaked with silver. "Werewolves don't use those stupid titles unless they work for the Council."

"I… I didn't know that. Sir?" The officer tried again, raising a hand to his throat. Gabe tried not to laugh. Ben was intimidating, but he'd never bite unless he had good reason.

"Now, move it. Your daddy wants his badge back." The officers skirted to the side, eyeing him as if they thought he'd suddenly go feral and attack.

Ben stopped, peering down at the kids. His mustache twitched as he offered them a smile. His silver eyes were steely as he set his sights on the officers. "These kids were reported missing twenty-four hours ago. Their parents miss them. They're under the protection of the Lycanthrope Protection Agency. Clear?"

"Yes, Stroud. Sorry. We had no idea this guy was one of yours."

"Sure, you thought he was some irresponsible werewolf you could hassle, right?" Ben's smile showed his fangs.

The officers backpedaled. "Not at all, we—"

"Now you can clear off. And I better not catch you hassling werewolves again. Clear?" His voice got gravelly and low, and he curled his lip to show more of his fangs. The officers hurried back to their cruiser, throwing looks over their shoulders.

"Wow," the little girl whispered. Her brother rolled over, showing his belly.

Gabe hid a smile behind his hand. He wasn't afraid of Ben. He'd been a friend to Gabe's family for years. He was barrel-chested and rugged, but Gabe would always think of him as the man with whipped cream on his beard, staying up past midnight drinking hot cocoa with Gabe's baby sister when she had nightmares of their father's death.

Ben patted Gabe's chest. "Next time show 'em your badge. It's not a pretty trinket."

Gabe reclined against a streetlamp, catching his breath. "No? It brings out my eyes so nicely."

Ben chuckled, rolling his eyes, and nudged the pup to his paws. "Let's get you two home." Ben escorted them across the bike path and walked them to his truck as Gabe followed. Ben exhaled once the kids were inside, then leaned on his Chevy Silverado and ran a hand through his beard. "Can't tell you how relieved I am they aren't feral."

Gabe sighed his agreement. He'd never been happier not to have to use the tranquilizing gun in his bag. It was hard enough when grown werewolves went feral, but kids were already wild. "Yeah. Really wasn't looking forward to that conversation with the parents. 'Sorry, ma'am, I shot your kid in the ass with a dart.'"

Truthfully, Gabe had doubted they would be feral; it took longer than a few days for werewolves to go feral when separated from their pack unless they struggled with control already.

This world wasn't a kind place to werewolves. Some went feral due to extreme stress and trauma or because they lost their connection to someone that reminded them of their humanity, usually in a highly traumatic way.

A wolf's anchor was almost always their pack, their mate, or both. Some could be brought back and most usually recovered. There was no telling what damage remained, however.

Ben's heavy hand clasped his shoulder. "Good work, kid. Those assholes give you too much trouble?"

Gabe shrugged. "The usual lycanthrophobia. Nothing new, *Alpha* Stroud."

Ben growled. "Not you, too..."

"Hey, you gotta admit it's not a bad title."

Ben pulled a face. "It reinforces stupid human stereotypes about us. I'm your friend, not some controlling asshole who asserts his dominance over his pack."

Gabe supposed by now it shouldn't surprise him how negatively humans reacted to their kind. It was no wonder many werewolves chose not to live in populated areas and if they did, they usually stuck to more rural areas with lots of wide-open space to run and hunt in peace.

Werewolves had coexisted with humans ever since the Witch Hunts of the late seventeenth century, when both sides had teamed up to defeat the tyrannical druids. After that, werewolves had earned the trust of humans and had begun to blend into society. This hadn't been without its protests from fearful, thickheaded humans, of course. It had been a long, bloody road to equality, and things still weren't perfect even now.

Gabe wasn't about to pretend that all werewolves weren't as animalistic as they appeared, but personally he wanted the right to live in peace like anyone else.

"Better get these kids home," Ben said. "Wanna come see the happy reunion?"

"Sure..." But distant police lights grabbed his attention. "Maybe in a minute. Those cops said something about bodies."

Ben's bushy brow furrowed. "Bodies? In this cushy neighborhood?"

"Yeah." Unease tightened in Gabe's stomach. "I wanna have a look."

"Not gonna invite me?" Ben locked the doors and motioned to the kids that he'd be back. He followed Gabe toward the red and blue lights. Several squad cars were parked along the highway at the entrance to an old warehouse with shattered windows crawling with vines. The interior was pitch black. Gabe froze as he smelled it, coppery and thick. Blood.

Ben sniffed and his face paled. "She-Wolf's tits. The hell happened here?" He approached the police crowding the entrance and flashed the badge of the LPA, a solid pewter paw print inscribed with the agency's initials and his name. The police let him in without protest.

Gabe's feet splashed in something and looking down, his stomach lurched. A river of crimson spilled across the dusty concrete. Gabe curled his fingers. Oh, it was bad. He tried to brace himself, but nothing could have prepared him.

Like butchered pigs, two men hung from beams stretching across the ceiling. They were upside down, cut from throat to groin and drained completely of their blood.

Blood splashed under Gabe's shoes as he approached one of the corpses hanging upside down, squinting in vague recognition at the young shifter's face. He had black hair and vacant brown eyes. "Shit." His stomach clenched. "This is Adam Farley." Frustration made his fangs come out. The metal wall screeched as he lashed out, slashing the wall in his anger. "Damn it!"

The scent of their fear and pain still lingered in the air, stifled under the pungent scent of blood. Painted onto the dusty ground was a symbol, a lotus flower blooming against the full moon. The lotus flower was a symbol of purity, and every shifter no matter how agnostic could agree that the moon was synonymous with the She-Wolf, the mother of lycanthropy.

Gabe's stomach turned upside down. This symbol had barged into his life when he was thirteen. It'd been there when he was taken from his family and had been sprawled over the walls of that dark basement he'd been locked in. It was the last thing he'd seen as his father carried him to safety, right before— He closed his eyes tight, breathing hard as his fangs punctured his lower lip.

This was the work of fanatics with hate in their hearts for any werewolves whose "pure" connection to the goddess was corrupted by human influence, whether they were humans bitten and turned to wolves or hybrids born through human-werewolf couplings.

The Moonborn cult had no tolerance for such a slight against their species. Such influence, they claimed, was an insult to the goddess. Gabe couldn't comprehend such hatred. It made no fucking sense. Hybrids weren't even that different from regular werewolves depending on how much wolf they had in them. It made his damn head spin and his stomach churn.

This crime bore the signature of John Stone.

"Fuck," Gabe snarled, feeling sick with despair and fury.

"Easy, kid." Ben squeezed his shoulder, voice low and silver eyes darting around the room. "Don't lose your shit. There are cops everywhere."

Adam Farley had disappeared on his walk home from work in the dead of night a few weeks ago. He was not the first missing hybrid to turn up mutilated in some odd location.

No, hybrid werewolves had been terrorized by Stone's Moonborn cult for over two decades. Farley's human mother had come to the LPA desperate for help after she'd been dismissed by her local police station—and the LPA had failed her, too. Now she'd wake up every day for the rest of her life with a piece of her heart missing.

Ben sighed. "Yeah. Adam Farley was a hybrid, but do you smell anything weird about him or the other boy?"

Gabe sniffed. He could only catch the scent of blood and cops. "They have no scent. They don't smell like wolves, not even hybrids."

It was said the blood of werewolves carried a whiff of lunar flowers from the days when their ancestors ran as wolves beneath a full moon in a cosmic realm called the Hunting Grounds. Hybrids carried the scent of lunar flowers but it was diluted by their human blood—these victims only had human scents.

Over the years, there'd been copycat killers, psychos trying to earn their place in the cult by abducting and killing hybrids, but those victims lacked the telltale missing scents of a corpse robbed of their inner wolf.

Bile scorched the back of his throat. As a shifter whose mother was human and whose father was a hybrid werewolf, these murders clawed their way under his skin. They set his blood damn near boiling, made his claws extend and his fangs sharp.

Ben's lighter clicked, illuminating the hard gray of his eyes. He stuck a cigarette in his mouth and lit up. Ben took a drag and exhaled, face twisting in bitterness. "This is revolting. To go so far as to rip out their inner wolves, as if they were undeserving of the She-Wolf's gift... You never get used to this shit."

"How is that even possible?" Gabe growled.

Ben approached the corpses, examining the knife wounds that cleaved the bodies in two. He wrinkled his nose. "Smell that? Like ozone. It's magic. Some real fucked-up kind of magic." Ben's silver eyes were dark, like the moon concealed by clouds. "These wounds were made by a druid artifact that was stolen from the Council of Lycanthrope Affairs by John Stone. I was there the day it was stolen."

Gabe had seen enough. He left the bodies to be combed over by the police. He stopped at the street corner and sucked in a breath but the fresh air he sought was denied to him. The scent of blood clung to his clothes and brought bitter bile to the back of his throat. His stomach lurched, and Gabe doubled over as his dinner came back up. He braced his hands on his knees, coughing and gagging until his stomach had emptied.

His claws pierced his palms and blood dripped hot between his fingers. A snarl rumbled deep in his chest as his wolf bared his fangs, longing to come out and attack.

"Easy, kid." A hand fell heavy on his shoulder and squeezed. The warmth and weight was familiar, achingly so. Nights like these, he missed his father something awful. His animal rage calmed, he took in a breath and willed himself to stay in control. "You can't lose your cool."

"It's him, Ben. It's John Stone. This is his work."

"Easy." Ben's hand tightened on his shoulder. "I know." Gabe stumbled as Ben turned him around. Ben's eyes flashed and though anger thrummed under Gabe's skin, he knew better than to argue with the old man. "I know. This is personal, but if you're gonna let anger cloud your head, then you've gotta take a step back. You start acting reckless, you're gonna wind up like them."

As a hybrid, his life was in danger, too, but like hell Gabe would let that stop him. He eased out a slow breath and urged his wolf to settle. "I don't care, Ben." He stepped out of Ben's reach, needing space. "I don't care what happens to me. I'm going to find this son of a bitch, or I'm going to die trying."

He wouldn't die in some dusty old warehouse, not before he'd taken these fanatics down with him.

Darkness blanketed Central Park. Warm summery wind whispered through the trees, and the sweet green scent of grass soothed Gabe's nerves. Breathing in and holding his breath, he heard the frantic heartbeat of a rabbit on the run.

Birds sang in the night, flying in front of the moon. His heart rate sped up. He stepped off the asphalt, removing his shoes to savor the cool grass that tickled the soles of his feet.

Concealed within the elm trees, he removed his jeans and tossed aside his T-shirt. Shifting in public was illegal, but there was no one around to stop him at this time of night. His heart thundered, blood pumping as the thrill of the change swept over him. The grass tickled his paws and he shivered as the wind swept through his fur like a gentle caress.

The trauma of his past that had been ripped wide open by those poor murdered hybrids, the whirlwind thoughts tearing up his mind—it all vanished as he left his human mind behind. He threw back his head and howled, calling out for any like him to join him in his hunt. A distant howl answered and sang a song of *pack.* The familiarity of it made his heart sing. He wasn't hunting alone tonight.

The earth was soft and springy beneath his paws as he ran, the wind whipping back his fur. He could practically taste the blood pumping through his prey as it ran, tiny paws turning up leaves and dirt as it darted ahead. The frantic race of its heart spurred him on and made his jaws froth. His paws thundered the earth in time to a single racing thought, *prey, prey, prey!*

The rabbit dove into its burrow and a snarl of disappointment ripped from his throat as he resisted the urge to shove his snout in there even at the risk of getting bitten. A deep bark turned his head as a familiar wolf with mottled brown fur emerged from the trees, moonlight gleaming on a thick, impeccable coat.

Zachariah DeShawn's tail swished in greeting, his brown eyes intent upon a second burrow nearby. The rabbit bolted and Zach pounced, nipping at its hind leg. The rabbit tumbled over within jaw's reach. Gabe bared his fangs, and then the smell of blood left him frozen.

He recalled the blood, wet beneath his feet, the smell of it.

Zach charged past and caught the rabbit, breaking the small neck between his jaws. He carried the rabbit by the neck and set it down before Gabe.

Together, they ate beneath a moonlit sky.

"That's a new one." When Gabe shifted back to his human form and looked up, Zach was a man again. He was freakishly tall, slender yet muscular, with moonlight glimmering on his copper skin and twinkling like stardust in the long braided locs that cascaded down his back.

Gabe eyed his prominent Adam's apple with hunger. He recalled the taste of his sweat, the way he'd shivered, heart beating fast as Gabe's mouth fluttered over his warm racing pulse.

Though it had been weeks since they'd lain naked under the sheets, he could still remember it. And judging by the way Zach wet his supple lower lip, he could, too.

Gabe swallowed hard. Best not to encourage those thoughts, though he would have loved to hook up with Zach again. They weren't together. They'd been hooking up on and off for three months, but Gabe had brought an end to it a month ago. It had been a hard decision, but with how uncertain his future was, it made sense to him.

He had to find John Stone and kill him or die trying.

How could he promise himself to anyone when he might lose his life?

Gabe shivered as slender fingertips grazed his cheek where a new scar had been added to Gabe's collection. "What did you get up to while I was gone?" Zach's tone was lightly scolding.

Gabe moved his face away from Zach's touch before he could stop himself.

"Sorry." Zach's smile faltered, and Gabe wanted to slap himself.

Gabe cleared his throat. "Same as usual. Just catching ferals off the street. Ran into some asshole humans hurting this one feral wolf, so I maybe bloodied them up a bit."

"By yourself? Gabe, come on."

"It was fine, mother hen." Gabe barely refrained from rolling his eyes. "Reinforcements showed up, but what was I supposed to do, sit around and watch?"

"At this rate, there won't be an inch of your skin that isn't covered in scars. You're too reckless." Zach looked away, lips thin and eyes narrowed.

Gabe shrugged, picking some rabbit meat out of his teeth. "So I got scars. Rather me than you or someone else in the pack." He could shoulder his own pain easily enough. Seeing someone he loved in pain, knowing there was nothing he could do to help or any way he could have prevented it—that he couldn't cope with so easily.

Gabe rolled over on his back, folding his arms beneath his head. "I didn't know you were back."

Zach yawned and rolled out his shoulders. "Yeah, our flight got in this morning. I'd have texted but I was exhausted."

"You and Ryan have any luck?"

Zach's wide mouth curled in a charming, droll smile as his eyes lit up. "Yeah, we tracked the missing kids to some weird cave pretty far upstate. These sick hunters wanted to torture them, induce so much pain they shifted so they could skin their pelts and sell them."

A growl vibrated in Gabe's throat. Just when he thought he'd seen the limits of man's cruelty, humans surprised him.

"But Ryan and I rescued them. They all went home. The story had a happy ending." Zach leaned on the tree, smiling contentedly.

Happier than Adam Farley and that other boy. Poor kids. Gabe preoccupied himself with picking the last scraps of meat off a rabbit bone.

"What's up?" Zach must have sensed the distress his thought had caused.

"Nothing. Just wanted a hunt, same as you." Gabe tossed aside the rabbit bone.

"Yeah, that's why you watched the rabbit flail around within your reach. It almost got away. You've never been that shoddy before." Zach's inquisitive eyes peeled away Gabe's layers like they always did.

Gabe's jaw tightened. He sighed. He and Zach had known each other since college, and they were twenty-seven now. Trying to hide anything around his friend of eight years was pointless. Trying to hide anything as a werewolf was even more pointless when scents betrayed every emotion.

"There were another two murders. First ones since January. It had... *his* handiwork all over, Zach. The symbols, their wolves ripped from them like..." His throat tightened and he blinked hard.

Zach frowned, gnawing at his lower lip. "I'm sorry you had to see that."

"It's been years, Zach! Years! How can werewolves still refuse to acknowledge people like me as one of them? How can we as a species still be so fucking narrow-minded?"

Zach rolled his shoulder, sighing up at the stars. "Hey, I get it. I'm Black and a werewolf. I've been getting shit from day one. Feels like two steps forward, ten steps back."

Gabe squeezed Zach's knee. Gabe was half Spanish and half Mexican, but he'd inherited the fair skin of his European ancestors. With Gabe's fair skin, some people didn't realize he was Hispanic, at least until he started speaking Spanish. Then came the dirty looks.

"It's hard enough looking different. The world already thinks we're savage animals without werewolves killing each other and proving them right." Gabe wrestled with his own bitterness, but the words flowed out anyway like water from a dam. "Why do I bother trying to make a difference, huh? When humans aren't killing us, we're killing our own. Sometimes, I... fuck. Never mind." Shame gnawed at him.

"What?" Zach drew his knee to his chest, his pointed chin propped on his kneecap. His considerate, open expression compelled Gabe to speak up.

"I wonder what it's all for. That's all. It's like, you know, clearing out a rabbit burrow, only you come back and there's ten of them. Shit. That's not really a bad thing."

"Yeah, that was a pretty crap analogy. But I get it. It's frustrating. But someone's gotta do it. And I'm glad it's us, Gabe. I'm glad we're trying to make things safer for our kind, for our future generations."

Gabe nodded, seeing the sense in his words.

A large warm hand squeezed his shoulder, and the moonlight twinkled in the soft brown of Zach's eyes. "You care, Gabriel. You're trying to make the world a better place. That's all you can do. That's enough."

Gabe, feeling bitter, didn't agree and rolled his shoulder, dislodging Zach's comforting hand. It would be "enough" when he'd caught the monster responsible for these killings.

Zach sniffed the air. "Hold on. You smell that?"

Gabe took a whiff of the night air. The green smells of the trees mingled with the rich scent of soil and the mouthwatering smell of the blood and meat of the rabbit—

Gabe sat up straight, sniffing. On the wind was a smell unlike any other. It was another wolf, but it was... Oh man. It was so much more than that. His breath caught, surprised by the feelings this scent stirred in him. This scent—it made him happy. Like all the trauma today had stirred up was fading to background noise.

His wolf stirred inside, tail wagging. *I want him,* the wolf howled. *I need him! Find him. Find him now!*

"Uh, Gabe? You good? Your eyes are glowing."

Gabe gave his head a shake. Whoa. What in the hell was with his wolf tonight? He sniffed again, needing more of that scent. A growl rumbled in his chest. Damn, the beast within was practically purring. "Chili and cinnamon." He smiled, though he was confused.

"Huh?" Zach took a whiff of the air. "The hell you talking about?"

Gabe breathed in deep and for a moment he was walking the streets of Mexico City.

The sounds and smells of the marketplace enveloped him. The air was scented with spices, especially cinnamon and chilis. He breathed in a lungful and coughed when the spices tickled his throat. His father smiled down at him and laughed.

"I love that smell," his father said, breathing in deep. "Chili peppers over an open flame."

"It's stinky," Gabe said.

His father smiled and tousled his hair. "It smells like home, Mijo."

Gabe had never thought of that. Of home having a smell to it. But that was what this wolf smelled like, like home, somewhere safe and familiar.

Gabe blinked away the memory. "Our last family vacation with my dad. We went to Mexico to visit my grandparents. We cooked chili con carne for dinner and..."

Zach looked bewildered.

Gabe scoffed at him. "You really don't smell that?"

"Smells like blood. Dirt. Fur." Zach squinted at him. "Trust me, I wish it smelled like cinnamon. Something's wrong."

Gabe scoffed. "You're joking, right, man? This smell is..." It brought a grin to his face. "Amazing." It made his wolf want to howl and run, run toward the source of that beautiful smell and roll around in it.

Zach gave him a cockeyed looked. "Smells like blood to me."

Humoring him, Gabe took a few more whiffs, practically sighing as more of that lovely aroma caressed his senses. There was something else buried deep beneath that pleasant scent. Fresh urine and dirty fur. Blood. The wolf was hurt. Fury surged within him, and a snarl ripped from Gabe's throat.

"Gabe? Whoa!" Zach lurched away from him as the shift burst from Gabe's skin. Gabe ran as a wolf, pursuing that scent through the trees, and the scent of blood and fear got stronger and stronger until he could taste it.

Paw prints in the earth led to a thick clump of bushes. The tracks were inconsistent, as if the shifter had been stumbling along. Gabe's fur bristled. Fear hung heavy in the air. A frantic heartbeat whispered in his ear, growing louder as he and Zach approached the tangle of bushes.

Zach shifted, reaching out his hand to part the bushes. "Oh shit. Gabe, take a look."

Gabe assumed his human form, his heart in his throat as he leaned over Zach's shoulder. All the breath left his body.

A wolf huddled beyond the bushes, and not just any wolf—a red wolf. There was no mistaking that orange-red hue mottled with gray and the splashes of cream on his legs and underbelly. Coyote-like in appearance, he had big pointed ears and a narrow face.

Those wide eyes full of fright reached into Gabe's soul and twisted. There was a cry for help in his eyes. They were a blazing yellow, the pupils constricted. He wasn't like those two kids from the piers. They'd shifted out of fright but they'd been in control.

This wolf had lost his connection to his humanity.

"Wow. A red wolf," Zach whispered. "If Ryan were here, he'd flip out. I've never seen a red wolf before. Have you?"

No, not ever, but Gabe was more concerned about what such a wolf was hiding in the bushes for—and why he smelled so pleasing to his wolf.

Gabe's knee hit the dirt. "Hey. It's okay, Lobito. We're like you. We aren't gonna hurt you."

Gabe shifted closer, reaching out. It was a mistake. He'd underestimated the fight response of a wounded, cornered wolf. He got no warning, not even a growl. Fangs gleamed white and the wolf charged from the bushes, his fangs bared for Gabe's throat.

CHAPTER 3

LOBITO

THE WORLD SPUN AROUND as Gabe tumbled over, spraying dirt and leaves. A snarl vibrated the earth. Zach stood over him as a wolf, ears flattened, fangs bared at the red wolf. *"Back off!"* Zach's furious voice echoed through Gabe's mind.

Panic twisted up Gabe's insides. He sent soothing thoughts Zach's way. *"Easy, Zach. Back down. He's scared."* It was his mistake; the smell of fear should have been enough to warn him away from reaching out. He didn't want Zach getting hurt because of him.

The red wolf didn't share their pack bonds and was unaware of their telepathic communication, but he must have gotten the message. He retreated back into the bushes, tail between his legs.

Gabe sat back on his haunches and cursed. He'd nearly lost his damn fingers there. He'd been working with the agency for four years. He knew better than to reach out to a feral like that but something about this frightened red wolf was shaking him up.

This was the kind of encounter with ferals that he dreaded. This wolf had been hurt so badly he'd disassociated from his trauma by surrendering control to the animal within. That hurt to even think about.

Gabe had been there himself, had the scars to prove it. He knew the depths a werewolf had to sink to before their control *snapped* like that. Only unimaginable pain and trauma could make a werewolf willingly throw away memories of their loved ones in exchange for a wolf's feral mind.

Gabe swallowed bile in his throat. Zach touched his back, the warm glow of their bond like a fire in a dark blizzard. *"I'm here. It's okay. We'll help him,"* Zach whispered along the bond that connected them. The waves of comfort flowing from Zach to Gabe helped soothe the pain in Gabe's heart.

Gabe exhaled. "I know," he replied aloud, too drained to bother with telepathy right now. In any case, something had to be done about this red wolf. He was fearful and aggressive, desperate to defend himself from anything he perceived to be a threat. He was a danger to himself and others in this state and couldn't be allowed to roam around the city.

"We need to bring him in," Gabe said, the words heavy on his tongue.

Zach shifted partially, his face covered in dark fur, his fangs leaving indentations on his lower lip. "Gotta go back. Get my stuff. Stay here, watch him."

The wolf would surely hurt someone if they happened upon him. The responsible thing was to capture him and take him back to headquarters, see if they could help him. It wasn't impossible for a werewolf to recover from disassociation, but it was challenging. They were burying painful experiences by going feral.

For those cases, Ben would authorize the Humanity Restorative Treatment, a process designed to restore the link between a shifter's wolf and their humanity. It could help with bringing a wolf out of their shift, but ultimately it was the survivor's choice whether they stayed human or not. Gabe wondered what Lobito here would choose.

Zach left for a while, and Gabe lingered by the bushes. The smell of the wolf's fear and fury made him growl. His inner animal wanted to find whoever had hurt the red wolf and tear them apart. What was his story? How had he come to be alone and frightened in the park, smelling of dried blood and fear?

Zach appeared between the trees fully clothed and with a gym bag slung over his shoulder. "We're taking him to headquarters?" Gabe asked.

"Yeah." Zach dropped the bag and knelt, pulling out a tranquilizer gun and loading it with darts.

Gabe frowned at the tranquilizer. "Is that necessary? Poor guy's already traumatized enough."

Zach loaded another dart into the gun. It was tipped with silver. Silver weakened wolves, causing them to shift back to a human. While the red wolf might be too feral to shift back to human, it would weaken him regardless. "He's feral. If he's unresponsive to communication and resorts to snapping and biting, we've got no choice. Try and coax him out. Watch your fingers."

His heart heavy, Gabe shifted back to a wolf. He parted the bushes with his snout. Wide yellow eyes gleamed at him from the darkness, and a snarl tore from between pointed fangs. The wolf pressed his body up against a bush, fur bristling and fangs shining in the darkness.

Gabe flattened his ears, trying to appear as unimposing as possible, but the wolf snapped and barked as he came closer. When his warnings failed to make Gabe back off, the red wolf sprang at him.

A blur of red fur plowed into him. Gabe fastened his fangs into the wolf's scruff, and they tumbled out of the bushes together. Claws sliced like little daggers against his belly as the wolf thrashed and struggled to escape Gabe's grip on his scruff. Gabe threw himself atop the smaller wolf, crushing him into the grass.

"Come on, Zach! Hurry up!"

White exploded in Gabe's vision as a claw flew into his face, shredding the skin near his eye. His skin burned hot, and the coppery smell of his own blood hit his nostrils. The wolf scrambled away, panting and frothing at the mouth. He advanced on Gabe again, eyes crazed in fury. He sprang toward Gabe.

Gabe braced himself, but the wolf cried out and toppled to the ground in a tangle of limbs. A dart protruded from his hind leg. The wolf licked frantically at the leg, yelping in a way that made Gabe want to run over and pull out the dart.

The wolf struggled to stand and stumbled, weaving side to side. He collapsed, sides heaving. His breath slowed, wide eyes becoming slits. He was asleep in seconds.

Gabe shifted back and Zach tossed him a spare change of clothes from his gym bag. Werewolves always carried extras. "Are you hurt?"

Gabe shook his head as he stepped into the jeans, rolling up the ankles so they didn't sag over his feet. Zach was a damn giant. The scratch by his eye burned, but he could tolerate it. If he were a pure-blooded werewolf, the wound would have healed in seconds. Gabe knelt by the red wolf. He was fast asleep.

"Poor guy." Gabe stroked his fur. "Let's get him back to headquarters. Ben should know how to help him." Gabe hoisted the wolf over his shoulder. He was far too easy to carry; Gabe could feel every rib.

Zach led the way to his pickup and Gabe set the wolf into a large cage underneath a tarp in the bed of the truck. Zach started the engine and Gabe climbed in.

"I am way too tired for this," Zach confessed. "If I see a convenience store, I'm getting coffee. Don't care how crap it is."

Gabe leaned his head back against the seat. "Grab one for me, too."

They drove out of the city, stopping only to grab crappy gas station coffee for the road. It was a long drive to Fire Island but at this time of night, the road was quiet. Only weirdos like them were driving at this hour.

Times like these, Gabe wished the LPA headquarters had a location in the city, but they needed somewhere quiet and secluded to work in peace and being by the serenity of the ocean was beneficial to many of their patients.

Zach's phone buzzed from the dashboard, a text message popping in front of the GPS. Gabe caught Rebecca's name—Zach's mom—before Zach swiped the message away with a scowl. "Damn. Forgot to turn on drive mode."

Gabe noticed Zach's frustrated sigh. "Your parents still trying to guilt-trip you back into their claws?"

Zach scoffed, a twinkle in his eyes. "You've got no idea. Mom sent me a Tesla for my birthday last month."

Gabe rolled his eyes in mock frustration. "Oh man. I hate it when my ma sends me Teslas for my birthday. What a drag. Tell me you kept it."

Zach made a face that implied Gabe was stupid.

"Zach! Come on, a Tesla! You coulda given it to me!" Gabe smacked his shoulder, grinning. "I thought we had something."

Zach shook his head, locs swaying against his cheeks. "No way. First, it's Teslas, the next it's a lecture about how I'm wasting my time with the LPA. They'll be fixing me up with rich snobs and trying to trap me in the business for the rest of my life."

Gabe sighed, imagining that beautiful car. "For a car like that, I think I'd settle." Still, he was proud of Zach for turning his back on the family fortune and pursuing his own dreams.

They drove over a bump and the cage rattled around in the bed of the truck, turning Gabe's attention toward their passenger. Gabe asked, "Have you worked with ferals before?" Gabe wasn't familiar with treating ferals. He was good at tracking them, and he'd been trained to capture them off the streets, but that was the extent of his role in the LPA.

Zach took a sip of coffee and grimaced. "God, that's bad. A few times, yeah." Zach mostly handled search and rescues, but when he was at the estate, Ben had been training him to rehabilitate feral werewolves.

Gabe glanced out the rear window at the tarp concealing their wolf. "Is he beyond hope?"

The idea that they might not be able to save this wolf had his inner animal whining in anguish. It was strange. Now that he had a moment to think, he had to wonder why he was so invested in this wolf's recovery. He'd been around plenty of ferals and while they always tugged at his heart, he'd never felt anxious over them. He and his wolf *needed* this feral to be okay. Why?

Zach's brow knitted, his lips pursed. "It's hard to say. I can't tell if he can shift back or not. Maybe he doesn't want to, or maybe he can't."

"If he can't shift back, could he still be helped?" Gabe squeezed his hands into fists, trying to contain his anxiety.

"That's what we gotta determine." Zach met his gaze and offered a smile. "One step at a time."

They drove across the Robert Moses Causeway and arrived on Fire Island. Cars weren't allowed on most of the island but the road that connected the lighthouse and tourist centers also connected to the agency grounds. Fog hung heavy over the ocean and mist settled on the windows. Zach switched on the windshield wipers as they drove.

Nestled among untamed island greenery was the Lycanthrope Protection Agency, close enough to the beach but with enough distance from the beachfront bungalows to offer some seclusion. Zach drove them down a long stretch of road, the surrounding forest thick enough for Gabe to believe they'd left the world behind. At the end of the road was the headquarters of the LPA surrounded by a tall stone fence crawling with stubborn ivy.

The gates opened at their approach and Zach parked in the garage beneath HQ. Together, they hoisted the cage and took the elevator up from the garage to the west side of the estate where the patients dwelled. They set the cage on a cart and rolled it through the halls until they reached the kennels where feral werewolves were kept until they were deemed safe enough to have their own room.

The snapping and snarling made Gabe uneasy. Curtains concealed the wolves to offer them some privacy and keep them calm, for the most part. They set the cage down and transferred the wolf to a kennel after snapping a muzzle on him.

Gabe hesitated at the door, looking back at the sleeping wolf. He would wake in a few hours, alone and in a new place. Gabe only hoped they could help him.

GABE SPENT THE NIGHT in his bungalow tucked away on the estate grounds. He and other high-ranking LPA members had their own houses there, making it easy to stay near during especially busy times. Gabe wanted to be with the feral red wolf the minute he woke up. He'd seen many feral werewolves over the years, but those wide frightened eyes lingered in his mind, though he couldn't be sure why.

He ate breakfast and walked to the main building. Howling carried to him on the wind, the distant barks and yelps echoing. Unable to resist, he tipped his head up and howled back, and other howls answered him.

He could smell them, wet fur all tangled up with the green smell of leaves and soil. He longed to shift then and there and join the wolves running and playing in the acres of land beyond the estate, but he couldn't digest his breakfast in peace until he knew how the newcomer was doing.

He stepped through the oaken double doors of the estate and the delectable smell of sizzling sausages and scrambled eggs made him regret his boring but healthy oatmeal breakfast. He passed the dining room, peering inside to where Ben and Zach ate. Ben met his gaze and stood, dabbing at his mouth with a napkin.

"Let's go meet this new wolf," Ben said, leading the way up the stairs. "Zach administered a sedative this morning, so he should be calm enough for us to examine him."

"Someone hurt him. Bad," Zach murmured, his eyes dark. "He's got scars, fresh wounds."

Gabe's jaw clenched. He didn't even know who had hurt him, and he already wanted them dead.

"There's a problem, though," Ben grumbled. "I had Izzie look around online, trying to see if anyone's filed a missing person report. There's nothing matching his description, which means we can't get in touch with any family he might have. I had Izzie update the database with what little info we have on him, so there's still a chance someone could get in touch. In the meantime, Zach—"

"Right. We'll get to work. Also, Ryan wants to come meet him."

Ben sighed. "We can't freak the pup out by bringing the whole pack into the room."

"I know, but he flipped out when he heard we'd caught a red wolf. He'll kill me if he isn't here for this. Come on, Ben, he really wants to come. He said he'd bring some extra stuff."

Ben sighed. "Fine."

Zach got in touch with Ryan while Ben and Gabe went on ahead to the kennels. The wolves barked and snarled as they entered. Gabe swept aside the curtain, looking in on the wolf. The meat in his bowl was untouched and the wolf lay in the farthest corner of the kennel eyeing them warily.

The sedative seemed to be keeping him calm. Scars cut through the wolf's red fur, which was matted with old blood and tangled with leaves and dirt. He was a hybrid, judging by the way the wounds hadn't healed. Gabe's fingers curled.

"Interesting," Zach said. "Hybrids don't usually have such a powerful scent of lunar flowers."

Gabe couldn't smell any flowers, just delectable spicy notes emanating from the red wolf. Lunar flowers were of course synonymous with the She-Wolf since they bloomed under moonlight. If the stories from his childhood were to be believed, lunar flowers were plentiful in the goddess's realm, hence every werewolf smelled like them.

Ben leaned on the wall next to the cage. "It's not unusual for a hybrid's scent to be stronger than most pure-bloods. Depends on how much shifter they inherited over their human side."

"Look." Zach pointed to a large cream-colored paw. There were cuts on each of the wolf's legs. "Looks like rope burn. And he smells strange. Like a lab, you know?"

"I hope you mean a laboratory and not the retriever." Ryan Kelly flashed them a cheerful grin as he strode in lugging a box in his arms. Gabe didn't know how he managed such energy this early in the morning, so he had to assume Ryan woke up with a grin plastered on his face.

Though he and Zach had been away together a whole week, he still greeted Zach with a back-slapping hug as if he hadn't seen him in a month as usual while everyone else got handshakes or waves. It was pretty funny considering Zach dwarfed Ryan and had to lean over all the way, which he always gladly did, to hug his childhood friend.

"There's my favorite hombre! Qué pasa, man?" Ryan gave Gabe's hand a hearty shake then lunged to catch the box before it slipped from his arms.

"Don't qué pasa me! Qué pasa you!" Gabe clasped his hand and shook. "Nice to see you, Ry." He'd missed Ryan's snarky sense of humor during dull workdays.

"Whoa, man! I can't believe it!" Slack-jawed, Ryan ran over to get a better look, adjusting his big dorky glasses that made him look like a nerd. His green eyes sparkled with intrigue. "I've never seen a red wolf before! You guys know how rare they are?"

Gabe scoffed at his excitement, but Ryan was honest as always. He looked like he'd run his fingers carelessly through his brown hair and he'd thrown on a Yankees T-shirt backward in his excitement to meet their new wolf.

"Ryan, he's not an exhibit in a museum." Gabe already felt a headache coming on. "And of course we mean a laboratory."

"He smells like he'd been drugged with something," Zach added as an explanation. "A powerful sedative by the stink."

"Just making sure. Ferals will do all sorts of weird shit, even if it means getting too friendly with the neighborhood dogs. I mean, they're pretty much pure wolves at this stage, so..."

"Can you not?" Gabe growled.

"Damn. Poor guy. What happened to him?" Ryan observed the red wolf.

"Anything," Zach admitted, shaking his head hopelessly. "He smells like he was drugged, probably with a nonlethal dose of wolfsbane so he couldn't fight back. He could have been tied up. Kidnapped. Experimented on. Used for fighting. It's up in the air and I don't want to know. We need to make him better."

Ryan set down the box. "I brought stuff that could help him remember he was human."

Gabe sighed, worrying his lower lip. "Here's to hoping that stuff helps."

"You good?" Ryan shook his shoulder. "You seem a little more upset than usual."

Need to help him. The wolf panted in Gabe's head. *Need to lick his wounds. Curl around him. Keep him safe and warm.* Gabe shook the thoughts right out of his head. What was *with* him? His wolf was never so vocal over just another rescued feral. Somehow, this one was different.

"Nothing. It's nothing. What did you bring?" Gabe asked.

Ben interrupted. "Zach, he's waking up. Help me move him to an exam room."

Gabe didn't think he would be any help with his emotions boiling so close to the surface. He'd seen his share of beaten-bloody shifters over the years. The red wolf's case wasn't any different or any more unusual than most cases, yet the scars marring that beautiful red fur wouldn't leave his mind. He kept seeing the cuts on those paws and the fear and desperation in those wild eyes.

It was the eyes that got to him most. They cried out for help, for someone to turn to, and he wanted badly to give the little wolf the safety he yearned for. He envied Ben and Zach for being able to keep levelheaded but then again they had to be. This was their line of work.

Ben and Zach carried the wolf to one of the empty rooms near the kennel. It was usually used as an exam room, but it was quiet enough for the work they had to do. They set the wolf in a cage and slowly the wolf came to. He growled at the sight of them, tucking his tail. Gabe's stomach churned. The smell of fear suffocated all other scents in the room.

The door opened and Izzie, his sister, walked in. She waved but her smile was heavy. Bags hung under her pretty almond-shaped eyes, and her mascara was smudged from a restless night of sleep. Her black hair lacked its usual glossy sheen and was tied back lazily in a frizzy ponytail. At twenty-one, she was Gabe's younger sister by six years and one of the youngest to work in the LPA.

"Whoa. You sleep at your desk, Izzie?"

Izzie smiled in a way that made Gabe fear for his life. "Actually, yes, I did."

"Any luck finding his family?"

"None," she admitted, stifling a yawn. "No one's responded to our posting yet, but it's only been up a few hours. We'll see. He's a red wolf, so who knows how many will claim to know him so they can come and ogle him."

"Guys, can we focus here?" Zach knelt before the cage and opened the box Ryan had brought. He reached in and made a face. "Really, man?"

"What?" Ryan approached.

Zach threw a couple of porn magazines at him. "Get that shit outta here."

"Hey, people read them!"

"You don't read that trash, do you?" Izzie asked.

Ryan didn't answer her question. "Hey, if he doesn't like ladies, I brought the gentlemen, too." With a wink, he unfurled a gay porn magazine.

Gabe rolled his eyes and leaned over Zach's shoulder. Inside the box were numerous items that might be relevant to a guy the wolf's age, which they speculated was his early to late twenties based on his size—phones, sports equipment, and books popular among young adults.

"It would be easier if we had something that belonged to him." Zach sighed. "But this'll have to do."

"What's a baseball supposed to do exactly?" Gabe asked, not understanding the point of all these random items.

"Usually with Humanity Restoration Treatment, we'd have family or friends bring objects that hold significant meaning to him. Could be anything: a picture, a shirt he likes to wear, sometimes it's even a person.

Anything to remind him of his humanity. But since he's alone as far as we know, we need to make guesses." Zach reached into the box and pulled out the baseball. He slipped it through the bars of the cage, and it rolled across the tiles. The red wolf retreated, eyeing the ball with confusion. He bent his snout and sniffed, then ignored it.

"Alright, let's try something else."

One thing turned into two, object by object, until they'd emptied the box. Books and graphic novels, various sports balls and equipment. The wolf disregarded everything, never taking his eyes off them.

Izzie shrugged. "Maybe he doesn't like typical macho stuff?"

"I hate to say it," Ryan said, "but I think it's time to bring in the big guns." He reached for the Playboy magazines.

"Keep them!" Gabe snapped. He was growing wearier by the minute. "Say this doesn't work. What's our next action?"

Zach reclined back on his heels and regarded the wolf. "We could wait until someone responds to our posting about him."

"And if they don't respond?"

Ben's lips thinned and he stroked his beard as he eyed the wolf. "What we're looking for is recognition, a sign that he understands what we're saying to him. Something to show us his humanity is still in there. I'm not getting that."

Gabe's stomach tightened. "So? That doesn't mean he's beyond hope. Right?"

"He might still come back. It's always possible but based on his behaviors, he might already be too far gone. At this point, it would take a person he knows and trusts to bring him back, and since we don't have that..."

Gabe's mouth ran dry. "What are you saying?"

Ben said, "The poor guy's been through hell. It would take something very powerful to remind him of his humanity. If no one comes looking for him, which unfortunately is pretty common, then we're going to have to consider—"

Zach suddenly stood, his face twisted in bitterness. He made for the door.

Ryan looked after him. "Zach, you're doing all you can."

"And it's not good enough." Zach's voice was sharp. He exhaled. "Give me a minute." The door slammed behind him. Frowning, Ryan pursued him out into the hall.

Gabe reclined against the wall, stomach churning. "There's gotta be something."

Ben sighed, folding his arms over his barrel chest. "Our options are limited right now. But if no one comes looking for him and if he doesn't get better, he can't be released. He's too aggressive. There's a chance he could be accepted by a wolf rescue center. They'll accept feral werewolves who can't shift back, but he may be too aggressive. If that's the case, we need to consider a permanent solution."

Cold dread ran down Gabe's back. He looked at Ben, unable to believe he'd suggest such a thing. Ben stared back, his eyes heavy. "It's hard. I know. But Gabriel, not everyone can be saved. Sometimes, it's kinder to understand that."

Throat tight, Gabe turned to the red wolf pacing in the cage, panting and growling. At the sight of the scars cleaving through the red fur, his vision blurred and he blinked hard.

No. I won't give up on him. I can't lose him. I—

Gabe's fingers trembled as he popped the button on his shirt. "Open the cage and leave." If this went sideways, he didn't want Ben or Izzie caught in the crossfire.

"Gabe, what the hell do you think you're doing?" Ben asked.

Gabe strode toward the cage. "I'm bringing him back."

CHAPTER 4

FLOWERS AND SPRINGTIME

"MY NAME'S GABE REYES. I don't know your name, so can I call you Lobito for now?"

Something about Gabe's scent broke through the feral fog in the wolf's mind. He remembered his name. The terrible events at Bad Man—*Richard's*—house. His mother. Goddess, he hoped his mother was okay.

But he remembered something else, too. When he'd been trapped in that tiny pantry, all he knew was darkness and isolation. Sometimes, it had been easy to forget the outside world existed at all, that there was anything beyond the darkness of that cramped, lonely space.

One day, the window in the kitchen had been left open. A breeze drifted in from under the slit in the door, bringing in scents he'd forgotten could even exist.

Max had crowded up against the narrow gap between the door and the kitchen tile and breathed in the smell of springtime that drifted in through the open window beyond his prison. The sweet, calming scent of flowers and warm air that carried the aroma of the cherry blossom trees in the backyard—the scents of life carrying on beyond the darkness, smells of a spring in full bloom that no darkness could touch.

Gabe smelled like flowers and springtime, like hope and life.

Max's trembling stopped and all he could do was sniff the air and drink in that soothing scent. His wolf whispered, *Him... We can trust him. We're safe. Finally safe.* Something in that flowery scent implored Max to let his guard down. To trust. His instincts weren't usually wrong, but the human in him was too wary.

Gabe stopped outside the cage and turned the latch.

"Gabriel! What the hell are you doing?"

"Let me do this, Ben!" Gabe threw off the older man's hand and knelt outside the cage. The growl rumbling in Max's chest died down as Gabe met his gaze and held it. He had kind amber eyes. "I see you're quite the warrior. You've got your share of scars. I do, too. Look and see." He unbuttoned his shirt and let it slide from his shoulders.

Scars marred Gabe's skin, cutting across his shoulders, embedded in his chest, tearing across his abs. Scars spiraled down his arms, ending at his hands. A whine pulled from Max's throat just imagining the pain Gabe must have gone through. He wanted to lick and soothe each scar.

For so long, he'd thought his own body bore more scars than anyone else's ever could. That anyone he met would look at him and see his own weakness slashed across his body.

"A lot of scars, eh?" Somehow, Gabe smiled. "I'm going to tell you a story about a hybrid boy and his family. Maybe he's like you, I don't know. Once upon a time, a hybrid boy lived with his father, mother, and sister in Manhattan. Their mother was a human, their father a hybrid werewolf, but it didn't matter to them. They were happy, and their father worked hard so his cubs could have a future where they didn't have to fear being who they were.

"But, and I think you know well, there are monsters in this world. Well, a monster came for the hybrid boy and took him away. Locked him in the dark. Hurt him so badly, he couldn't remember what happiness felt like. He told the hybrid boy he was impure because of the human blood in his veins, and because he was impure, he deserved suffering."

"You're a freak, boy." Bad Man's teeth gleamed in the dark as he smiled.

"And for a long time, the hybrid boy believed everything the monster told him."

He forgot. Everything faded except for the pain, the loneliness. Nothing existed, only darkness, only the throbbing of his wounds.

"He was wrong."

The door opened and shafts of light penetrated the darkness. His mother opened her arms for him. Something touched his head, warm and gentle and kind. His eyes flew open. Gabriel knelt outside the cage, his hand resting warm on his head.

"My father came for me. He never forgot about me. We lost him, but my family went on loving me, supporting me."

Could he have that, too? Had he found it at last? Someone he could turn to, someone he could trust? That warm hand ran along his head, caressing between his ears. He'd forgotten what it felt like, to be touched like he was loved and cared for.

"Maybe someone out there will come for you, too, my friend. Until then, you'll be safe here. I swear on my life, as long as I'm here, you'll never be hurt again."

His eyes closed. He couldn't resist leaning his head into that gentle touch. He stumbled from the cage. Two powerful arms wound slowly around his weary, aching body and he stumbled into a warm, muscular chest.

The darkness returned. The Bad Man's knife dripped with blood. *"No one loves you, boy. No one can love something like you."*

Those warm arms held him tight, contradicting everything he'd been told in that dark, painful room. "I got you, Lobito. We're going to look out for each other."

Whining, he nuzzled into Gabe's chest and let those strong arms soothe all his broken pieces.

Never had another person's scent brought him so much comfort and peace.

For now, in Gabe's arms, he knew he was safe.

THE NEXT DAY ARRIVED and Gabe left his bungalow and made a dash for the estate, jumping up the stairs until he arrived near the red wolf's room. They'd moved him from the kennels to a bedroom now that he wasn't feral. Gabe breathed in and sighed as that familiar, pleasing scent brought a smile to his face. Angry barking made his heart lurch, and he rounded the corner.

"I hear you, I hear you!" Ryan threw up his arms and paced away from the bedroom door.

"What's going on?" Gabe asked, observing that Izzie was here as well, clutching a tray loaded with meat and vegetables.

"I was about to call you," Izzie said. "Our friend is proving to be difficult."

Gabe frowned. "Why?"

"He won't let me in to feed him! Zach tried and he got bit in the ass on his way out," Ryan explained, all flustered. "I thought maybe he's more of a ladies' man, so I called Izzie over."

"Bit?" Gabe repeated, disappointment walloping him in the chest. "He's still a wolf?"

Izzie flung up her hands. "He chased me out of the room and started throwing himself against the door like he wanted to eat me. Poor guy."

"Yeah, he hasn't taken a human form, but his eyes aren't all glowy and yellow like before. Think it's easier for him to stay as a wolf right now." Ryan nudged Gabe. "But old Ben says you have the magic touch. Wanna give it a try?"

Gabe accepted the tray and approached the door. There came a snuffling sound from beyond the door, then a welcoming *awoooo*!

Ryan's mouth fell open. "He's literally wooing you!"

Izzie grinned, her eyes sparkling.

A grin tugged at his lips, too, and Gabe tipped his head back and howled in response. "Next time there's trouble, call me." He nudged open the door and the red wolf jumped up to greet him. "Easy, Little Red."

The wolf growled in response and gave a disapproving sneeze.

Gabe chuckled. "Don't like being called little?" His wolf form was much smaller than Gabe's big and bulky black wolf but he definitely wasn't a pup. "Is Lobito okay?"

The wolf barked his approval and jumped up on the bed. Gabe sat beside him and set the tray down. "I guess it'll have to do until you tell me your name." The wolf gave the food a sniff, then hesitated to eat. "It's good. See?" Gabe picked up a chunk of meat and ate.

The wolf sniffed once more at the food, then snapped up a piece of meat. Gabe's chest tightened, hoping the little wolf would put more meat on his bones soon.

"Listen, everyone here is your friend. Even Ryan. I know he's annoying but he's a good guy. The people here want to help you."

The wolf lay down and ignored his meal. A sigh shivered from him and he looked utterly defeated. Gabe wished he would shift and say something, anything at all. He was curious to hear what his voice sounded like.

"You've got a long road ahead; I'm not going to pretend. But we've got your back." He wanted to reach out and lay a hand on the wolf's bushy fur, but he wasn't sure if their contact yesterday had been a one-time-only thing. It was hard to resist.

Now that he wasn't feral, the wolf had these big orange eyes that simply demanded love and care. Figuring he'd said and done enough, Gabe left the wolf to do what he wanted with his food.

Ben awaited him outside, leaning on the wall. "How's he?"

"Shy but sweet. What a scent, too. Have you smelled him?"

Ben wrinkled his nose. "Yeah. Smells like dirt and blood. We ought to give him a bath if he'll let us."

Gabe frowned. "Sure, he could use a bath, but he smells amazing!"

Ben's mouth quirked. "Really, now?"

Gabe scoffed. "What, you haven't noticed? It's like... I don't know, all these happy feelings bundled into one. Wonder if he uses a fragrance or something."

Ben's eyes twinkled, his face alight with a knowing smile, and Gabe's face warmed, wondering if Ben was teasing him.

"His name's Max. Maxwell Gallagher."

Gabe looked up into Ben's narrowed eyes.

"His mother called. She's coming for him."

CHAPTER 5

FILTHY HYBRID

BEYOND THE GATES, A black car pulled up. A woman stepped out, and the wind carried her scent to Gabe's nose. She smelled like sweat, and her heart rate was elevated. She wore a dirty, wrinkled T-shirt and sweatpants. Her blonde pixie cut looked as if she'd run her fingers through it.

Max hadn't inherited his beautiful ginger locks from her, that was for sure. Only as she hurried closer, sneakers slapping the ground, did Gabe take a guess at her age. Her blue eyes were baggy, and the corners of her mouth were lined.

Gabe exhaled and let the tension in his body relax. He hadn't been sure if she could be trusted, but her harried appearance set him at ease. She was clearly worried about her son. "Nice to meet you, Ms. Gallagher. I'm Gabriel Reyes."

"I'm Kendra, Mr. Reyes. Where's my son?" Her voice was clipped, her lips thin and eyes wide with worry.

"He's resting, Ms. Gallagher. He's been through a lot."

"I need to see him, please." Her voice broke, tears springing to her eyes.

"Sure thing. Follow me." Gabe led the way through the building and up to the second floor.

"Where did you find him?" Ms. Gallagher asked.

"In Central Park."

"Was he hurt?" she asked, her voice frayed.

Gabe rounded the corner toward the bedrooms. "He had cuts on his legs like he'd been tied up, but otherwise no." No, Gabe suspected the damage was more psychological. That was the worst kind of wound, and it always took longer to heal than any cut or scratch, if those inner wounds ever healed at all.

Gabe stopped outside Max's room and motioned for her to go ahead. Kendra approached the door and raised a trembling hand to knock. "Max? It's your mother. May I come in?" Silence answered her.

Gabe said, "He's stayed as a wolf since he arrived here, so he's not too talkative."

Kendra gripped the knob and turned slowly. A sliver of light spilled into the bedroom and she entered. Gabe slipped in behind her, keeping the door open to let in some light. His eyes adjusted fast, and he could make out Max lying in bed where he'd made a den out of the sheets.

"Max." Kendra's voice trembled. "Sweetheart, are you all right?"

Max sat up, ears flicking. His tail wagged, and he squeaked out a happy whine.

"Oh, Max!" Kendra began to cry, wiping her eyes. "I'm so glad you're okay!" She knelt and opened her arms.

Max bunched his muscles, preparing to jump, but he didn't. His tail slowly stopped wagging. His ears drooped. With a whine, he hung his head, circled, and lay down with his back to her.

"Max? What's wrong?" Kendra's voice shook. Max didn't look at her. The sour scent of his shame hit Gabe square in the heart. He wanted to go to Max and comfort him, his wolf was damn near commanding it, but he didn't think that was what Max needed right now.

"I'll... I'll leave you alone. Let you rest." Shoulders slumped, Kendra turned away. "I'll be back. Okay, Max? I promise." She walked out the door, sniffing, and Gabe sighed.

Not the happy reunion he'd been hoping for.

Kendra's soft sobs reached his ears. She leaned on the wall outside the bedroom, covering her eyes as her shoulders trembled.

Gabe reached into his pocket and pulled out a tissue. "Here."

"Th-thank you," she choked out, dabbing her eyes.

Gabe opened an arm, motioning toward the stairs and away from Max's room. "I'd like to talk to you, if that's all right."

"Of course." Sniffing, she followed him.

Gabe led her to the dining hall where banquet tables were loaded with pancakes, eggs, sausages, and bacon along with various teas, coffees, and juices. "Hungry? We have tea, coffee."

"Tea, please."

"Sure. You can go sit outside. I'll be there shortly." Kendra went outside to sit on the wraparound porch. Gabe poured hot water in a teacup and grabbed himself a hot coffee. He barely refrained from making it Irish. His stomach twisted whenever he tried to imagine what Kendra would reveal to him.

Gabe carried their steaming drinks outside where Kendra sat on a bench overlooking the lawn. On the horizon, storm clouds gathered, the clean smell of moisture heavy in the air.

Gabe set the teacup down on a side table and handed Kendra an assortment of herbal teas. He sat in a chair across the way from her, his coffee warming his hands. Kendra took her time choosing her tea and stirring in sugar. Her hands trembled, and her heart beat fast in Gabe's ears. He exhaled, trying to brace himself for whatever story she'd tell that was making her so anxious.

Kendra took a sip and stared into her lap, her expression twisting as if the tea were too bitter. She was silent, twisting her fingers together. "I don't know where to start," she finally admitted.

Gabe took a swallow of his coffee and tried to smile. "Can you tell me about Max's homelife? It might help me understand what's going on with him."

"Right. Well, for the basics... He's going to be twenty next month. He was studying prelaw in college until recently... He was—*is*—cheerful and sweet, and he's so independent and hardworking." She exhaled and sipped her tea as she gathered her thoughts. "When Max was a baby, his father left. He was a human, and he'd never wanted a family life. For a time, it was me and Max. Then I met Richard a year ago, Max's stepfather. We met at a supermoon festival. It was like something out of a romance novel. He was so taken with Max, and he was kind to me. At first."

She took in a breath, hands clenched in her lap.

"We became mates. He helped pay for Max's college tuition and treated Max like his own son. I was so, so happy. Max never had a father figure, and Richard was just what he needed. That's what I thought, anyway. But over time, he... changed. He had this temper. Sometimes, he'd blow up over the smallest things. He'd... hit me. Yell at Max. He always apologized afterward. Said his wolf ran too close to the surface, made him angrier than most."

Gabe scoffed. "Right. 'Cause that's a thing."

Kendra closed her eyes tight. "I believed him. I felt so awful. Like there was something wrong with me for making this kind, sweet man blow up at me."

"That's not your fault, not at all." Gabe held her gaze, needing her to believe him. "He didn't change because of you. He just revealed who he really was now that you were mated."

She sniffed. "I wanted to give Max the family he'd never had and for a time, Richard fit the mold. Until he didn't. His outbursts got worse. He didn't understand why a pure-blooded werewolf like me had a 'mutt' for a son."

Anger made her voice shake. "It was so shocking to hear him talk about Max that way. He'd always apologize. He felt so guilty for getting angry, he'd cry. I believed he was sorry, that he wanted to change. Since Max was having a bad time at school, he started taking Max to his upstate home for getaways. I'd go, too, sometimes. I thought they were connecting. I thought..."

Gabe took in a deep breath. In his chest, his wolf snarled and threw himself up against the walls of his restraints.

"Then one week, Max got into a fight at school. Some hybrid-hating werewolf started it, but the school sided with his family. Max was expelled. Max was really depressed, so Richard took him upstate for a getaway. He called me one night. He told me Max had had a breakdown from the stress and run away. For weeks, we searched for him. Richard went to your agency every day for help. Or so he said."

Gabe shook his head. "He lied."

A pained expression twisted her face. "One night, Richard came home smelling like Max. He wouldn't tell me where he was. I got this horrible feeling, so I stole the keys to his home and drove upstate. All this time, he'd had Max locked up in some dark, cramped pantry. He'd... he'd tortured Max." Fury and pain made her voice break, and tears spilled down her face. "I tried to get him out, but Richard showed up."

"It's not your fault." Gabe cleared his throat, choking down his growl. "No one should have been put in your situation."

"How could I not have known he was hurting Max? How could I have let Richard take him out of my sight?" She scrubbed her eyes furiously. "I thought Richard was genuinely changing. I thought—I was so stupid!"

"No, you weren't. He took advantage of your trust." Gabe stayed quiet and waited for her to collect herself. "But Max did escape. How?"

She blotted her eyes with a crumpled tissue. "I don't know." She must have scented Gabe's disappointment because she added, "I'm sorry. Richard knocked me out before I could escape with Max. I woke as he returned. He... he tried to kill me." Her fingers touched her throat. There was no bruising to indicate a struggle, but that didn't mean a struggle hadn't occurred. Werewolves healed fast, but the scars that remained weren't always physical.

"I ran. Stayed with a friend. I called the police, but Richard wasn't home. The officers told me their hands were tied, so they suggested I check the LPA database for missing werewolves. I was starting to think Max was dead until I saw your posting." She dabbed her eyes. They were red and blotchy. "Thank you, Mr. Reyes. Thank you for finding my son."

Gabe let her hug him, putting one arm around her shoulders in return. "Of course." When... if Max decided to return to human form, hopefully he would be able to fill in the blanks in his mother's story.

Gabe shuddered to think Max could have ended up like Adam Farley or any of the other hybrids, butchered like pigs. "You're welcome to stay here. I can send the police to apprehend Richard. You can get justice. Please, tell me where he is."

Her cracked lips parted but words didn't come.

"Ms. Gallagher."

Her eyes blazed with apprehension. "If it were that easy, I'd have taken Max and left myself."

Gabe held her gaze. "I swear to you. You and Max will be safe here. Safer than either of you will be when he discovers Max is still alive."

Her eyes, weary and dark with exhaustion, met his, searching for someone she could turn to. "And your people can keep us safe?"

Gabe held her gaze and nodded. "I swear it."

BEYOND THE DARK AND quiet confines of Max's bedroom, all was still. The scent of Gabe and his mom was growing stale. The rage and self-loathing had quieted for now, but his ears flicked every time footsteps approached his room.

His mother was alive. He vaguely remembered her coming for him and Richard knocking her out. It had crossed his mind that she could be dead, but he'd denied it with everything he had. She'd survived. She'd come for him. But Max's relief had been torn to tatters when he saw her face. How exhausted she looked, how scared and broken. All because he hadn't been strong enough to keep her safe.

Panting, Max jumped from the bed and paced, toenails catching on threads in the carpet.

Growing up without a father, Max had promised his mother he would be the man of the house. Not because she'd ever asked him to, but because he wanted to. He'd started working on the weekends, poured his all into his studies so he could earn a degree and get a high-paying job, even if he wasn't passionate about legal work.

Then they'd met Richard during the supermoon festival a year ago. Richard and his mom had hit it off right away and at first, things were fine. Richard had seemed like a nice guy while he and his mother were dating. He was friendly and charismatic, generous with his wealth, and Max had liked him. Max knew his mother's heart was wary after being left by his father, so he'd been delighted when she'd accepted Richard's proposal, and they became mates.

Then, once they'd moved in with Richard, things had shifted so gradually Max couldn't be sure when it had happened. Richard had become a little controlling and possessive of Max's mother at times, but Max had chalked that up to newly mated pheromones and let it lie. Then when his mother wasn't around, the insults had started. Richard couldn't believe such an upstanding werewolf had a "filthy mutt" for a son.

Max had kept it to himself when his mother came home after work and hugged Richard, smiling in a way she hadn't in so long. His mother was happy. Her happiness was everything. Max could be a man and stomach Richard's petty insults for his mother. Besides, he was saving up enough to move out soon.

Then Richard hit his mother for the first time. Max wasn't sure what happened. He had been in the next room studying when they'd started arguing. Their voices had gotten louder. Richard hadn't liked that his mother was friends with another man. His mother had shouted, "I can be friends with whoever I want!" and then cried out in pain. Max's stomach had dropped. He'd run into the living room and found his mother clutching her cheek. Richard's balled fist had trembled.

"I…" Richard had croaked. "I'm sorry. Kendra, I'm so sorry! I just… I lost it, okay?"

Max had been too stunned to speak, even though he'd wanted to demand Richard never touch his mother in anger again. All he'd felt was noxious horror.

Goddess. How he hated himself for having been too stunned to speak. For not insisting his mother leave Richard then and there. His mother and Richard had cried. They'd hugged. Richard had apologized again and again as he cried, even though the scent of tears had been oddly absent.

When Max had tried to talk to his mom about it, she'd brushed him off. "It's fine," she'd said, smiling in a way that didn't reach her eyes. "It was my fault. Of course it made him uncomfortable. I should have been more understanding."

They hadn't talked about it again.

Richard had felt terrible for losing his temper. He'd started bringing home gifts. Cooking dinner more. Watching TV with them, even helping Max with his coursework. Max had tried to forget and just enjoy the feeling of having a normal family. Richard had insisted he and Max go on father-son trips to Richard's upstate home. His mom had sometimes gone with them, but she'd wanted them to get in some bonding time.

But when they were alone away from Max's mom, Richard's true colors had shown. He'd yell at Max for seemingly no reason. Hit him in the stomach and back, places where his mother wouldn't see the bruises. When Max would choke out, "Why? What did I do?" Richard would only sneer.

"Can't help myself. Sight of a hybrid like you just gets my blood boiling." Then he'd smile and say with the most dangerous gleam in his eyes, "Be grateful I'm hitting you and not your mother. She'd deserve it for bringing impure filth into this world."

So he hadn't told. Not a word. He'd accompanied Richard upstate again and again, even knowing what awaited him. His stomach had bruised in yellows and purples and greens. Max hadn't let his mother see. He could handle it. If Richard was hitting him, it only meant he wasn't directing his rage at Max's mother.

Then the shifting had started. It happened at school. Max had been in the bathroom and Dean had strutted past. He was always giving hybrids at the school shit. Max must have stared too long, wishing Dean would slip and fall into the urinal. Dean's body had slammed Max against the bathroom stall.

"Fucking crossbred freak," Dean had snarled, fangs bared. Something had snapped in Max. Fury had swelled within him and he'd seen Richard standing before him, mocking him. Max had lunged and he must have blacked out after he shifted because he woke later in some alley far away with a scrap of Dean's shirt and blood in his mouth.

There had been a meeting with the dean of students, Dean and his snobby parents complained, and Max had been expelled before he'd started his second year of college. His mother had told him he deserved better and promised he'd get into a better school. Max hadn't known what to do. He'd thought it was a one-time thing, that he'd had a shitty day.

Until it had happened again in the middle of work. He didn't remember how or why, but he'd woken up far from work in the rain. No blood, not this time. His manager had fired him, and Max had crumbled. He'd locked himself away in his room and hadn't talked to anyone, sure he would hurt someone because he was losing his mind.

Richard had been more irritable than usual, yelling at them, being verbally abusive to Max's mom. Then he was apologizing and trying to make nice with her, but Max had known this side of him wouldn't last long.

Max had worried his mom would get the brunt of it when Richard did lose his temper, so when Richard had offered to take Max out of the city, Max accepted. A part of him had almost wanted the fight he knew was sure to come. Wanted to hurt Richard like he was hurting. They'd driven for miles and arrived at Richard's home in the country.

Something had been different about Richard this time. He'd been muttering to himself the entire drive and when they arrived at the house, Max had braced himself for a fight. Richard wasn't expecting him to shift and fight back. Wasn't expecting Max to tower over him, his fangs at Richard's neck.

Richard had snapped then. He'd gotten the upper hand, his jaws around Max's throat until Max passed out. When he'd woken up, he was locked in the pantry. Richard had been holding a knife, but he hadn't killed Max. No. He'd just wanted to break him, and he'd succeeded.

Max had thought he'd known the extent of Richard's rage, but the things Richard had done to him in that dark room—he hadn't known the first thing about how deeply Richard's hatred toward him ran. The pain, fear, and fury had kept him shifted, ready to bite and tear if Richard should so much as open the door. He'd been totally powerless. A weak wolf. A useless son.

Someone knocked on the door. "Max? Can I come in?" It was Gabe's voice.

Max hesitated. His snarl died in his throat. What was he conflicted about? He should chase him off and shut him out. It was bad enough the pack had seen his scars, seen him at his absolute lowest. He wished they'd leave him alone—or that was what he told himself, not what he truly believed.

Feet shuffled on the carpet, and the door creaked and leaned forward ever so slightly. Was Gabe sitting on the other side? Max's defenses threatened to crumble. He didn't have to choose between fight and flight. The tension seeped from his body and he stood before the door, at a loss for what to do with himself.

"Max," Gabe's low voice said. "Your mother's going to stay with us."

Max's tail drooped. How could he look her in the eyes knowing how badly he'd failed her?

"I won't pretend to know what's going on in that red head of yours, but you should try talking to her, huh? She's hurting, too, Max. She's suffered, too."

Oh no. Did Gabe know everything? Did he know what his bastard stepfather had done? What did he think of Max, knowing he'd been too weak and powerless to prevent it?

"Max." Gabe's voice stilled the hurricane inside him. "She feels terrible. She really wants to speak to you, whenever you're ready."

The air became trapped in his throat. Was that true? Was it possible she still loved him despite his weakness? No. It couldn't be possible—could it?

"She still cares, so maybe go easy on her, huh?"

He wanted to open the door. Reach out his hand and find Gabe on the other side. A voice inside him whispered louder than all his hopes. It whispered through a mouthful of fangs in his stepfather's voice, *"He's lying. He hates you. Your mother hates you. You're weak. Pathetic. Filthy mutt."*

And it was that voice Max listened to as he turned away and dragged himself back to bed, curling himself into a ball as small as he could get and burying himself among the sheets. He closed his eyes tight.

The distant crunch of gravel made his ears twitch. Curious, he jumped off the bed and put his paws up on the windowsill. His heart sank. A black BMW pulled up to the front gate. An icy chill ran down Max's back.

That was Richard's car.

He'd come for Max and his mother.

CHAPTER 6

YOU'RE SAFE

THE SMELL OF LUNAR flowers, freshly shined shoes, and an expensive woodsy cologne spilled across the driveway, carrying into the yard like the scent of rot on the breeze. Like a missile, Gabe cast his gaze toward the man striding from the passenger side door of the black BMW and toward the gate. Gabe couldn't get a glimpse of the driver through the tinted windows.

Stocky and of medium height, with broad shoulders and a crooked jaw, Richard possessed a face like granite, made sharper by a severe buzz cut, with steely eyes that glanced hungrily at the doorman's throat and thick, heavy fists like miniature wrecking balls. He smiled at the doorman. His smile was all teeth beneath a thick coating of stubble, sharp and predatory and practically a snarl. Gabe barely suppressed a growl.

Ryan and Zach, who had just come up behind him, were quiet. They could likely sense Gabe's fury at the pure threat prowling ever closer.

Richard growled something to the doorman, and then those heavy-lidded eyes met his gaze. Gabe didn't move and neither did Richard. He had the feeling if he got within reach, Richard would lunge for his throat.

"Hey, fellas. Maybe you can help me out here." Richard smiled and Gabe was surprised worms didn't slither from between his teeth.

Gabe put himself in front of Ryan and Zach. Richard's eyes never blinked, watching him from beyond the gate like a beast in a cage. "That depends, man. What do you need?" He knew full well, and it was all he could do to keep his claws from coming out.

"Name's Richard Moray. I'm looking for someone. Was told your agency might know where he is."

"Depends," Gabe growled, not caring if his fangs showed. Would Moray still smile if he knew what despicable things Kendra had told them about him, or did he know and was smiling regardless?

Richard narrowed his eyes, an arrogant tilt to his head. Gabe knew that look—how dare a filthy hybrid show his teeth to a pure-blooded werewolf. "But where are my manners? Who might I be speaking to?"

"Agent Gabriel Reyes. What do you want?"

Richard said, "I want my son. His picture turned up on your website last night and he's supposed to be here." Cold eyes swept around, then widened.

Gabe turned, and his heart dropped at the sight of Kendra.

"No..." Kendra whispered. "What are you doing here?"

Richard bared his teeth at her, then snapped his gaze to Gabe. "What has she told you? Whatever it is, it's all lies."

"Be quiet," Kendra whispered, her voice quivering.

Richard slammed a hand against the bars. Kendra flinched. Gabe put himself between her and Richard. "That bitch abducted my son. Tormented him. Carved into his skin with a knife!"

"I'd never!" Kendra cried, furious tears in her eyes. "You're the one who hurt him!"

Gabe crossed his arms and stared Richard down. "That's not what she told me."

Richard barked a laugh. "Let me guess. She spun some story about how I abused her? What horseshit. I did nothing but provide for her and my son, and this is how she repays me. Women, am I right?"

"That's enough!" Gabe growled.

"The crazy whore tried to kill me when I attempted to save him from her abuse."

"He's lying!" Kendra screamed, latching onto Gabe's arm in desperation. Gabe squeezed her hand, assuring her that he knew, and kept his eyes on Richard.

"Whatever she told you, Mr. Reyes, she's delusional. You can't trust her. Now, let me see my son."

"He's *my* son!" Kendra snarled and though she trembled in fear and anger, the wolf was ready to burst from her skin to protect her son. "You will never hurt him again!"

A blur of red streaked from the front door and tore down the courtyard toward them. With a snarl, Max leaped in front of his mother, fur bristling and lips pulled back from glimmering fangs. Kendra's face was stark white.

Richard smiled. The sight made Gabe want to put his fist through his teeth. "Max. Sonny boy. I've been so worried. Come with me, kid, and your mother won't be able to hurt you anymore."

Max trembled, ears flattened against his head. His snarling only got louder.

"Max," Richard growled, his poor attempt at a loving façade cracking to pieces. "I said *come here.*"

The threat in those words had Gabe's wolf surging to the surface. He lunged, fist shooting between the bars, and fisted the front of Richard's shirt. He pulled and Richard crashed into the gate, fangs bared as he continued to smile.

"Here's how we're gonna play this. You're not stepping foot past this gate. You won't lay a hand on Max or his mother."

Finally, that infuriating smile fell away and a snarl took its place. "The bitch finally grew a backbone, did she? I shared my wealth, put up with that hybrid brat of hers. And this is how she repays me."

At the mention of Max, Gabe's fangs extended, piercing his lower lip. "Put up with? You tortured him!" His claws itched to rip, to tear.

Richard narrowed his eyes as he sneered in Max's direction. "That *thing* is a mutt! It's a disgrace to werewolves everywhere!"

Gabe bared his fangs in fury. "Touch him again and I'll fucking kill you."

Richard snapped his fingers. The driver side door flew open. A hulking man lurched out, fabric ripping as the driver grew fur and fangs.

"Watch out!" Ryan shouted as an enormous mass of muscle and fur leaped over the gate. He was huge, body straining out of his clothes, snarling face a hairy combination of man and wolf as it bared salivating fangs and roared. Ryan got between Zach and Richard's bodyguard.

With a single swipe of the bodyguard's clawed hand, Ryan tumbled down to the dirt. Blood spattered. Zach roared his fury and Gabe answered. The howls of the wolves within the estate filled the air. Zach's claws came out, he bared his fangs, and he charged Richard's bodyguard.

Richard scaled the gate and crashed down before Gabe, sending him flying back. Richard approached him, claws long and sharp. What little humanity he possessed was crumbling, and he snarled through a mouthful of fangs, the whites of his eyes turning an inky black with blazing pupils. Fur grew from his jaw and his ears were sharp points.

"Good." Gabe panted as his wolf snapped and strained at his chains. "I was hoping you wouldn't make this easy for me."

They circled. Gabe didn't dare blink, eyes fixating on Richard's razor claws. Richard's tongue swiped at his upper lip as if he couldn't wait to taste Gabe's blood. "Wanted to kill me a hybrid today. You things are a blight on our kind. An ugly sore that has to be cut out."

Look who's talking, Gabe thought, sneering his contempt.

Richard sprang, claws poised for Gabe's throat. Gabe bunched his muscles, and a flash of red soared in like a fireball. Richard fell mid-leap, tumbling over in the flower beds. Max stood in front of Gabe, shielding him. The little wolf trembled, but his fur bristled as he bared his fangs in fury. Gabe was in awe of the strength such a small wolf possessed.

Richard rose on all fours, panting harshly. He was shifting by the second, his clothes stretching to tatters as his wolf surfaced. He grinned, eyes blazing with hatred as he set his sights on Max. "Maxie boy. I missed you. Why don't you come home with Daddy? The pantry's empty without you." He rose, towering over Max.

The fear in Max's eyes spurred Gabe forward. Gabe's clothes ripped and tore as he shifted, his feet turning to paws as he charged. Richard leaped, changing into a big black and white wolf. He and Richard collided in a tornado of claws and fangs. Blood gushed coppery in Gabe's mouth as his fangs pierced Richard's shoulder, bone and muscle crunching under his teeth.

Richard slammed a heavy paw into his ribs, knocking the air from him as he tumbled over. Before Gabe could recover, Richard had his neck between his jaws. He hurled Gabe against a window. The glass cracked and shattered, stabbing into his skin. He tumbled through the shattered window and rolled to a stop. Stinging pain sliced into him as he landed on broken glass scattered on the hardwood. His vision darkened.

MAX HELD HIS BREATH, unable to look away until Gabe heaved himself back out through the shattered window. Blood dripped from his fur. Max felt sick, another person hurt because of him. His paws trembled when he stood. For the first time in months, something was rising in his throat, pressing against the back of his lips. He opened his mouth, but nothing came out, only a whine as Richard stood.

Blood dripped from his inky black pelt and he gave a shake, scattering shards of glass. Those burning eyes set their sights on him.

Richard shifted, teeth bared and streaked with crimson. "Come on, let's go home."

Gunfire cracked, ringing in Max's ears and thrumming deep in his chest. Richard howled and collapsed, smoke curling from a hole blown into his leg. The bullet hole sizzled as if the flesh were burning from the inside out. Gabe's friend, the tall one with long braided hair, lowered a smoking pistol. Richard's anguished scream split the air and Max couldn't help feeling a twinge of satisfaction. No one had ever made his stepfather scream so loudly before.

Richard collapsed as he seethed through gritted teeth. "Gonna kill you. Kill you this time. All of you hybrid-loving motherfuckers."

Behind his stepfather's crumpled form, the large black wolf that was Gabe rose. Gabe shifted, his paw becoming a hand as he fisted the back of Richard's thick neck. Richard's back collided with a tree and Gabe loomed over him in his human form, blood running in rivulets down his naked, rippling muscles. He pinned his elbow against Richard's throat.

"No," Gabe growled, his voice never wavering. "You'll never hurt Max again."

Since Max had known Richard, his stepfather had been a dominating force. No one had been able to stop him. His mother had tried and been broken. Max had fought at first, but as he'd become more and more malnourished and his stepfather's words had cut deeper than his blows, he'd lost the will to fight back.

Gabe was the first to stand up against Richard and leave him utterly powerless. More than anything, it was the promise in Gabe's words that left Max breathless. The way he glanced at Max and not at Richard as he spoke—it was a promise to Max, a promise that he'd never be hurt again, that so long as Gabriel Reyes drew breath, Max would always be safe.

It was like Gabe had said from the start, but Max hadn't wanted to believe him. Talking was easy. Now, having seen how far Gabe was willing to go, that he could back up his words with action, Max believed with every fiber of his being.

Gabe's friends got Richard on his knees and slapped cuffs on him. Max couldn't look away. The fear that had stolen his voice for so long disappeared. Words were rising from somewhere deep inside him. He'd never wanted to speak again after weeks in that pantry. Words only got him hurt and there was no one to listen even if he did want to speak.

Even after he'd been taken to the agency, words had still felt meaningless. The hurt, the loneliness, the fear—it was all too much for words to suffice, so he'd stayed quiet.

But now... *now*—

The change came over him. His paws became feet, the wind cooled his skin and pushed back his hair. He reached out, unafraid for the first time in months. Gabe's arms opened and Max fell into the warmth and strength of his bare upper body. Max's arms trembled as they flew around broad shoulders. He breathed in the smell of uncut grass and elm trees, pressing his face to a hard chest. A heartbeat thrummed in his ears, his or Gabe's, he couldn't tell.

"You're safe, Max. I got you." Strong arms went around his shoulders and held tight.

Against his will, tears squeezed from his tightly closed eyes and for the first time in what felt like forever, a single word spilled from his lips, a name he uttered in reverence.

"*Gabe.*"

CHAPTER 7

FILET MIGNON

"YOU KNOW THIS IS touching and all, but there's three grown-ass men standing around naked," Ryan remarked.

Heat rushed to Max's face, and he realized he was naked and huddled up against Gabe. "Sorry!" He'd been so overcome that he hadn't been thinking. Running to Gabe was as natural as instinct.

Gabe offered a smile but rejected the clothes Ben brought to him, instead handing them to Max. "Don't be. Here." Max couldn't help feeling disappointed as Gabe's warm arms fell away.

"Gabe, catch!" Zach tossed Gabe a robe.

Max pulled on Gabe's oversized tee and the jeans. Gabe made a face as he lugged a naked Richard to his feet. "Have to say, Mama Gallagher, you can do way better than this guy."

Zach hurried over, fixing Gabe with a wary stare. "Where are you going?"

"Gotta toss Richard into a cell where he belongs."

"You're hurt. Stop by the clinic. Max, too." Ryan and Zach took Richard by both arms and dragged him toward the main building. A crew arrived to take the dead bodyguard to the morgue.

"Where is Richard going?" Max croaked, voice hoarse from disuse.

"The basement," Gabe answered. "We have cells down there, reinforced with silver and guarded twenty-four seven. He won't get out."

Max shivered, not sure how he felt about Richard being in the same building as him.

"This way, people," Ben shouted, waving toward the manor. "I'll show you to the clinic."

"Max, honey?" His mother hurried over and inspected his scratches, and then her blue eyes met his. "Are you hurt badly?" Max looked away, a spasm of guilt racking his insides. Was she upset he'd spoken to Gabe first instead of her? Max hadn't been able to help it.

Speaking to Gabe was easy. There wasn't any guilt to paralyze him when he looked Gabe in the eyes. No memory of bruises on Gabe's cheeks that wouldn't be there if he'd been stronger. Max balled his hands into fists and stared at the ground, determinedly avoiding his mother's eyes.

Fuck. She must have thought he hated her, and his silence would only make things worse. He wet his lips, trying to figure out how he'd assure her he could never hate her.

"Coming in?" Gabe grunted, holding the door for them. The smell of his blood made Max's stomach clench. Gabe had been hurt fighting for him and his mother. He wanted to apologize, but what good would it do? Gabe would bleed regardless.

Max and his mother followed Gabe to the clinic on the manor's ground floor. Heads turned as patients and residents eyed Gabe, who was dripping blood on the floor. They stopped in a waiting room with a reception desk and several chairs. Kids, both in wolf and human form, played on the colorful carpet under the watchful eyes of their parents. The air conditioner blasted them, and Max sighed in contentment.

"Is Luke in? I'm in a bit of a fix," Gabe asked, grinning through his pain. They were asked to wait a moment for a room to open up.

As they sat, Max said, "Thank you."

Gabe's eyes opened and he quirked a brow.

Max realized Gabe mustn't have heard him. "Th-thank you." It sounded so stupid now he was saying it aloud, and he blinked hard, overwhelmed when he remembered Gabe standing up to Richard. Words didn't come close to expressing the gratitude he felt, but he had to say something.

A smile tugged at Gabe's lips. It made Max's stomach flutter and scrambled his brain. "It's my pleasure."

Max looked out the window, alarmed as tears burned his eyes and his throat tightened. Alone in that dark pantry, his body aching and bruised, all he'd wanted was for someone to come and help him. In his eyes, Gabe was a hero.

Gabe was called by a nurse. Max's mom remained in the waiting room, but Max had a few scrapes from when he had scuffled with Richard, so he accompanied Gabe. The nurse led them to an empty exam room. Gabe briefed her on their injuries and she left, informing them the doctor would be in to see them. Gabe sat on the exam bed, Max in a hard chair as the silence pressed in on his ears. Gabe met his gaze and suddenly looked away, scratching behind his head.

"Does it hurt?" Max asked before he could stop himself. Stupid. Of course it hurt! Guilt gnawed at him.

"Stings a little, but I'll live. Times like these, I wish I had pure blood. I once heard a werewolf complain his wounds took fifteen seconds too long to heal. Boo-hoo."

Max smiled. He supposed that would be nice. His own cuts were stinging pretty badly. His eyes shifted from tile to tile, toes tapping while he thought about what to say.

"You seem to be in a good mood, twinkle toes."

"Sorry." He stopped at once, not wanting to annoy Gabe. His ears burned. "Just... relieved, I guess."

"Sorry?"

Max grimaced, realizing he was speaking too quietly. He squeezed his fingers together in his lap. "I'm relieved," he said, meeting Gabe's eyes and regretting it as his stomach fluttered. Sudden nerves threatened to chase away his words as Gabe's full lips quirked into a warm smile. "That Richard's locked up. What a thing to say about your stepdad..." Max cleared his throat, his voice unused to speaking. "He'll... he'll really be contained?"

"Yeah. He'll be heavily guarded while he recovers. Zach shot him with a silver bullet, so he'll be too weak for questioning right away."

"Won't that kill him?"

Gabe shook his head. "Silver bullets aren't for killing, though I imagine eating a ton of them will do you in. Silver bullets subdue our inner wolves, force us to assume our human forms like you saw with Richard. It's a nonlethal way to end a fight. Depending on how feral a wolf is, though, they may not always shift back."

"Oh." Max had never been taught much about werewolf lore. His mother was no historian, and Richard... to Richard, a hybrid like Max was unworthy of werewolf lore.

"Aconitum, or wolfsbane as it's more commonly known, now that's a killer. Silver bullets poisoned with aconitum will kill the wolf *and* its host like that." Gabe snapped his fingers for effect.

"What'll happen to him? To Richard?" Max asked. He nibbled his lower lip. Would he go to jail?

Gabe fiddled with the sash to his robe. "Between you and your ma, there's enough evidence for him to go to trial. You'll have to testify against him."

Max's heart threw itself into his throat. He'd have to speak in front of people? Relive those terrible weeks locked away in the dark, Richard looming over him, saying those horrible things, the gleam of his knife—

"We don't have to worry about this yet, Lobito," Gabe's low voice assured him.

Max exhaled, squeezing his fists until his knuckles whitened.

"But yeah, he could go to jail."

"He'd deserve it." The venom in his own voice took him by surprise.

"He would," Gabe agreed, an edge in his voice.

A shaky exhale fell from Max's lips. Wanting to clear the air, he said, "Sorry if this is a stupid question, but what does Lobito mean? I've wanted to ask since you first called me that."

"It's not stupid," Gabe assured him with a carefree smile. "It's Spanish, means 'little wolf.'"

His own laughter sounded strange to his ears. He didn't remember the last time he laughed. Cheeks warm, he said, "You think I'm little?"

"You looked so little the night I saw you. I wanted to take that and turn it into a strength."

Max smiled down at his lap.

He wanted to talk more, but the door opened and in walked a surprisingly young man with thick chestnut hair and neatly trimmed scruff. He smelled of lunar flowers. "Hey, Gabriel. Got yourself in trouble again?"

They fist-bumped. "You should see the other guy. Max, this is Luke Collins."

Luke offered a kindly smile that lit up his blue eyes. Max shook his hand.

"Goodness, Gabriel. What did you do this time?"

"Not only me." Gabe pouted as if wounded. "Max here hurt himself, too."

Max raised his hands to ward away the doctor. "It's nothing! Gabe's the one who needs your attention. But thanks," he added.

"Very well." Luke approached Gabe. "Now, what might be the problem? If I had to guess... you landed on glass." Luke scrutinized Gabe's numerous cuts.

"Yup. Got thrown through a window while fighting his stepdad."

Luke's eyebrows disappeared into his bangs. "Now, that's a story you'll have to tell me over a drink."

"Will I need stitches?"

Max covered his mouth to suppress a laugh. Gabe was practically squirming like a panicky dog at the vet's office.

"No, but these need to be cleaned. You're sure you're alright, Max? This will take a while."

"I'm fine." His cuts stung, but he was more concerned about Gabe.

"No, do him first," Gabe insisted.

"Okay, you both have to decide. Who's going first?"

"He is." Gabe pointed to Max.

"No, really, I'm fine!"

With a sigh, Luke made the decision for them and promptly cleaned and wrapped Max's wounds before moving on to Gabe. Gabe shrugged his shoulders out of his robe, and it pooled around his waist. Max swallowed at the sight of his lean, muscular body lined with scars. Max's scars were ugly, but Gabe's made him look powerful.

"I don't know if he's told you this," Luke said, chuckling as he cleaned Gabe's cuts with a cotton ball, "but Gabriel was quite the rebel in his youth."

"What do you mean 'in my youth'? I'm twenty-seven!"

He didn't look it. Not that it mattered—Max's first boyfriend had been an older boy. The comparison made Max's face heat up. Not that Gabe was his boyfriend...

Did Gabe have a mate? Mated pairs usually had mating bites on their necks. He glanced over, trying to take a peek at Gabe's neck. His eyes wandered right into the golden amber of Gabe's and he looked down at his feet.

"You see"—Max became aware Luke was still talking—"Gabriel fancied himself a vigilante type, running around fighting against bigoted humans and pure-blood supremacists."

Max smiled, thinking that was the coolest thing he'd ever heard. He wished he could be that strong. "That's awesome."

"No, it's not," Gabe said, fixing Max with a stern look. "Running around without a pack doing that kinda shit will get you killed. Which I learned pretty quickly. Ben found me and told me to get my act together and join the LPA when I was old enough."

Luke concluded his examination with a final bandage across Gabe's back. "All done."

Gabe jumped off the table, touching the bandages on his back. "Where's my lollipop?"

"Where it always is. Nice to meet you, Max. I don't mean to be rude, but I hope we don't see each other again quite so soon."

Nestled among the blankets and encased in the darkness of the bedroom, Max closed his eyes and tried to sleep. It had been an exhausting day. Distant sounds carried to him: laughter, indistinguishable chatter. His wolf whined but Max pulled the covers over his head.

Ever since he was expelled from college some months ago, his social life had diminished. Wolves craved a pack and after months alone, all he'd waited for lay beyond the door to his bedroom.

When he'd met Gabe, he'd finally found someone he trusted enough to speak to without fear of being reprimanded, but Zach, Ryan, the older man, Ben—they were all strangers to him. He had nothing in common with those wolves. He wasn't part of their pack. He was a freeloader seeking sanctuary. Once they felt safe, he and his mother would leave and never see any of them again, so what was the point in being friends?

Laughter echoed from down the hall. His wolf whined, itching to rush to the door and join them. To be *pack.* The thought made cool sweat break out across his body. He'd never been part of a pack before, and they'd make fun of him for not knowing what to do around them. He was still malnourished and weak, and they'd sense his weakness and take advantage of him. It was better to stay in his room.

His stomach rumbled, making that difficult. The distant smell of sizzling beef made him salivate. They'd all be down there eating together: Gabe, Ryan, Zach, and the others, maybe even his mother.

There came a knock at the door. "Hey, Max, dinner's ready." Max recognized Ryan's Brooklyn accent.

Max stared at the door, torn between whether to speak or not. Did he eat with them or stay in his room? If he ate with them, what would he say? The thought of being surrounded by people he barely knew made his heart race.

"I'll leave it here," Ryan called. "Night, kid."

Max exhaled, shoulders drooping. He slumped back in bed. Bitter frustration came rushing in. At this rate, they'd all think he didn't like them. Would he ever be able to leave this room and be part of the pack?

He left the food outside and fell asleep with an empty stomach.

Darkness pressed in on him. His whole body ached and throbbed. Light came streaming in.

"Max? Honey? Come here. We're leaving, I promise. I promise."

Don't go, don't go, he tried to say, but his legs carried him anyway, out the door and beyond.

Tobacco burned his nostrils. A clawed hand fisted his scruff. Bad Man bared his fangs.

Don't kill me. Don't kill me. Please, someone help—

He woke to a shredded pillow, feathers in his mouth. His thrashing legs had torn apart the sheets. He'd gone to bed a man but woke a half-formed beast.

Stumbling from his bed, he threw the sheets out the window and crammed the pillow under his bed. He wanted to go to his mother's room down the hall and make sure she was okay but worried he'd wake her up.

No one could know. He had to be strong.

Bury it.

He would bury it all.

THE NEXT MORNING, A tray of food awaited him outside his door. Additionally, a bag full of things he'd left in Richard's apartment sat beside the tray. Inside was his wallet and phone. On the tray was a dish of yogurt, some bacon, and fried eggs. It was a feast.

Guilt chased away his hunger when he realized he'd let such delicious food go to waste last night, and he carried the tray into his room and sat at a small table by the window. These people were treating him like one of their own, and he couldn't even thank them in person. He made sure to clean his plate in appreciation and leave it outside the door.

He settled back into bed wearing sweats and Gabe's oversized T-shirt. It smelled like him, blanketing him in a sense of comfort and safety. Tired from his broken sleep, he slept the day away until dinnertime. He picked at his food, still full from his late breakfast, until someone knocked on his door. "Max? Would you like dessert?"

He didn't recognize the voice, which was female. He sniffed and caught a whiff of berries, chocolate, and whipped cream. Man, he couldn't resist chocolate.

"Sure."

A pretty young Latina woman entered the room with a tray, her long black hair in a ponytail. He thought she looked familiar but embarrassingly he couldn't remember her name or where he'd seen her.

All warmth, she graced him with a brilliant smile and set the tray down on his table. "How are you feeling?"

He shrugged. "Okay."

"That's good. My brother told me you kicked your stepfather's ass."

This was Gabe's sister then. She had the same black hair, similarly colored eyes, though not nearly such a radiant amber color, and she had a deep olive complexion.

"Are you older than Gabe?"

She grinned. "I like you. No, we're six years apart. But between me and my big bro, I'm the smarter of the two of us." She winked.

Max laughed as his eyes wandered the carpet.

"You and I actually met once before, but you probably don't remember. You were under a lot of stress. It was after you arrived. I'm Isabella, but call me Izzie. Everyone does."

Max couldn't remember her or much of anything before the moment Gabe had shown him his scars and held him in his arms. How could he forget the first tender touch he'd known since leaving the pantry?

"Yeah. I can't remember much," Max admitted.

Izzie smiled. "It's all right. We were worried, you know. We thought you were lost to us. I put up a posting online about you and fortunately your mother got in touch."

This revelation made Max see her in a new light. She was the reason he and his mother were reunited. "Thank you."

"Of course, Max. Nothing makes me happier than helping people find their families. Anyway, this looks great. I hope you enjoy." She had her own plate of dessert on the tray next to Max's serving.

"Uh, you can eat with me. If you want." He immediately regretted speaking. Why would she want to eat with him, this weird, quiet guy? "If you're not busy! I understand if you are, so—" By the She-Wolf, he needed to shut up.

A smile lit up her face. "Sure, I'd love that!" She pulled up a chair. Max ambled to the table and sat across from her. He dug his fork into the chocolate mousse and ate. It practically dissolved in his mouth. "So good..." He sighed.

"Isn't it? Try it with a raspberry."

Max did, enjoying the tart sweetness in contrast to the dark chocolate. He nodded his approval.

Izzie swirled the mousse in a patch of whipped cream, moaning in bliss as she popped the spoon into her mouth. "I think this is one of my favorite desserts. Oh, but that's only next to the cherry pie. You have got to try it!" She sighed dreamily. "We have some of the best cooks here. What's your favorite food?"

Max thought back to dinners with his mother, before Richard. "My mom always made this amazing filet mignon roast for Christmas dinner. It's a tradition of ours." Remembering those dinners brought back the scent of the Christmas tree and holiday-themed candles.

Izzie gasped. "That sounds so good! We should make it."

"It is. It's so tender and juicy. It melts in your mouth. We only have it once a year, so it's something I look forward to." The year Richard lived with them, they'd stopped celebrating Christmas. Richard believed no werewolves should celebrate a human holiday, especially a religious one. It was "an insult to the goddess" to acknowledge any "pitiful human gods." Max and his mom weren't Christian, but it was a tradition Max's birth dad had introduced to Max's mom, and one his mother enjoyed for the ideas of giving and family.

There was a knock. "Max?" His mother's voice made him pause. "Can I come in?"

Max hesitated. Izzie looked to him, waiting.

Max cleared his throat. "I'm, uh… getting dressed."

"Oh. Okay. Did you have anything to eat? I brought some food. I thought we could maybe have dinner together."

It had been a long time since he and his mother had sat down to a meal together. Max opened his mouth, but the words wouldn't come. He kept seeing the bruises on her face. Kept hearing her cry of pain when Richard hit her.

"I'm not hungry," he answered, the lie falling heavy into the pit of his stomach.

"Oh. That's fine." Her voice was light, as if she were trying to convince him his rejection hadn't hurt. But he could smell the salt of her tears beyond the door.

"Yeah," Max said. "That guy, Ryan, brought me some."

"That's good. Great." She laughed. The sound made Max flinch, suddenly wishing he was alone as Izzie furrowed her brows at him. "Well… I'll be downstairs if you change your mind. Goodnight, sweetie." Her footsteps grew farther away. Max swallowed down the urge to call her back and apologize. He slumped, chin to his chest. Izzie frowned but didn't say anything.

Izzie stretched and yawned. "It's been a long day." She took their plates, which were wiped completely clean. "Hey, tell you what, how about to-morrow night you can join us for dinner? This pack's a bit crazy, but I promise to smack the boys around if they get too rowdy."

Unsure how to reply, Max nodded. He didn't know what to do. He wasn't sure how he'd fit in. Then again, if they were all as nice and easy to talk to as Izzie, how hard could it be?

Once she was gone, Max lay back in bed and let the quiet of his bedroom lull him to sleep.

MAX SPENT MOST OF the next day alone but when the housekeeper arrived to tidy his room, she asked him about his missing sheets. Unwilling to answer, Max left the bedroom. He decided he might as well explore the estate a bit.

The upper levels seemed to be primarily sleeping quarters for guests and patients in the west wing, each with their own bed and bath. The kennels were further in the west wing, but Max wasn't in a hurry to go back in there. Exam rooms and offices occupied the east wing.

Down the stairs was the kitchen and dining room in the south wing with a recreation room on the other side of the manor boasting things like a gym, a painting studio, and other various artistic pursuits. There was also a basement where staff scurried in and out. Max sometimes heard barking and snarling down below and supposed it was another place ferals were kept.

Thinking he'd seen enough of the interior, Max headed out the back door into a courtyard. A garden of fruits and veggies grew beyond a tall fence, and Max could smell tomatoes and onions, leeks and eggplants as well as apples and carrots. An enormous swimming pool dominated the courtyard. Werewolves and hybrids occupied the pool.

Wolves dog-paddled while toddlers giggled as their parents dipped them in the water. People sat on the edge of the pool talking and laughing, and wolves ran past shaking their pelts and scattering water everywhere. Something twanged longingly in Max's chest. They all looked like they felt right at home, untroubled by whatever hurts and pains had brought them here.

Distant howls caught his attention. His sneakers splashed in puddles of pool water as he hurried to take in the miles of land beyond the courtyard stretching off into the island forest. Families sat on blankets, wolves basked in the sun atop boulders, and whole packs of wolves charged across the lawn, tumbling together, yipping and barking. Pups frolicked together, struggling to keep pace with the older wolves.

Max's wolf itched to break free of his skin. What he wouldn't give to run with them, feeling the wind in his fur, smelling all there was to smell, chasing and giving chase, euphoric and carefree as he ran.

If he could keep up in his malnourished state. He was still skin and bones. He didn't want people to stare or feel sorry for him. His wolf whined in disappointment as he forced himself to turn onto a trail away from the estate, passing bungalows with darkened windows, the scent of other wolves declaring the spaces to be homes.

He caught Gabe's scent tangled up with many others and stopped outside a blue house with tiled eaves. Gabe's smell was all over this place. This was his home. He wondered if the black wolf was here. There was another smell, familiar. Like clean clothes, coffee, and sand.

As he passed in front, his heart raced as he caught sight of Gabe standing around the side of the house holding a hose in his hand. He wore only swimming trunks, and he smelled of salt water and sand. The hose sprayed water across his skin, cascading down the flat muscles of his stomach.

Max swallowed, suddenly finding breathing to be difficult as he watched the water race down his body. Gabe ran a wet hand through his dark wavy hair that cascaded down to his broad shoulders.

Max hadn't seen him so relaxed before. Gabe had the pretty, clean-shaven face of a boy band front man when he wasn't snarling at his foes and the lean, toned body of a fighter. Gabe's lips curled into a smile that made Max's heart lurch into his throat.

It was such an honest smile, all teeth, and brought a boyish charm to his already youthful face. He motioned someone over. A great brown wolf lumbered toward him, shaking sand and water from its pelt. Max recognized Zach's scent right away.

Zach shifted, long braids swaying around his broad shoulders. He was tall and handsome, trim and fit, but somehow he didn't hold Max's attention like Gabe did. Zach reached for the hose, but Gabe smiled that megawatt grin and blasted him with the water.

"You bastard!" The smile lighting up Zach's eyes contradicted his harsh words. They tussled, skin to skin, and Zach pushed Gabe up against the side of the house, dousing him with the hose. Gabe shrieked like a boy, laughing so hard he doubled over.

They like each other, Max realized as the musky scent of Zach's arousal hit his nose, and he was unable to look away as Zach's large hand ran up Gabe's shoulder to play with his hair. Zach smiled, vulnerable and warm, and Gabe smiled back, lightly punching Zach in the chest.

Max didn't know why, but there was a sinking feeling in the pit of his stomach as he turned his back and walked away. He was hungry, he supposed. He'd feel better once he ate. And yet the image of the two of them stuck around in his mind as he returned to the manor.

Ryan strode out the doors as Max approached. "Hey, Max!" Ryan offered him a high five and his glasses slipped off his nose. "What's up, man?"

"Nothing much." Max returned the high five and missed, slapping the air. Ryan sucked in his lips to keep from laughing at him.

"Nice to see you out and about. Where'd you go?"

"Around." Max motioned toward the courtyard. "I've never been on Fire Island before."

"Yeah? You go to the beach, get some sun and fun?"

Max shook his head. He always felt like Ryan was laughing at him.

"Anyways, stick around. We're having dinner in a bit. Come on over, it'll be fun."

"I don't know. Maybe." Max offered a smile and left. He returned to his room and was thinking about going back to sleep when someone knocked on his door. The familiar smell of cherry trees mixed with the smell of the ocean and tickled his nose.

"Max? You there?"

Max answered the door and Gabe smiled at him. "Hi," Max said, feeling strangely out of breath. He hadn't spoken to Gabe since their appointment with Luke yesterday.

"Dinner will be ready in ten minutes if you wanna join us. We're having filet mignon. Thought you might be interested."

"Oh. Yeah. Yeah, sure." Had Izzie told them that was his favorite meal? Gratitude left him warm all over. Unless it was a coincidence, but how likely was that?

When the dinner bell rang, Max hurried downstairs, his stomach twisting into knots. He hoped the pack usually dressed casually for dinner because that was all the clothing options he had right now.

In the dining hall gathered around an eight-seater table was Ben at the head of the table, Max's mother next to Izzie, Ryan and Zach joking around at the far end, and Gabe on Zach's right. Max felt a twinge of disappointment that they wouldn't be sitting next to each other. It would have made him feel more comfortable.

Izzie waved. "Max!" She squealed and ran over to give him a kiss on the cheek. Max's face felt hot enough to catch fire, but he returned her one-armed squeeze.

"Hi, sweetheart!" His mother's eyes sparkled with delight.

"Hey, sweetheart!" Ryan waved with a big grin, candlelight glinting in his glasses.

Ben's weathered face brightened. "Come and grab a seat, pup."

Face still hot, Max sat across from Gabe. Gabe smiled at him in a way that made his stomach flutter, and Max suddenly felt he'd made the right choice. The staff carried plates of buttery mashed potatoes, roasted vegetables, and the sizzling filet mignon to the table. A rush of different memories swept through Max as he recalled Christmases he and his mother spent together.

At the sight of the meal, Kendra's eyes widened and shone with happy tears. "Thank you so much. All of you." Izzie squeezed her shoulders.

Max swallowed the lump in his own throat and wished he'd sat next to his mom so he could hold her hand. The moment the tender roast touched his tongue, all feeling was swept away except the pleasure of eating good food, and this time there was good company to enjoy it with.

Ben shoveled down his food like a starved beast and got potatoes in his beard, Izzie and his mother talked fashion and complimented each other's makeup, and Ryan stole food off of Zach's plate while Zach chastised Gabe for wolfing down his potatoes and getting food on his shirt.

Looking around at them all gathered together in good cheer, a feeling unlike any other swept through him, and Max realized he was happy for the first time in a long time.

He hoped that someday he could be part of their pack.

CHAPTER 8

A FRESH START

MAX KNEW HE SHOULDN'T, and yet he found himself standing outside the basement door. It stood out from the other doors in the estate with the nose-burning stink of silver.

"Help you, kid?" The guard grunted, looking Max up and down.

Max wet his lips, trying to find his courage. He should walk away. He shouldn't engage in his own revenge fantasies but the anger was eating him alive. He was sick of the nightmares. Sick of the person he'd become, whittled down to nothing but skin and bones, fear and mistrust of everyone around him. "I want to speak to Richard Moray."

"Five minutes." The guard grunted, unlocking the door. He slipped on a glove and grasped the silver knob. "Stay at least six feet away from the bars and watch out for the line of silver at the foot of the stairs."

"Thanks." Max exhaled, balling his hands into fists. He walked down the stairs and the barking and snarling of furious wolves assaulted his ears. He walked over the line of silver at the bottom of the stairs and jumped when a wolf hurled itself against the bars near him, jaws snapping at him. The wolf screamed, flesh and fur burning. It ran into a corner of the wall and huddled, snarling and salivating. Its eyes burned with yellow light. All of their eyes did.

This was where the agency kept wolves who couldn't be fixed, Max realized. Wolves who'd lost their connection to their humanity for good. As he entered, a wolf was carried from one of the cells, a silver dart incapacitating it. The workers carried the unconscious wolf beyond a door that smelled like ash and burnt fur. Death. He shuddered. Would he have ended up in a cell down here if Gabe hadn't been able to bring him back from feral madness?

The man he was looking for was easy to find. He was in the last cell on the left and the only one who wasn't a wolf.

Richard Moray wasn't looking so hot. They'd at least dressed him in sweats and a tank top, but his arms were chained with silver cuffs with thick gloves on his hands to keep them from burning his bare skin. As Richard's narrow eyes met Max, icy dread ran down his spine. His heart began to race, and his palms grew slick with cold sweat.

Richard bared his teeth in a grin. "Hey, boyo. Come to see me? I've missed you."

Richard could smell it, Max's terror.

He can't hurt me. He can't. He—

Richard stood so swiftly, Max jumped back from the bars even though he was already a reasonable distance. "Where's your mother? Tell her to come and visit. I miss her."

Fury grabbed hold of Max, making his fangs long and sharp in his mouth. "You... You won't ever touch her again. I won't let you!" His voice was feeble from weeks of feral quiet. He sounded like a frightened child.

He'd come here for a reason. To threaten him the way he'd threatened Max. To tell him *he* was the weak one, *he* was the one who was filthy. But he couldn't. As a sneer curled Richard's face and he advanced on the bars, Max's words retreated like they always did in his stepfather's presence.

"Oh? You won't let me? What a shame." Laughter crawled, gravelly and low, from Richard's throat. "Look at you. You think you're a big man because those mutt lovers upstairs protected you. But you're not. I can smell it. Your fear. Your eyes, they're flickering. You're nearly feral with terror at the sight of me, filthy hybrid."

"I'm not," Max rasped. His knees quivered and he balled his hands into fists. His claws cut into his skin. "Tell me why. Why did you barge into our lives? Why did you hurt my mother? Me? Why couldn't you just stay the hell away?"

Richard's slimy gaze crawled over Max's skin. "That night at the supermoon festival, I saw your wolf and I... I knew you were different. And oh, I was right." A nasty grin curled his lips.

Max laughed, the sound harsh in his throat. "What the hell are you—"

"I figured if I hurt you enough, you'd reveal yourself to me. Show me why I was right to suspect what I did." He shrugged his bulky shoulders. "But you were a stubborn little shit. Stone did a better job than I ever could at bringing out that side of you."

"I don't get it. What are you *talking* about?"

Richard rolled out a crick in his neck. "As for your mother, well... she just pissed me off. A fine, upstanding wolf like her mated with some lowly human? Bore some crossbred little whelp? Made me fucking sick." A growl rumbled in his chest. "Had to put her in her place."

Guilt wrapped around Max's insides. "You turned our lives upside down. Hurt my mother. Because of..." Because of him. All of this had happened because of *him*. His knees trembled. Bile scorched his throat. His mother had been hurt because this nutjob thought Max was special for reasons Max didn't even want to understand. He'd lied to their faces, upended their lives, all to get at Max.

Max left without another word. He returned to his room and locked the door. He sat at the end of his bed trying to breathe. A snarl pulled from Max's throat. His claws cut into his palms. Fury swelled within him, and a red haze fell over his eyes. His mother had been targeted because of Max.

Max lunged off the bed and slashed at the wall. *"Fuck!"* He roared. Splinters of wood ripped from the wall. It wasn't enough. He needed to shatter something, break apart everything in his room, rip and tear with his fangs and claws and—

The window shattered. Shards of pain stabbed into Max's fist. The pain brought him out of his fury. Shit. *Fuck.* That hurt. Gasping, Max stumbled to the bed, cradling his fist. "Fuck. Shit! Why did I do that?" His voice cracked from pain and fear. Bits of glass had lacerated his knuckles, glittering shards protruding from the flesh. His blood spotted the blankets.

The door rattled. "Max? Are you okay?" It was Gabe's voice.

Fuck. He couldn't let Gabe see him like this. "Go away," Max snarled.

The doorknob shook. "It smells like blood in there. Are you hurt?"

Max squeezed his eyes shut. "I said go away!" He'd already caused Gabe so much trouble. Gabe had seen him at his worst time and again. Max had thought he was getting stronger, better. "Please." His voice was a whimper.

"I can't do that, Max. Not if you're hurt. Can you let me in? I want to help."

Max wanted to scream at him to leave, but he couldn't find his voice. Blinking fast, Max stumbled to the door and fiddled with the lock. He closed his eyes tight.

How could this get any worse?

GABE HAD BEEN GOING about his business when his wolf started nagging at him. His instincts screamed at him to check on Max *right now*, so he did, and he was glad because it sounded like Max was having a bad day. Gabe's heart pounded as he turned the knob.

The smell of Max's blood upset his wolf. He wanted to show his teeth and hunt for whoever had been the cause of Max's pain. "I'm coming in." His voice was rough, and he cleared it. He opened the door. Max was gone, the bathroom door open. A whiff of coppery blood hit his nose, and fury lit Gabe up from the inside out. A thousand different possibilities whirled through his head.

It was Richard. He'd gotten out. No, that wasn't possible. Was someone at the agency harassing Max? He wouldn't stand for that. Gabe would let them fucking have it if—

He kicked a piece of glass. The window had been broken. What the hell? Exhaling some of his fury, Gabe called out, "Max? You okay?"

"Fine." It was a lie from between clenched teeth. Max stood over the sink running his hand under the water. There was so much blood spattering against the porcelain, the water ran crimson.

Gabe's heart thundered. "What happened?"

Max tried to smile. It broke on his face. "Nothing. It's nothing. I—"

Gabe touched his shoulder. "Go sit down. I've got this." He nudged Max aside and knelt, finding the first aid box under the sink.

Head bowed, Max sat on the closed toilet seat. He smelled of sour shame and blood. Max's emotions flooded over Gabe until he thought he'd drown in Max's misery. Gabe didn't stand up right away. He took in a few breaths, unsettled by how emotional he was getting. He had to be the one with a rational head here. He had to be strong, but Max's hurt cut him deeply. It had never been this way with other wolves.

Gabe went to Max's side with the medicine box.

"I'm really fine," Max said.

Gabe snorted. "You look like you had a boxing match with that window."

Max extended his hand. Gabe tried to keep his face blank, but the sight of the cuts on Max's knuckles made him swallow a pitiful whine in his throat. He wanted to lick away the blood. Not exactly sanitary, but his wolf was pushing at his chest, aching to come out and lick and nuzzle and care for Max.

"I'm sorry," Max murmured. "I didn't mean to worry you."

"Well, you won't need stitches at least. The cuts aren't deep." Gabe forced a smile. "You showed that window who was boss, huh?" Gabe grabbed some tweezers, plucking little shards of glass from Max's skin.

Max winced. "I... I don't know what happened. I got so angry."

"Any reason?" Gabe wet a cotton ball with rubbing alcohol.

Max licked his lips. They were soft-looking, full and plump. There was a little freckle above his cupid's bow. Gabe didn't know why he was noticing that. "I saw Richard."

Gabe dropped the cotton ball. The idea of Max being anywhere near Richard made his hackles rise. "They let you down there?"

Max flinched. "I know. I'm sorry. I shouldn't have."

"No, Max, that's..." Gabe took in a breath. "You were brave to confront him like that."

Max sniffed, eyes narrowed in anger. "More like stupid."

Gabe plucked another cotton ball from the bag. "Why did you go?" he asked, careful to keep his voice calm. He wasn't angry at Max. The idea of him and Richard being in the same room made him want to bare his teeth. He thought he had a clue why Max had gone, though.

"Don't know," Max said, laughing bitterly. "It was stupid."

Gabe wet the cotton ball. "Ready?" Max nodded, his lips set in a tight line. Gabe dabbed the cut on Max's first knuckle and he jumped, gritting his teeth. Feeling bad, Gabe took his hand. Max exhaled, squeezing tight when Gabe cleaned the rest of the cuts. Max's hand was warm in his, his grip tight but not uncomfortably so. His fingers were longer than Gabe's, their fingers interlacing easily.

"All done." Gabe squeezed Max's hand and pulled away. He wasn't sure why he'd done that. It'd felt like a nice thing to do, rather than yanking his hand away. He fumbled in the box for Band-Aids.

"I can do the rest," Max mumbled. His cheeks were scarlet and the blush contrasted nicely with his fair skin.

Gabe wanted to do more, but it looked like Max would combust from embarrassment. "Sure." He handed Max some Band-Aids, and he pressed them over the wounds. Gabe said, "I had fantasies. For years. About con-fronting the man who hurt me." He still did.

Max grinned. "Bet you'd kick his ass."

Gabe chuckled.

Max hesitated, his eyes closed tight. His hair was long, framing his face. He'd shaved his wiry beard, revealing the dimples in his chin and his angular jawline. He looked younger without it, skin smooth and freckled. Gabe wondered how soft his skin might be under his fingers.

"I wanted him to see he hadn't broken me, I guess. But... He looked at me, and... And I felt like a scared little pup again." Fury and despair twisted Max's voice. "He... broke something in me. I don't know how to fix it. If I'll ever—" Max swallowed, his eyes bright in the darkness. He didn't finish, just stared into his lap. He took deep breaths, shuddery and wet in his chest. "I used to be strong and confident. Now I feel like a victim."

Fuck. Gabe hated this so much. "Hey." He patted Max's leg, unsure what to say. "You're not a victim. You're a survivor."

Max hung his head and rubbed his fist into his eye.

Gabe nudged him. "Wanna get out of here?"

Max looked over, surprise in his wet eyes. "Huh?"

Gabe smiled. "Off the estate for a bit."

"Is that allowed?"

Gabe chuckled. "Yeah. It's fine. We can go into town, get you some clothes that fit. Maybe a cool haircut. Lunch. Whatever you want." Max was still wearing Gabe's T-shirt and some loose cargo pants, the same clothes they'd tossed him after the fight with Richard.

Max twirled a lock of his red hair. "That... Yeah. That sounds good. My hair's crazy long, and I could do with a change of clothes. Okay. Let's do that."

Gabe jumped up. "Great! Wanna head out now?"

Max nodded and stood.

Gabe bounded from the bathroom and Max followed him downstairs and out into the driveway. Gabe called over his shoulder at Ben in passing, "We're getting out for a bit! Tell Kendra, okay?"

Ben raised a hand. "Have fun, crazy kids."

It was a fifteen-minute walk from the agency to a small harbor town. Seagulls cried and the warm summer breeze carried the salty scent of the ocean to Gabe's nose. The wind whipped Max's red hair around his face and he scowled, trying to tuck wayward locks behind his ears. Max went to the bank straight away to check the funds in his savings account. He'd said he'd thought for sure Richard would have drained his bank accounts, but it looked like that wasn't the case.

"I guess what little I have in savings was chump change to a millionaire like Richard," Max mused, rejoining Gabe outside the bank. Gabe was glad. At least Max could be financially independent.

"What's there to do here?" Max asked, looking around the small town.

Gabe shrugged. "Not much. Parties. Sunbathing." There were a few small towns spread out across Fire Island. The one closest to the agency boasted a tiny village with a few shops, a diner, and boating activities. "You've never been to Fire Island before?"

Max shook his head, hands stuffed in his pockets as he walked beside Gabe. "My mom and I went to Long Beach a lot in the summer."

Gabe smiled, remembering summer days spent on the beach. "Same. Hey, there's a diner up the street. We go there all the time. Hungry?"

Max shrugged. "Sure."

They stopped inside. Gabe waved at Betty, the waitress, and she got them a booth. Gabe ordered the meat loaf and Max ordered a burger. Gabe sipped his Coke and asked, "So, you grew up in New York?"

Max swirled his straw around in his ginger ale. "Yup. My family lived upstate. Then Mom moved into the city to open her business when I was five."

Gabe was impressed. "Your ma's a businesswoman?"

Max nodded, smiling. It looked like he was proud. "Yeah. She worked so hard for years to get it off the ground, and it finally took off a few years back."

"Awesome. What's she do?"

"She designs and sells clothes." Max sipped his ginger ale. "She has a store in the Village. It's pretty popular. Lots of fashion magazines have interviewed her."

Gabe's jaw dropped. "I didn't know you were the son of a celebrity."

Max's face colored. "It's not... I'm not..." Max pushed his hair away from his face. "I helped out around the store when I was younger. Think I disappointed her a bit when I decided to strike out on my own."

The diner was mostly empty, so their food arrived shortly. Max took a big bite of his burger, making his cheeks bulge. Gabe smiled and tried not to laugh.

"What about you?" Max asked, wiping his mouth with a napkin. He had a glob of ketchup he missed.

"Huh? Oh." Gabe tore his eyes away from Max's mouth. "Yeah, I grew up in the city. My parents immigrated to the States before I was born. My ma's from Madrid. My pa grew up in Mexico City."

"Cool. How'd they meet?"

Gabe smiled, but there was a twinge in his heart at the memory of his father. "They went to the same college in the same tiny town upstate. My mom's human, but my dad knew she was his mate the moment he smelled her. Took a while for her to come around, but he won her over." Gabe poured some gravy over his mashed potatoes. "It's crazy the experiences people miss out on when they judge others for looking different. They never let their differences divide them, and they had a beautiful life together." Throat a little tight, Gabe drank the last of his Coke.

"Is that why you joined the LPA? To make a difference?"

Gabe nodded. "Yeah. Getting angry and picking fights is easy. Helping others... It can be healing. It makes me feel like I'm making the world a better place." Even if on most days, it felt like two steps forward and ten steps back. "The world might never get better for hybrids and werewolves. At the end of the day, at least I can say I tried."

Max wet his lips and looked down at his food. His fingers curled in the napkin, then relaxed. "You have made a difference. To me."

Gabe's heart tripped over itself. Day after day of bringing feral werewolves off the streets, it became difficult to see how he was making a difference. All he saw were werewolves like Max, frightened and scared, feral at worst. It was never-ending.

"To my mother, too," Max continued, clearing his throat. He opened his mouth, then shut it. Gabe waited for Max to find his words. The low chatter of the other customers and the scrape of utensils on plates filled in the quiet. "We have a chance now. Because of you and the others. We didn't before, but we do now. So..." Wide eyes blinked at Gabe underneath a mop of ginger hair. They were the color of honey. "Thank you."

Gabe blinked, at a loss for words and worried he might suddenly start crying. Max looked away as his tongue trailed over his bottom lip. Gabe smiled, admiring the flush on Max's face. "That's great." He cleared his throat, voice thick. "I hope that when you and your ma have found your way again, we can still be friends."

Max's eyes widened. "I..." He smiled. It was all teeth. Radiant. "Yeah! Yeah, of course. That'd be great."

Gabe's heart felt lighter in his chest, and he couldn't wipe the grin off his face.

"Your food's gonna get cold," Max pointed out.

Face warm, Gabe shoveled meat loaf in his mouth.

Max's smile stuck in his mind throughout lunch as he kept smiling more and more. They talked about the agency. Gabe told Max about Ben and his twin teenaged sons. How he'd met Zach and Ryan during his training at the Lycanthrope Academy and the years they'd studied together to join the LPA.

The bell jingled and two men walked in. One was tall and Black with short curly hair. The man he was holding hands with was Japanese, his hair buzzed short on the sides and long on top. They were dressed in shorts and smelled like sand and the ocean, so Gabe assumed they'd been at the beach. He recognized them right away.

Max gasped. "I know them! They were students at the same college as me." Max waved. "Jin! Marcus!"

Gabe's face broke into a grin. "Oh, hey! Fancy seeing you guys here."

Marcus, the tall man, waved. "Jin, look, it's Max! Hey!"

Gabe shook their hands. "Good to see you guys again."

Max looked at Jin. "How do you know the agency?"

Jin's smile faltered, a haunted look in his eyes. Marcus squeezed his hand, offering support.

Jin cleared his throat, saying, "It was awful. I won't go into detail. But I'd be dead if it weren't for you and your friends, Gabe. Thank you." He smiled his gratitude.

"Of course," Gabe said. "I hope you're both doing well."

"We are," Marcus said, his deep voice sincere. "I can't thank you guys enough for all your help."

Gabe's heart squeezed in his chest. "It was good seeing you guys again."

"You, too," Jin said. "Thanks again, Gabe. Tell the other agents I said hello."

Max said, "And thank you, Jin, for sticking up for me back at my old school."

Jin clapped his shoulder. "No problem, Max. We hybrids gotta stick together. You're in good company."

Marcus put an arm around his shoulders. "Babe, our food's ready. Bye, guys!"

Jin and Marcus went to pick up their food at the counter.

"Think we should head out, too." Gabe waved the waitress over for their bill. Max reached for his card and Gabe said, "I got it."

"You sure?"

"Positive."

Max ducked his head. "Next time, lunch's on me."

Gabe thought that sounded great, especially the "next time" part.

After their meal, Gabe and Max stopped at a clothing store up the road. It was a small boutique store that Max said reminded him of his mother's store. Max changed out of his loose cargo pants and Gabe's T-shirt in the dressing room and emerged in some black skinny jeans that hugged his long legs and a black cotton shirt that fit tight across his chest.

Max tugged at the shirt. "I used to wear a bigger size than this. I lost so much weight when Richard locked me up."

Gabe hated the smell of Max's shame. He squeezed Max's shoulder. It was bony but strong. "Keep eating dinners with us and you'll gain it all back and then some. Especially the chef's mac and cheese. That stuff will blow you up like a balloon."

Max picked out an extra pair of jeans, a leather jacket that made him look badass, and a few T-shirts. Outside the store, Max handed Gabe's old T-shirt back to him. Gabe waved it away. "That's fine. It looks better on you than me."

They'd spent over an hour at the diner and a while shopping for clothes, and the hair salon had closed early since it was the weekend. Max frowned. "Great. I was hoping to get this mess trimmed." He shrugged. "I'll just do it myself when I get home."

Gabe frowned. "Are you sure? Have you done it before?"

"How hard can it be? I'm just buzzing it off."

Gabe winced. "But your hair is so nice... I mean, sure. If that's what you want."

Max wanted some agency in his life. Who was Gabe to stop him?

They walked back to the estate under blue skies. Gabe helped Max carry his new clothes into his room, and then Max made a beeline for the hair clippers in his bathroom. Max switched them on and hesitated. "Huh. This is going to be harder than I thought. Hey, could you give me a hand?"

"Sure." Gabe walked up beside him hoping his hands stopped shaking. "Tilt your head back."

Max did, and their eyes met. A current of... something swept down Gabe's spine. Max smelled relaxed.

"Do you trust me?" Gabe asked.

Max said, "Yeah. I do."

That shouldn't have made Gabe's heart clench so tightly, but now that he had Max's trust, he'd never abuse it. Gabe ran his fingers through the long ginger locks. "Okay…" Gabe breathed. "I'm feeling awfully protective of your beautiful red hair. Do I have to shave it all off?"

Max blinked, eyes widening. He squeezed his hands in his lap. His scent soured with sadness. "I thought about it. Richard said the color was ugly, that I looked like a girl with it so long. Not that that's wrong, but the way he said it…"

Gabe hated Richard. He hated him so much. Gabe brushed a lock of copper hair from Max's cheek. "Fuck him. Your hair is beautiful, short or long. And so is your red fur." Fuck Richard to hell and back.

Max's Adam's apple bobbed when he swallowed. He looked down, and Gabe smelled his salty tears. Gabe rested his hand on Max's head, closed his eyes, and felt for Max's thread, feeble and small but *there. "It's okay. You're okay. You're going to be okay."* He pushed as much comfort and kindness into their bond as he could, nurturing it the way a gardener might tend to a wilting rose.

"Can we do this?" Max asked, his voice low and rough.

Gabe switched on the razor. "Shaved?" he asked, holding his breath.

Max tilted his head right and left. He wanted to keep it. Good.

"Head back," Gabe instructed and Max did as asked. His eyes were wet, and a tear left a shimmery track down his cheek. Gabe ached to wipe it away, but he let Max pretend he hadn't noticed. Chunks of red hair drifted to the floor at their feet. It was matted in some places quite badly, but the razor cut through it with ease. Gabe hated to think of how long it had been since Max had been able to care for it.

"Sorry," Max mumbled. He smelled ashamed again. "I washed it and conditioned it but the mats were too painful to get out."

"It's okay," Gabe said at once. He didn't want Max to feel like he had to explain a thing. "Think of this as a fresh start."

Max let out a shuddery breath. "That sounds nice."

Max winced a little at first but gradually settled. Their toes nearly touched, and Gabe never wavered far from Max's side. He tilted Max's head left, right, up, and down, and Max let him.

Max closed his eyes and let Gabe's hand guide his movements, trusting Gabe to give him what he needed. Gabe's hands stopped shaking. He could see the end result as he worked, and he grew more confident knowing Max wouldn't be wincing the whole time. Knowing that Max trusted him.

Gabe buzzed the sides and back short but left a little length on top. Gabe took a step back, relieved to realize it actually didn't look that bad, not at all. Of course, that was all Max. He had a lovely face, masculine and gentle all at once. Gabe could see his ears now.

The haircut gave him an edge without stealing away his vulnerable softness. Of course, it was a little rough. Gabe wasn't a professional. But with some product to bring out his natural curls, it would look great. Max had the kind of face that worked well with about any style.

He was... beautiful. Gabe only hoped Max saw himself the way Gabe did, that he liked it... "Okay... Ready?"

Max's mouth quirked at Gabe's nervousness. "Didn't make me look ugly, did you?"

That wasn't funny. Gabe held his breath while Max walked to the mirror, chuckling at Gabe's nerves. Max stopped laughing and Gabe winced. "Sorry. Sorry, I think I cut it too short. Is it uneven? You still look great, Max. Really. You do, I—"

"Gabe, stop." Max's voice, low and husky, shut Gabe up. Max reached out, running his fingers through his hair. He blinked and a smile brightened his face. "It looks... perfect. It's exactly what I wanted."

Gabe exhaled. "Oh. Phew. I thought you were gonna scalp me for a second."

"No. No, I..." Max hung his head. He was crying again, but the scent wasn't soured by shame and sadness.

Gabe smiled, face warming. "I'm glad, Max." Figuring he should give him some space, Gabe stepped back, but Max reached back and grasped his shirt, holding him in place. Max took in a few deep breaths. Gabe breathed with him, waiting.

"Th-thank you," Max croaked. He looked back at Gabe, his face red and splotchy, and smiled. It was beautiful, cracked, and precious. Gabe wanted to see more smiles like that. He clasped the hand Max had curled in his shirt and gave an inviting tug. Laughing and sniffling, Max went to him, and Gabe put his arms around him.

"Anytime, Max."

It happened then, right there, as Max tucked his head under Gabe's chin, as he wound his scarred arms around Gabe and held on tight, as he laughed and cried into Gabe's chest. The bond between them surged from a spark to a roaring flame, glowing bright and warm in Gabe's chest.

It was different. Different from the bonds connecting him to Izzie and Ben, Ryan and Zach.

It was more, so much more, more than he could hope to comprehend.

Gabe nestled his nose into Max's ginger curls and breathed in the scent of cinnamon, chilis, and everything good and right and wonderful.

And later that night, with the stars bright and the moon overhead, his wolf tilted back his head and sang in a way he'd never sung before.

Chapter 9

DESIRE

The next night while they were having dinner, Ryan set down his empty wine goblet and said, "Let's watch *The Thing* at Zach's place!"

Izzie cocked a neat brow. "What thing?"

Zach snorted. "What is your obsession with that movie?"

"It's only the best horror movie ever made!" Ryan exclaimed, glasses askew on his pointed nose.

Izzie rolled her eyes. "You're going to scare yourselves silly, boys. Count me out. Sorry, Zach." She patted his cheek.

"We are *not* watching *The Thing!*" Zach declared. "Since Max is new, how about we ask him what he wants to watch."

Max was pleasantly surprised by Zach's dedication to including him. All their eyes landed on him. Max began to sweat. He really wasn't a big movie person. Ryan looked at him with wide, hopeful eyes. "*The Thing*?" Max suggested. He didn't even know what that movie was about, but he didn't mind scary movies.

"Yes!" Ryan punched the air. His glasses fell onto the table, and Zach laughed at him. "You and me are gonna be good friends, kid!"

Zach rolled his eyes. "Fine."

Ben stretched. "I'd join you kids, but I don't like shitty movies. See you lot in the morning."

Ryan bounded to the door and Gabe followed. Max set off after the pack. The air was moist and warm as they walked fifteen minutes to get to Zach's bungalow. Max trailed behind, unsure how to join in the conversation as Ryan playfully boxed with Zach and they wrestled on the way, Gabe laughing at their antics.

Zach looked over his shoulder at Max. "It's good to see you in human form!"

Max smiled. "It feels good."

Zach smiled back, warm and friendly. "How are you doing? Settling in okay?"

"Sure."

"Every Wednesday we go for runs as a pack. You should join us sometime."

Max liked the sound of that. "Sounds like fun."

They passed Gabe's blue hut and arrived at Zach's, a yellow two-story cottage with an outside seating area on the roof. The living room was open to the dining room, with a kitchen in the back of the house where a doorway led out to a little tomato garden. A spiral staircase led up to what Max assumed were the bedrooms.

"Bathroom, anyone? One's upstairs, another's right over there if you need it, Max." Zach pointed to a door just off the kitchen. "Anyone want snacks?" Zach asked, making a detour through to the kitchen. "Drinks? I got beer, soda—"

"I'll have a beer," Ryan called, sprawling out on the sofa. "You got a lager?" he asked, polishing his glasses.

"An ale!"

"That's fine."

Gabe said, "I'll have one, too."

Zach returned with the beers. "What about you, Max?"

"No thanks." Max wasn't even slightly curious. Richard always smelled of beer.

Grinning, Ryan adjusted his glasses with the air of an evil scientist cooking up a scheme. "You can have some. We won't tell."

Max shook his head and smiled. "I'm good."

"Here we go," Zach said, handing out the beers. He turned on a streaming service and located *The Thing*. He shot Ryan a look. "This is the last time." He smiled to show he was kidding.

"Love you, man." Ryan grinned and squeezed his shoulder.

"Max, do you wanna sit here?" Gabe asked, motioning to the couch.

"This is fine," Max said as he took the single armchair.

"Great. Then I'll take the couch."

Max didn't want to sit next to Zach for some reason. He didn't know him or Ryan enough to feel comfortable sitting with them.

"Excuse me, ladies." Gabe sat between Zach and Ryan and Ryan's smile faltered. Max's stomach twisted as Zach playfully bumped his shoulder into Gabe's, coaxing a shy smile to Gabe's mouth. Ryan was grimacing and Max wondered what the problem was.

Zach dimmed the lights as the movie started with a cheesy shot of outer space and a UFO. Max drew his knees to his chest. Out of the corner of his eyes, he could see Zach lean over and whisper something to Gabe. Laughter rumbled from Gabe's lips. His smile, all teeth and bright enough to rival the sun, made Max's chest hurt. Max wondered if he'd ever made Gabe smile like that.

Max kept his eyes glued to the screen, but he was uncomfortably aware of every shift in his peripheral vision. He glanced over, something ugly growing inside him as Zach laughed and wiped away the foam mustache on Gabe's mouth.

About halfway through the movie, Ryan said, "I'm feeling sick all of a sudden." He stood.

Zach looked away from Gabe, brows pinched in concern. "What's wrong?"

"You know, I'm not sure. Gotta run to the bathroom. Be back." Ryan shuffled into the bathroom around the corner.

Zach paused the movie. Gabe was snoozing beside Zach and didn't protest the movie being paused. "Ryan told me you've never been on Fire Island before," Zach said, fixing Max with a pleasant smile. "What part of the city are you from?"

"Mom and I lived in Midtown for years, but we moved to the Financial District after my mom and Richard mated. We're not rich or anything. Richard owns a big business, so we live in one of those fancy high-rises now. Or lived. We'll never go back to that place." Max stared down into his lap, wondering if he'd rambled too much.

Zach took a swig of beer. "I like the Financial District. There's a bar Gabe and I always go to round the corner from the Park Place station. The burgers are amazing."

They went to bars together, touched each other... Well, Zach did most of the touching. Gabe didn't seem like the PDA type.

Are you and Gabe dating? Are you mates? No. No way could he ask any of that.

"How long have you two known each other?"

Zach looked skyward, reflecting. He smiled. "Since college. I was going to NYU at the time. Gabe was training at the Lycanthrope Academy. Gabe's the one who introduced me to Ben and the agency. I decided I wanted to help others rather than join my family business. Now we work together."

"Wow…" They were close; there was no denying that. Zach likely knew so much about Gabe.

What does it matter? Why do I care?

And right away, a low voice growled in the voice of Richard, *Stupid mutt. Zach's his friend, but you're just a job to him. You may like him, but to Gabe, you're a messed-up kid to fix. You're not like Zach. You'll never be.*

Gabe yawned, rubbing his eyes. "Shit. I fell asleep. Anyone die yet?"

Zach frowned. "Man, is Ryan still in the bathroom? He must be really sick." Zach rose on those long legs and went and knocked on the door. "Ry, you okay, man? Need me to get you some medicine?"

The door opened and Ryan stepped out, head low and shoulders slouching. "I'm good. Think I need to go to bed."

"You sure?" Zach's fingers settled on Ryan's forehead, brushing aside chestnut brown locks.

Pink bloomed in Ryan's cheeks. Ryan ducked out of reach and slipped past to the door. "I said I'm fine. I'll see you guys tomorrow."

Max suddenly wanted to leave, too. "I'm pretty tired, too, so..."

Gabe's brow furrowed in concern. "Feeling all right, Lobito?"

Max's body flushed at his concern. "Yeah, it's nothing."

Ryan waved him over. "I'll walk you back."

Max followed Ryan out the door. Ryan said nothing as they walked, a surly frown on his face and the occasional sigh carrying off into the night. Max couldn't fathom what had soured his mood. "Are you okay?"

Ryan shrugged. "Yeah, just... worried about Zach."

"About Zach? Why?" He'd seemed to be in a good mood to Max.

"He's the one flirting with Gabe, and Gabe doesn't even seem like he cares. If he doesn't feel the same, he should just tell Zach."

No, the wolf within whined. *Gabe. Want. Mine.*

Max coughed as if to physically push that bizarre thought out of his body. "So, they're dating?" He tried to ignore the disappointment that walloped him in the stomach.

"Hell if I know what they are to each other. They've been on again, off again for maybe three months. I just hope Zach doesn't get hurt." Ryan sighed and ran a hand through his hair.

Max's wolf rumbled low in his chest. For some reason, his wolf hated the idea of Zach being with Gabe. But it wasn't any of his business.

They passed through the agency gates. Ryan waved once they arrived outside the doors. "Night, man."

Max said goodnight and went up to his room. His jeans pooled at his feet, and he searched among his things for something to sleep in. Gabe's oversized tee caught his attention. It was too big, but it was comfy, more comfortable than wearing pajamas—and it smelled like him. Cherry trees, flowers, soil, and sweat, like his skin. Heat blazed in his cheeks.

It was comfy. He'd go with that.

Max pulled it over his head and let the shirt swallow him. His breath hitched as Gabe's scent enveloped him and he felt for a moment like he was wrapped tight in Gabe's arms. He pulled the collar up and breathed in slowly, drinking in the smell of him, then tugged it down to his collarbone.

He turned off the light and stumbled to bed in the dark, curling up atop the cool sheets. The window was open, and the salty smell of the ocean wafted in with the distant crash of the waves and the wind through the palms.

What were Gabe and Zach doing in the bungalow alone? Had they grown bored of the movie? If Max were the one alone with Gabe, he didn't think the movie would have held his interest for long. Sooner or later, the heat of Gabe's body and his scent would have become overwhelming.

His hand wandered over his chest, tugging the collar of the tee to his nose again, and he breathed in Gabe's scent. Warmth tingled pleasantly between his thighs, making his breath hitch again.

He thought back to the pair of them outside Gabe's cottage, Gabe's body dripping wet, smelling of sand and salt water. Gabe would have tasted like the ocean under Max's tongue, hair slick and sandy between his fingers, his lips like salt.

His cock twitched and his boxers strained, growing tighter by the second. He was feeling short of breath as his hand wandered past his hips, tracing the swell of his cock with a finger. He hissed, alarmed by how sensitive he was. He hadn't felt this turned on in... he couldn't even remember. Fuck. Even the slightest touch felt amazing.

Zach knew everything about Gabe. He knew the taste of Gabe's skin. Knew the way he kissed, where he liked to be touched. Knew the way he looked in the heat of the moment, sweaty and flushed. The way he moaned. The way he fucked. The heat and feel of his cock.

Max bit his lip as he wrapped his fingers around himself. He stifled a whimper, toes curling as he found himself at the mercy of every slow stroke. Shallow pants fell from his lips, and he rocked his hips, pushing himself faster into his fist.

His arousal only heightened his sense of smell and Gabe's scent enveloped him, burning his nose, so potent and overwhelming it was as if he was in the room with him. In this bed with him, watching him with those fiery eyes, his large hands hot against Max's skin as he squeezed his cock, penetrating him with those long, slender fingers.

Max pressed against his swollen knot and saw stars, biting his lip to stifle his whimpers and gasps as Gabe took him from behind. It hurt, but Max raised his ass high in the air like a bitch in heat. He pleaded for more, for harder, for faster, totally shameless as his toes curled and he tore at the sheets.

There wasn't any part of himself he wouldn't give to Gabe. He trusted him with his heart, with his body. Gabe's fangs found that spot between his neck and shoulder and bit. Gabe's knot expanded inside him until Max was full to bursting as Gabe mated him, claimed him.

Yes! He was Gabriel's. He belonged to him and only him. The only one Gabe kissed, touched, and fucked.

"Gabe," he whispered before he could stop himself. "*Fuck.* Gabe!"

His moans filled the room, hips launching off the bed as he came into his fist. Shuddering, he collapsed into the mattress. His hand was completely drenched and he struggled to catch his breath, face burning hot as he realized what he'd done. He'd gotten off to the thought of his friend.

Guilt gnawed at him. He'd crossed a line, but he'd worry about that in the morning. Right now, he wanted to bask in the pleasure still hot in his veins. It had been too long since he'd felt anything other than pain. Too exhausted to clean himself off, he dried his cum-slick hand on the inside of Gabe's shirt.

Now it would smell like him, too.

Lost in a fog of bliss, Max looked out the window at the stars as they winked at him from the sky. Exhausted in body and soul, he squeezed his pillow and fell asleep with Gabe's scent wrapped around him.

In his dreams, his mother screamed for help. He had to find her. Save her. He ran, shifting to a wolf, and fastening his fangs into Richard's arm. Bones crunched beneath his teeth.

Kill him. He would kill him this time.

He woke half man and half beast, with claws embedded in the sheets. He tasted blood from where his fang had pierced his lower lip. He shivered, drenched in sweat from yet another nightmare, still able to feel a clawed hand at his scruff. He rolled over and something spiny stabbed him. He panicked, throwing off the sheets to discover sand all over the mattress and the remains of a crab torn apart across his bedsheets.

Sand was scratchy between his clawed toes. The window was wide open, the curtains blowing in the wind. Terror left Max frozen. There were claw marks on the windowsill, but Max didn't scent anyone except himself in the room.

What the fuck is going on? Did I sleepwalk? Did someone prank me?

He smelled of the ocean, and the taste of crab was in his mouth. Then he tasted bile. He ran to the bathroom and rinsed his mouth in the sink.

What in the hell was happening to him?

During the day, he felt good. He was making friends. He was safe and happy.

So why in the hell couldn't he forget the things Richard had done to him when he was alone at night?

If the others knew, if Gabe knew, he'd feel bad. Gabe would think he wasn't good enough, that he couldn't help Max. Gabe had done so much for him. They all had.

They couldn't know, not any of them. Max wouldn't be a burden to them.

Gabe woke in a cold sweat, holding his breath. The room was so dark he could barely see more than a few inches in front of him. His scars ached and the chill of a rusty blade still lingered on his skin. He breathed in, chest tightening, but couldn't manage a full breath. Fuck. He was about to have a panic attack. For a moment, he smelled his own blood, the rot of the basement, the stench of John Stone's unwashed body.

Gabe forced himself to breathe, shallow as his breaths were, and pushed away the panicked thoughts of *I'm dying, I'm about to die, he's here with me, he'll never let me go, he's going to kill me this time.*

No. He wasn't in the basement. He was in Zach's bungalow. He was safe. After a few minutes, the tightness in his chest eased enough for Gabe to take in a full breath. Shaking, he slumped over and leaned on his knees. Fuck. That hadn't happened in a long time.

"Gabe?" He jumped at Zach's voice, gentle and so unlike Stone's cold rasp. "You okay?"

The mattress shifted behind him, and Zach's body warmed his back.

"Fine," Gabe said, his own voice unconvincing. "A nightmare, that's all."

The lamp went on and Gabe found breathing to be easier as the shadows were chased away. Zach sat up behind him, a hand going to his wrist. Gabe flinched before he could stop himself.

"Sorry..." Zach pulled away fast and he felt a rush of guilt. "Do you want to talk about it?"

Gabe shook his head. He didn't want to let the darkness back in. He didn't want to burden Zach. He smiled over his shoulder and took comfort in Zach's warm brown eyes. "Sorry for falling asleep. I don't know what hit me."

"You've had a rough week. Are you feeling better than before?"

"Huh? Oh. Yeah."

They were supposed to be broken up, but this week had been hard. Seeing Max's scars, the two murders—it had opened old wounds. He'd turned to Zach for comfort, and Zach had been all too eager to let him back in. They'd come up to Zach's room with the intention of having sex. But the moment Zach had touched him, something bizarre had happened.

The touch had felt noxious down to Gabe's bones. His wolf had revolted at Zach's touch and snarled, *No. Not him.* Gabe's instincts had been so strong, he'd asked if he could just lie down and rest his eyes instead. Zach, of course, let him. Gabe couldn't explain why he was suddenly so against Zach touching him. Why, in that moment, he'd thought of how much better it would be to kiss Max instead.

"Gabe," Zach began and abruptly went quiet. "No, never mind. I'm here for you, okay?"

"What is it?" Gabe didn't want Zach to hold back what he felt.

Zach ran a hand over his long braids, tucking one behind his ear. "I don't know how to help you. I hate that you're still going through this trauma alone. I wish you'd let me help you."

Guilt gnawed at his insides. Zach couldn't mean to make him feel guilty, but knowing Zach was hurting too only hurt Gabe in turn. But the fact was Gabe simply didn't know how to talk to him about his trauma. He wasn't comfortable opening that door and bringing Zach into the darkness with him.

"You do help, Zach." Gabe touched his hand.

Zach had opened up about his love for Gabe a few months ago. Gabe saw Zach as a friend, though Zach believed those feelings would change in time. Since then, they'd been on again, off again. Zach was kind and good. He'd make anyone a fine mate.

Yet Gabe had never once felt the urge to claim him. Zach smelled good. He always did, like deodorant and clean clothes and coconut shampoo. But he didn't smell like *mate.* Not like Max, who had such an amazing scent.

Damn it. Why can't I get him out of my head?

"Zach, my future isn't clear. For all I know, I'll be dead the next time I face Stone. How can I make any promises about our future?"

"You won't die." Zach clasped his hands and held tight. "Gabe, you won't. We'll be together."

Gabe sighed, wishing he could believe him. "You've got the patience of a saint."

"You're worth the wait," Zach assured him, his hand warm on Gabe's arm. He leaned in to kiss Gabe and—

No, the wolf growled. *Not this one. Not him.*

Gabe flinched away from Zach.

"Gabe?" Zach began, brown eyes wounded.

Gabe didn't know how to explain himself. He'd never pulled away from Zach before but for some reason, the very idea of kissing him, touching him, was repellant.

"I shouldn't have come..." He'd craved the comfort Zach offered, but it wasn't right. "I like you, Zach, but I don't know what my future holds. I can't make any promises I don't know I can keep."

Zach's face softened when he smiled. "I believe in us, Gabe, no matter who else might come between us until you figure things out. You know that."

Gabe wasn't sure he deserved that devotion, but he didn't say anything.

A glance at the clock revealed it was late. It was time to be getting back to his place. In the morning, perhaps Richard would be well enough for interrogation. He still wanted to ask Max about where he'd escaped from the night they'd found him. If there was any chance his abduction and the killings were intertwined, he could finally be one step closer to answers he'd been seeking since his father's murder.

"Where are you going?" Zach sat up as Gabe jumped out of bed, tugging on his jeans and T-shirt.

"Gotta go home, check my emails."

Zach smiled, but it didn't reach his eyes. Gabe was hurting him. "Okay. I'll see you around the agency then."

Gabe walked home. The cry of seagulls and the salty sea air usually relaxed him, but he kept recalling how hurt Zach looked whenever Gabe pulled away from him.

If he and Zach really were meant to be, wouldn't he have realized it by now? What was wrong with him? They'd known each other since college. Zach had been there for him during days when the world was fogged and bleak. Who was a better match for him than his dearest friend?

You know, the wolf rumbled in his chest.

Gabe shook away the memory of cinnamon and chili.

He hurried into his cottage and took a long, hot shower. In his bedroom, he dropped the towel, pulled on some sweatpants, and turned on his computer. He checked his emails one more time before bed.

Ben had emailed that Richard had recovered enough of his strength to be fit for interrogation. He had a goal, a way forward. If Max's story lined up with the other hybrid disappearances, then he was one step closer to finding the man who'd torn a hole in his family.

Falling asleep was nearly impossible, but when he opened his eyes, golden sunlight glowed on the walls of his bedroom. Once he was ready for the day, Gabe left the house. As he approached the agency gates, he caught a familiar scent that made him sigh. A smile curled his lips, his worries dissolving as if he'd sunk into a hot bath. Max had been through here.

He turned to the guard at the gate. "Did you see Max?"

"He went over to the beach."

That was unusual. Max stuck to his bedroom most days, but Gabe was pleased he was venturing out, although he'd prefer if he stayed within the gates for his own safety. Gabe followed his scent to the beach across the road.

A short hike through the woods and the grass gave way to warm sand. Waves crashed and lapped at the shore, and gulls flew overhead, diving to pluck fish or crabs from the water. The gray clouds didn't inspire much confidence, and very few people roamed the sandy shores.

A familiar head of windswept red hair grabbed his attention. Max walked along the shore, running away from the waves. They lapped at his toes, making a grin bloom across his freckled face. The sight of Max soothed Gabe and his wolf.

Max's rare smiles made this windy gray day brighter. If Max could smile after all the terrible things he'd been through, he was stronger than he knew. Gabe hoped he could find strength of his own someday.

He removed his shoes, sand warming the bottom of his feet and gliding between his toes as he went and stood behind Max. Max's shoulders stiffened and he turned, a flush coming to his cheeks as their eyes met. He quickly averted his gaze, frowning. "Am I in trouble?"

A smile tugged at Gabe's mouth. He made his expression as dour as he could. "Big trouble."

Max's eyes got wide.

Gabe gently punched his shoulder. "Relax! I'm kidding!"

A burst of breathy laughter spilled from Max, his ears reddening. "I knew that," he mumbled.

"What would you be in trouble for?" Gabe asked.

A shrug of thin shoulders. "I don't know if I'm allowed to go outside the estate."

"You're not a prisoner. Just don't go too far."

Max would one day leave, possibly once this ordeal with Richard was over. He and his mother would begin anew somewhere else. The thought made something in Gabe's chest ache. He'd miss seeing him at dinner, watching him open up to the others and grow more comfortable in his surroundings.

"Is something wrong?" Max asked.

Gabe forced a grin. "Got a minute? There's something I wanted to discuss."

Max's face fell. "Did something happen?"

Gabe wanted to wrestle him into a hug to see one of those smiles again. "No. I wanted to talk, that's all." This wouldn't be an easy discussion. They sat on a sand dune overlooking the water. Sand clung to Max's bare feet, and he smelled of salt water. Gabe had a sudden desire to reach out and dust away the sand on his clothes.

"Have fun last night?" Gabe asked, unsure where to start.

Max's ears reddened. "Yeah. Sure. I'd like to watch the rest of that movie. I was tired."

Gabe wondered what was provoking the color in his cheeks and swallowed the urge to tease him about it. He had to stay on track. He exhaled, trying to find the words. "Max, Richard is well enough for interrogation."

Max's eyes went wide with fear. "Do I need to see him?"

The fear in those eyes made Gabe want to bare his teeth and snarl at anything that might try and hurt Max. "No. No, you don't. But the agency needs to know what happened to you the night he sent you away."

Max looked away, drawing his knees to his chest and making himself smaller.

Gabe placed his fingers on Max's shoulder. "I know this is hard. You're not the first hybrid to disappear. Others like you have gone missing. Many of them have turned up dead, if they turn up at all. I think you might be connected in some way."

Max exhaled. "So, if I tell you, I might be able to help others like me?"

"More than you could possibly know."

Max nibbled his lower lip, brows knitting tight. "Okay." His voice was quiet but firm.

Gabe's chest filled with admiration. "Whenever you're ready. Remember, you're safe. You're never going back there."

Max nodded, squeezing his eyes shut. He forced himself to sit up straight, chin sticking out defiantly. He exhaled, a fire burning in those orange eyes. "I was feral when this happened. I don't remember much. Sorry."

"That's okay. Tell me what you remember."

Max nodded resolutely, wetting his lips as he struggled to find his voice. Then he began his story.

CHAPTER 10

LAY OUR DEMONS TO REST

THE WEREWOLVES CARRIED HIM from Richard's lawn toward the white van. From within came the anguished cries of fear and pain. The van doors flew open, and the smell of blood, suffering, and sour fear made Max's fur stand on end. His captors removed the rope muzzle and bindings. They snapped silver chains around his paws. The silver burned, and he was too weak to fight. A muzzle silenced his bark for help.

Wolves yipped and cried out in the dark. Their fear and despair choked him, crawled into the pit of his stomach and became his own. They drove on and on.

Rain lashed at the windows, thunder rumbled like a beast on the horizon. The occasional burst of lightning illuminated the interior of the van and the wolves huddled in on themselves, snapping at their chains, pawing at the muzzles around their snouts. Wide eyes shone at him from the darkness.

He was finally free of his stepfather, but here he lay in the dark at the mercy of his abductors. Everything spiraled, soaring out of his control. He closed his eyes. He surrendered. No one was coming for him. No one cared where he was. He was alone.

He wondered about the woman. His... his mother? Wasn't that who she was? She'd tried to help him, and Bad Man had hurt her. He hoped she was *okay. He* needed *her to be okay. He had to see her again. She was important. Even if he couldn't remember why.*

The van stopped, doors opened and slammed. The wolves paced, their unease and fear clawing at Max's throat. The doors opened and sneering faces leered in at them. Max bared his fangs, wanting to snap and bite, but the muzzle prevented him from defending himself. One of the robed wolves gripped the scruff of his neck and tugged, forcing him toward his captor.

"Get the rest of them. Hurry up!"

More robed men and women materialized from the darkness, wrestling the other wolves from the van. Their robes bore the insignia of a lotus flower blooming under a full moon. They were in the countryside.

The crumbling smokestacks of an old factory spiraled into the dark clouds. The windows were covered in ivy or shattered. The coppery scent of blood crawled into Max's nose, so pungent he could taste it. It was a warning to any would-be vandals or explorers to stay away.

The wolves whined in fear as they were shepherded toward two enormous rusted doors that were grinding open at their approach. Graffiti covered the walls, curtains of ivy swayed in the breeze, and the smell of blood grew more and more potent the deeper into the factory they went.

Lightning flashed, casting shadows of the windows high above onto piles of rubble. Torchlight flared from above and Max's heart lurched into his throat. On the upper floors, hooded figures had gathered, observing them.

A chant echoed through the dilapidated halls, a single word repeated over and over in reverence. "Stone. Stone. Stone."

A hooded figure strode into the torchlight on the platform above. "Bring them forth." A shudder ripped through Max. If a demon could speak, it would sound like this man. Stone. "Tonight, the world becomes a cleaner place."

Max dug his claws in, strained against his chains, but he was powerless. His captors forced Max and the other wolves up the rickety stairs. That symbol was carved into the metal, a lotus in the middle of a circle depicting the moon.

Old bloodstains spattered over the lotus, claw marks bright against the bloodied metal. The metallic taste of blood flooded Max's mouth when he breathed in. So many had died here, their blood had stained the channels of the strange symbol.

I'm going to die.

His legs went weak, the terror closing his throat. The cultists dragged him up to the hooded man. A shadow fell over him. He looked up into the face of his doom, torchlight illuminating dark, sunken eyes, a bearded face, and long, stringy hair swaying like tentacles from the hood of his robe. A cold hand fisted in the scruff of his neck. Max's heart pounded in his ears, and he trembled so badly he could barely stand.

"A red wolf. How intriguing. You must be that 'special boy' Richard found. Such a pretty coat, but I don't see what's so special about a pitiful little mutt like you." Cold fingers delved into his fur like worms. Max shuddered. "All hybrids taint the She-Wolf's blessing with the human blood in their veins. Tonight, we purify!"

The cultists dragged Max to a metal table caked in dried blood and rust. Beside the table was a smaller table with syringes full of purple liquid. Aconitum, by the burning stink.

Someone had to come. Someone would save him. His life couldn't end this way.

"Hold him down and give him the injection!" Stone commanded.

Hands shoved him, and his collision with the ground knocked the wind out of him. The needle bit into his skin, and he howled in agony when the aconitum burned its way into his bloodstream. Drowsiness overcame him. The cultists laid him across the stone altar.

I want to go home.

Never in his life had he expected to find himself missing the darkness of the pantry and Richard's cruelty by comparison.

Please. No. I want to go home. I want to go home. Goddess, please. Help me.

Through the hole in the roof, the moon shone brighter and moonlight obscured his vision.

"What's happening?" Stone's voice snarled. "Everyone, get back!"

Metal groaned and glass shattered. Screams and terrified howls split the air. Sudden pressure pushed him down into the altar, crushing his bones.

There was an explosion of sound all around, ringing in his ears. He couldn't see, his vision blurry, and he was caked with dust and dirt.

Then Stone's breathless voice. "Oh, you... You are no ordinary hybrid, are you? That fool Richard was right!" His cold, manic laughter rang in the night.

"Max!"

The chill of the warehouse faded. He opened his eyes and found himself nestled against a warm, firm chest. Two strong arms held him tight. The roar of the ocean chased away the terrified howls of the wolves. His lips were moving, the words "I want to go home!" dying on his tongue. His chest heaved and his heart thudded so hard he thought it would burst. He jumped as the tip of an icy wave brushed over his toes. The tide had come surging in. Grunting, Gabe picked Max up and carried him to higher ground.

Max shuddered and gasped, unable to draw breath as Gabe set him down. "Hey. Hey, Max." Gabe knelt before him. "You're safe, Max. I promise." Gentle hands gripped his shoulders. "Breathe with me."

Max's frantic gasps struggled at first to follow Gabe's slower rhythm, but he managed. Gabe's scent filled his nose, sweet and strong, warm and soothing, and his heart slowed, his breathing settled. Clasping Gabe's shirt, Max squeezed tight, relishing the feel of the soft fabric between his fingers. He inhaled Gabe's scent and it was as if an anchor were wrapped around his leg, keeping him from drifting away.

"We don't have to talk about this anymore," Gabe murmured. His low voice vibrated pleasantly in his chest, soothing Max.

Max didn't want to leave it there. He wanted to get all this poison out of his system. "There's not much more to tell. I thought over and over that I wanted to go home. I even pleaded to the goddess to save me. I was that desperate."

Gabe smiled, sweet and kind. "You're a brave wolf."

Max scoffed. He wasn't brave at all.

"But you escaped. That's when we found you in the park."

Max closed his eyes, trying to recall the moment it happened. His brain felt fuzzy, scrambled. "I don't even remember how. It's all a blur. I broke out of my bindings, I think."

Gabe's brow furrowed. "How?"

"I don't know. I don't remember. Something happened. The building came crashing in. It was an old structure, so..." Max couldn't fathom how he'd escaped. He'd been too drowsy to fight one second, and then next he recalled, he was running for hours until he arrived in the park where he passed out. Something was missing from his memory. He glanced up at Gabe and heat rushed down his spine as he caught him staring pensively over the ocean. "Did that help you?"

Gabe smiled. He ruffled Max's hair. "Yeah. It did."

Max's face felt hot enough to catch fire. "That's good."

"That man who spoke to you, I know who he is."

Max's heart lurched. "Really?"

Gabe nodded, jaw tightly clenched. "He's the man who killed my father. His name is John Stone. He's behind the murders and disappearances of hybrids. And Richard is in league with him."

Max's stomach twisted. "I remember... Richard mentioned a Stone the night those cultists abducted me. He mentioned someone named Farley."

Gabe rumbled a growl in his chest. "Adam Farley?"

"I don't know. Sorry."

"Fuck." Fury thickened Gabe's voice. "Richard was responsible for that poor kid's disappearance. He turned up dead the night I found you."

A shiver ran through Max. Richard was a horrible man, but to think he'd participate in the capture and murder of other people like Max brought bile to the back of his throat. "How many others has Richard had kidnapped and taken to Stone for sacrifice?"

The uncertainty made him sick. He swallowed hard, shivering. Gabe shrugged off his jacket, offering it to Max. He wasn't cold, but he didn't want to turn it away, so he pulled it on. It smelled like Gabe, still warm from his body.

"I don't know," Gabe admitted.

"What is this Stone guy's fucking problem?"

Gabe's voice was barely above a growl when he answered. "Stone was once a member of the Council of Lycanthrope Affairs, a sort of governing body for werewolves and pack territories. Ben could tell you more about it. My father was a councilman. He represented New York State, the first hybrid to serve. Stone couldn't stomach that a 'weak mongrel' had a place among pure-blooded werewolves. So he threw a fit and by that I mean he betrayed the Council and went on a murder spree across the country. My father was one of his victims. And Stone used me to... get to my father."

Gabe's voice broke, his throat clicking as he blinked hard. "He captured me. Took me away. Hurt me for hours until he got bored and told my father to come and get me. My father escaped with me, but he was shot while we were crossing a flooded river. He kept himself above water long enough to hand me off to the cops, then... the river dragged him under."

Max winced, breath hitching. Gabe's claws had come out and were leaving dimples in Max's shoulder. Gabe's eyes widened as he remembered himself. "Sorry. It still makes me so angry to talk about it." He tried to smile and to Max's astonishment, it softened the hard lines around his eyes. Max hoped he could smile like that someday in the face of such pain and anger.

"Stone took a few fanatics with him when he fled the Council. His open hostility toward anyone who wasn't a pureblood gave bigots the confidence they needed to come out of hiding and seek Stone out. They became the Moonborn cult."

Max's heart ached for him. "Stone needs to pay for everything he did."

"I'll be the one to do it, mark my words. But there's a silver lining in this. That symbol of the moon and the lotus you saw in that warehouse has been a part of my life since my father's death. It was written all over the walls of that room he kept me in. The room where he broke my fingers 'cause he knew I couldn't regrow my own bones, cutting me everywhere he could."

Anger thickened Gabe's voice. The whites of his eyes turned inky black, his eyes flashing yellow.

Max's chest ached to see him so lost in the past. Max reached out and touched Gabe's shoulder without thinking. Max froze as Gabe's eyes widened, and his sensitive hearing caught the hitch of Gabe's breath. Fearing he'd made him uncomfortable, Max pulled away.

"Gabe, it's okay." The growl vibrating deep in Gabe's chest lessened and Max hoped he'd soothed his inner beast, even if only a little. "Richard probably knows where he is. You can make him talk. He'll give away Stone's location and you'll get vengeance for your father."

Gabe nodded, but the anger in his eyes never wavered. "I will. For years, Max, I've been hunting this guy. I'm so close now, and it's all because of you." He exhaled shakily, his eyes gleaming with emotion as he held Max's gaze. Max's breath hitched, his heart thundering as their eyes met.

Nervous, he let his eyes stray, admiring Gabe's plump lower lip, so caught up in his scent that for a moment he couldn't think of a reason not to lean in closer.

A hand settled at the nape of his neck and squeezed tight. Gabe met his gaze, eyes radiating with a promise. "I swear, Max. We're gonna put our demons to rest soon. Both of us. We'll do it together."

Max closed his eyes with a shiver, basking in the warmth and strength of Gabe's touch. Gabe's breath quickened and his big warm hand cupped Max's cheek. Max barely suppressed a moan, angling his head into the gentle touch. Their hearts beat faster when Gabe's breath warmed Max's lips. Curling his fingers in Gabe's shirt, Max urged him closer. Gabe's eyes, dark and heavy-lidded, slowly closed.

"Max," he whispered, as if Max were precious beyond all else. The longing in his voice took Max's breath away. With a sudden gasp, Gabe lurched away and Max caught himself against his shoulder. Gabe's eyes widened as he stared up the road. "Fuck!" He bolted to his feet.

"What's wrong?" Max followed him.

Gabe touched the side of his head. "The pack just spoke to me through the bonds. They're under attack! Stay here."

"No way!"

Gabe rounded on him. "Stay! You'll be safer here."

CHAPTER 11

BLOODLUST AND FURY

THE WIND CARRIED THE howls of pain and fury to Gabe's ears. Gabe stripped completely and left his clothes behind. His feet became clawed paws as he shifted, and the wind whipped his fur back. They were fighting without him, hurting or being hurt. And he wasn't there. He had to hurry. A song of bloodlust and fury tore from his throat.

Hang on, pack. I'm coming!

The gates to the headquarters had been sabotaged, the bars bent and forcefully ripped open. An empty car, looking worse than the gate, had crashed in the front yard. Claw marks riddled the dirt. The doorman lay facedown, his blood a stark crimson as it spilled across the asphalt driveway.

Gunfire cracked and Gabe raced beyond the gates. A partially shifted werewolf howled in pain and fury as it collapsed, writhing as a silver bullet smoked in its chest. One of their bodyguards fell to his knees, blood gushing from his throat.

He was dead before Gabe knelt at his side. Gnashing his teeth as a storm of fury possessed him, Gabe surveyed the courtyard where the bodies of werewolves and bodyguards lay mangled and disfigured.

Horror clawed at Gabe's heart. He closed his eyes, terrified he'd see the bodies of Izzie, Ben, Zach, and Ryan among the dead. To his relief, their bonds still glowed in his chest, stretched taut with fear and anger. They were alive, but they were fighting.

Gabe didn't have to know who these werewolves were. He knew from the fury curdling his insides that any who dared fuck with the LPA pack and their patients would die screaming under his fangs. Howls of battle echoed from within HQ.

Gabe's blood pumped as he ran, charging through the battered double oak doors. Gabe leaped over the corpse of a werewolf in the doorway. By the smell, it wasn't one of theirs. A howl echoed through the halls. "Find the red wolf!"

Gabe growled, fur bristling. They were here for Max, and he'd be damned before they laid a claw on Max.

A blur of brown and gray fur tumbled down the stairs, leaving spots of blood. Ben, an enormous wolf with silver fur, pinned the wolf beneath him and lunged. His fangs crunched in the wolf's neck and with a single tear, ripped out the wolf's throat. Blood streaked his snout.

"Where the hell have you been, Gabe?" Ben turned toward him, tongue swiping at the blood on his mouth.

"Where's everyone? Zach? Ryan? Izzie?" Was his sister all right?

"Kendra ran off to find Max, and Izzie pursued her. I'd have followed but this shitsack kept me busy."

A snarl tore at Gabe's throat. If Izzie was hurt, there'd be hell to pay. *"Where'd she go?"*

Ben turned his snout toward the courtyard. *"Izzie's probably sneaking her out the back way. Hurry!"*

Gabe's vision blurred as he pelted past, claws scrabbling at the tile as he ran toward the back door. He hurled himself at the door and stumbled out into the courtyard. Blood turned the pool red.

A howl of pain ripped through the air and sent Gabe's heart into a frantic race. Three wolves tussled on the ground, their pelts matted with blood. An unfamiliar white wolf that smelled like Kendra's perfume collapsed. A black wolf towered over her, lips pulled back from his fangs in a snarl.

In a blur of fur, Izzie pounced, seizing the wolf around the neck. The pair rolled over together, clawing and biting.

Gabe charged and his fangs pierced the flesh beneath the wolf's matted fur. They tumbled toward the edge of the pool. The ground disappeared beneath his paws and the water of the pool crashed over his head. The surface grew farther away as the wolf dragged him under. Gabe thrashed, twisting to try and free himself as his own blood rose like mist around him. His paw collided with the wolf's stomach. The wolf let go, jaws opening wide and swallowing water. Gabe paddled, one paw breaking the surface of the water.

Fangs clamped around his leg and dragged him down to the depths, the fog of Gabe's own blood clouding the water. It pressed into his ears, muting all sound. Gabe kicked and clawed but the wolf bit down on Gabe's ankle and dragged him deeper and deeper toward his demise.

Waves buffeted them as Izzie sprang into the water. Izzie rammed into the wolf and a spray of bubbles rose from the enemy's maw. They struggled, but Izzie got her jaws around his neck. The pain in his leg, like dozens of daggers, relented, and Gabe swam for the surface.

He shifted as his head burst above the water, sucking in frantic gulps of air. Izzie came up behind him, her fur soaked and floating in the water around her. Blood turned the pool water crimson. His leg ached, and Gabe struggled to stay afloat. Water forced its way back into his mouth, and he choked. As a wolf, Izzie paddled up to him and ducked under his arm. She whined when Gabe's weight threatened to pull her under, water rising up to her snout.

"Let go, Izzie!" Gabe choked out, terrified he'd make her sink.

Growling, Izzie kicked her way toward the pool's edge, bringing Gabe with her.

A few feet from the edge, Max leaned over the bloody water and reached for Gabe's hand. "Gabe, grab on!" He clasped Max's hand and Max pulled him up against the wall of the pool. Relief flooded through him as he touched solid ground and collapsed on the edge of the pool. Rolling over, Gabe retched chlorine-tasting water from his lungs. He struggled to breathe between body-shaking coughs. Max handed him the clothes he'd discarded on his run to HQ.

"Told you to stay." Gabe gasped around a hacking cough.

"Thank the goddess! You're all right!" Kendra threw her arms around Max. Max held her tight and quickly offered her his beach towel as sudden torrents of rain came lashing down from above. "Where were you?" Kendra demanded, securing the towel around her upper body.

Max raised both hands in surrender. "I went for a walk!"

A howl echoed through the storm. It wasn't a song of pain or fury but of sorrow. A shiver of dread ran down Gabe's spine. "That's Ryan."

Ry? What happened? Gabe asked through the bond connecting him to Ryan.

He didn't receive a response. Gabe took off toward the building, ramming open the double doors. He bounded up the stairs toward the library, the others in pursuit. Gabe threw open the library door and stopped in his tracks.

The library had been torn apart, shelves knocked over, books strewn across the carpet. Dead wolves lay in heaps of bloody fur. Ryan was the only wolf still standing, and the white timber wolf howled his grief over a crumpled body of mottled brown fur. The smell of blood hung so thick in the air, Gabe didn't realize who it was, not until he caught Zach's scent.

A strangled cry tore at his throat, so pained that a howl alone wouldn't cut it. He stumbled on trembling legs to Zach's side and laid a hand on his blood-soaked fur. Dozens of deep scratches and bites ripped into his skin. Small scratches healed before Gabe's eyes, but the bigger bites and cuts were too severe for his body to heal on its own.

Izzie hurried to Ryan's side and nestled close to comfort him. Ryan only whined with his head on his paws.

Gabe's breath hitched as Zach's sides rose and fell, each breath so slow it was hard to detect. "He's still alive." Relieved tears burned his eyes.

"He is?" Max hurried forward.

Ryan's hackles rose. Gabe's fangs came out before he could stop it, and he lurched in front of Max with a hand to his chest to keep him back. Ryan snapped at Max, snout wrinkled in anger. Izzie leaped away from him, eyes wide in alarm.

"This is all your fault!" Ryan's voice boomed in Gabe's mind and made him jump. Max flinched.

Kendra growled and stepped in front of Max. "Leave him alone!"

The fury pulsing through Ryan's bond threatened to raise Gabe's hackles in Max's defense.

"Ryan! Gabe!" A deep voice turned their heads. Ben's eyes flashed as he strode toward them, showing his fangs. "Back down. Both of you. Now! Zach needs to get downstairs to Luke. Ry, give me a hand!" Ryan shifted, and he and Ben hoisted Zach's limp body into their arms and carried him from the room.

"Are you okay?" Max touched Gabe's arm, eyes wide and unsure.

His mouth twitched. Max was sweet as could be. "Tired," he said with a grunt.

Max's ears reddened. "Ryan seemed pretty pissed at me."

Gabe was grateful Max wasn't part of their pack bonds yet. Max already had enough on his plate without feeling guilty. "Not your problem, Lobito. Ryan's just worried about Zach."

Izzie shifted and tugged on Gabe's arm. "Get up. You need to go to the infirmary, too."

Max helped Gabe stand and they followed Ben and Ryan to the clinic downstairs. Luke and Ryan were carrying Zach into an exam room as Ben slumped against the wall, exhaustion sagging his broad shoulders. Gabe limped into a chair next to Ben and a nurse rushed over to check the injury on his ankle.

"Gabe." Ben's gruff voice made him look up. Ben's eyes were worn and dark, his face grim. "It's about Richard."

Gabe faced him, mouth suddenly dry. He didn't want to ask.

Ben sighed, thick fingers scratching through his salt-and-pepper beard. "Bad news."

"Worse than this?"

"It's the flies on the pile of shit that's been today."

"Great..."

Ben looked him in the eyes. "While we were busy fighting, Richard broke out of his cell. He's gone, Gabe."

Gabe slumped against the wall. "Well, shit..."

How in the hell would he tell Max?

Chapter 12

KEEP YOU SAFE

Two hours passed before they had any word about Zach. Gabe, Ben, and the other agency wolves brought the dead agency members to the morgue, got in touch with families of the deceased, and burned the Moonborn cultists bodies. Max felt useless just sitting around, but was at a loss for what he could do to help.

Finally, Luke emerged from the operating room smelling of blood and chemicals. Max rose with the others, stomach twisting. Luke offered a smile. "He'll be fine. He's very weak right now. His wounds could barely heal on their own, so I gave him a blood transfusion to speed up the process. He'll need to spend the night to regain his strength."

Ryan exhaled and dropped into his seat, his face in his hands. His shoulders trembled and Gabe's hand settled there and squeezed.

The depressed air of the pack finally lightened. Max smiled.

"Got it," Ryan said, drying his eyes on the back of his hand. "What else does he need?"

"Lots of protein and rest should do the trick."

"You got it, Doc. I'll look out for him, make sure he doesn't do anything stupid and wind up back in your clinic," Ryan vowed.

Izzie sighed her relief. Max glanced at Gabe. He'd been pacing as much as his injured ankle would allow since their arrival and had finally settled into a chair. Relief glimmered in his eyes, and he was laughing breathlessly with Izzie. The smell of his worry had only been second to Ryan's, who'd gone between bouts of angry pacing to sitting slumped in his chair.

"Can we see him?" Ryan asked.

"He's going to be asleep for some time, but he'll surely appreciate the company."

Max imagined Gabe would want to see him. He squeezed his fingers together, fixating on the tiles.

Ben shook Luke's hand. "Thanks for looking out for him, Luke. Who's hungry?" A show of hands from the pack made Ben chuckle. "The cafeteria is trashed, but there's a diner nearby. Let's grab dinner; then we can talk."

Ryan didn't follow them to the door. "I'm gonna stay with Zach."

Gabe said, "Ry, if you're hungry, I can stay with Zach. Keep an eye on him while you get some food in you."

There it was, making Max's fingers curl and his wolf growl, *Mine. You're mine. Stay with me.* Guilt gnawed at his insides. How could he feel that way? Zach was Gabe's friend and possibly more. Or not. Gabe had almost kissed him on the beach before the attack... unless Max had just projected his own desires onto Gabe. Which was probably the case. Gabe liked Zach, not Max. Of course Gabe would want to be with him. Max swallowed a sigh.

Ryan shook his head. "That's okay, man. I'd rather stay with Zach."

"'Kay," Ben said. "Want us to bring you something back?"

Ryan shrugged. "As long as it's not salad, I'm not picky."

"I'm going to check on Zach. I'll meet you guys there," Gabe assured them.

Max lingered in the doorway as Ryan and Gabe went to Zach's room. He forced himself to look away and followed Izzie, his mother, and Ben to the car. Ben drove them into town and stopped outside the quaint diner Gabe had taken him to. They found a booth big enough for four and pulled up an extra chair for Gabe. Max's stomach rumbled at the smells of charred meat, salad dressings, and creamy pasta sauces.

Once they were seated, Ben declared, "Take your pick of the menu. It's on me."

"Oh no, I can pay for myself and Max," his mother assured him.

Ben waved a hand. "Don't worry about it."

Max sought out anything under twenty dollars on the menu, knowing he'd feel guilty if he made Ben pay for something overtly expensive, and settled on a pasta dish.

"Thanks, Ben." Izzie squeezed his hand. "We lost a lot of good people today. We should toast their memory."

"Goddess, what a damn mess," Ben grumbled, slumping in his seat. He closed his eyes tight. "Think I'd be better at telling folks their loved ones aren't coming home, but it's never easy."

Kendra rubbed his arm. "I'm sorry."

"You did all you could," Max said.

Ben scrubbed the wetness from his eyes. "Four people lost their lives on my watch. If I'd done all I could, they'd still be here." Ben slapped down the menu. "Damn it. I need a drink. What about you, Max, you drink?"

Max shook his head. "Should we order for Gabe?"

"I got it. He usually gets the meat loaf," Ben mumbled. "Guess I'll order the steak for Ry to go. We should treat Luke for all his help, and he usually likes the gyro..."

Once they ordered, Max found his gaze straying to Ben. While Izzie and his mom chatted, Ben remained silent, staring into his whiskey like he was looking for answers. Max hated that he was blaming himself. Ben ought to be blaming Max. Moonborn wouldn't have targeted the agency if they hadn't been after Max.

Their food arrived shortly after their drinks and when Max looked up from his food, his heart gave a pleasant jolt as Gabe settled into the seat at the end of the table.

"How is he? Still sleeping?" Ben asked.

Gabe tucked into his meat loaf. "Yeah. He's worn out. Those bastards got him good."

Max's food turned into a lump in his stomach. Zach had been hurt because of him. Those wolves had come for him. "I'm sorry to all of you." The words spilled out before he could stop them. His eyes stung.

Gabe's brows furrowed in concern. "Why?"

"The Moonborn wanted me. If I... If I'd just..."

Gabe's hand fell warm and heavy on his shoulder. "Listen to me. None of that was your fault."

Izzie exclaimed, "Absolutely not! It's not your fault you have crazies hunting you."

Ben set his fork down. He'd already cleared his plate. "They were after you, kid. That doesn't mean it's your fault, but you're in danger."

Ben looked at Gabe. Gabe's jaw tightened and he stopped eating.

Unease settled into the pit of Max's stomach. "What?"

Gabe said, "I wanted to wait until after dinner, Ben."

"We don't have time. He needs to know."

Max's heart raced faster. He looked from Ben to Gabe. "What happened?"

Ben exhaled, and gray eyes as dark as storm clouds found Max's gaze. "Richard escaped during the fighting."

An icy wave of fear ran down Max's back. Richard would come for him; he'd come for him and his mother and take them away. He'd hurt Max again, maybe even kill him and his mother this time.

"Max. Hey." The hand on his shoulder pulled Max from the icy waves of terror. Gabe looked him in the eyes. "He can try all he damn well wants but he's not coming near you or your mother."

"How can you promise us that?" Kendra's voice was low and shivery. "What do we do?" Her arms went around Max's shoulders, holding him close. Max grabbed her arm without a second thought, squeezing tight. If Richard came for them, Max would make sure he never touched his mother again.

Ben's low voice rumbled. "That's what we're here to decide. You can't stay on the estate, that's for damn sure. You'll have to stay with one of us. When we aren't on estate grounds, we all have apartments in the city. Between so many of us, they'll have a harder time figuring out where you are. They'll have to go through all of us if they want to get their hands on either of you."

"No." Max couldn't bear the thought of more people getting hurt, or worse, because of him. "There's got to be another way. We can leave the city, go far away."

Ben sighed, running a large hand across his smooth scalp. "Kid, the cult has its eyes on you. Richard must be helping them. He's the closest link Stone has to finding you, so he's important to Stone."

Max squeezed his fists. "What the hell is Stone's deal?"

Ben raised his hands in a who-knows gesture. "John Stone is obsessed with cleansing hybrids of their wolves. The sick fuck's done it to every single corpse we've found, ripped their wolves right out with that magic dagger of his. In his eyes, hybrids are undeserving of being werewolves. Of course, he's never gone this far to target a hybrid, not since he killed Gabe's father. There's gotta be something about you that intrigues him, but I'm not crazy enough to get in his headspace and figure out why. He'll find you, doesn't matter where you go. Until he's dealt with, you need to be among a pack to protect you."

Max's throat tightened and tears burned his eyes. "He'll hurt you. All of you. And I have to let him? I don't care what happens to me; I don't want anyone getting hurt because of me!"

He moved out of his mother's reach as she tried to console him.

"We know the risks, Max. Every agency wolf knows the risks when they sign up to help others." Gabe's voice stilled the fear inside him.

Ben looked Max in the eyes. Max swallowed, shivering under those intense wolf's eyes. They glowed, and Max could see the wolf lurking behind those eyes, powerful but contained. Max felt safe, like he could entrust everything he had to the older wolf.

"My grandfather founded the LPA to help shifters like you and your mother, kid. I've built my entire life around this line of work, so don't tell me that you don't care what happens to you and expect us to let you waltz your little bubble butt outta here. We care. And we're gonna protect your family no matter what those cultist bastards throw at us."

"Hell yeah," Izzie said. She walked around the table and took Max's hand. "They want you, they're going to have to get through me."

"You guys..." Max's face burned hot. His throat tightened until he couldn't speak, until all he could do was nod his acceptance.

Kendra whispered, "Thank you. All of you." The salty scent of her tears made Max's throat thicken and ache.

"Now," Ben said, his voice gentler, "we need to decide who you're staying with."

Max looked to Gabe before he could stop himself. He knew Gabe more than Izzie or the others. He trusted Gabe, and he knew he'd feel safe with him. Gabe wet his lips as their eyes met, brows furrowing as if trying to read him. Max's heart thundered and he tore his eyes away.

I couldn't burden him like that. If he got hurt because of me... What am I thinking?

He would have to stay with someone else.

Ben continued, "Heather, my ex-mate, brings my teenage sons over on the weekends, so I haven't got the room."

Izzie frowned. "I'd love for you two to stay with me, but my boyfriend lives with me."

Ben said, "So, Izzie's out. Zach's gonna be out of sorts for a while. We'll ask Ryan."

Max's stomach turned over. It didn't take a genius to see Ryan blamed him for Zach's injury. "I'm pretty sure he'd object to that."

Gabe said, "You can move in with me."

Max's heart flew into his throat. "But—"

Gabe frowned. "You don't want to?"

"No, I..." Damn it. Why did words have to fail him now? His heart soared at the possibility of living with Gabe but then Zach's bloodied body resurfaced in his memory. "No. If you got hurt—"

Gabe shrugged, a smile playing on his lips. "So I won't."

Max growled, wishing he'd take the risks more seriously. "Gabe, if they find me, they'll hurt you. Stone probably wants you as much as me."

Gabe rolled out his shoulders and cracked his knuckles. "Let them try. If John Stone decides to show himself, that'll be a little added bonus."

"You're not taking this seriously." Max seethed, fingers curling. Gabe's devil-may-care attitude scared and impressed him.

Gabe grinned, making Max bristle. "I'm dead serious. My apartment's got a foldout sofa and an extra bedroom. We can make it work."

Max couldn't speak. If he did, he would be selfish. There was nothing he wanted more than to say yes, and he hated himself for it. "Mom? Would this work for you?"

She looked to Gabe, her eyes glimmering with emotion. "You'd really do this for us?"

Gabe smiled. "We're a pack. This is what we do."

His mother dipped her head, a watery smile making her lips tremble. "Thank you. So much."

If it worked for his mother, then it worked for Max. He nodded, hoping Gabe didn't see the tears he was fighting back.

Silence descended over the table. Max dried his eyes on the back of his hand as casually as he could, even if everyone could smell his tearful gratitude. Words couldn't express what it meant to him to finally have people he could turn to and trust.

He would find a way to repay their kindness someday. That was a promise.

"Someone order steak?" Gabe called as he tossed the foil container of food into Ryan's lap.

"If you'd spilled that..." Ryan muttered, digging in with a gratified sigh.

Ryan seemed to be in better spirits, Max noticed. "How's Zach?"

"Sleeping," Ryan said. "Luke says he should be awake tomorrow, though."

Max nodded, unsure what else to say. "Ryan, about before… I'm sorry Zach and so many others got hurt because of me."

Ryan waved a hand. "Don't worry about it."

"But you were upset with me. I understand why. They were after me. If they hadn't been, Zach wouldn't have gotten hurt."

Ryan shrugged. "He's not a puppy. He can make his own choices. He chose to stay and fight. Look, and Gabe can attest to this, I'm an asshole sometimes."

"You are," Gabe agreed.

Ryan jerked a thumb at him. "See?"

Max smiled. "At least you're aware of it?"

"Right?" Ryan grinned around a mouthful of steak. "Nothing's worse than an asshole who doesn't know they're an asshole."

"But you had every right to be angry. You've known Zach a while, right?"

A smile lit up Ryan's face. "He's been my best friend since we were kids."

He declared it so wholeheartedly, with a sweet little dopey smile, that Max saw him for who he was right away. He was a bit smart-alecky, but he was honest and he cared about his friends. A growly wolf with a soft, vulnerable underbelly, or a hedgehog, cute but prickly.

"So yeah, I worry about him, but I know it was important to him that you and your ma were safe. So, if it's important to him, it's important to me, too. Those jerkasses come for you again, they're gonna have to go through me."

Max's face warmed. "Thanks."

"Since you two aren't gonna kill each other, I'll wait outside, Max." Gabe stood and headed for the door.

Ryan snorted. "Wait, are you two going somewhere?"

"Yeah, Max and Kendra are moving in with me. It's something we all agreed on."

Max vaguely remembered Ryan being excited to learn Max was a red wolf. Most people were curious about his fur color, but Ryan had seemed genuinely excited. "So, you know about the cult?"

"Yeah, fun guys. What about 'em?"

"Their leader, that Stone guy, he said something to me the night he captured me. Something about how my red wolf was rare. He seemed especially interested. Can you think of any reason why?"

Ryan chewed his steak, brows knitted. "Well, he ain't wrong. Red wolves are rare. Super rare. There have only been two or so in recorded history."

Max shook his head. "I just don't get it. Of course I know my fur color is rare. People have made that obvious to me my whole life. But I can't say anyone's wanted me dead because of it."

"Hey, you don't gotta understand their special brand of crazy." Ryan punched his shoulder and grinned. "Just keep your head down and let us worry about the rest. Cool?"

Max smiled. "Cool."

Ryan extended a hand for a high five. Max didn't miss this time.

Once they returned to Manhattan, Kendra and Max wanted to be helpful guests and offered to go to the grocery store around the corner from Gabe's apartment.

While they shopped, Gabe set about cleaning his apartment in preparation for their arrival. He changed the sheets in the guest room and set some blankets by the sofa bed. Gabe seared some white fish on the stove and had finished cooking it by the time the doorbell rang.

Gabe jogged to the door, grinning at his guests. "Hey, welcome! Come on in."

Kendra and Max hurried in with their bags of groceries. The bodyguard who'd accompanied them waved and went on his way. Kendra looked around in wonder. "Your apartment is beautiful."

Gabe was rather proud of his den, a two bed and bath with an open kitchen and living room. Being a penthouse, it offered high ceilings and large windows with views of Central Park. "Thanks. Working for the LPA is tough, but it pays well."

"This well?" Kendra gaped at the windows and their stunning views of the park.

Gabe's face warmed. "Well, that and my pops comes from a long line of defense lawyers and left Izzie, me, and Ma a nice slice of inheritance money."

Max whistled. "It's way better than Richard's fancy place. It's cozy."

"Make yourselves at home. I'll have dinner ready soon." Gabe couldn't help being excited. He hadn't cooked for anyone in a long time. Sharing his den with Kendra and Max would be good for shaking up his routines. Using the ingredients they had bought, Gabe made a salsa to pour over the fish and toasted some tortillas.

Gabe grinned when he caught Max and Kendra roaming around the living area and circling the sectional sofa. Max ran his hand across the fabric, then over the top of the HD TV. They were making the place their own, getting their scents on the furniture. It made his heart sing. No wolf enjoyed living alone and he wanted Max and Kendra to feel at home here.

"Can we help at all?" Kendra asked.

"Yes, you can sit down."

Gabe carried dinner to the table, and they dug in. Max nudged his food around his plate, glancing at Gabe beneath his thick auburn lashes. "So, am I under your strict surveillance?" he asked, a teasing smile on his face.

Gabe felt an odd flush of heat despite the AC being cranked high. Max's playful tone could be mistaken for flirting, but Gabe was sure he was just overthinking things.

"No, not really. It's a big city. It's impossible for the Moonborn to know where you could be. I won't imprison you, but you should stay inside after dark and keep your phone on you if you go out. Maybe take me or someone else with you if you go outside the neighborhood. If you go to work, someone—me—should stay with you during your shift and drive you there and back."

Kendra cleared her throat.

Gabe's face reddened. "Right, you're not going to college or working, so those rules don't apply."

Max nodded, taking a bite of food.

"I've got time off to look after you and your ma, so I'm at your disposal. I'll accompany you if you need to go anywhere. Reasonable?"

Max smiled. "Sounds like a plan."

"You're so close to the park," Kendra said, gazing out the window.

Gabe took a sip of his water. "Yeah. One of the reasons why I love the location. We should go for a run tomorrow night."

Max looked up from his taco. "Won't we get in trouble?"

Gabe winked and enjoyed the pretty flush that colored Max's freckled cheeks. "Only if we're caught. Would you like to run?"

Max's eyes lit up. "Sounds awesome. I haven't done anything like that as a wolf in a long time."

Kendra smiled. "That sounds nice. Is it all right if I join you boys?"

Max frowned. "You should probably stay close to the house. Just to be safe."

Kendra folded her arms, arching a brow playfully. "I don't think it would hurt to get a little fresh air. Richard can't know where we are all the time."

Max's fist tightened around his taco, squeezing out the insides. "Mom…"

"I'm just saying. We've been cooped up in the estate for a while. It would be nice if—"

"No!" The word erupted from Max, making Gabe jump and Kendra wince. Max's shoulders slumped. "I mean… can you just… You need to stay where it's safe."

Kendra laughed softly, but it was a clipped sound. "I know, but—"

Max lurched to his feet. "There's no 'buts'! If he finds us, who says Gabe will be able to stop him from hurting you again? I sure as hell couldn't!"

Gabe looked down at his empty plate. "Max," he began, wanting to tell him to go easy on his mom.

Max sighed shakily. "Shit. I'm sorry, Mom. I... Thanks for dinner, Gabe." He went into the bathroom and shut the door.

Kendra sighed and rubbed her hands over her face.

After dinner, Kendra insisted on helping with the dishes. He'd brought out the fancy plates, which needed to be washed by hand rather than in the dishwasher, so Gabe washed and she dried. His skin prickled as he smelled her distress, like gray clouds over the kitchen. "Are you okay?" he said without thinking.

She shook her head. "I don't understand." She wrung the dish towel in her hands, lips pursed in frustration. "Does he blame me for not leaving Richard? Does he feel guilty somehow? I can't find out because he won't let me talk to him."

"He'll get there." At least Gabe hoped so. "Hey, want me to talk to him, figure out what's going on in his head?"

Kendra offered a smile that didn't reach her eyes, fingertips whitening as she squeezed the plate she was drying. "Don't worry, Gabe. You've already done so much. You don't need to do more."

"I can always do more. Like catch the bastards who keep coming after you." Gabe handed her another plate to dry.

She laughed gently. "Even if you don't, you'd have done enough."

Gabe shook his head. He wouldn't rest until the man who'd taken his father from him was rotting in a cell with Richard Moray or Gabe was dead himself. If they didn't die by a lethal injection of wolfsbane, they'd spend a lifetime in a cell and be lucky to do so.

"You don't agree."

Another shake of his head. "I'd be doing a pretty poor job if I didn't catch them."

Kendra hummed, moving the rag in a slow circle against the plate. "I'd love it if Richard was caught. I'd love to see him hurt for what he did to our family. To Max. But even if justice never comes to pass, it won't diminish what you've done for us. But I understand if you can't see the light you've brought into our lives. And Goddess, did we need some light. All I wanted was to give Max a family, to bring back that happy pup with dimples in his smiles. Instead, I killed him the minute I brought Richard into our lives."

Gabe's chest hurt. "You didn't know."

Kendra blinked fast. The salty smell of her guilt stung Gabe's nose. "There were signs. There are always signs, and I ignored them. I brought that monster into my life and watched him destroy my son. Gabe, I thought Max was broken. I thought he'd never trust again. Then I see how he is with you, smiling, laughing!"

Gabe smiled, his neck warming. "He's stronger than he thinks he is."

Kendra shook her head, smiling exasperatedly. "You listen to me." She set the plate on the counter and turned, clasping his damp, soapy hands in hers. "You saved my son. No matter what happens with Richard, you've given us the chance for a new beginning. So, from the bottom of my heart, thank you."

Her hand settled on his arm and squeezed tight. Gabe nodded, throat too tight to speak. He couldn't argue, but what he wished he could say was that he never wanted to see Max broken ever again. He wanted Max to keep flourishing, like a flower in the sun.

To that end, he wouldn't stop hunting until he could say with certainty that Max would never know cold, unloving darkness again.

CHAPTER 13

SCARS DON'T DEFINE YOU

He's coming. There's nothing I can do.

Cold sweat left Max in shivers as he woke suddenly, gasping. Dread brought bile to the back of his throat. He closed his eyes tight, squeezing the sheets. If he lay still enough, Richard would think he was sleeping and leave him alone. *Please, let him go away...*

"Nightmare, Lobito?"

Max lunged, claws slicing at the shadows.

"Whoa! Watch the face. It's me, it's Gabe."

His eyes battled the darkness, heart racing as silhouettes were chased away by shafts of light from the windows. Gabe stood to the right of the sofa bed, hands raised in a calming gesture. His lips quirked. "I know, the scars make me look pretty spooky in the dark."

Max slumped, his heart rate slowing. He breathed in deep, sucking in the scent of Gabe that clung to every piece of furniture and hung in the air like a soothing mist. His hands shook and he clenched the sheets tight. He wasn't in the pantry. Richard was gone, for now.

"You're safe, Max." Gabe sat on the side of his bed. "He can't find you here."

"I know." But his shaking dismantled his pitiful attempt at a lie. He gnashed his teeth, wishing he could be strong. "I'm fine."

A warm hand fell upon his shoulder, fingers pressing into the taut muscles. "Felt like you were locked up again, right? Alone, helpless."

Max tried to respond but his throat ached. He didn't even have to explain himself. Gabe knew. Gabe got him. Max didn't have to reopen old wounds and relive the nightmares all over again. "Does it get better?" He swallowed hard.

Gabe wet his lips. "In time. But it never goes away. Not entirely. Trauma, it becomes a part of us, but it doesn't have to define who we are." Gabe's throat rippled as he swallowed, his face looking suddenly bleak.

The light outside illuminated the scars on his bare arms. They were thin jagged lines that had been made by a knife.

"Sometimes, I wake up and I'm cold all over, Max. It's like I'm back in the basement." The sofa bed creaked. Gabe was sitting beside Max but he looked miles away, eyes dark and face haunted.

Gabe swallowed, a shiver racking his body. "I asked him why once. Why he hated me. He told me hybrids were a pestilence. A poison perverting the natural order of the world of werewolves. That the only way the world could return to its natural balance was if hybrids were eradicated."

Max felt sick to his core.

"Sometimes, I'd tell myself to imagine a special place. A memory, maybe. Somewhere I felt loved and safe. Happy. I thought that if I could build a fortress around myself, then maybe everything he did to me would hurt less. Every time, he tore it down. Every wall I built around myself. Until I felt as naked and weak as a newborn, lying out in the open."

Max couldn't take another word. Oh Goddess, he knew exactly what Gabe felt. Yearning to make him understand, Max leaned in and nuzzled into the crook of his neck. He rubbed his nose along Gabe's neck, blanketing Gabe with his scent. Gabe's breath hitched, the sound sending Max's heart into overdrive.

Before Max could move away, worried he'd made him uncomfortable, a warm hand settled on his head, fingers curling softly in his hair. Max's face warmed and he was grateful for the dark. He hadn't expected to be touched in return but he liked it. Having Gabe's hand on him was soothing and pleasant—and his heart wouldn't stop racing.

He was so sorry. So angry that anyone had ever hurt Gabe. If he ever met John Stone again, he'd kill him with his bare hands. He wasn't strong but he would kill for Gabe if it meant he'd never be hurt again. Gabe's hand was unsteady as it drifted through Max's hair, his touch so gentle yet it killed every doubt, every fear.

"Go to sleep, Max. I'll watch the door."

"You don't have to." Max didn't want to be alone in the dark, but he didn't want Gabe losing sleep.

"Maybe I want to?" Gabe's lips turned up in a smile that made it difficult to argue. "I can't sleep either, anyway. Must have been the fish or something..."

Max closed his eyes and lay back down. Before he knew it, sleep came for him. The nightmares returned, a twisted conjoining of beasts that looked like Stone and talked like Richard. Max whimpered, paralyzed as the shadowy things circled him.

Knives gleamed, ribbons of spit and blood dangled from the tips of fangs, and yellow eyes burned away the darkness. Something touched him. He jumped but there was no pain.

"Shh. I'm here, Max. I'm here."

The monsters retreated to the shadows where they watched him, eyes burning, jaws drooling. "Stay," Max whispered. He couldn't fight them on his own.

"I will."

When Max opened his eyes, morning had come and cast out the darkness. A second heart pumped in his ears. The gentle rise and fall of Gabe's chest had been soothing enough to lull him back to sleep. Max's face warmed, heart pounding so loudly he worried it would wake Gabe up.

He'd stayed with Max all night. Max hoped he'd slept well. Gabe's wavy locks tumbled across his cheek, lips slightly parted while he slept.

Max couldn't look away, enraptured. Gabe's brow furrowed, his wide mouth scrunching in distress. His chest rose and fell faster as his heart rate increased. The smell of his fear made Max wrap himself around him, fingertips drifting over Gabe's cheek. He brushed a lock of ebony hair from Gabe's face and murmured, "It's okay. You're safe, Gabe. I won't let anyone hurt you."

The frowning lips lifted in a small smile, tense features melting into bliss. Max wondered who he'd thought about then, who it was that had made him smile and brought him comfort. Probably Zach. Max closed his eyes tight and nuzzled into Gabe's chest, clinging on to the memory of Gabe's brief happy smile. He wished he'd been the one on Gabe's mind, that he could be the one to make him feel safe and happy.

THE FIRST FULL DAY in Gabe's home wasn't without a few bumps. Max had only woken up when his phone started blowing up with messages. His mother had snapped a picture of him and Gabe and shared it in the pack's group message. "Mom!" Max growled, shooting his mother a glare over breakfast.

"Relax, honey! It's adorable."

Gabe's face was the color of a rare steak. "We do look pretty cute," he mumbled.

And the rest of the pack seemed to think so, too.

Izzie: Somebody slept well!

Ryan: Gabe, come on. I thought snuggling was our thing!

Gabe: I hate all of you. (except you, Ry, love you)

Ben: How do I get off this group?

If Zach was awake, he didn't have anything to say. Max didn't know how to feel about his silence. He knew he ought to feel bad for sleeping, literally, with another wolf's possible mate but he didn't. He still felt warm and fuzzy when he recalled waking up next to Gabe, bundled up in the warmth of his body and strong arms.

"Zach's mad at you, huh?" Max asked. Gabe had been on the phone for five minutes, texting back and forth.

"Huh?" Gabe offered a lopsided smile.

Max hoped he wasn't in trouble. "He didn't get the wrong idea, did he?"

"No, no! He's cool," Gabe stammered, flushing up to his ears. "I told him everyone needs a good puppy pile once in a while." Gabe hastily ate a mouthful of cereal.

Max's chest ached and he wished he could rewind to the early hours of the morning when Gabe had lain in his arms, back to a moment when Gabe Reyes was his.

Max dozed on the sofa for a bit and woke with a bladder fit to burst. Afternoon sun warmed the carpet as he stopped outside the bathroom door. He grabbed the knob and pulled it open, walking right into something warm and damp and very naked. Max's head smacked into a powerful chest that smelled of soap and deodorant, cherry trees, and spring flowers. Max sighed. Gabe smelled good enough to roll in.

"Sorry!" Max lurched out of Gabe's personal space.

Gabe laughed, cheeks dusted pink. "No biggie. Not like I've got anything secret on me you haven't seen before." He adjusted the fluffy white towel around his hips. It hung low, revealing spirals of short curls that trailed from his navel and disappeared below the towel.

Water trickled, dripping over V-cut abs. He had a birthmark Max hadn't noticed before next to his navel. His nipples were hard, practically begging for Max's attention. His hair was longer when it was wet, tumbling past his shoulders, sleek and glossy.

Fuck. Rooming with Gabe had been a very, very bad idea.

"Sorry. I'll get outta your way." Gabe stepped to the right, and Max mirrored him. Max's face was ready to catch fire. Max stepped left, the blood pumping in his ears, and Gabe copied him. They both laughed. Suddenly, big hands clutched Max's shoulders and he found himself being spun around until his feet touched bathroom tiles. Max was red in the face, he knew it, as he laughed breathlessly.

"I gotta run out for a bit, run some errands." Gabe's voice sounded as if it were coming from miles away. Max jerked his eyes from Gabe's perky nipples to his face, praying Gabe hadn't noticed him staring.

"Huh? Sure. Okay."

Gabe nodded wordlessly, swiping a pink tongue over his supple lower lip. Crap, had Max made him uncomfortable? "But hey, when I get back, we can go for a run in the park later. Okay?"

"Sure, yeah," Max babbled, looking at anything other than Gabe.

Gabe clicked his tongue. "See ya." He raised a hand, laughing. He had a little gap between his two front teeth, and Max was utterly charmed. He couldn't resist grinning back, even if he wanted to sink into the floor.

The door closed, and Max collapsed against it. In the mirror, his face was practically scarlet. His hand trembled as he covered his mouth, breathing fast. He closed his eyes so tight they ached.

It was a crush, just some silly childish crush. He was being stupid and latching onto the first person to show him any kindness. Though was that really true? Ryan had been kind to him. Izzie, too, and Ben. His stomach lurched when he thought of cuddling with them or letting them see him at his most vulnerable.

He raked a hand through his hair, fisting the roots and squeezing tight.

It would go away.

Please let it go away.

GABE WAS GONE FOR a long time. Max was watching *Friends* reruns when the door flew open. Gabe walked in whistling, his arms filled with groceries. "Hope you like strip steak." Kendra jumped up from the couch and went to take a bag from Gabe's arms.

Max's stomach growled longingly. "I'll help." Max stood and froze, reeling at the scent permeating Gabe's clothes.

He smelled like Zach. Max sniffed, smelling sweat but nothing to indicate they'd done anything. They didn't have to because Zach had made his point perfectly clear: stay away from what's mine.

Max squeezed his fists until his nails dimpled his palms. His fangs lengthened and he exhaled a growl. He'd never felt his wolf so close to the surface over another wolf. Maybe when he'd been at Richard's mercy, scared and helpless, but this was different.

This was fury, turning his insides upside down, making his arms tremble. This wasn't some stupid crush. This was eating him alive, filling him with so much pain and fury all he wanted to do was howl to get it all out. Howl and bare his fangs and claws, tear down anything that tried to take away his—

His... what had he been about to call Gabe? His *mate?* Horror seized hold of Max's heart.

Gabe wasn't his.

He was only being kind to Max because it was his job. Max wasn't special. He wasn't like Zach, who was an experienced agent and a respected member of the pack. He was worthless. Gabe would never care for someone like him the way Max wanted him to.

"Max?" But Max ran, ducking into the guest bedroom before Gabe and his mother could ask what was wrong. The door slammed and Max caught his breath. His wolf clawed against his chest, all fangs and fury. Max wrapped his arms around himself, urging his claws to dull, listening to the slamming of his heart against his ribs.

He'd been so happy this morning when he woke up in Gabe's arms. If he could begin every day like that, he'd never ask for anything else. His jaw tightened, smothering his wolf's song, a song for Gabe that he could never hear.

He'd wanted so much in that tiny dark pantry. Someone to come and rescue him. Someone to love him. To be stronger than those who hurt him.

Gabe would leave Max someday soon. He knew that, had thought it didn't bother him.

That was before he'd woken up to Gabe's sleeping face nestled so perfectly against him, like they belonged together. Right now, he had it all. Happiness at his fingertips when he touched Gabe's sleeping face and whispered soothing words to him.

Happiness, so frail yet so bright that he wanted to cradle it in his hands so no one and nothing could extinguish it before it went out and left him in the dark again.

Please. Can I keep this? Just for a little while longer. Can I keep him?

Gabe wasn't his to keep. Gabe would never be his. Gabe would leave eventually, and the memory of him would fade like a scar on his heart. And Max would have to let him go because he had no right to ask Gabe for anything more than he'd given already.

"The trees are so big here! This is awesome!"

"So many smells! Grass, birds, dirt—oh my gosh, is that a rabbit? Can we hunt it?"

"Gabe, Gabe! Are there ducks in that huge pond? Can we hunt them?"

"What's that smell? Holy crap, it's horse crap! Can we hunt horses?"

These were the kinds of questions Gabe had been putting up with during their hour-long jaunt through the park. Well, perhaps *putting up with* was a bit harsh considering Gabe laughed at most of Max's questions.

"The horses are gone," he responded telepathically. *"They're here during the day."*

Max whined his disappointment. *"So let's come back during the day and hunt them!"*

Gabe yawned and sat in the grass on a hill overlooking the duck pond. *"Sure, knock yourself out. Just don't get kicked in the head."*

"Tired already? We just got here." The red wolf shuffled his paws impatiently. Gabe was pleased he was having a good time. All night long, he'd been sniffing frantically at the air as if he thought he'd lose his sense of smell and wanted to breathe in everything while he had the chance.

Gabe shifted back to human form, fur receding and bones reshaping. "Let's sit for a bit. The night's still young." And he was a bit tired of communicating telepathically. He was thrilled, however, that Max's pack bonds with him were strong enough for such communication. He hoped someday Max would be able to communicate with the others like this.

The grass rustled. Gabe turned and his breath ran away from him. Moonlight glimmered on Max's pink skin. The smattering of freckles on his shoulders was like a constellation of stars. His beautiful ginger hair looked curly and soft. He'd put more weight on since he'd come to them, no longer skin and bones.

While his scars still hurt Gabe's heart to see, they only served as proof of what Max had survived. He was strong, so much stronger than he knew, and Gabe ached with fierce pride.

And tonight the sight of his slender body stirred something else in him, something that simmered hot in the pit of his stomach and shortened his breath.

Something that made him notice the attractive shape of his jaw, the sprinkle of copper hair that glimmered like gold on his chest and stomach, the smell of chili and cinnamon that clung to his skin and made Gabe want to bring his face to Max's chest and bathe in those pleasant smells.

Max was changing, that was for certain, changing in the way he interacted with others and the world around him, growing stronger in body and spirit.

It was impossible not to be swept away by him, to feel that strange warmth in his chest that was spreading throughout most of his body but most noticeably in his loins, a pulsing, pounding heat that grew ever stronger as Max met his gaze, a curious smile tugging at his full lips, a delicate flush on his cheeks.

"Wh-what is it?" Laughter spilled from Max's lips. "Do I have dirt on me?"

You're fucking perfect.

"Uh, yeah. A bit. There was a leaf on your... Never mind." Shoulders tight, Gabe exhaled all the air lodged in his chest and looked out over the pond. What in the hell was with him?

Max sat beside him. Gabe suddenly had trouble focusing on the pond, his gaze longing to stray in Max's direction. Should he look? Would not looking make Max worry Gabe was annoyed with him or something? Fuck, what did he do?

"Are you okay? Your heart's pumping like crazy," Max said.

Damn. Sometimes being a werewolf was a blessing and a curse.

"I'm fine." Gabe cleared his throat. "Just enjoying tonight. With you."

"Me, too." Max laughed and the sound made Gabe's stomach flip over. He was quickly coming to adore that laugh. He hoped Max would laugh more often.

Sighing, Max gazed up at the moon. "Wow. It's really beautiful tonight. We picked a good night to come out here." Thank the goddess they were moving on from talk of leaves and dirt on Max's beautifully naked body.

"How was Zach?" Max asked, clearing his throat. "You saw him today, didn't you?"

Gabe tried to smile. "Yeah. He's feeling better."

Zach had left the agency's care and returned to his apartment. Gabe had gone to check in on him, and updated him on the situation with Max and Richard.

Zach's smile was strained when he said, "Seems like Max really likes you, huh?" He was staring at the picture of them in the group chat.

Gabe's skin flushed. "No. No, he just... We get each other. You know? I think he relates to me."

Zach met his gaze. "I missed you. Would have liked having you around while I recovered." He worried his lower lip. "Gabe, I gotta know... I almost died. That didn't make you feel something? Anything?"

Gabe lowered his gaze, unprepared for the question. "I was worried about you. Of course I was." But he hadn't had the realization Zach wanted. His feelings for Zach were as fond as ever, but not romantic.

Zach closed his eyes, face twisting into a frown. "Sorry. Forget I asked. Thanks for stopping by. I'll see you." They hugged goodbye. The air was heavy with Zach's sadness.

Gabe's wolf had howled for Max the moment Zach held him. Being in Zach's arms had felt... wrong, down to his very bones. Like he wasn't meant to be there. He was meant to be with someone else... with Max. Gabe shook away the thought. He couldn't offer Max the future he deserved.

He jumped as fingers suddenly darted across his ribs. Max withdrew, chuckling. "Sorry. You looked all serious for a minute there."

Gabe's heart pumped faster. The spot where Max had touched him tingled. Two could play at this. Once Max turned his gaze to the moon, Gabe's fingers shot out, tickling his ribs. Max batted him away, his laughter carrying into the night. Max growled playfully in response, snapping his fangs. He pounced on Gabe's back, laughing as he tried to pin Gabe in the grass. The sound was infectious. Gabe had to hear more.

Gabe put up a fight, but he ultimately let Max tackle him into the dirt. "You win, you win!" Gabe declared as Max pinned his arms to the ground.

Max grinned triumphantly, his eyes aglow. "You let me."

Gabe wriggled to free himself from Max's grip. "I'm tired."

"Right." Max collapsed onto the grass, laughing between gasps for air. The smell of his joy was like cookies, warm sunshine, the smell of fresh clean laundry—dozens of little happy feelings bundled up into one.

Gabe rolled over and found himself nestled into the crook of Max's arm. Gabe's heart lurched. They were so close Gabe could appreciate the flecks of green and gold in his eyes.

"Gabe?" Max's breath warmed his lips.

Something cold ran down Gabe's back. Shit. He'd crossed a line; he knew it. What was he doing, getting so close to him?

"Yeah?" Gabe swallowed.

Max's tongue peeked out when he wet his lips. Heat rushed down Gabe's spine as the musky scent of Max's arousal sent a heady pulse straight to his cock. And, oh Goddess, the way he lay beneath Gabe flat on his back, exposing not only his throat but his stomach, so trusting and vulnerable. His heart melted.

Fuck. Fuck! What are we doing? This is fine. This is normal, right? This isn't awkward at all, just two guys lying in the grass, naked and turned on. Happens all the time.

Like that time on the beach when Max's breath had warmed his lips and he'd felt so small and fragile in Gabe's arms. And Gabe had leaned in and—

But that hadn't been anything. Gabe had just wanted to comfort him, nothing more. Right?

"Thanks. For bringing me here. It made me happy." Max swallowed and Gabe's eyes were glued to the rise and fall of his Adam's apple. Max's heart raced in his ear and he longed then to drag his mouth across the soft skin of his throat, to feel his pulse under his lips.

Would Max trust him to get so close to the most vulnerable part of his body? He bit back a whine. He wanted to know, wanted to take all of Max's trust and lock it up tight, keeping it close to him always so no one could ever betray it.

The fear washed over him then. If he did anything to hurt Max or upset him, anything to damage the rickety bridge of trust they'd built between them, he'd never forgive himself. So he took in a deep breath to keep his desires in check. He blocked his ears to his wolf's howl, crying out to Max's wolf in a way he'd never cried out for anyone.

Gabe said, "I'm glad. If anyone needs to have fun, it's you."

The little smile on Max's lips set his blood on fire and made moving away physically painful but Gabe forced himself to roll onto the grass. They sat side by side, which was somehow even harder than when Gabe had lain atop him. The scent of Max's arousal faded slowly, but every second was torture until Gabe was digging his nails into his arms to keep from reaching over and—

Damn it. Just stop! Max is... off-limits.

Max needed a friend, not all the complications Gabe would bring to their relationship. It was for the best if Max recovered, moved on, and left Gabe behind, even if the thought drove a dagger between his ribs.

"It is a beautiful night," Gabe said, his voice cracking. He cleared his throat, mortified. "Your mom should join us next time."

Max growled lowly. "No. I like it when it's us." There was something possessive in his voice that threatened to make Gabe hard. He looked at Max, hoping to get through to him.

"Max, you need to talk to her."

"No. I don't." Max's eyes blazed, and the anger thickening his voice made Gabe want to apologize and pull him close.

"Max. Life is short. Things are uncertain right now. If something happens to her, you're going to beat yourself up the rest of your life for not settling things between you two."

"I don't know why she acts like everything's normal between us!" Max's fangs came out, his eyes wide with fury. "It's not! Nothing about what happened is fucking normal!"

"Max—"

But Max withdrew into himself, trampling the grass under his feet as he moved away. With a snarl, he slammed his fist into the trunk of a tree. His claws pierced the bark. "I promised. I promised I'd be a man. But I let him hurt her! I'm weak! A weak wolf. Weak man. Weak, stupid boy."

Gabe shivered, cold all over as Max started to shift, growing fur and fangs and claws. He was trying to repress his guilt, escape it in the only way he knew how. Fuck. How had Gabe missed this? Just because Max was doing so much better than before didn't mean the trauma he'd suffered had magically gone away. To his horror, Gabe realized he had let Max's sunny smiles and infectious laugh blind him.

"Max. Easy."

"Won't let Bad Man hurt her. Bite him, rip him, tear his flesh!" With a snarl, Max raked his claws across the tree trunk, scattering shards of bark.

"Hey, what did I promise you, huh?" Gabe's voice trembled, his hands unsteady as he reached out to Max slowly. "Tell me, Max. What did I promise you?"

"That...?" Max blinked frantically, sclera black and irises flickering between yellow and honey orange. "That you'd... that as long as I was...?"

"As long as you stayed with us, I would keep you safe. That hasn't changed. If Richard does come, you won't face him alone. It's not on you to protect your mother and yourself anymore. Max, she doesn't hate you, okay? You know that back when the estate was attacked, she was out there looking for you. She loves you, Max."

Max's fur disappeared, the inky blackness in his eyes creeping away, letting white shine through. Tears gleamed in his eyes. His entire body shook and his hand trembled as it covered his face. He pushed Gabe's hand away weakly when he reached out, sobs tearing from his throat that hurt Gabe's heart to hear. "Don't. Please." Gabe froze. Max's heart sounded as if it were breaking apart.

"I'll call Ben in the morning, Max. We're gonna work through this. Okay?"

Max sucked in a breath and leaned on the tree, wiping furiously at his eyes.

Gabe opened his arms, wanting so badly to go to him and give him the comfort he needed, if only Max would let him. Max hesitated then took one step toward Gabe. He dropped his head against Gabe's chest, and Gabe put his arms around Max's shoulders.

Closing his eyes tight, he laid his cheek on Max's ginger locks. Max sighed and nestled his face in Gabe's shoulder. Max's trembling stopped, his breathing slowed, and Gabe felt a wave of peace wash over him like Max was an anchor in a vast, churning sea, keeping him grounded. Gabe's heart wanted to burst.

When did I let him so close?

He was *too* close. He'd let Max wrap himself around his heart and blind him to the turmoil going on beneath the surface. He only hoped Max wouldn't suffer from his ignorance.

"Listen, Max." When Max nodded against his chest, Gabe ran his hands up and down Max's shoulders. "I've struggled with control over my wolf my entire life. My grandparents were a human-werewolf couple, so were my parents. I don't know if it's true what all these fanatics say, that my human blood has messed with the connection to my wolf.

"Or... or if it started after I lost my dad. He was my connection, taught me everything I knew about being a werewolf, and I lost him. After that, I'd shift whenever I was angry or scared or feeling helpless. But I found a pack, and they put me back on my feet. And they... they saved my life. This isn't over for you. Don't let your blood define you, or your scars."

Max shuddered in his arms and didn't speak.

Gabe kissed his hair. "You can come back from this. I know it."

CHAPTER 14

BLOOD-CRAZED BEAST

Gabe was hoping for a quiet Saturday morning. It sure started off that way. Max slept in, tired from the night before. Kendra tiptoed around the kitchen, whispering questions like, "Where do you keep flour and sugar?"

Gabe poured boiling water from the kettle into his coffee filter. "In the cabinet on the right. Making something?"

Kendra pulled down the sugar and flour bags. "Pancakes. Max loves them."

"Sounds good. What flavor?"

"Banana pancakes are his favorite. Do you have any?"

Gabe checked the fruit bowl and handed her two slightly overripe bananas. Gabe set aside a cup of coffee for Max and handed a mug to Kendra. She thanked him and took a grateful sip.

Gabe slurped his coffee. "You know, I can't figure out why the cult wants Max."

Kendra grimaced. "They're crazy, the lot of them."

"No doubt about that, but it can't be a coincidence, you know? I've been paying close attention to the Moonborn killings. Stone has never targeted a hybrid like Max before. They know we rescue hybrids. They've had plenty of opportunity to strike back at the agency for that, but they haven't. It has to have something to do with his fur color, don't you think?"

"I have no idea." She scoffed, shaking her head.

Gabe took a gulp of coffee, gathering his thoughts. "Have you noticed anything that might indicate he's special somehow? I don't know, anything about his birth that was unusual? Oh! Maybe he was born under a special lunar phase?" As far as he knew, lunar phases did nothing to influence a werewolf's birth, but nothing was outside the realm of possibility.

Kendra choked on her coffee. She quickly cleared her throat. "No, no! Max's birth was..." She became oddly flustered, tucking her hair behind her ear and looking anywhere but at him. "H-How did the run go last night? Did Max have fun?"

That was weird. Why would Kendra not want to discuss Max's birth? Unless it had been a difficult, traumatic labor, he didn't understand why a woman might not want to talk about the birth of her child. His mom could talk about his and Izzie's births as if they'd been born yesterday. He was curious, but being a man, he didn't want to push in case he was being insensitive.

Setting his curiosity aside, Gabe took another swallow of his coffee, trying to gather his thoughts. "Max is..." How did he tell her without upsetting her? He realized there was no easy way to tell her Max was still struggling. He had to be honest.

Before he could speak, his phone rang in his sweatpants pocket. Gabe jumped to answer, worried the ringing would wake Max up. "Hello?" he murmured, darting across the room and into his bedroom.

"Hey." Ben's voice was groggy. "I wake you?"

"No," Gabe assured him, leaning on the door and closing it. "Is everything okay?"

"There's been an update on the Moonborn situation."

Gabe nearly dropped his coffee. He took a seat on the bed, heart hammering. "Tell me."

"Early this morning, a woman came to us. A hybrid. She escaped an abduction attempt. She was bleeding badly. Looked like she'd been through hell."

Gabe felt terrible for the woman, but he was thrilled. "She could know where to find them! Did you ask?"

"Slow down there." Ben yawned. "She was too shaken up to question. She's recuperating at the agency. Between her and Max, they are the only two who have had experience with the Moonborn and lived to tell the tale. Thing is, she's real clammed up. Doesn't feel comfortable talking to pure-blooded werewolves about her experiences."

"She and Max should meet," Gabe said. "Maybe it would help Max to talk to someone who has shared his experiences."

"Bring it up with him. Her name's Gemma." Another long yawn. Ben's jaw cracked.

Gabe chuckled. "Get some rest, Viejo. I'll talk to Max about meeting Gemma."

They hung up and Gabe exhaled. This was good, so fucking good. Not for the woman, of course. He felt terrible for the things she must have endured. But a living witness to the Moonborn's crimes was nearly unheard of. They were so meticulous about never letting hybrids leave captivity alive. Perhaps they were getting sloppier over time. If Gemma could tell them what she knew, she'd be a hero.

Gabe left the bedroom. Kendra was mixing up ingredients in the kitchen and Max was mashing up bananas. Gabe smiled at the sight of them, watching as Max handed the bowl of banana mash to his mother, who dumped it in with the wet ingredients. They looked like a normal family, and what a blessing it was to see.

"Morning!" Gabe said.

Max smiled, though he had bags under his eyes. "Hey. You're in a good mood," he said.

Gabe sat at the breakfast bar and took a gulp of coffee. "How's the coffee? Did I make it okay?"

Max swirled the contents around in his mug. "Sure."

Gabe drummed his fingers on the marble counter, considering. "I have news about Stone. A hybrid escaped from the Moonborn cult."

Kendra dropped the measuring cup of pancake batter on the floor.

Max's eyes widened. "What?"

"Her name's Gemma. She's shaken up, but she's alive. She could tell us where Stone's fanatics are holed up."

Kendra said, "That's wonderful! Not about the poor girl. I hope she'll make a full recovery." She picked up the measuring cup. "But this is huge."

"It is," Gabe agreed. "Would you like to meet her, Max?"

Max handed his mother a wet paper towel and she knelt and scrubbed the floor. "I thought I wasn't going back to the agency."

"She's not feral, so she won't have to stay long term. She'll be able to go home, and Ben would probably assign someone from the agency to guard her until she feels safe. If she agrees, maybe you two could visit. I think having someone to talk to who's had similar experiences to yours could be helpful, for both of you."

A frown furrowed Max's brow, and he hummed thoughtfully. "Yeah. Maybe. When could I meet her?"

"I'll ask Ben." He was pleased that Max was receptive to the idea.

Stone felt closer than he had in fourteen years.

A FEW HOURS LATER, Gabe and Max rode the train into Harlem, where Gemma lived. Her wounds had been treated, and she'd insisted on returning home. After all, the same thing couldn't possibly happen twice. She'd refused an armed bodyguard, demanding her independence, and the agency couldn't exactly force her to comply.

Max was pleased she'd agreed to talk to them. She sounded eager to hear Max's story, and Max was excited to speak to her.

As they neared Gemma's apartment, Gabe gripped Max's shoulder. "Is this okay?"

His stomach squirmed from the anticipation, but Max found that he was okay. "Yeah. This is fine. I'm excited to talk to her."

Gabe nodded, squeezing Max's shoulder. "Good."

His skin tingled from Gabe's touch. "Thanks for checking. I promise I won't go all crazy like I did last night."

Gabe chuckled. "No. I know."

Max's skin warmed. He still wasn't in a hurry to talk about what happened in the park last night when his wolf surfaced. It embarrassed and confused him.

"Max," Gabe began.

Max turned away. "Let's focus on Gemma right now."

"Okay. But we're going to get to the bottom of what's going on with you, too. Who knows, maybe talking to Gemma will be healing for you."

Max wasn't sure what to expect. He approached the front door. "What buzzer was hers?"

Gabe reached over and buzzed an apartment on the third floor.

"Hello?" The voice was quiet and soft.

Gabe waved at the intercom. "It's Gabe and Max from the agency!"

Max somehow liked the sound of that. Gabe and Max from the agency. Like they were partners, working together to help others.

She buzzed them in, and they rode the elevator to the third floor. Max's heart beat faster, and he put his hands in his pockets to keep them from twitching. Gabe glanced his way and offered a reassuring smile. That only accelerated the beat of Max's heart, and his face warmed. Before Gabe could tease him, they were striding down the hall to Gemma's front door.

Gabe knocked and waited. Floorboards squeaked beyond the door. The chain rattled, the locks clicked, and the door opened slowly, revealing a bedraggled woman with a long morose face. Her red-dyed hair was wispy, tied back in a ponytail from which it was coming loose in long strands.

A bruise purpled her right cheek. She smelled faintly of blood, and Max's stomach churned.

She sniffed the air, and the tension in her shoulders loosened. "Hi," she said quietly. She sounded tired and scared, and Max's heart went out to her.

"Is it okay if we come in?" Gabe asked, hands folded neatly against his waist.

She nodded, her eyes heavy-lidded from exhaustion. "Yes. Of course." She held the door for them. "You can leave your shoes on. I don't mind." Max didn't usually, but he left them on and followed her inside, Gabe shadowing him. "I'm grateful for your agency's help, but I couldn't stay there. All the suffering in the air... It was overwhelming."

Max nodded, understanding. "The wolves howling in the kennels was pretty distressing to me, too."

"Can I get you both anything? Tea, water?"

Max was thirsty, but he didn't want her to go to the trouble. She wobbled side to side, clearly half-dead on her feet. She arched a brow at Gabe, who shook his head. "I'm good."

She led them to the living room. It was a small apartment, neat and clean with the scent of lemony cleaner and cigarette ash. A half-filled ashtray was on the coffee table. "Do you mind?" she asked, holding up a smoke. They didn't, so she lit up. She sat on the sofa and drew her knees to her chest, looking anywhere but at them. The summer breeze through the open window diluted the ashy scent of smoke.

Max cleared his throat. "I was a victim of the Moonborn cult, too. They abducted me, but I managed to escape. Are you able to tell me what happened to you?"

Gemma exhaled smoke. "I was walking home after work. It was dark. No one was around. Someone grabbed me, stuck me with a dose of wolfsbane. I woke up strapped to an altar in the woods. I don't know where. They were going to sacrifice me. I escaped." She scratched the back of her neck, claws prickling over her skin.

"Okay," Gabe said. "Can you tell us anything about where they took you? Any details that might help us figure out where their hideout is."

"Don't remember. Sorry." She dragged on her cigarette and sighed, smoke curling from her nose. "Did you feel... blessed, Max?"

Max frowned. "Blessed? No. I was terrified."

Gemma hugged her knees to her chest with one arm. "All my life, I've felt filthy. Disgusting. All for being a hybrid. And John Stone... he wanted to sacrifice me. Rip out the wolf I don't deserve. We hybrids dirty the goddess's gift. Stone wanted to make me pure. I wasn't terrified; I was relieved." She smiled, cold and bitter.

Max was too stunned to say anything. Gemma shook her head. "The wolfsbane is still clouding my head. I'm sorry I called you down here. I really did want to talk to you, but I don't think I'm ready yet."

Max nodded his understanding. "Of course. If you want, we could exchange numbers. You can call me when you're ready. Or if things get tough. Maybe we can lift each other up."

Her mouth twitched in an attempted smile. "You'd do that?"

"Yeah, totally." Max pulled out his phone.

She told him her number, and Max gave her his.

"Thank you, Max. It would mean a lot to have someone I can talk to who gets what... happened to me." She blinked fast, eyes watering. Max wished he could give her a hug but refrained.

"Me, too."

Max bade her goodbye and went downstairs with Gabe.

"What was that all about? Why did she feel blessed?" Max was still struggling to comprehend Gemma's words.

"With all the hatred toward hybrids out there, it wouldn't surprise me if she internalized some of her own. Besides, she's been through a lot." Gabe stepped onto the stoop, the summer sun bringing out the natural blue highlights in his black hair. Max wanted to run his fingers through it but settled for touching his shoulder.

"At least she gave me her number," Max told him. "When she's ready to talk, she'll call me."

"That's good," Gabe said.

"I know you want answers," Max said, sighing as they set off for the subway. "If she tells me anything, I'll let you know."

They descended into the subway. They swiped their MetroCards and walked to the platform where they could catch a downtown train. At this hour, the platform was empty. Most commuters were already at work or school. Max sat on a bench and Gabe paced, nose in his phone by the edge of the platform. Max wanted to tell him to move away from the platform edge but didn't want to sound like a worrywart.

Footsteps echoed and a tall man in a hood came down the steps, his hands in his pockets. He walked up to the edge of the platform. He was standing close to Gabe in a way that made Max uncomfortable, though he didn't understand why.

Max opened his phone and stared at Gemma's number. He wondered if she would call. Perhaps he could make the first move and check in on her.

"Max, train's coming." Gabe waved him over, peering around the edge of the platform toward the tunnel.

The man in the hood lunged for Gabe, arms outstretched to push him onto the tracks.

"Gabe!" Max screamed, bolting to his feet and running.

Gabe whirled around and grappled with the man. The lights of the train illuminated the tracks. Gabe spun his attacker around and hurled him against the train as it roared into the station. The man tumbled to the floor, a snarl twisting his face. His claws scraped against the tile. Max kicked him in the face, bowling him over. His hood fell down, revealing a claw mark tattoo across his furious face.

A clawed hand swiped at Max, tearing the front of his T-shirt. Gabe seized Max by the arms and wrenched him behind himself, urging him toward the train. "Get on!" Gabe yelled, shoving Max through the open door. Gabe's claws popped out, fur sprouting on his arms. The man on the platform roared, fangs bared.

Max yanked Gabe inside by the shirt as the doors closed. The man crashed into the doors and snarled, claws scraping the glass. He punched, raining blows down against the door until the glass cracked. Then the train pulled out of the station. The man chased after them but was left behind as the train sped away into the dark.

Max collapsed into a seat, gasping. Gabe knelt between his legs. "Are you okay? Are you hurt?" His big hands fumbled blindly, running up Max's arms. Max slumped, shaking violently. "Hey. You're okay. We're okay." Gabe's hands were unsteady when they framed Max's face.

Max struggled to catch his breath. "What was that? Who the hell was he?"

Gabe's face was sweaty and pale. "I don't know. Some crazy person, maybe?"

Max hoped that was all it was and nothing more.

MAX CALLED GEMMA ONCE they were home, warning her about the crazy guy near her subway building.

She was quiet a moment. "So, neither of you got hurt?"

"No, we're fine."

"Oh. Well... that's good." She didn't sound especially relieved.

"I was worried he might be Moonborn. That's why I wanted to call you."

"No!" She snapped, and Max jumped. "He's not Moonborn. He's... He's some crazy guy, all right? There have been police reports about some nutjob pushing people in the subway. It usually happens at night, so I thought..."

Max was relieved he wasn't a Moonborn hunting for Gemma. "Shit happens. New York's full of weirdos. Just be careful. I wouldn't want you to get hurt."

"Thanks, Max. You're great." After a pause, she added, "And don't waste your agency's time, okay? He's not Moonborn."

Max wanted to believe her. The thing was, how could they really know unless the weirdo screamed fanatical things? He exhaled, trying to let it go. "Bye, Gemma. We can talk in the morning."

She hung up and Max went to eat dinner with Gabe and his mother.

Later that night, Gabe locked the front door while Max huddled beneath the blankets of his bed. Gabe went to the bathroom, then came back out and checked the locks again. Sighing, he waved to Max and went to his room.

Trying to relax and forget about the insanity of today, Max watched a movie but he barely paid attention to the plot. He kept remembering the bruises on Gemma's face, the fear in her eyes.

Before he knew it, his eyes were closing, chin slumping to his chest.

He woke in the night for reasons he wasn't sure of, lying beneath the blankets of Gabe's sofa bed. Muffled voices came from one of the rooms, loud and indistinguishable. His mother's room. She started screaming and didn't stop. Max tried to throw himself from the bed, but he was paralyzed, a weight pressing down on his chest.

The screaming got louder, drilling into his ears. Tears burned his eyes and his throat tightened but he couldn't move. He couldn't help her.

A growl rumbled through the floor and Max realized then that something was behind him, lurking out of his field of vision. He couldn't move to look. He could only lie helpless as heavy paws came toward him. It wasn't a wolf. Nothing in this world had ever felt so evil, except—

Coppery blood flooded his mouth as a shape loomed over his bed, baring a mouthful of bloodstained fangs that spattered his face with crimson rain. It had the long, stringy hair of John Stone and the skeletal face of a wolf with hateful human eyes—Richard's cold silver eyes. He wanted to scream for Gabe but his mouth was trapped shut. His claws pierced the sheets, but he couldn't lift his arms; they weighed more than his body.

Its jaws opened impossibly wide, drowning him in darkness.

Max's eyes flew open and he sucked in a gasp as cold sweat chilled his skin. The taste of blood flooded his mouth and he swallowed hard, trying not to be sick. The wolf-human thing was gone. He could move again. His mother's room was silent, deathly silent. Fear clawed his throat. He needed to see her. Right now.

He sat up and touched something wet and sticky and cold. He lunged for the light switch. His heart and stomach changed places. Blood spattered the sheets, cold to the touch as if from something dead and frozen. His hands trembled as he raised them to eye level, and he swallowed his scream when he realized they were soaked in blood.

His toes touched something cold and slimy under the blankets. Gasps spilled from his lips as he felt across the sheets and squeezed a bulge beneath the blankets, squishy and cold, oozing blood into the bed.

He'd snapped. He'd wandered in his sleep again and this time he'd killed someone. Who? A human? A child? His gasps turned to pants as his fangs came out. His claws pierced the mattress and ripped at the sheets.

No.

How could he have done this? How could he have let it get to this? He should have died at the hands of the cult if this was what he'd turned into.

Fur sprouted thick across his arms and legs. He wanted to forget. He needed to forget. He gritted his jaws against a scream as his body shifted. He had to get out and get away before he hurt more people.

This was all his fault. If he'd talked to someone, it wouldn't have gotten this bad. He wrestled with the chain on the door and then the knob went flying off as he ripped the door open. He ran to the elevator, heart in his throat, waiting for someone to come upon him and see all the blood. Max hurled himself into the elevator and dropped to all fours, clothes ripping. The fear, the horror, the guilt—it all faded away as he assumed his wolf form and tore out of the elevator and into the warm, dark night.

A scream ripped Gabe from his sleep. Panic chased away the sleep fogging his brain. It was Richard; he'd come for Max and Kendra. Hurtling from his bed, he kicked open his bedroom door and Kendra screamed at the sight of him.

"Get down, Kendra! I'll—"

The living room and kitchen were empty. The house was still and no unfamiliar scents stood out to him—except the smell of blood. Fear rushed in. Kendra stared at the sofa bed, face pale and eyes huge. The sheets had been torn to shreds and the blankets were crusted with dried blood.

"What happened to Max?" Kendra gasped. "Where is he?"

Gabe's legs trembled as he approached the bed, heart pounding hard in his ears as he ripped the blankets back, revealing chunks of some kind of meat. His stomach lurched and he urged himself not to throw up. There had to be an answer. This didn't make any sense. He sniffed. This blood wasn't Max's or even a werewolf's. He reached out, tentatively cradling the slimy lump of meat in his hands. He sniffed. It was... beef?

Understanding dawned on him. He dashed to the kitchen, following dried bloody paw prints on the zebrawood that trailed from the kitchen to the bed. The fridge door hung open, and packages of meat had been torn into. "Shit..."

"What?" Kendra's voice was thin with tension.

"He got into my meat supply." He'd devoured most of it, from sheep's intestines to cow's tongue to ground chuck, and he'd even had a bite of a pig's heart. His gaze wandered to the bloody paw marks on the floor. His stomach twisted. "He was a wolf when he did this."

He recalled Max the other night, on the brink of losing himself to his inner wolf.

"Oh shit."

Max had gone feral.

He turned to Kendra and found his horror reflecting back at him. Her trembling hand covered her mouth. "Oh, my poor boy."

The front door hung open with claw marks in the wood from where the knob and chain had been ripped right off the door. He was loose out there in the streets and at the mercy of humans who wouldn't take kindly to seeing a wolf running through Manhattan.

Gabe hurled himself into his bedroom and lunged for his phone. How could he have let this happen? This was his fault for not being more perceptive. Now Max could be anywhere. He could be lost, or hurt, or—

"Ben, we have a fucking problem! Max is gone!"

"She-Wolf's tits, Gabe! Stop fucking yelling. It's eight in the morning!"

Gabe snarled, squeezing the phone until he thought he'd crack it. "Did you hear me? Max is—"

"Calm down! I was about to call you! He borrowed someone's phone and got in touch with me. I'm en route to get him right now."

The world stopped spinning. His breath caught up with him. "Is he okay?"

"Depends. He's real shaken up. He was ranting that he needed to be locked up or something, claimed he'd killed someone."

"No, just tore into my meat supply." Gabe swallowed, remorse eating him from the inside out. "It's my fault. He's got a lot of pent-up anger and guilt. A night ago, he almost shifted involuntarily."

Ben growled and Gabe could hear him running a hand through his scratchy beard. "Fuck. We need to do better. Security was patrolling the other night, found some torn-up sheets in the bushes outside his window. This has been going on for a while."

Gabe sat up. "We're going to help him."

"Right. This can be fixed, Gabe. His connection to his humanity is still unsteady. His wolf is still in charge and is internalizing the trauma by shifting to cope with it. He's in a fight he's losing and if we can't help him, then he could be consumed by his wolf for good. Who knows if we'd be able to bring him back?"

Gabe swallowed his guilt and panic. This wasn't about him. "How can I help him?"

"Slow down. First, I'll bring him back." A sigh. "This is going to be hard for him, Gabe. But you have to stick with him. He's not going to want this, but he needs to face his trauma. All of it. And you need to be there with him."

"I..." Was Gabe really what was best for him? "Okay, Ben." Gabe hung up and soft sobs reached his ears. His heart sank. "Kendra?" He found her in the living room, her face in her hands. He touched her shoulder but she wouldn't look at him. "Hey, don't worry about Max. Ben's got him. He'll be back soon."

She snorted and when her eyes met his, they were blazing. "I'm not worried. I'm pissed."

Gabe blinked. "Really?"

She marched around him, wiping furiously at her eyes. "What kind of mother am I? He's been struggling so much, and I haven't even tried to help him."

Gabe frowned. "You were giving him his space. Besides, it's hard to help someone who keeps pushing you away. Max could have made an effort, too." It wasn't that he didn't understand Max's guilt, but the lack of communication swung both ways.

Kendra whirled toward him, blonde hair flying around her face. Her eyes were red and wet, but they were fearsome in her anger. "Things used to be so different between him and me. Him and his wolf. He always had such a strong connection to his wolf. He was proud. He never let anyone make him feel ashamed for being a hybrid.

"We used to talk, him and me. Every day, we'd sit down and have dinner together and talk. I always encouraged him to open up about his feelings, none of that toxic masculinity crap in our house. But Richard... He drove a canyon between us, and I couldn't tell! I couldn't tell if I helped or hurt him when I tried to get him to open up to me. So I stopped trying. I thought I'd make it worse. And now look at us!"

With a snarl, she paced up and down, bare feet slapping the floor. "My son's suffering! Because he didn't feel like he could open up to me. Because he felt guilty. And he didn't feel comfortable telling me any of this because I couldn't be strong for him. I—I should have packed my bags and taken him away from Richard earlier, consequences be damned!" She stopped, covering her eyes with her hand.

Gabe squeezed her shoulder. "It's not your fault. You didn't know the full story. Richard and Max hid the abuse well."

She looked at him, tears drying on her cheeks. She laughed, revealing a pointed fang. "Enough's enough." She curled her fists, head held high and defiant. "Enough fear. Enough guilt. Enough bullshit." And she left the apartment and went downstairs to wait for her son to come home.

GABE LURCHED TO HIS feet when Ben walked in through the ruined door, Max trailing bleary-eyed behind him. Gabe wanted to go to Max's side, but then he noticed it. Max's hands were covered in red fur, his nails long and sharp. The rest of him looked human, except for his hands. The sight made Gabe's stomach churn in fear.

"You go and get some sleep. Right now." Kendra had her arm around Max's slumped shoulders.

Max nodded, eyes heavy-lidded with exhaustion. "Sure."

Gabe hung back, suddenly reluctant to approach. Inwardly, he kept wanting to hit himself, frustrated that he hadn't seen the signs. He kept his arms to his sides and his feet rooted, even though all he wanted to do was go to Max and offer him support and comfort. His lack of professionalism had gotten them into this. He'd let Max get too close, and he'd suffered as a result.

Across the room, Max didn't even look at him before he let Kendra usher him into her room for some peace and quiet. Ben spoke briefly to Kendra, and then he marched over to Gabe.

"Something's wrong," Gabe said, feeling sick.

Ben sighed, folding his arms over his chest. "Yeah. Parts of his body are stuck in his shift."

"Fuck!" Gabe paced, wringing his hands together. "This isn't normal. I thought he was all right. He's pack now! I can feel him. Why isn't our bond enough to keep him human?"

"Because his life's been turned upside down. His relationship with his mom is shaky. And sure, you two are close, but he needs more than that. He needs a pack. He needs a family. With all that's going on, we haven't been able to be that for him. There's been no opportunity for bonding as a pack with him, and his wolf's suffering for it."

"Ben..." Gabe's heart thundered. "What happens if we can't fix this? What happens if Max goes feral again?"

Ben's nostrils flared as he breathed in deep. He looked Gabe in the eyes. "Since Max keeps regaining control, that means he's fighting. But he can only fight for so long. Based on what happened the last time, how deep he fell into his wolf... It's not gonna be good, Gabe. You were enough to pull him out of it, but even now with that bond between you two, it's not enough to keep him there."

"Ben," Gabe said through gritted teeth. "What will happen to him?"

"If this goes on, he won't be able to come back out of his shift, Gabe." Ben glowered at the floor. "He could be lost to his wolf for good."

Gabe's heart thumped wildly in his chest and despair gripped his heart. He might lose Max. He'd been so blinded by their bond and because of it, Max's suffering had gone untreated.

Ben cleared his throat, pushing off from where he'd leaned on the wall. "Right, so Kendra's gonna gather some more things from Richard's apartment that might mean something to Max. Don't worry, I'll send some bodyguards to accompany her. Tonight take him somewhere he'll feel comfortable. I don't know the kid that well, so I'll leave that to you. After he's talked out his issues, we'll go for a run as wolves. It'll be good for him, help strengthen his ties to the pack."

"Viejo." Gabe's voice tried to retreat down his throat the minute he spoke. He balled his hands into fists. "Listen. Maybe I should take a step back from this."

Ben's bushy brows furrowed, the creases in his forehead more prominent.

Gabe swallowed as his throat tightened. "I know what I said over the phone. But my being there for Max, that's what got him into this whole mess. I thought our bond meant he was better. That he was okay. It's all too personal for me. He's too—we're too close. I can't do my job. So…"

Ben's lips thinned. Was he disappointed? Angry? "You are close, but that's what Max needs right now. He doesn't need a doctor to give him some diagnosis. He needs a friend. He needs you."

"I failed him!" The words came flying out before he could stop them. He took a step back, suddenly feeling as if all the air was being sucked out of the room. He blinked hard, mortified as his emotions flared to the surface. He paced to the window, clasping the windowsill for support. "You said it yourself. Our bond isn't enough. It doesn't make a difference if I'm there or not. I'm not… I'm not qualified." The words hurt, and he couldn't look Ben in the face.

"Fine. Take a step back. I'll handle tonight. But you can't run away from this, Gabriel. It's not right, not for him or you."

Gabe hardly heard him. He wanted what was best for Max. His own feelings, his desire to be near him, to see him smile and laugh and flourish—none of it mattered. This was the right choice, if not for himself then for Max.

CHAPTER 15

THREADS OF LIGHT

THE MOON ROSE OVER Central Park. Max watched TV, barely hearing a word or focusing on the story. All his senses were amplified. The TV noise. The clashing smells of the apartment. It all kept him grinding his teeth and growling low in his chest.

He jumped when the intercom buzzed, the sound piercing his ears. He rushed to cover them and winced when his claws scratched his face. "Shit!" It had been hours, but his hands were still furred claws. He didn't need a doctor to tell him that wasn't normal. His heart thumped fast, his stomach churning.

"It's Ben," Gabe announced from by the door.

Max nodded, worrying at his lower lip until Ben walked through the newly fixed door. Max had cleaned the kitchen, and the dryer was almost finished running the sheets he hadn't torn up. Gabe had opened his home to them, and Max had wrecked it. Maybe it was better for all of them if Max just wasn't here anymore.

Ben raised a hand when Max attempted a small smile. He almost waved back but put his messed-up hands in his pockets instead. "Moon's out, kid. It's time."

His mother approached, holding a box under one arm. "Sleep well?"

"Sure," Max replied, his voice gravelly with exhaustion. It was lie, but he didn't want to burden her with any more of his drama.

165

His mother tucked a lock of blonde hair behind her ear. "Your friend Ben said I should come tonight. He thinks it might be helpful if I was there."

Max was tired of being a burden to her. "You don't have to."

"I want to," she said, sticking out her chin defiantly.

Max nodded at his toes, knowing it was futile to argue. And... a part of him that was scared and unsure wanted his mother to be there tonight as he faced down painful memories. "I've been such a disaster lately. Soap operas have less drama than me." He attempted a laugh.

"You stop that talk, you hear?" His mother grabbed his hand and looked him square in the eye. "And after this, you and I are going to sit down and talk. Clear? Enough trying to be a man and bottling up your feelings. That's not how we Gallaghers roll."

Max smiled. She was beginning to sound like her old feisty self. "Yeah. Okay."

She patted his cheek. "Now, carry this. It's heavy!" She set down the big cardboard box and pushed it toward him with her foot.

She walked away and Max exhaled long and low. She had bags under her red-rimmed eyes. Her skin still smelled faintly of salty tears.

He'd made his mother cry today. The shame could have doubled him over, but he refused to cave to it and balled his hands into tight fists. Enough. Fucking enough. Enough making his mother worry over him. Enough pushing her away and causing her pain. All this time, he'd wanted to protect her from more pain, become strong enough, be the son she deserved. Instead, he'd only hurt her more.

His decision to withdraw from her out of guilt had caused so much more heartache than he'd ever wanted. He was hurting his mother, not keeping her safe.

Something had to give, and he wasn't looking forward to a big heart-to-heart, not when his own was so frayed and vulnerable. But it had to happen. He needed to get his shit together and become stronger, but he needed to do it with his mother at his side.

Max looked around, realizing Gabe wasn't with them. He was in the kitchen, pouring himself a glass of whiskey that smelled like peanut butter. Was he not coming? Gabe turned around and froze when he met Max's gaze, like a deer in the headlights. Max struggled to find his voice, anxious about what answer Gabe might give him.

"Aren't you coming?" They'd done everything together so far.

"Uh…" Gabe offered a smile that didn't touch his eyes. "No. I think it should be you and your mom."

"Ben's coming." Max's voice was smaller than he'd expected, unprepared for how much Gabe's answer stung.

"Yeah. He is. He's more experienced in this weird moon ritual than I am." Gabe didn't look at him as he slipped past to an armchair by the window. "Max…" Gabe hesitated.

He's angry at me for wrecking his apartment. Or disappointed. I don't blame him.

But what Gabe said next was so much worse.

"I'm not qualified to look after you anymore. So, Ben's going to take over from here."

The ground cracked under Max's feet.

So that was all this had been, this whole time? Max had just been Gabe's responsibility, some broken thing to fix? His claws punctured the palms of his hands and his hurt turned to fury.

It was happening, so much faster than Max had thought it would. He was losing Gabe, and he'd had no time to prepare himself. His chest felt like it was caving in. He wanted to ask why, what he'd done, to apologize for anything that might have caused Gabe to distance himself, but the words were trapped behind a wall of hurt and anger.

You promised. The wolf inside panted, feral and hurt. *You promised!*

"Fine," Max growled. And in his mind, he snapped the bond between them. Gabe stumbled, one hand going to his chest. Max's own heart ached, but in his near feral state, he didn't fucking care. He hoped it hurt.

"Max," Gabe began, his voice small and oddly breathless.

With a snarl, Max turned his back on Gabe and walked out the door with his mother and Ben. *Screw him.* He didn't need Gabe. He didn't need a pack.

Out in the hallway, Ben pushed the button to call the elevator. "So, for this ritual to work, we need to be somewhere you feel safe. Anywhere you can think of?"

Max struggled to think, lost in a fog of feral anger. Central Park came to mind and not only because it was close. His wolf had felt so free and safe roaming the park. He'd been in control of his shift for the first time in the months since Richard's abuse. "The park."

"Let us know when you find a spot you like. Then we'll get started."

They roamed the park for some time, passing homeless people asleep on the benches. Otherwise, the park belonged to them. Moonlight glimmered on the duck pond before clouds obscured its light. "Down there is fine," Max said, motioning toward the pond. They descended a short hill to reach the shore where the water was lapping gently at the soil. Ducks foraged for food, diving under and pointing their tails in the air. Max breathed in the sweet smell of uncut grass and mossy water.

"This is good," he said.

Max set down the box. Ben said, "It's a full moon tonight. That's good. Our wolves are closest to the surface on nights like this. It's the perfect time to bond as a pack. Izzie and Ryan texted me. They're on their way. Zach would come if he could."

"What does bonding entail?" Max asked.

Ben shrugged. "We all shift and do what wolves do. Run. Hunt. Play. You've been making progress. If I close my eyes, really concentrate, I can feel your wolf reaching back. But the Moonborn divided us after the attack on HQ. And then there's the trauma you're still working through. All that guilt. It's interfering with your wolf's ability to reach out to us, keeping us apart. So I think it would be helpful if, before we shift, you could talk to us about how you're feeling."

Ben held Max's gaze. "I'm not going to bullshit you, Max. This is going to be difficult, but you need to stick with it, no matter how painful these memories might be. Let us know when you're ready."

Max's stomach twisted and his breath became short. He didn't want to remember. His claws lengthened. He wanted to forget. Forgetting was fine. It was easy.

"Max." His mother's voice was soft. "Breathe."

Max sucked in a deep breath and exhaled, relaxing his shoulders. He forced his palms to open so he didn't cut himself with his claws.

"Do you want to see the first object?"

"Fine. Sure." He knelt in the grass before his mother and Ben. His mother retrieved a gold engagement band from the box that was tarnished and cold. It had belonged to his father.

"You kept this?" Max murmured.

"Yes," his mother replied, her voice barely a whisper. "He put it in our bedroom the day he left."

His father. Max had never known him, but he'd taught Max a lesson—Max wasn't worth sticking around for.

"Max," Ben's low voice rumbled. "Focus on the item, the memories."

"I don't—"

There was nothing about the man Max *could* remember. He'd left before Max was born. All Max had of him were fragments from pictures his mother had put away. Max would go into her room while she was working and unearth those pictures, the memories of a man he'd never known. Max tried to imagine what kind of man he was, what his voice sounded like.

"Max?"

His eyes opened. The grass was cool and ticklish against his knees. His face was wet. For a moment, he didn't recognize the people in front of him. Their voices came from far away.

"Do you want to see the other items?"

He recognized his mother, then the old man. Ben, was it?

"Why did he leave?" Max asked. He'd never understood why.

"He left because he was selfish. It had nothing to do with you." His mother took his hand and held tight.

He didn't believe her. They'd looked so happy in their wedding photo. It surfaced to his memory suddenly, like salvage from a shipwreck. His mother in her white gown, his father holding her face as if she were something precious. Werewolves didn't get married but his mother had agreed to a traditional wedding for his father. Because she'd loved him, and he'd loved her. Had Max's birth destroyed their marriage?

Forget, the wolf growled in his mind. *Forget. I want to forget.*

No. No, he couldn't. He had to focus.

The next item his mother showed him was... Oh Goddess. It was Max's favorite shirt. He thought he'd hidden it. Richard had ripped it up during a fit of rage, claws gouging Max's back.

"Max?" Ben whispered. "Can you tell us about this shirt? Can you tell us about when this happened?"

He panted and whined. "No. No, I can't. I—" The shame burned.

Tears spilled from Kendra's eyes. "Max, why didn't you tell me he hurt you?"

"Because..." His fang cut his lower lip. He tasted blood, metallic in his throat.

No, the wolf whined. *No, no, no. We were supposed to protect her. Protect pack. Protect Mother. She wasn't supposed to see! She wasn't supposed to know!*

"Max, breathe," Ben said. "We're your pack. Find us. Find our bond. Grab onto it."

"I'm *trying,*" Max said. It came out high and strained. He closed his eyes and gasped for breath, felt for the thread connecting him to his mother and, though faint, Ben. There was a hole where Gabe's bond used to be. Gabe wasn't here. Gabe had left him because Max was weak, because he was stupid, because he was a pathetic mutt. No, no, no... Find it!

There. It was there. Warm and bright. His mother's bond was lavender, sweet and soothing. Frayed. It was frayed. Because of Richard. Because of Max. Because he'd failed her.

A snarl built in his throat. His wolf was rankled by these warm reminders of love he didn't deserve. He hated it.

"Max. Keep talking, okay?" Ben said. "Can you answer your mother's question?"

A whine pulled from Max's throat. "I didn't tell. Because," he said around a sudden snarl, "because if he was hurting me, he wasn't hurting you."

And yet, growled Bad Man's voice. *And yet she still got hurt. You weak little fool. You stupid, pathetic mutt.*

"Weak." The wolf panted, claws clutching at his face, nails biting into his skin. "Weak wolf. Weak boy. Sorry. So sorry."

We'll run away, the wolf whimpered. *We'll run far away so we can never fail her again!*

That sounded good. So good. Far away from pain and shame. Somewhere dark and quiet, away from all the hurt.

He cleaved through the fragile bonds connecting him to his pack. Good. *Good.* He was untethered. Free. He could never hurt anyone again. He could never disappoint them.

"Damn it! Max, no!"

"Max? Honey, no. Oh Goddess, no. It wasn't your fault!" The woman reached out and he lunged, batting her hand away.

His clothes ripped. Fur sprouted all over his body. His shoes ripped around his clawed toes.

Who were these people? He didn't recognize them. Where was he?

Who?

Who was he?

Oh.

Yes.

That was right.

He was—

A growl rumbled in his throat.

The pond water churned, splashing up over his clawed feet. The moon's light blinded him.

Who was he?

"Max? *Max!*"

No. Not Max. Max was dead, and he was...

Wolf.

He was wolf.

"I'M ALMOST HERE, GABE," Izzie said through the phone.

"Yeah, I can see the park," Ryan's voice chimed in.

Gabe sighed in relief. "Thanks for coming. Max needs this. He needs your support."

"Glad to help, man. He's a nice guy. Okay, I'm parking now." Ryan ended their group call.

"I hope we can help him, Gabriel." Izzie's voice was fraught with worry. "I'm heading into the park. You should come. I think Max would really appreciate it."

"Bye, Izzie." Gabe kicked the sheets off the bed with a growl. It was too hot, even with the AC on. His heart pounded, his stomach twisting. He hadn't drunk enough whiskey to numb his anxiety.

Was Max all right?

Was he upset as he confronted old unwanted memories?

Was the treatment working?

He closed his eyes and felt for Max's bond, trying to see if he was all right. Pain twisted through him. Right, Max had severed their bond like it was nothing. He touched his chest, trying to rub away the ache, but the absence throbbed like a missing tooth. He knew Max had only done it in his feral anger, but still. Knowing he'd hurt Max so badly made him feel like a colossal fuckup. He'd truly thought he was acting in Max's best interest.

Fuck. He couldn't sleep like this, not with his wolf itching to run to Max's side and make sure he was all right. He lurched out of bed, pushing damp hair back from his forehead as he went to sit in the living room. He wished he'd gone, but he'd been so sure it was for the best that he and Max had some distance.

Instead, he'd just hurt Max even more. His feet carried him to the window where ivy crept across the glass. The streets were empty and quiet, headlights illuminating the road as cars drove by.

The wind swayed the trees in Central Park. Max was there somewhere with Ben and Kendra, confronting hurtful things without him. He'd promised, hadn't he? He'd promised to be there for him and instead he was running away. But if all he did was be oblivious to Max's inner turmoil, then what good was he?

His cell phone rang on the nightstand and his heart jumped up into his throat. Gabe marched to the bed, Ben's name sending a jolt of panic into his stomach.

"What's up, Ben?"

"The ritual wasn't enough." Ben's voice was panicked, breathless. "Get down here, now. Max needs you."

He threw the phone on the bed and ran, bouncing the door against the wall as he pelted into the hallway and punched the button for the elevator. It wouldn't come. Cursing, Gabe tore down the stairs, grabbing the railing when he slipped on the smooth marble.

I should have gone. Fuck! I should have gone!

If anything had happened to Max, Gabe wouldn't be able to live with himself. The moment the elevator doors opened, he tore out into the night air. His feet pounded the asphalt as he ran along Park Avenue toward the stone walls surrounding Central Park. He hadn't even put shoes on in his panic, he realized as broken glass cut his feet.

The pavement turned to warm soil as he ran through the park. The wind carried scents to him. He smelled Ben's sandalwood cologne and beard oil. Blood. Kendra, her sweet perfume overpowered with the smell of what

Gabe could only describe as despair. Izzie and Ryan had arrived, too. Fury overwhelmed the scent of cinnamon and chili.

I'm sorry. I'm so sorry, Max.

He rounded the curve in the trail and the duck pond came into view. Down the hill, three figures tussled. Gabe ran, sliding down the hill and catching himself on his hands, skinning his palms on the rocks.

"Stay back!" Izzie shouted, a hand out to keep Gabe at a distance.

Ryan lay in the grass, a hand over his face. "Gabe, be careful!" he croaked, and his hand came away from his face to reveal a slash across his cheek.

Ben, a deep gash oozing blood carved into his face, had shifted halfway between man and wolf as he struggled to keep a half-shifted beast at bay, their feet splashing in the water that overflowed from the pond. A beast with honey orange eyes who hurled himself at Ben, fangs gleaming as he lunged for Ben's throat. His shirt lay in tatters, and thick red fur covered his body.

"Max, stop!" Kendra begged, her arms around his torso. The thing wearing Max's skin flailed, whipping around to catch her across the face with his claw. She crumpled into the grass.

"Max! That's enough!" Gabe's voice trembled.

Blazing feral yellow eyes set their sights on him. His eyes flared, like flames in a fire. For an instant they changed color, turning as pale as the moonlight above. But Gabe thought he must have been seeing things because when Max blinked, his eyes were a furious honey orange.

"You left." The voice was hoarse, snarled through a mouthful of fangs. It was Max's, and it wasn't. He was still in human form, but he was losing himself before Gabe's eyes.

"I know. I'm so sorry, Max. I thought—"

"You promised, and you left!" Fangs bared, Max charged at him. He flew as if suspended in slow motion, hair rippling around him as if he were underwater. Moonlight silhouetted Max, glimmering in his hair. Gabe blinked, now sure he was seeing things. He could swear Max was floating. Or maybe Gabe had entered fight or flight and things were... slower?

The wind flew out of him as they collided. Gabe had to do something, stop him from hurting more people. His arms flew around Max as they rolled over, and he trapped Max beneath him in the flooded grass. Pond water splashed around them, small waves crashing over their ankles. If Gabe didn't have a feral werewolf beneath him, he'd be more concerned about why the hell the pond was overflowing on a rainless night.

Claws carved into his back, and he bit off a scream as his blood ran in hot rivers, soaking his shirt. Even through the pain Max inflicted, he nuzzled his face into Gabe's neck, clinging to him like a lifeline. "Mine," Max growled, trembling breaths puffing hot against his neck. "Gabe. Pack. *Mine.* Stay. Please."

"Max, don't hurt him!" Izzie implored, yanking Max's clawed arm off Gabe's back.

"Hey, Max, cool it! You need to remember us!" Ryan hugged Max's other arm.

Gabe's throat ached and his arms shook as they went around Max's shoulders and held him tight. Max was still in there somewhere, and Gabe would fight to bring him back. "I won't leave you. I swear, Max. I'm sorry I let you down."

"Don't believe you," Max snarled, and his claws cut deeper. "Weak wolf. Worthless wolf. Everyone leaves. Hate it!"

Gabe's eyes blurred from tears of pain and he pulled back far enough to look into Max's snarling face. He hardly recognized him in his betrayed fury. "I'm here now. I'm not going anywhere. Remember, Max. You've gotta remember. You've gotta come back. I didn't give up on you. Now you've gotta promise me you won't give up on yourself.

"You have to come back, Max. So we can eat dinner together. So you can get to know Ryan, Zach, Izzie, and Ben. And if you can't think of a reason to come back, then come back for me, 'cause I need you. Okay? You have no idea how much you're worth, and I'm gonna remind you every single day."

Please come back. Please.

"I know your father left you. You thought your mother left too, but she's here now, Max, she's right here. Izzie's here, Ryan's here. Your pack is here. I'm here, and I'll never go away again. Remember, Max. The day we met, I promised you'd be safe. I held you, remember? You ate dinner with us at the estate. Your favorite's filet mignon. You ate so much you said you didn't think you'd ever eat again. Richard came for you, but I looked out for you, didn't I? You held me tight, spoke for the first time since we met. What did you say?"

His name. Uttered like a prayer by a man who'd found his salvation. Tears scorched his eyes. His fingers trembled as they carded through soft hair matted with leaves and dirt.

Come back. Please. Come back.

The claws driving into his back lost their grip.

Those eyes flickered. Honey orange to yellow. Yellow to orange. Yellow. Orange.

A hoarse voice trembled, sucking in a gasp.

"Gabe. Gabe. Gabe."

WHEN MAX WAS A baby, his father left.

For a while, it had just been Max and his mother, the two of them against the world.

Then Richard had come. Max hadn't liked him or his greasy smiles or the way he'd touched his mother, like she was his property. He'd been kind, supportive, like a father. But it had all been a lie. His outbursts and insults had gotten worse and worse. His mother had stopped laughing. Max had stopped talking. What was the point when every word had been met with insults or hurt? His friends had stopped reaching out to him because he didn't say a word.

Richard had hurt his mother. She'd tried to hide it, but Max had known. He'd known, and he'd wanted to hurt Richard badly. He'd wanted to take his mother away, somewhere no one could ever hurt her, a place where it was just them, like it had always been.

But he was weak. A weak son. A weak wolf. The pantry had been dark and dusty. He'd been alone all the time except for when Richard visited. Sometimes he'd sat there and done nothing but talk. The words had cut deep, deeper than the lash of his belt, deeper than the kitchen knife against his skin. He'd been alone. Being alone was easy. There was no one to hurt or be hurt by.

Forget. Bury it. Lock it all away.

Arms around him held tight. A voice whispered, trembling and broken, in his ear. "I'm here, Max. I'm here. I promise I'll never leave again."

"Max. Honey, you're going to be okay. I'm here. We're all here."

The door to that dark pantry opened. His mother walked toward him with open arms. She'd come for him. Richard had tainted things, like he'd always done. But she'd come for him.

His life was dark, like the pantry. It was full of hurt and pain and loneliness. He feared and hated that dark place. In the dark, he was lonely. In the dark, he was safe. No one could hurt him, no one could help him.

We're safe here, the red wolf snarled, huddling in the darkness beside him. *People are trouble. People hurt.*

The door opened. Shafts of light penetrated the dark. Voices called out to him.

Gabe's voice. "Max, you're safe. I promise. I'll never leave again."

Ben said, "We got you, kid. Come on now, fight. You can do it. Come on, don't give up on us."

"Max, come on, man, you got this!" Ryan's voice was wet with tears. "If you don't come back right now, I'm spoiling the ending of *The Thing* for you. So, you gotta come back so we can watch it together as a pack."

"We're here for you, Max. We've been reaching out to you all this time," Izzie said, voice shaking. "I want us to be friends."

His mother sang to him like she did when he'd been small enough for her to rock him to sleep.

They'll hurt us, the red wolf growled. *They always do, even if they don't mean to. I want to run. Let's run.*

He wanted to run away, too. Somewhere far away. Wanted to forget.

"Lobito. Come back. Okay? Please, come back."

The smell of springtime penetrated the dark around him.

He had a choice. A choice to sing the feral lullaby that howled in his mind, sweet and tempting. Or to reach out to the frayed, tattered threads of light and mend them.

Forgetting meant letting go of everything that hurt him, but it also meant forgetting Gabe and his mother, forgetting Ben and the rest of the pack. Forgetting all the good times they'd shared since he'd come into their lives. The good times yet to come, but only if he didn't run.

He didn't want to run anymore. Not from pain. Not from shame.

Not from his pack. He wasn't alone anymore. No matter how bad things were, he could weather the storm with them.

He laid a hand on the wolf's head, fingers delving into bushy fur. He pulled the wolf close and held tight, running his fingers over scar tissue. Those scars would always be there. Nothing would take them away. Richard had carved himself into Max's skin and he would never get him out. But that didn't have to define him, like Gabe had said all along. He could still be strong, and he wouldn't have to be strong alone.

People are more than pain, he said, and though the wolf growled, he didn't fight as Max guided him toward the open door. He stepped into the light. The wolf hesitated, then put one paw forward and followed. They walked toward the tattered, glowing threads, the only light in the dark.

The voices got closer. Fur rippled and receded over Max's skin. His fangs lengthened. His claws retracted in and out. The tug was still there, the feral call. He took one step then another, fighting it. His hands and feet turned to paws and back again. He was a wolf, and then he wasn't. A wolf, then a man. Wolf. Wolf. Wolf. And then... *then—*

Max.

He was Max.

He was wolf.

He was both. He was human. His father had left, and then it was him and his mother.

He loved her. He loved her so much.

He had a pack.

They loved him.

Even though he was a mess.

Even though he was broken and imperfect.

That was okay.

No. That was a lie.

But it would be okay. He would be okay. Soon. Someday. He knew he would. And even if he was never okay again, even if pieces of him were cracked and broken, that was okay, too.

Because he wasn't alone.

A door opened in his heart. The warm golden glow of *pack* burned bright inside, casting away the darkness of his animal urges. Golden psychic threads tied the wolves of the LPA to one another's hearts and minds, threads that kept them connected and reminded them of their humanity. Gabe's thread was tangled up with Ryan's, tangled with Izzie's, and Ben's, and his mother's—and Max's own thread was tangled up with theirs. They'd been reaching out to him all this time and at long last, Max let them in.

He reached for the threads of light, dancing like fireflies in the dark.

Clutched them to his chest.

And let them make him whole.

GABE FELT THE MOMENT Max returned to them, their severed bond knitting itself back together in his chest.

"Max?" Gabe held his breath as the feral light in Max's eyes dispersed. Max blinked slowly, looking upon them in recognition. The world had stilled around them. The pond water had receded and lapped gently at the shore. The moon hid behind a blanket of clouds.

Max sat up and fell backward against his mother. "Ryan... Izzie? When did you guys get here?"

Izzie wiped her eyes. "Gabe called us, told us about the ritual. We wanted to be there for you."

"Of course we came, man!" Ryan sniffed hard. "You're pack, Max. I can feel you now!"

Ben grinned. "I can, too. It's faint, but it's a start. If we all spend more time together, those bonds will grow stronger and stronger."

"I'm glad you guys are here." Max breathed out, smiling a tired, beautiful smile.

Gabe looked all over Max's body for signs of the wolf's influence. There was no red fur. No lingering claws or fangs. His eyes were a beautiful honey orange. The bond between them glowed warm and bright, untainted by feral madness. Max was here, and he was here to stay. Gabe's eyes burned, relief leaving him breathless, and he wasn't sure whether to laugh or cry.

"Damn it, Max, you made me cry!" Ryan choked, yanking Max and Kendra into a group hug. "Never pull that shit again, you hear?"

"Thank the goddess," his mother gasped, enveloping him in her arms. "We thought you'd never come back."

"I didn't, either," Max admitted, closing his eyes as his mother cradled his head to her chest.

Gabe couldn't look away from him, drinking in the way his lashes rested against his freckled cheeks, and reached out to brush a leaf from his tousled red hair.

Izzie said, "The night's still young. How about a run if you're up for it?"

Max blinked sleepily and rubbed his eyes. The drowsiness there dispersed. "That sounds... Man. That sounds amazing."

Ryan was already stripping. "Hell yeah! Let's go!" He turned into a white wolf with black-tipped fur. With a howl, he took off splashing in the water. Laughing, Kendra undressed and shifted, and Izzie was seconds behind. The two wolves chased each other around the trees, and Ben's big silver wolf followed. Gabe and Max undressed to prepare for the shift.

Gabe chuckled. He loved this rowdy pack. "Ready, Max?"

He could see the fear in Max's eyes. "What if it isn't enough?"

Gabe squeezed his shoulder. "It will be."

Max exhaled, closing his eyes. "Okay, but if I go crazy, bite my butt." The shift started, but it was slow. Max was uncertain, taking his time. His body rippled like he was underwater, fur sprouting and face elongating into a snout. Gabe smiled when he felt the tug in his head and heart whenever anyone else in the pack shifted. Max was doing everything right, using their bonds to stay in control when he shifted. Before he knew it, Max's red wolf stood before him. He dropped into a playful bow and barked.

The shift rolled over Gabe, and all thought fled his mind except the urge to run, hunt, and chase. He pursued Max through the trees, high off the scent of cinnamon and chilis. Ryan pounced on Gabe's back, yipping playfully. Ben growled nonthreateningly when Izzie pulled on his ears. Kendra and Max rolled around in the leaves. Panting, Gabe lay down, tail thumping when Max curled up beside him. Ryan loped over and woofed at Gabe, tail wagging, and Max growled at him.

"Mine," Max's wolf snarled along their bonds, and Gabe had never felt so happy.

But all good things had to end. Max yawned, curling up to sleep on the forest floor.

"Let's get him back," Ben said, stepping into his jeans.

Ryan tugged on his jersey. "His bond feels even stronger after the run. If we keep this up, we'll be tight knit in no time."

Kendra propped Max's limp body up. "Oof. He's too heavy."

"Need help?" Izzie asked, buttoning her blouse.

Gabe finished dressing. "I got him," Gabe said, reaching out to take Max as Kendra struggled to lift him.

Gabe hoisted Max into his arms and Max's head settled against his shoulder. His body heat blazed through Gabe's wet clothes, his breath hitting his neck in slow bursts, sending a shiver down his spine. His fur tickled Gabe's cheek and Gabe couldn't resist leaning his cheek against Max's fur, breathing in his scent. He brought his lips to Max's head and let them linger there, closing his eyes tight.

"I'm so happy you're still here," he whispered, arms holding him closer. "Let's get you home."

MAX WOKE SOMETIME LATER in his human form. His eyes adjusted to the darkness of Gabe's living room. His whole body felt too heavy to lift, broken and bruised like he'd been stampeded on by elephants. He caught a familiar scent of lunar flowers and rolled over. His mother lay on the foldout bed beside him, hugging her pillow to her as she slept.

Max nestled closer and she stirred, waking slowly.

"Sorry," Max mumbled.

Her arm went over his shoulders in response. "Is it over, Max?"

Max exhaled, closing his eyes. He'd thought it was before because he was away from Richard, out of the pantry, and making friends in the agency. He'd lied to himself that everything was okay because he hadn't wanted to face all that was still hurting and broken. But he finally had, and from those shattered pieces, Max wanted to make something new. He squeezed his mother's hand for what felt like the first time in years.

"I'll be okay," he told her, and he meant it. "I'll get there."

"How are you feeling?"

"Horrible," Max admitted, and it wasn't because of his tired, achy body. "I'm sorry, Mom. I've been so selfish." He felt unworthy of her embrace.

"How so?"

"I thought I was doing the right thing by staying away. I knew it hurt you, but I thought anything was better than being a burden to you." His throat closed up and he thought he'd choke on the guilt.

"Honey, no." She cradled his face, wiping away the tears he couldn't fight back. "You're not a burden. Not ever. How could you even think that?"

"I couldn't protect you," Max confessed. "I was weak. I let him hurt you." His chest hitched, his throat aching.

She shook her head, tears glittering on her lashes. "Oh, honey. No, no, no." She pulled him to her and Max clung to her, holding her so tightly he worried he'd break her. He sobbed like a child, saying, "I'm sorry," and "I'm so sorry, Mom," and "I should have protected you. I should have done more to keep you safe."

"I'm the one who's sorry." She sniffed hard and pulled away to look him in the eyes. Max sucked in a gasp as she stroked his hair. Her eyes were red and glossy and tears streaked her face, but she wiped them away with a steady hand, then put her hands on his shoulders. "I'm the one who should have kept you safe."

"You did everything you could. We both did. It's Richard we should be blaming." Max kissed her cheek. "Thank you for being there tonight and for trying to take me away from Richard. I'll be better, Mom. I'll be stronger."

She held him tight, sniffling into his shoulder. "That's my line."

Max laughed and managed to smile. "Let's be stronger together, then."

He would be stronger, for her. Always for her.

Chapter 16

A LIGHT IN THE COLD DARK

The savory smell of beef, chicken stock, carrots, and potatoes made Max's stomach roar. He'd slept the day away into the late evening and woken with a ravenous appetite. His mother was singing in the guest bathroom while she showered, and Max wasn't sure where Gabe was, so he helped himself to the stew on the table.

"Finally awake, Sleeping Beauty?" Gabe's face brightened as he walked through the front door. He smelled like the outdoors, like clean air and elm trees. Gabe's warm amber eyes lit up as he smiled. "How are you feeling?"

"Like I got hit by a bus. Hungry, too."

"Yeah, you slept the day away. You had one crazy night."

"Yeah. It was hard at first, but then..." Max surprised himself by smiling. "I had fun afterward. Running with everyone felt great."

"Totally. We'll have to do it again sometime soon!" Gabe sniffed the air and swooned. "Damn, your ma can sure cook." He turned away and made for the kitchen.

Max's heart lurched. Blood seeped through Gabe's shirt, oozing from wounds on his back. "Your back is bleeding!"

Gabe stopped, frowning as he reached behind himself and felt the dampness on his shirt. "Shit. I thought Ben bandaged it."

Did I do that? Guilt tore into him. He grabbed Gabe's wrist and led him to the bedroom. He left Gabe standing there and searched the en suite bathroom. "Where do you keep bandages?"

"Under the sink. Max, it's fine—"

"No. It's not 'fine.' Did I do that?"

Gabe chewed his lower lip and didn't answer. "You were lost to your wolf. You didn't recognize any of us. It wasn't you."

Max yanked a roll of bandages from the medicine cabinet. "I'll fix it."

Gabe didn't argue, popping the buttons of his shirt and letting it glide down his broad shoulders to his forearms. At first, Max had been horrified by Gabe's scars. Now they were a reminder of how strong Gabe really was, of the things he'd been through and come out the other side of alive and stronger than ever. "Um... Sorry, you can sit down?" His face burned hot as he realized he'd been staring.

"Yes, Doctor." Gabe sat on the edge of the bed, eyes never leaving Max.

"Okay..." Now what? His brain was short-circuiting as the lamplight glimmered on Gabe's toned upper body, his scars pale as they twisted over his skin. His chest rose and fell, fuzzy with dark hair that stopped over his abs but resumed in a little happy trail that disappeared below his pants. Not to mention the way he sat on the bed, thighs parted ever so slightly—

Max looked at the floorboards to avoid gazing in a lustful stupor at the outline of Gabe's dick through his tight sweats. Why had Max decided to do this in the bedroom of all places?

Gabe shuffled his feet, one hand combing through the thick, wavy locks that tumbled down the back of his neck. "Uh... Ready?" Face hot, Max held his head high and walked around on wobbly knees behind the bed and knelt on the mattress. The springs creaked and the bed gave a little under their weight. Max tried not to imagine those springs creaking in... other scenarios, preferably with Max's back to the mattress and his arms full of Gabe Reyes.

Holding his breath, Max settled his hands on Gabe's shoulders, muscle and bone hard beneath his fingers. Was he imagining it, or had Gabe tensed beneath him, drawn in a little gasp? *Focus, come on!* "Sorry. My hands are cold."

Gabe chuckled. "It's fine."

Max removed the bloody bandages and swallowed a remorseful sigh at the claw marks curling across Gabe's back. Max bit back the apologies surging to his lips and focused, blotting at the injuries with a cotton ball soaked in disinfectant. His skin was so warm under Max's hand. Max came closer without realizing until Gabe's wavy curls tickled the tip of his nose. Gabe squirmed as Max glided the cotton ball over the last area of the cut.

Hating to be the one who made him uncomfortable, Max rubbed the bridge of his nose against the back of Gabe's neck in apology. A quiet exhale fell from Gabe's lips and he leaned back into Max's body. Heat rushed to Max's face, and his heart jumped up into his throat.

"Does it hurt?" Max asked.

Gabe jumped as if he'd been stung. "Not anymore. You're doing a good job."

That was a relief. He couldn't stand being the cause of any pain for Gabe, who deserved so much more for all the kindness he'd shown Max and his mother.

Max reached for the roll of bandages. One of the wounds was deep and would surely scar. The sight of it brought his wolf to the surface and he dipped his head, licking at the cut. A shiver ran through Gabe, but he didn't rebuke Max.

"I'm sorry," he murmured, throat thickening in remorse. He gripped Gabe's shoulders and squeezed tight. "I hate that I gave you more scars."

Gabe graced him with a sweet smile. "It's fine, Max. I don't mind."

Max blinked hard, unable to fathom how Gabe could be so forgiving. "I feel like shit, you know? You opened your home to me and my mom, and I hurt you."

Gabe's shoulders rippled under Max's hands as he shrugged. "Actually, back scratches are kind of sexy in... other scenarios."

Max snorted as he covered the wound with bandages. "Shut up."

"What? They are. I can say some sexy guy gave me these, and—"

The thought of Gabe with another guy had him swallowing a growl. He didn't want to see Gabe with someone else. Not with Zach, not with anyone. The thought made his wolf bare his fangs and growl, *mine, mine, mine!*

But Gabe wasn't his. He and Zach were together. Weren't they? These ugly jealous feelings were meaningless.

"Max?"

Gabe looked over his shoulder at him. If they were any closer, Max could easily brush their lips together, feel the rough scratch of Gabe's stubble against his skin, Gabe's hot mouth beneath his. Max screwed his eyes shut. He couldn't. Gabe had Zach.

"Hey. You okay?" The bed squeaked as Gabe turned around. The warmth of his bare upper body seeped into Max's shirt, and he knelt so close that his breath warmed Max's mouth.

Max's heart pounded and his breath caught when Gabe touched the side of his neck, fingers weaving through his hair. Max shivered and leaned into his touch, so warm and gentle.

What if he'd misread everything and he and Zach were friends with benefits or something? Maybe they had an open relationship? If that was the case, would Max be okay sharing Gabe with Zach? Maybe. Possibly...

"Max?" Gabe's eyes were heavy-lidded, his chest rising and falling fast. His voice, low and oddly scratchy, made Max's dick twitch.

No. No, Max was definitely *not* okay with sharing this gorgeous, kind, protective man with anyone.

Max tore his eyes away from Gabe's lips, parted and oh so inviting. "I..."

What if Gabe and Zach were mates? What if Gabe loved him? Why would Gabe want Max? Max had baggage. He was damaged. He'd been nothing but trouble for Gabe since he arrived.

"How's Zach?"

Gabe blinked as if coming out of a daze. "Oh. Uh..." Gabe shifted out of Max's reach. Max missed his body heat. "He's fine, I guess. He made a full recovery."

He had to know before he fell in even deeper. "You and he... what is he to you?"

Gabe got up and grabbed a fresh shirt from his drawer. "We're friends, first and foremost, but Zach's got it in his head that I'll return his feelings eventually."

"You mean you don't return his feelings?" Max hadn't known Gabe's relationship with Zach was so complicated.

Gabe averted his gaze, rubbing the back of his neck. "I... No. I don't. We're not together. We've been on and off for a few months. I like him, but it's never been more than... physical for me. There have been other people. He knows; he's fine with it. He's so sure that I'll eventually find my way to him. But I've felt more and more distant toward him as of lately." He squirmed, biting his lower lip. "Not sure why."

"So, he's not your mate?"

Gabe shook his head emphatically. "No. I've never felt that kind of connection to him."

Max exhaled. Okay. That was better than he'd hoped for, but he couldn't help feeling there was more. Gabe seemed so uncertain, as if he didn't know whether he would or wouldn't be with Zach, and it made Max anxious. It was better for his heart to walk away, to let him go.

"Sorry. For all the trouble." He stumbled off the bed and winced as he bumped into the dresser. "You should rest."

"Max, wait." The bedsprings creaked, and a hand closed around his wrist. Max froze, powerless under the weight of Gabe's anguished eyes. "I'm... I'm the one who should apologize." Tears brightened Gabe's eyes. Max held his breath, stunned to see him so vulnerable. "I left you. I promised you we'd face our demons together, but I left."

Neck burning, Max counted the floorboards. "You don't owe me anything. I'm grateful you've stuck with me this long. I've been nothing but trouble to you and the others."

"Max." The guilt in Gabe's voice shifted to a growly undercurrent, desperate and driven. Gabe took one step, then another, and Max swallowed as he found himself trapped between the dresser and Gabe's warm upper body. Gabe looked as if Max had struck him. "I knew what I was getting into the minute I saw your scars. You're not nothing. You're not trouble. You're—"

Gabe laughed and shook his head. He sighed and ran a hand through his hair, a determined set to his jaw. "I showed you my scars when we first met because I knew you were someone who would understand, who wouldn't judge me and think I was weak. You didn't pity me or freak out. You made me feel like I was strong, despite it all."

Max blinked hard, at a total loss for words as Gabe's walls came down before his eyes.

"Max, I looked at you and I knew you'd get me. You were someone I could confide in, someone I could open up to about the parts of myself I hate the most. Since the day we met, I wanted to keep you safe but... I let you down last night. I've let you down for a while probably."

"Why weren't you there?" Max asked, and he didn't mean it to be accusatory but Gabe winced regardless.

"I got... distracted. Seeing you start to heal, it threw me off. It blinded me to everything else going on under the surface." Gabe's hands dropped from Max's shoulders to his forearms, squeezing gently. "I felt totally useless. 'Cause you were still suffering, and I didn't see it. I was so wrapped up in..." His face reddened. "Stuff. I thought you'd be better off without me there." He deflated with a sigh.

"But that's not true," Max said. If Gabe hadn't come for him last night, he didn't know where he would be now. What he would have become. Just like he'd done from the beginning, Gabriel Reyes had pulled him from the darkness and into the light.

"Gabe, that's not... You're not..." Words wouldn't suffice. He couldn't describe what this man meant to him. Max hung his head, at a loss as to how he could make Gabe understand. "No, I get it. I'm not angry at you. I'm relieved, that's all. I thought I'd done something wrong."

Somehow, that seemed to make things worse. Gabe looked horrified.

Max said, "No, I mean—I know I'm a mess. I'm sorry if I made you feel bad."

Gabe hid his face in his hand. "No. No, no, no..." He looked hopelessly at Max. "No, you don't get it! I'm doing this all wrong."

"Get what?"

Gabe raised a hand to cup Max's cheek, and Max was powerless to look anywhere but into his molten amber eyes, fiery with sudden determination. Gabe was so close to him. Their body heat mingled, and Gabe's breath caressed Max's cheek. He smelled like elm trees and peppermint toothpaste.

"I care about you, Max. I care too much, and—" Gabe's face reddened and he looked down at his feet. He let out a frustrated growl. The sound sent a shiver down Max's spine. "And it's not because it's my job to. It's not even because of our shared pain. It's because you're so strong. Because you've been through so much but you can still smile and laugh like it's nothing. Because I..." Gabe wet his lips. "I..." He laughed, the sound breathy and nervous.

Max wondered if it was possible for the whole world to hold its breath. Gabe's eyes were impossibly wide, his face flushed and vulnerable as he searched for words.

"I'm sorry," Gabe said at last in a breathless gush. "I... This is what I meant." He raised both hands and took a step back. "You don't need this. Whatever 'this' is."

"No," Max said, and he clasped Gabe's face in his hands. "Tell me what you meant. I want to hear it."

Gabe's throat bobbed when he swallowed. "Max, you don't need—"

Max wouldn't let him take it back. Gabe was wrong. Max needed. He needed so badly. "Please," he whispered, so close he could practically taste Gabe's scent on his tongue.

Gabe's eyelids fluttered, as if he were sinking into a warm bath. His nostrils flared, drinking in Max's scent. Max wondered what he smelled like to him. His chest swelled against Max's, bare and warm.

Gabe's eyes left Max's and glanced at his lips. It happened so quickly Max might have missed it. He didn't, and in those few seconds when he realized Gabe wanted him, everything in this crazy, messed-up world suddenly righted itself.

They were so close, their chests touched with every quickening breath. Max leaned in slowly, waiting for Gabe to push him away. For this delicate moment to shatter like so much glass. But Gabe didn't push him away. He closed his eyes, angled his head, and met Max halfway.

Their lips brushed. The air between them sparked, ignited, and Max burned from the inside out. It didn't last a minute, this gentle kiss of theirs, but hadn't the Big Bang happened in less than that? Gabe's chest expanded against Max's, their lips parting ever so slightly. Gabe's lips were soft and warm. Max raised his hand, his fingertips settling on Gabe's hip.

Max huddled close to him, like someone lost in the cold and seeking the fire that burned so bright in Gabe Reyes, the promise of warmth and safety, a flame in a world Max had once thought of as cruel and dark. Max inhaled and felt woozy as Gabe's scent seeped into his lungs.

From the moment they'd embraced, Gabe's scent had brought his most treasured memories to the surface of his mind, chasing away the darkness like a candle. He hadn't understood why Gabe's scent brought him so much joy. Not until now.

When had it happened? When had the scent of safety, comfort, and home become *want, mine—mate?*

Cold dread extinguished any joy at finally kissing Gabe. He'd opened the door, unleashing feelings he'd tried so hard to fight. What chance was there that Gabe felt the same way? He pulled back with a thousand apologies ready to pour from his throat. He'd ruined everything.

"I'm sorry. I'm so sorry, I didn't mean—I mean, I did mean to, but I shouldn't have and—Shit." Gabe blinked at Max with eyes big as the moon itself, his chest rising and falling fast. Max wanted to sink into the floor. "I've sort of really liked you for a while, but it's fine. Everything's fine."

No, it wasn't. A lump formed in Max's throat. *Fuck,* he'd let his stupid childish crush ruin their friendship. He couldn't lose Gabe, he couldn't. "I'll go. Okay?"

Gabe took hold of his wrists and Max found himself being pulled back to him. Gabe crushed their mouths together with a low moan, leaving Max frozen but not for long. Relief and joy surged through Max, and he threw his arms around Gabe's waist, curling his fingers in the fabric of his shirt.

Gabe's scent blanketed Max, his arms warm and strong as they flew around Max's shoulders, bringing their bodies together until there wasn't a single inch of space between them. Gabe's chest pressed against Max's, rising and falling fast with every breathless moan and sigh they passed between their lips.

Shifting his hips against Max's, Gabe coaxed a gasp from his lips. Gabe was hard for him, and Max's head spun from the realization. They broke apart and Max struggled to catch his breath. Gabe's sharp teeth captured his lower lip, biting hard as if to devour him piece by piece.

Max rocked his hips, unable to tell if it was him moaning or Gabe as their erections rubbed together through the fabric of their jeans. More. He needed more, and Gabe obliged, slipping his hands into the back pockets of Max's jeans. Gabe cupped and squeezed him, thrusting Max's pelvis against his. Gabe parted his lips against his neck, sucking and nibbling.

His stubble scratched Max's neck and he groaned when he imagined what Gabe's scruff might feel like against his thighs. Hot, heavy puffs of air dampened his skin, and Gabe's fangs came out, nipping at the spot between his neck and shoulder—where werewolves claimed their chosen mates.

Max squeezed Gabe's hair, urging him to stay right there. It wasn't a full moon but if it were, he thought for sure he'd let Gabe bite him, claim Max as his. Fuck, he could come at the thought.

It scared him and enthralled him, realizing how much of himself he was willing to entrust to Gabe. He shouldn't be so trusting. By all accounts, he should be bent and broken and weary. He knew how easily trust could be shattered but Gabe made it so easy to trust him.

Then Gabe was out of his reach, yanking his lips from Max's neck. His eyes flew open, his arms falling to his sides. Gabe retreated, chest heaving as he caught his breath. One hand covered his fanged mouth and his eyes were wide with surprise but Max didn't scent any distress.

Something cold fell into Max's stomach. "I'm sorry. Did I do something wrong?"

Gabe laughed, running his tongue over his lips, chasing the taste of Max. "No. No, that was... That was a *very* good kiss."

"Then?"

Gabe sat at the edge of the bed, running a hand through his disorderly locks. Hunger gnawed at Max, and his cock twitched against the crotch of his pants. He already missed the heat of Gabe's powerful body. He had to remind himself to look Gabe in the eyes, though the tent in Gabe's pants demanded his full attention.

"I'm in the wrong here, not you," Gabe confessed, his eyes dark and wounded.

Max laughed this time. "What? No, you're not. What are you talking about? I'm the one who kissed you."

"And I shouldn't have encouraged it."

His words cut deep. Max struggled for words, but his mind was fogged.

Gabe bit his lip and looked away, shoulders rising and falling in a long, low sigh. "Max, it's not that I don't like you. I just..."

"Is it Zach?" Max curled his hands into fists, suddenly so jealous he thought it would burn him up inside.

Gabe slumped with a sigh. "I can't be with you, Max. I can't be with anyone."

Max held his breath. He hadn't realized he'd handed Gabe his heart, not until Gabe was in danger of breaking it. "Why not?"

Gabe paced to the window, his back to Max as he leaned on it for support. "Because I can't offer you a damn thing." Gabe sighed, hanging his head. He turned to face Max, teeth worrying at his supple lower lip. Max swallowed and tried to ignore the pang of desire that shot through him.

Gabe said, "You believe in the power of sight?"

Max blinked, not expecting Gabe's question. "Like... the power to see the future?"

Gabe's mouth twitched. "Yeah. That."

Max shrugged, at a loss. "I mean, anything's possible in this world, right?"

"Sure." Gabe cleared his throat, running a hand through thick, wavy locks. "I was in a real bad place a few years back. Stone was out there killing. No one knew where he was. Izzie insisted we take a trip, get a change of scenery. We went to London."

Max smiled. "Why London?"

Gabe rolled his shoulders, grinning. Max let himself admire the little gap between his two front teeth. "I don't know. Izzie said she threw a dart at a map and it landed on London."

Max chuckled, plopping down on the edge of the bed. That sounded like an impulsive, fun, very Izzie thing to do.

"Anyway, we went. Drank enough gin and tonic to kill a human and decided to get our fortunes told." Gabe crossed over and sat on the bed beside Max, their shoulders almost touching. "I was ready to laugh the seer outta the room. Instead, she was pretty on point."

Gabe's expression had darkened as he stared straight ahead at the white wall.

"What did she tell you?" Max asked, not sure he wanted to know.

Gabe swallowed, throat bobbing hard. "It was a prophecy. I wrote it down after I left." He reached over and fumbled in his bedside table. He withdrew a rumpled scrap of napkin with smudged blue ink that had seeped through the thin layers of paper.

He recited, "When the full moon bleeds red and the She-Wolf hides her face, the black wolf of vengeance will clash with the beast of hate. One will rise, the other will fall, and the wargs of war will howl for man's doom." Gabe tossed the napkin back in the drawer. "Not too poetic, is it?"

Max's stomach twisted. "That... doesn't sound good."

Gabe smiled sardonically. "Right?"

Max's head spun. "When the moon bleeds red... That sounds like a blood moon. But what about when the She-Wolf hides her face?"

Gabe shrugged. "Could mean the moon turns red and then is eclipsed? Like a super flower blood moon. It's a rare phenomenon."

"What about the wargs of war?"

"No idea. Sounds like a bad metal band."

It was a lot to take in, and he couldn't pretend to understand what most of it meant—except for one small part. "The black wolf of vengeance... A beast of hate... One will rise, the other falls..." Stomach churning, he looked over at Gabe, a black wolf seeking vengeance for his father's death. "Did..." Max swallowed and his throat went dry. "Did she mean you will fall... or Stone?"

Gabe raised his shoulders and dropped them. "She wasn't sure." He spoke calmly, as if it didn't trouble him one way or the other what became of him so long as he put his teeth in Stone's throat.

Max struggled for words. "She might have been a phony."

Gabe's lips twitched in a ghost of a smile, dead before it could blossom over his face. "No, Max. I don't think she was, because the path I'm walking leads straight to Stone, and either he dies, I do, or... or something happens to you or someone else. And I can't deal with that."

Gabe pushed off from the bed, floorboards squeaking under his bare feet as he paced. "Max, ever since we met, all I've wanted is to protect you. To care for you. To keep you safe. But I need to protect you from myself, as well."

Max lurched to his feet. "No, you don't. I'm not some fragile thing, I—"

"Max, you don't need me." Gabe slumped. "You've been through so much. I'm trouble. I'm no good. You should find a guy who isn't haunted, who isn't broken. Someone better." He snorted. "Ryan might be a better choice for you, honestly."

"No. Would you... Stop, okay?" The hurt was gone. Anger curled his hands into fists. "You know what? You don't get to decide what's best for me. 'Cause you don't know. You don't have a clue. You know, you weren't the only one reaching out to me. Izzie, Ben, even Ryan were all there for me. But I didn't choose them, Gabe. My wolf chose you! So don't treat me like I'm some messed-up kid who doesn't know what the hell he wants!"

"Max," Gabe began, eyes wide in guilt.

"I don't need some stupid kid my age who doesn't have a clue what to do with his life. I don't need to be sheltered and protected, and I sure as hell haven't been for years. You're what I need, Gabe. You. If Ryan or Ben or any man in the world had found me that night, I would still fucking choose you! Every time!"

Gabe's guilt-ridden face became a blur as Max's eyes stung. "Max, you've been through so much hurt. So much pain from the Moonborn cult. And I'm pursuing them. Don't you see? I have nothing to offer you but uncertainty and pain."

"That's not true." Max looked down, trembling from head to toe as the weight of it all came crashing down on him. "Is... is that the kind of future you want?"

"No!" Gabe shook his head emphatically. "No. Of course not. I..." A pretty flush colored his cheeks. "Never mind."

Max wouldn't let him off that easily. "Tell me."

Gabe rolled his shoulders, a smile chasing away the darkness that had come over him. "I had this... fantasy. You know? That I'd meet the perfect guy. We'd become mates. Or get married, if he were human and that's what he wanted."

A smile tugged at Max's mouth, pleased to see Gabe bare his soul in ways that weren't quite so painful. Gabe ran a hand through his hair, his smile soft and shy as he opened up about a future free of darkness and pain, of Stone and his cult.

"We'd have a couple of kids. A big house in the countryside with a few miles of land so we could all shift and go for runs as a pack. Teaching them how to howl and hunt..." A shadow stole away his light. "Now... I'm not sure if that's who I am. If there'll ever be a time when Stone isn't haunting my future. The kind of life I live, I'm not even sure that's the future I deserve..."

Max scoffed. "You are way deserving of that future." If anyone deserved peace and happiness, it was Gabe. "I want something like that, too."

Gabe managed a small smile. "Yeah?"

"Yeah. A partnership with someone I trust and love. A family. It sounds perfect, Gabe."

Gabe sighed. "That's the kind of life you deserve, Max. And that's not what I can offer."

"That's not true," Max said, sure he sounded stupid, sure he was muddling up the most important thing he'd ever told anyone. But he kept going because stopping wasn't an option. "You do make me happy, Gabe. When I met you, it was like all these happy memories I'd forgotten came rushing back. For so long, my world was darkness and then you came and it was like this... light came on. You were a light to me, Gabe, and I wanted to cradle your light in my hands before you disappeared."

Gabe's eyes were impossibly wide, his lips parted as he gazed at Max.

"I remember something," Max said, looking down at the floor. "When I was losing myself last night. You told me... told me that I didn't know my worth, that—"

"I was gonna remind you," Gabe whispered. "Every day. I meant that."

Max nodded, heart hammering fast. "You don't know yours either, Gabe. Because meeting you saved me."

Gabe looked down, scuffing his toe on the floor. "Ben and your ma helped—"

Something like fire blazed in Max's gut. "You brought me back, Gabe! You. Would you learn to take a compliment?"

"Hey." Gabe's voice was quiet and gentle as big warm hands grasped Max's shoulders. Max breathed in through a tight throat, scenting life and springtime flowers as Gabe came close. "It's not you, okay? I care about you, Max. But I don't know what the future holds. How can I commit myself to anyone if I'm not sure whether I'll survive the next encounter with Stone?"

Max wanted to say so much. That the future didn't matter, and it was tonight that counted. That he didn't care how much time they had so long as they were together, even if that would be the biggest lie he'd ever told.

"I know, I... It's complicated." Max sucked in a breath as waves of doubt crashed over his head. "We don't need to talk about this anymore. I should... I'll go." Max swept past Gabe, unable to even look at him.

"Max—"

"I'll see you later, Gabe." Max tried to keep his voice casual and failed as it came out quiet and choked.

He let the door slam behind him.

DINNER WAS AWKWARD. IF his mother could smell Gabe all over him, she said nothing and talked about the weather of all things while Max ate his beef and potatoes and ignored the carrots. Gabe ate in his room, only further spelling out that something had happened between him and Max. But Max cleared his plate without an awkward confrontation. "Thanks for dinner," he said to his plate and stood.

"Max, just a moment."

Here it was. Oh, by the grace of the She-Wolf, he'd been a good boy all his life. He didn't deserve this. Max dropped back into his seat.

His mother folded her hands together and stared into her plate as if searching for words.

Max considered bolting for the bathroom but his mother said, "You know it's never bothered me that you're gay. That's not an issue at all."

"I know," he assured her. He felt stupidly lucky in that regard. He still remembered his friends at school complaining about how their parents expected them to find mates by a certain age to carry on the pack line.

"Gabriel is a good man. A little old for you, in my opinion, but it's your life."

"Mom," he practically begged. "It's not—"

"It wasn't a problem with Jack since he was a werewolf"—Max cringed at the mention of his first boyfriend—"but since you're both hybrids, there's no guaranteeing you're immune to STDs. So, before things get too spicy in there"—*Oh Goddess. Kill me. End my life now*—"you should both get some bloodwork done to determine if you're immune. Okay, sweetie?"

"Mom." He groaned. "We're not... We haven't... I don't even know if he likes me that way."

She hummed, raising a brow. "It sure smells like he does."

Max stabbed at his carrots and potatoes. "Look, we just... you know. Kissed." His face felt hot enough to catch on fire. "That's it."

"Kissing leads to other things. Which is fine. You're both adults. Just be safe, all right?"

Max wasn't sure there'd be any more kissing. His blood still boiled when he remembered how Gabe had questioned his feelings. Who the hell was he to decide whether he was good for Max or not? What did Gabe even feel for him, anyway?

Max tossed and turned that night, uncomfortably aware of the light shining from the gap under Gabe's door. Was he still thinking about their kiss? The skin around Max's lips was chafed from his stubble. His lips still tingled when he remembered Gabe's hot, eager mouth on him. His blood burned, pooling hot in his groin when he recalled the scratch of Gabe's stubble, hungry lips parted around his neck. The front of his sweatpants grew unbearably tight.

Damn it. He couldn't sleep like this. He'd either have to jerk off or go and talk to Gabe.

What would he say if Max went to him now? Would he kill things between them for good? The doubt kept him rooted in bed.

Max knew he was younger than Gabe. He knew he'd been through more than most almost-twenty-year-olds. But he knew what he wanted. Mostly. He didn't know what job he wanted. He didn't know if he'd go back to college or what he'd study if he did. He didn't know much about relationships, but he knew what he wanted from a man and the kind of man he wanted to be.

He wanted to be everything his birth father hadn't been. He wanted to be there for the man he loved, for any kids he might have—and he would have kids. He'd decided that a long time ago, and he would never let them wonder if they were wanted and loved. Not like when he'd stayed up at night wondering why his father left, what about himself was so bad that not even his father would stick around for him.

He would be the most loving and supportive mate he could be. He wouldn't be like Richard. He would be respectful, faithful, committed. There were parts of himself that worried how he could keep those promises when his role models in fatherhood and love were so toxic, but to spite Richard, to spite his father, he would be the man they couldn't be.

He wasn't a confused kid. He knew what he wanted, even if he wasn't sure how to get it—and he knew who he wanted. Gabe wasn't perfect. He wore a dashing smile and possessed a disarming wit in the most perilous of circumstances, but there was darkness in him and he faced an uncertain future.

Tonight, though, Max had seen the light in him, too. He'd caught glimpses of hope in Gabe's smile when he talked about a big house in the country and a pack who ran and howled and loved beneath the moon. That wasn't the future of a man who believed he was destined to wander lost in darkness.

Gabe Reyes wasn't perfect, but he was close enough for Max's liking, and his dreams and hopes were so closely intertwined with Max's own. Gabe was everything good that Max had convinced himself he'd never find.

When he rolled over and found that the light under the door had gone dark, he realized he'd missed his chance.

Whatever they were or could be, Max wouldn't find out tonight.

CHAPTER 17

DESTINED

MAX'S CELL PHONE RANG in the night. Bewildered, he rolled over and reached for it on the nightstand. It was Gemma. Alarm shot through him. "Hey. Is everything okay?"

"Not really." She sighed. "I've had nightmares. Bad ones. Where I'm back there. Where they're hurting me." Her voice shook. "Did they... Did they tell you things? Like, that you were impure and filthy?"

Max swallowed, feeling sick. "My stepfather did. He was one of them."

Her voice was thick when she said, "My mother told me I was disgusting. A disgrace to the She-Wolf's gift."

Fury rose in Max. "She was wrong. That's bullshit. No one is superior to anyone else."

"But I believe her." Gemma's voice hitched. "And I believe the Moonborn. Maybe they were right. My bruises won't heal. My wounds are scarring. I'll have their marks on me for the rest of my life. All because I'm a hybrid."

Max's eyes burned. "No, Gemma. That's not true. We don't deserve suffering because of who we are."

She sighed wetly. "Max... If I tell you, you'll really be able to stop the Moonborn?"

Max balled his hand into a fist. "We'll try our hardest."

She was quiet, breathing in and out. Then she whispered, "I remembered where they're meeting."

Max's heart thundered in his ears. "Tell me," he said, voice low and urgent. "Gemma, please."

BEN'S EYES WIDENED. "THE Brooklyn Navy Yard?"

Max nodded, feeling the eyes of Ryan, Zach, Gabe, and Izzie intent upon him. They were squished into Ben's office at the estate. The distant howling of wolves filled the air beyond the windows. It was a clear and sunny day, but Max felt a storm coming.

"That's what she told me," Max said. "She overheard the Moonborn saying they would meet there for another ritual. It's happening tonight."

Ryan sighed, tweaking his glasses. "It can't be an abandoned ice cream store or a theme park. No, it has to be a creepy shipyard! Wait, I take that back. Abandoned theme parks are creepy as shit. Please, do not tell the Moonborn I said that when we kick their asses. Don't wanna give them any ideas."

A growl rumbled in Gabe's chest. Max jumped, alarmed to see him pacing up and down, claws sharp at his side. "So close..." He whispered, seeming to be in his own head.

"What are we going to do, Ben?" Zach asked. He was finally on his feet again. His wounds had healed and Max couldn't see a single scar. "We hitting them?"

Ben laced his fingers together. "We as in me and a few tough agency wolves."

"That's it, no outside help from the police?" Ryan asked.

Ben waved a hand. "Can't trust them after how dismissive they've been of missing hybrids in the past. They're more concerned with cases affecting humans."

"What about us?" Zach asked. "We can help."

"I'm not bringing all of you into danger." His eyes flicked to Gabe and Izzie. Max understood. If Ben asked Zach and Ryan to come, it would just be more obvious he was excluding Gabe and Izzie.

Izzie scowled. "Stone killed our father, Ben. He tortured my brother. Gabe and I have every right to be there tonight."

"I understand that," Ben said, his voice forcibly calm.

Gabe rounded on him. "Then let us go!"

Zach touched Gabe's shoulder. Max's skin prickled, his wolf growling low in his chest. "Gabe, think about your mother. How would she feel if something happened to either you or Izzie? It isn't fair to put her through that."

Gabe glowered at his feet, claws retracting. "I know that. But I can't sit there and do nothing while Ben faces down Stone's people!"

"Zach's right." Ben grunted, rising to his feet to face Gabe and Izzie head-on. "I promised Veronica that I would keep you both safe. I understand how important this is to both of you, but if either of you die or get hurt, V will kill me."

Max gripped Gabe's arm. "You shouldn't go. Stone might not even be there. You should save your energy in case we confront him later."

Zach's eyes locked on Max. He tightened his grip on Gabe's shoulder. Gabe looked from one to the other, wide-eyed. Zach bared his fangs at Max. Max growled back.

Izzie exclaimed, "Both of you cut it out! My brother isn't a scrap of meat!"

Ryan was snorting like a pig, laughing.

Zach had the good grace to look ashamed, though he still didn't let go of Gabe's shoulder.

Since they weren't getting anywhere, Max looked at Ben. "What's the plan?"

Ben ran a hand over his beard thoughtfully. "Once I have more details, I'll let you all know."

"Ben," Izzie began.

He held up a hand. "I'm not speaking about this further. We will talk more when we have a plan." His voice was decisive. Frowning, Gabe left the room with Izzie at his heels.

"Those two..." Ben sighed, massaging his temples. "The Reyes pack is as stubborn as it gets."

WHILE BEN CAME UP with a plan, Ryan invited the pack to The Slaughtered Lamb, one of the first werewolf-only establishments in the city. To pass the time until they left, Max retired to the agency's library for the rest of the day. He hadn't read for pleasure in a while and found a cheesy romance book to pass the time.

Around five when most members of the agency got off work, Max met up with Zach and Izzie in the courtyard. Zach glanced at him and Max looked away. "Hey," Zach said, polite and casual. He had a nice smile, and Max hated him for it. He bet Gabe had kissed those smiling lips many times.

Max nodded. "What's up?"

Izzie snorted. "Could you two be any more awkward? You know, polyamory is a thing. It might solve all your problems."

Max looked at her. "Did you really say you'd be okay with both of us doing your brother?"

Zach made a choking noise, turning his face away.

Izzie's olive complexion blanched. "Oh. Right. I hate myself sometimes."

It looked like everyone except Ben was coming. Max froze at the sight of Gabe's familiar shape striding toward them. After the awkward conclusion to their kiss last night, Max really wanted to be anywhere else. He turned to sneak back inside. A horn blared ahead of him as a car pulled out of the underground parking lot.

"Yo, Maxwell!" Ryan waved from the window of his car.

He froze. "Fuck me," he muttered.

Ryan pulled up to the gate, calling obnoxiously, "It is Max*well*, right? Not Maximus? Maximillian? Maxine?"

Max turned and found Gabe tugging down his shades, fixing him with a smirk that made Max's blood simmer—in rage or desire, he couldn't tell which. Maybe it was both.

"It's Maxwell," he grumbled, keeping his head down as he skirted around Gabe. Izzie climbed in the back and Max sat in the seat next to Ryan.

Gabe sat in the back, then Zach. Max's stomach churned when he realized Gabe was sitting between Izzie and Zach. Great. Max had a perfect view in the rearview mirror as Zach leaned over and whispered something in Gabe's ear that made him smile. He strangled the snarl rising to his throat. His wolf was close to the surface, teeth bared as he watched Zach cozy up to *his*—no. Gabe wasn't his mate. Gabe wasn't his anything.

In the seat next to him, Ryan was squeezing the steering wheel so tightly his knuckles were white. Gabe smiled at Zach but his smile seemed strained, uncomfortable. In the mirror, their eyes met and Gabe's smile fell away. Max looked out the window, replaying the moment Zach had leaned in, lips inches from Gabe's ear. It was clear as day Zach was head over heels for Gabe, even if Gabe didn't seem to return his feelings.

They drove toward the city. Ryan played the radio nice and loud, and he and Zach sang along to "Hungry Like the Wolf." Gabe howled out the window and made Max laugh.

After a couple hours in the car, Ryan parked on West Fourth Street. They crossed the cobblestone street where The Slaughtered Lamb awaited them, an Irish-style pub with a cool sign of a werewolf howling at the moon. Above the doorway, the flags of the USA and Ireland waved in the wind.

Max stopped to browse a menu, laughing at some of the names for various cocktails such as New Moon and the uniquely named Angry Werewolf Balls. The bouncer at the door sniffed people before he let them in. "Werewolves only!" he barked, scaring away a couple humans who tried to enter. He waved to Gabe and the others and asked to see Max's ID before he entered. He gave Max a wristband to wear in the bar.

The bartender and passing waiters waved and greeted Gabe and the others. The aroma of roasted pork made Max's mouth water as he followed Gabe and the others inside. Over at the packed bar, men and women drank various spirits still dressed in business casual from work.

Max jumped as a glass shattered against the wall and a man in a business suit transformed before their eyes, sprouting fur and claws and fangs as he tackled another werewolf who reeked of alcohol. The bouncer stormed over and threw them both outside to applause from the bar.

"Whoa!" Max whispered as the mate of one of the two men hurried out the door after them.

Gabe squeezed his shoulder. "Stay close. It gets wild in here sometimes."

Werewolves crowded the tables, some fully shifted into wolves, others somewhere between man and beast. A waiter whisked by carrying a steaming platter with a whole roast pig to a table of salivating guests. Max's stomach rumbled.

They crowded into a booth toward the back of the restaurant and the hostess left them with some menus. Max browsed, his mouth falling open as he read over the variety of UK-inspired meat dishes. There were also various vegetarian substitutes for some popular meat dishes.

"Why didn't I know there were vegetarian werewolves?" Max wondered.

Izzie said, "I tried going vegetarian. The meat withdrawals were too much. I feel bad, though. Werewolves consume so much meat. I'll have to try again someday."

The rest of the pack ordered a round of beers except for Gabe and Izzie. If they were meeting Stone tonight, they needed their wits about them, and hybrids had a lower alcohol tolerance than regular werewolves. Max ordered a root beer so he could at least pretend it was beer.

"Cheers!" The pack clinked their drinks together.

"Here's to kicking the Moonborn's asses tonight!" Gabe said, taking a hearty gulp of soda.

"Here's to the LPA and pack," Max said. Gabe met his eye across the table and smiled. Butterflies fluttered through his stomach.

Max couldn't decide between the elk burger or the rabbit stew, so when Gabe ordered the elk burger, Max copied him. Zach ordered beef stew, and Izzie ordered rabbit stew and made Max regret his choice until the burger arrived. Max cleaned his plate in what felt like seconds.

Across the table, Zach ate some of Gabe's fries. Gabe let him, clearly comfortable with sharing their food. Ryan sat on Zach's right, sulking down into his beer like it had wronged him.

Max excused himself and went in search of the restroom. Drying his hands, he stepped out, suddenly reluctant to rejoin the table. If he had to watch Zach touch Gabe one more time—

"Feelin' all right?"

Max jolted at the sight of Zach waiting outside the restroom. Max swallowed, craning his neck to look up at him. He was freakishly tall. With his pouting lips and that little mole next to his mouth, the cleft in his chin, it was easy to see why Gabe had been into him. Max hated him for it.

"I'm okay," Max lied, sidestepping him.

Zach blocked his path. "Hold on. I wanna talk to you."

Max squirmed at the thought and forced himself to meet Zach's gaze. He really didn't want to, but he didn't want to be rude. He didn't need Zach to see how much he envied his place at Gabe's side. Though hadn't Gabe said they weren't together? Or something?

"Here?"

"Outside. It's pretty noisy." Zach's smile was friendly enough. Max had to smell like Gabe, like what they'd shared the night before, but Zach wasn't being a huge prick about it. He was a good guy. He deserved someone like Gabe.

Max trailed behind him, squeezing past the packed bar and following him out an exit on the opposite end of the restaurant. Once they were outside, Max found himself looking around at the old brick buildings, trying to come across as casual and not like his insides were trying to flail out of his mouth. He'd wondered for a long time about Gabe and Zach and now he realized he might prefer wondering to the cold, hard truth.

Zach scratched at the back o swaying. He sighed. "Look, Max, I was hoping Gabe would say something to you. There's something you need to understand. About Gabe and me."

"I know you were together."

Zach cleared his throat. "We're not a couple, not officially. But we will be."

Max hadn't realized he'd closed his eyes until he was opening them. Utterly bewildered, he faced Zach. "What do you mean?"

"Three months ago, Ryan and I took a trip to London. Gabe and I had just started seeing each other, but neither of us were sure if we'd be more than just friends with benefits. I was bummed, so Ryan suggested we go to London and forget our boy troubles."

He frowned. "Ryan never told me what his boy troubles were. Huh. Anyway, Gabe told us this seer was legit, so I went to see her. Most humans think psychics are quacks, and maybe some are, but most of 'em are the real deal. I never believed in any of that stuff before, but this seer was unreal. I told her I didn't think Gabe would ever return my feelings. I asked if we would be together, and she showed me a future in that little orb of hers.

"It was him and me together on the porch of some little house somewhere. Upstate New York, maybe. The whole pack was there, celebrating something. A little girl with this cute pink hat came running to us and climbed into my arms. There was a bond between me and her, I could feel it. She cuddled up against my chest like she loved me, trusted me." Zach's eyes glowed, so full of hope and love it was unbearable. "She's our daughter, Max. We have a family."

Max's chest hurt. He couldn't speak.

Zach sighed. "Look, I'm sorry, Max." To his credit, he did sound genuine. "It's pretty clear you like him. To be honest, I think he likes you, too, and I'll admit, it hasn't been easy to see him with you when he's been pulling away from me."

"He has?" Max was surprised.

Zach folded his arms over his chest. "I think he's holding back. He doesn't want either of us to be hurt if he dies. Or... he knows what you two have might not last." He added the last part gingerly, eyeing Max carefully.

Max laughed, shaking his head. "Look, I'm sorry, but I don't believe it. If there wasn't some vision showing you two together, would you still believe you're meant to be? Is Gabe your fated mate, Zach?"

Zach took a step back. "I... No, he isn't, but that's never mattered to me. Werewolves can love someone other than their fated mate. It happens. That vision was the proof I needed that despite not being fated, we're still meant to be in some way."

"Zach, it could have been anyone's child."

Zach's eyes narrowed, the only indicator that his back was against the wall. "She was ours. I know it."

So if Gabe survived his destined encounter with Stone, Zach and Gabe might be together. Or they could start a family, Gabe could have his encounter with Stone, and die. Max didn't know what to believe and he couldn't find the words to challenge Zach. He wanted to go home.

"Do you think he survives?"

"I do. Wanna know why?" Zach brushed his braids away from his face and averted his gaze. "Max, you know Gabe. You know there's a darkness in him. It's impenetrable. It keeps him from letting people in. Like you, like me."

Max nodded, stomach clenching as he recalled the prophecy Gabe had told him about.

"But in this future the seer showed me... that darkness was gone, Max. He was happy. Finally happy. That could only happen if Stone was gone."

Max tried to speak but felt like he'd been punched in the chest.

Zach sighed. "Look, I didn't tell you this to be a dick. You've been through enough, Max. I don't want to see you get hurt even further." Without waiting for a reply, Zach let the door to the bar close behind him.

They were still in there, talking, laughing, probably wondering where Zach and Max had run off to. Zach would rejoin them, put his arm around Gabe, and maybe even kiss him away from prying eyes. Max couldn't sit at the same table as them. He couldn't even stomach thinking of Gabriel Reyes. If Gabe and Zach really were destined to be together, then what was the point in pursuing anything with Gabe?

He went back inside long enough to pay for his share of the dinner, hovering by the host stand so they couldn't see him. He needed to focus on something other than Gabe, like getting a job. If he kept growing his savings, he could eventually move and stop burdening Gabe. The thought of leaving Gabe twisted like a wire around his heart.

Max couldn't do it. He couldn't love Gabe for a day or a week, knowing he'd lose him one way or the other.

"Hey, Max!"

Ryan had followed him out the door, cheeks flushed from drinking and glasses crooked on his nose. He straightened them. "Leaving already?"

Max shrugged. "Not feeling too good."

"Oh. That's too bad. Yeah, I'm thinking I'll probably head out, too." Ryan made a face, as if he'd chomped on a lemon.

"Zach and Gabe making you sick, too?" Max asked.

Ryan groaned.

Max laughed.

Grabbing his car keys, Ryan made for his vehicle. "Come on. I'll drive you home."

"Are you good to drive?"

"Pure-blooded werewolves can't get drunk, remember? I'll be the one driving your drunk ass home when you're twenty-one."

Max smiled. He liked that Ryan thought they'd still be in touch by then. It gave him hope. Even if he and Gabe didn't get together, he still had friends in the agency.

Ryan asked, "Is your mom there?"

"She should be. Gabe gave me a spare key, so it isn't a big deal if she isn't."

Ryan climbed in and started the engine. The radio turned on. Ryan plugged Gabe's address into the GPS and they drove. Max hummed along to the song and Ryan began singing lowly. They began belting out the lyrics as they sped along toward Gabe's apartment. Ryan headbanged and drummed on the wheel while Max danced in the seat beside Ryan, shouting the lyrics until his voice was hoarse.

"Fuck!" Ryan exclaimed at the end of the final chorus and smacked the wheel. "That shit hits hard."

Max groaned. "I know."

"I love Zach, but he's totally blinded," Ryan said, venting. "That kid he saw in the seer's vision might not be his. Might not be Gabe's. He wants to be in love, and he wants Gabe to be the one for him. He's such a sap, you know?" There was admiration in Ryan's voice.

Understanding clicked. "You love him."

Ryan smiled. It looked painful. "Since I was a kid."

Max gaped at him. "That long? *You're* the sap! Why don't you tell him?"

Ryan grimaced, spinning the wheel. "The timing was never right. He's only ever seen me as a friend, and I'm fucking glad to be his friend. I wouldn't trade that for anything."

Max batted his eyelashes at him. "Except for a little kissy-kissy."

Rolling his eyes, Ryan stopped for the light. "Says the guy panting after Gabe's dick."

Max smacked his shoulder. "I am not!"

Ryan barked a laugh.

A ringtone distracted Max. His phone was vibrating in his pocket. He pulled it out and saw it was Gemma.

"Hey, Gem. What's up?"

"Max..." Her voice was small and frightened. "Can you come over?"

Max's heart sank. Ryan glanced at him. "Is everything okay?"

She began crying, gut-wrenching gasps that made Max's chest hurt. "I'm such a mess! I'm filthy. I'm impure. The Moonborn were right."

Max gripped Ryan's arm. "Hold on." Ryan arched his brows but stopped the car. Max cradled the phone to his ear. "You're not impure. There's nothing wrong with you."

"My—my mother," Gemma croaked. "She was right. We hybrids, we're abominations. We tainted the goddess's pure gift. We deserve to suffer." She sounded like she was having a breakdown.

Max said, "I'm coming over. Sit down and wait for me, okay?"

Gulping, she said, "Okay. Okay. I'll wait."

Max checked his texts. Ben had texted him Gemma's address a few days ago before he and Gabe had gone to meet her. He typed it into Ryan's GPS. "I'm coming, Gemma. I'll be there soon. Stay on the phone, okay?" She hung up. "Fuck!" He tried calling.

"Max?" Ryan's voice was unsteady. "What's going on?"

"The hybrid that escaped the Moonborn. She's having a breakdown. We need to go to her now!"

Ryan's eyes widened. "Shit!" He pulled out of their parking space and stepped on the gas.

Max took in one breath then another, terrified when Gemma refused to pick up. "Shit! What if she hurts herself, Ryan?"

"I'm going as fast as I can!" Ryan drove, slowing for turns but not stopping completely.

Max's heart sank when the call went to voice mail again.

Gemma, hold on. We're coming!

Chapter 18

I CHOSE YOU, TOO

Gabe checked the time. They'd already been at the bar for a little over an hour. His eyes kept flicking to the empty space where Max had been sitting. Had he gotten home by now? Why had he left without even saying goodnight? Ryan had texted Zach, telling him he was taking Max home. Apparently, Max had a stomachache. Gabe wanted to pick up some medicine for him on the way home.

He itched to say his goodbyes and go home. Waving over the waitress for his portion of the check, he whipped out his phone and sent Max a message.

Gabe: Get home safe?

He hit send and set his phone on his thigh, awaiting the buzz. The waitress set down the bill and Gabe asked if he could pay separately for his and Max's portion of the bill.

"He ordered the elk burger and the root beer," Gabe explained.

The waitress smiled. "That's fine. He paid on his way out."

Gabe frowned. He couldn't imagine Max had much money to splurge on expensive burgers. He supposed he hadn't wanted to burden them, but he'd have happily paid for Max's share of the dinner.

"Hey, I got it. Don't worry," Zach assured him, flicking his card onto the bill.

Gabe drummed his leg up and down under the table. Max still hadn't replied. He usually texted back right away. An exhale fell from his lips and he slid from the booth. "It's been real, amigos."

As Zach went to the bathroom, Gabe and Izzie stepped outside. Izzie frowned and checked her phone. "What gives? Has Ben called you? I thought we were hitting the Moonborn hideout tonight."

Gabe hummed and checked his phone once more. Still no reply from Max, and Ben wasn't answering any texts.

"Something wrong?" Izzie asked.

"Max." Gabe heaved his shoulders hopelessly.

Izzie frowned at him. "Is that supposed to mean something?"

"He's not answering my texts."

Izzie smiled and shot him a look. "So? Maybe he's asleep?"

Heat rushed up Gabe's neck. He sounded like a worried mate or a clingy boyfriend.

"Oooh, Gabriel!" She smacked his shoulder. "You like our Lobito! I knew it!"

Gabe growled and quickened his pace.

"This is perfect. You and he are so cute together."

Gabe's phone rang. It was Max. Thank fuck. Apparently, he'd spoken aloud because Izzie laughed at him. He flipped her off. "Lobito. Hey."

"Gabe, something's wrong with Gemma." Max's voice was fraught with panic. "She needs my help."

Gabe's heart sank. "Shit, Max. Are you okay?"

"I'm scared. Really fucking scared. I think she might hurt herself unless I get to her now."

Gabe paced, feeling helpless. "Max, you shouldn't have left without me."

"Ryan's with me."

"Do you need me?"

"I think we can handle it."

That wasn't what he was asking. "Max. Do *you* need me?"

Max made a strangled sound. "I... I don't know yet. If it's really bad, I'll call you."

Gabe wished he was there to help him. He wanted to go to Max now and hold him close, tell him it was okay, tell him how much he—

How much I... what?

Gabe squeezed his eyes shut. "Okay, Max." He hung up, sighing.

Izzie gazed at him. "You love him," she stated, and there was no teasing this time.

Gabe's face warmed. He couldn't do this right now.

His phone rang again. Now what? It was Ben this time. He held up a hand to Izzie, freezing her in place. It was a video call. That was odd. Ben usually hated those.

"What's up, Viejo?" His freaking heart couldn't take much more excitement.

Ben looked off. Tired. "I've got bad news."

Gabe's heart rate accelerated. His fangs sharpened. "What the hell do you mean?"

Ben said, "My wolves raided the hideout an hour ago."

"What?" Gabe snarled. Izzie turned, eyes wide. "You..." Fury surged within him. In that moment, he hated Ben Stroud. "How could you? You didn't even fucking tell me!"

Ben closed his eyes, rubbing them. His hand was bloody.

"Did you go?" Gabe exploded. "You went without telling us! What if something had happened to you?"

Izzie marched over. "What's going on? Ben, what happened to your hand?"

"It's not my blood," Ben snapped. "Okay. Maybe it is."

Gabe was so angry, he wanted to hang up. "How could you?" he said through gritted teeth. "How could you go without telling us?"

"You mean, without telling you," Ben stated, silver eyes hard.

He didn't try to deny it. He was so pissed, he wanted to shatter his phone to pieces.

"Talk," Izzie said, yanking the phone from Gabe's hand. "Tell us why you did this."

"Because I couldn't have you both getting hurt on my watch!" Ben said, his frustration erupting. Emotion thickened his voice. Gabe hadn't heard him that way before. It sobered some of his anger. Ben hid his face in his hand. "I made the right choice. My instincts were screaming at me to leave you out of this, and I was right."

Gabe rounded on him, nudging Izzie over so he could look at Ben through the screen. "The hell you did. Stone killed our father! You had no right—"

"It was an ambush!" Ben shouted.

Cold dread rippled down Gabe's back.

Ben's mouth trembled. "They were expecting us."

Izzie's hand shook, and Gabe took the phone before she could drop it.

Ben went on. "These wolves weren't Moonborn. They were something else entirely."

"What do you mean?" Gabe asked, throat dry.

A message pinged on Gabe's screen. Ben had sent him a picture. He opened it and saw a blurry picture of a wolf. It was dead. Gabe didn't recognize it, but his heart still skipped a beat.

"Look at the markings," Ben's voice said.

Izzie pointed to something on the screen. "There. What... what *is* that?"

Gabe zoomed in. It was blurry, but it looked like a tattoo. "Ben, what am I looking at?" He minimized the text screen and returned to the video call.

Ben's face was paler than usual. "It's one of the wolves who ambushed us. They all had that symbol painted on them. Like warpaint. It's not a lotus. It's a tree, a wolf howling beneath a tree."

That didn't make sense. "What are you saying?"

"These are a totally different pack of wolves. Their tactics were unlike anything I've ever seen. It means Stone's in league with a whole other pack."

Gabe leaned on a lamppost for support. The summer breeze made him shiver. "What happened?"

Ben blinked fast. "They waited until we stormed the building. Then... they fucking blew themselves to pieces."

Gabe struggled to make sense of what he was hearing.

"They were strapped up with silver grenades full of aconitum. They died instantly, and so did anyone who got within feet of them. My wolves." A tear slipped down Ben's face and disappeared into his beard.

"Oh fuck." Gabe clutched the lamppost. "Ben, I'm so sorry. Where are you? Are you hurt?"

"The hospital." Ben wiped his face. "No, I'm not hurt but the shock of it all..."

Gabe nodded numbly. "Yeah. Right. Of course."

"Ben?" Izzie whispered. "Who was the woman who came to the agency?" Her face was pale. "She told Max about the Moonborn hideout. They knew you were coming. Ben, she tricked us!"

Gabe's blood turned to ice.

Oh, no. No, no, no...

Ben's eyes narrowed. "This was a trap. An attempt to get the agency out of the way."

Gabe didn't care who those wolves were. Nothing mattered except the realization that Max was going straight to Gemma. To the woman who'd sent Ben into a trap.

Zach walked out of the bar, humming. Gabe lunged for him, claws digging into Zach's arms. "Drive us! Now!"

Zach jumped. "What's wrong?"

Everything. Everything was so wrong.

Max. Oh Goddess. *Max.*

RYAN PULLED UP OUTSIDE Gemma's apartment. Max leaped out and jogged toward the front door. He buzzed her intercom. "Come on... Come on!" The door buzzed open, and Max sighed his relief. She was all right. He jogged to the elevator with Ryan. His phone rang. It was Gabe. Max silenced the call and punched the button for Gemma's floor.

"Hey, easy," Ryan said, patting Max's back. "We got here in time. She's okay."

Max's phone pinged. Gabe was texting him. Max growled and ignored it. He needed to focus on Gemma right now. Gabe worried about him too much sometimes. The elevator opened and Max ran to Gemma's door. It was ajar. Ryan seized his arm in a death grip. Max whipped around but his retort died at the wide-eyed look on Ryan's face.

Ryan whispered, "Smell that?"

Max sniffed the air and his heart sank. There was a scent trail leading into Gemma's apartment. Wolves, two of them. Purebloods by the smell. He'd noticed the scents downstairs but had thought nothing of it at the time. This, though, was strange.

"We should go," Ryan murmured, eyeing the door warily.

Max couldn't. What if she was in trouble? "We can't leave her."

A scream came from beyond the door.

Max's heart froze in his chest. "Gemma!"

Ryan scowled and bunched his hands into fists. "Ah hell. Here we go!" He kicked open the door.

The pair of them sprinted inside, claws and fangs at the ready.

The apartment was dark, lights from the hallway spilling in and narrowly illuminating the front hall. Max's eyes adjusted to the dark as they pressed in, Ryan right at his side. A growl rolled from Max's chest up into his throat. The scent of the intruder wolves was overpowering—dirt and grime, blood and unwashed bodies. Fear. Sour, pungent fear.

They were in the living room. Gemma's wide eyes gleamed in the dark, her face pale with fright. The smell of her blood made Max's lip curl.

Two men flanked her, tall and bulky. Their fangs glistened when they bared their teeth at Max and Ryan. One of them was bald and square-jawed. The other Max recognized immediately by the claw tattoos on his face.

"You," Max growled. "You're the one who attacked us on the platform. You really were Moonborn after all."

Ryan looked from the men to Max, eyes narrowed. "What?"

Pieces were falling into place, and Max suddenly understood why Gabe had been calling him so desperately. He'd known somehow that something was very wrong.

The tattooed man sneered, his laughter gravelly. "We were all quite excited when Gemma convinced you to come to her apartment. Finally, we knew where you'd be. Stone could only send one of us without alerting you hybrid scum to our presence, and he chose me."

Savage pride showed in his cruel smile. "It was the opportunity I needed. One push, and that hybrid mutt would be dead, and you'd have been in Stone's hands. He would have rewarded me greatly." He dragged his claws over Gemma's face with a soft rasping noise. "But this, this is a far more interesting way to get you into our master's hands, red one."

Gemma let out an unhinged laugh. "This is what we filthy mutts deserve," she croaked.

"Gemma?" Max whispered, heart dropping into his stomach. "I don't understand."

Ryan growled beside Max, white fur rippling over his arms.

"I was scared at first," Gemma whimpered. "They abducted me. They hurt me. So badly. I thought they'd kill me. They let me go. Told me to go to the LPA. To cozy up to you and lie about a hideout so they could destroy the agency."

"You didn't have to do this. We could have kept you safe!" Max said.

She just laughed. "But I wanted to. I wanted to be cleansed. You don't understand, Max, but you will. You'll see soon enough. It's a fate all we lowly hybrids deserve!"

"Enough!" The bald werewolf growled and pointed a clawed hand at Max. "You're coming with me, red one. Rooks, grab him. Enough talk."

The tattooed werewolf—Rooks—sneered. "I'd let him leave with us," he suggested to Ryan. "Or things will get very bad for you and the girl."

"Like hell!" Ryan roared, claws long and sharp.

Max braced himself for a fight. "Let her go. You wanted me; I'm fucking here. Let her go!"

Gemma rocked back and forth in Rooks's grip. "Filthy. I'm filthy. Impure. John Stone will cleanse us all!" She laughed breathlessly, eyes wide and glassy.

Rooks tugged her hair, wrenching her head back and exposing her throat. Tears leaked from Gemma's eyes. "I think she's outlived her usefulness. Don't you?" His claws pricked Gemma's throat.

Max charged, but it was too late.

Rooks's claws flew across Gemma's throat, splitting it like paper. Max roared his despair and fury. Her body hit the ground as Max and Rooks collided, claws out. Max split flesh as he carved into Rooks's side, and blood spattered the wood floor. The other werewolf grunted as Ryan body-slammed him.

Rooks seized Max's neck and hurled him over the sofa. Max tumbled, crashing into the coffee table. A window cracked as Ryan flew into the glass and the other werewolf lunged for him. They both smashed through the glass and fell three stories to the ground below. A cry of terror spilled from Max.

"Ryan!" Max lurched to his feet and a gunshot split the air. Stabbing pain erupted through his leg as he collapsed, clutching it. Embedded in his calf was a dart. He yanked it out and saw it was tipped with silver. His claws retracted and his fangs lost their edge.

He snarled and tried to advance on Rooks, who stood tall and smug as he lowered the tranquilizer gun. Max stumbled as the room began to spin. He couldn't call upon his wolf anymore. He crumpled to the ground and felt as if he were spiraling down a whirlpool.

Chuckling, Rooks stood over him. The last thing Max saw was the bottom of Rooks's boot flying toward his face.

There was blinding pain, and then Max fell completely into darkness.

"Zach, drive faster!" Gabe urged. He cursed, throwing down his phone. Why wouldn't Max answer?

"I'm going as fast as I can!" Zach snapped, spinning the wheel as the car flew around a corner. He blared his horn at a couple of idiots crossing against the red light and they ran out of his way.

Gabe recognized Gemma's street. A pickup truck pulled away from the curb and drove at lightning speed toward them. Izzie screamed as Gabe latched onto Zach's arm. Zach cursed like a sailor and drove out of the way in time to avoid a collision as the truck sped off in the wrong lane.

"The hell?" Zach snarled, hitting the wheel.

Gabe slumped in his seat, his heart racing fit to burst. Was twenty-seven too young to have a heart attack?

Izzie lunged from the back seat, pointing at something. "What is that?"

A figure lay on the concrete, shattered glass glittering around them. Zach drove to the other side of the street and stopped, and his headlights illuminated the man lying on the ground. "Ryan!" Zach cried, throwing himself from the car and dashing across the street. Izzie and Gabe jumped out and ran.

"No! No, no!" Gabe had never heard Zach so terrified. He knelt, heaving Ryan into his arms. Ryan's face was blood-spattered, shards of glass protruding from his skin. Zach plucked glass from his face with shaking hands. "Ryan! Answer me!"

There was a big bloody stain on the side of Ryan's head where he'd struck the pavement hard. Gabe felt sick. Ryan's eyes weren't open.

"Please, please, please…" Zach whispered, closing his eyes tight, concentrating. Gabe searched among the tangled threads connecting him to Izzie and Zach. Ryan's bond hadn't severed. He was still alive.

Ryan's eyes fluttered. He gritted his teeth and groaned. There came a horrible snap as Ryan's shoulder jerked, the joint fitting itself back in the socket. Then he gasped, his face shiny with sweat.

"Are you okay?" Zach asked, voice shaking. "What happened?" He wiped the blood from Ryan's head. It wasn't flowing anymore, but there was a lot of it.

"Max." Ryan grunted, eyes wide with terror. His glasses had fallen off and were smashed nearby. "Where is he?"

Gabe's heart sank. "He's not with you?"

Ryan scrambled to sit up, pushing Zach away. "They took him! They're taking him to Stone!"

A wave of terror rolled over Gabe. The truck that had driven past, going faster than it had any right to… He whirled toward the road. There were tire tracks. A scent. He breathed in deep. Blood. Silver. Cinnamon and chilis. Max.

"They left a trail!" Gabe shouted. "Hurry! We can still catch them!"

Zach and Izzie helped Ryan into the bed of Zach's truck. Gabe jumped in beside him, and Izzie and Zach climbed in front. Zach slammed on the gas and they took off, following the tire tracks. When those disappeared, Gabe breathed in deep and guided Zach left and right in pursuit of Max's scent.

The Brooklyn Bridge loomed ahead and Zach cursed as they hit a wall of traffic.

Where in the hell were they taking Max?

As Max's scent grew stronger, Gabe stood in the truck bed and peered over a sea of cars. A white pickup truck stood out among the vehicles, a tarp thrown over the bed of the truck. One whiff of the air, and Gabe knew he'd found his target. Max's scent was stronger than ever.

"Found you," he snarled through his fangs, and he sprang.

"Gabe!" Izzie's voice became lost among the traffic noise as Gabe launched himself from one car to another, landing with a crash on the roof of the pickup. He ripped the tarp away. Max lay beneath, his hands and legs bound, wide eyes looking to Gabe for help.

With a swipe, Gabe severed the ropes, yanking the gag out of Max's mouth.

The truck's front door slammed. Max hollered, "Behind you!"

Gabe turned in time to catch the claw flying at his face. The passenger had come to investigate. He was bald and covered in blood, bits of glass glimmering in his jacket. He leaped into the truck bed and lunged for Gabe with a roar. Fangs closed around Gabe's arm, each one like a dagger piercing his flesh.

The traffic unfroze, and the driver slammed on the gas, shooting them forward. Gabe slipped and crashed down on the hood of the truck. The werewolf howled and collapsed as Izzie jumped into the truck bed, driving her claws into his back. She hurled the werewolf from the truck and into the road behind them, then helped Max to his feet.

Zach pulled up in the lane beside them. "Jump!" he shouted out the window.

The driver flashed a pistol through the rolled-down window of his truck.

"Get down!" Gabe roared.

Zach dove beneath the window as a bullet shattered the glass.

Gabe leaped into the bed of the truck beside Ryan's crouched form just in time to dodge another blast of gunfire. Gabe called, "Izzie, Max! Jump in!"

Izzie leaped, tumbling into the truck bed beside Gabe.

Gabe stumbled, clasping the roof for support as he faced Max, the gap between their cars widening by the second. "Max, come on!"

Max ran for him, leaping over the divide between their cars. A pop of gunfire split the air and Max crashed down into the bed of the truck. Gabe caught him as he landed, bringing him down behind cover as another burst of gunfire left his ears ringing.

The ground sloped as they drove off the bridge, and the abductor's vehicle wound up in front of them. The driver leaned out the window and aimed at their windshield. Zach accelerated and slammed into the rear of the truck.

Their hood popped open, and in an explosion of glass, the werewolf was thrown from the driver's seat and hurtled across the asphalt. His truck crashed into a streetlamp and lurched to a stop. The werewolf stumbled to his feet. Gabe recognized the tattoo on his face instantly. It was the asshole who'd almost pushed him into an incoming train.

Zach pulled over and Gabe leaped over the side of the truck and pursued the driver. Incoming traffic from the bridge cut Gabe off from the wolf. Across the sea of vehicles, the wolf disappeared around the corner.

"Gabe!" Izzie cried. Something in her voice demanded his attention. Gabe whirled around, saw Izzie's panic-stricken face, and felt his stomach drop. "Hurry and come here!"

Gabe looked over his shoulder. The asshole with the tattoo had made his escape. Nothing to be done about it now.

"What?" Gabe asked, heart pounding as he approached.

A sob tore from her throat. "Max!" she choked. "He needs help. Now."

Terror turned his legs to gelatin. Peering into the truck bed, he saw blood pooling, running in rivers and glimmering in the lights from the bridge. Max shivered, his face pale. Gabe hadn't seen him so small and weak since they'd found him in Central Park. Ryan sat beside him, crimson hands compressing Max's wound.

"Max..."

He had to make it stop. Stop the bleeding, stop his shivering, and wipe away the pain twisting his sweet face. Blood splashed under his boots and he slipped in it, landing on his knee. It was hot as it seeped through the fabric. There was so much of it. Too much. Max was so cold, so frail as Gabe gathered him into his arms, trembling so badly he could barely hold him.

"I got you. I got you."

Pale, cold hands clawed at his shirt and left behind warm, bloody prints. Max tried to smile. "I'm okay, Gabe... D-don't worry about me." Max grimaced in agony, each word gasped through chattering teeth.

"Max... Oh Goddess. Don't speak. Save your strength." He had to make it stop. He had to fucking do *something.* He peeled up Max's shirt, which was sticking to his bloody skin. There was a hole in him—oh fuck, there was a bloody hole right *through* him and the blood wouldn't stop. He was going to lose someone else he loved all over again because of John Stone.

"Zach, someone, can he have a—a blood transfusion, or—"

"Is the bullet still in him?" Zach asked, kneeling by them.

Gritting his jaw, Max gave a weak nod. "C-can feel it... Fuck. It hurts." He laughed, near delirious from pain. It was then Gabe noticed that Max's veins were turning black around the site of the injury.

Fuck. The bullet had been poisoned with enough wolfsbane to kill him.

Breathing hard, Zach shook his head. "He needs a doctor. If we give him blood, the wound will close but the poison will keep eating at him."

"We have to do something. There must be—" Max touched his face, silencing Gabe.

"Th-thank you," Max croaked, tears glimmering on his lashes. "For everything."

Gabe shook his head. "No. No, Max. Stay awake. Okay? Just—"

"Zach, start the car! We need to get him to a hospital!" Izzie's voice came from far away.

"Get me something! I need something, anything! He's bleeding so much."

"Gabe!" Ryan thrust his jacket at Gabe. Gabe ripped off the sleeve and held it to Max's side. Max's gasp of pain sliced right through him.

"So sorry, Max. I'm so sorry. I know, I know it hurts." His trembling fingers curled around the nape of Max's neck, guiding his head to his chest.

"Gabe, I..." Max's eyelids fluttered and closed.

He was weaker, Gabe realized in horror as those trembling, cold fingers loosened against his shirt. Those frantic gasps were turning into slow, shuddery breaths. Max's hand fell from his chest.

"Max. Max." Gabe's voice broke. The smell of Max's blood turned his insides upside down. Something ran hot down his face. His throat ached as he buried his face in Max's neck, pressing his lips to the shell of his ear. "Don't quit. You hear me, Max? You're a fighter." His trembling lips found Max's forehead. "Don't leave me. Don't—"

Wake up. Please. I have to tell you. I have to tell you how much I—

He could barely silence the howl rising to the back of his throat as his wolf cried out in a way it hadn't for anyone. Gabe had denied it from the moment they met, but the wolf in him had known. He needed to come home to Max; he needed to eat meals with him and hunt with him, needed to see more of the strength hiding behind his shy smile.

He needed to tell him that it didn't matter what the future held and that he was so, so sorry for being so self-absorbed and blind. He needed Max.

The minute they'd embraced, his wolf had found his mate.

"I chose you, too," he whispered.

Chapter 19

SOMEONE TO HOWL FOR

"Gabe, it's been two hours. Sit down," Izzie implored.

Gabe couldn't. If he sat still, he'd think. If he started thinking, he'd see Max's pale face, all that hot crimson blood.

Zach cleared his throat. "Does anyone need anything? Food, water? I can run to the store around the corner."

Izzie, bleary-eyed and slumped in her seat, shook her head. Ryan closed his eyes, running a hand across his short beard.

Max's mother hugged herself. "I'm fine."

Exhaling, Gabe turned away and paced. What was taking so long? "Luke would never take this long to remove a bullet. We should have taken him to Luke."

Izzie sighed. "Gabe, he's too far away. We had to go to the closest hospital."

Gabe chewed on the back of his knuckles. "The doctor smelled human. Does she know how to treat wolfsbane poisoning? Does she even have werewolf patients?"

Zach said, "Gabe, it's a bullet removal. They're trained for this."

Right. Of course. He was being stupid. Had something happened? No, surely the doctor would come and tell them if something serious came up.

Unless it was so bad she couldn't take a break. Unless Max was in there now, dying, while Gabe was out here doing fuck all to help him.

Kendra sniffed, wiping her eyes. Izzie put her arm around her shoulders.

"She'd tell us if something was wrong," Gabe said, more to himself than anyone. "Come on, she'd have to let us know if something had—"

"Gabriel, please." Kendra barely suppressed a sob. Izzie took her hand and shot him a look.

"Ry," Izzie said, eyes brightening. "Your stomach's growling. How about you and my brother go grab some snacks?"

Ryan quirked a brow. "I'm not—" He went quiet as Izzie's brow furrowed. "Sure. Gabe, come on."

What if something happened while they were gone?

"If Max is out of surgery, I'll call," Izzie assured him, likely smelling his distress.

Gabe's stomach twisted itself into knots as he followed Ryan to the elevator and out into the streets. Most stores were closed except the 7-Eleven up the street.

The air conditioning in the store made Gabe growl. The hospital was already so cold. He couldn't stop shaking.

"Coffee sounds great right about now. Wish I could spike it," Ryan said, stopping at the caffeine machine. "Want some?"

"Sure." Gabe didn't care. His twitchy legs forced him to wander the store, eyes darting around without really looking at anything. He realized he was holding his breath when it became hard to breathe. He kept waiting for his phone to ring, for someone to call him in tears to tell him that Max was—

He blinked hard, sucking in a gasp. Max wasn't going to die. He wasn't. He couldn't. Not before Gabe had the chance to tell him how he felt. To apologize for being so pigheaded. For wasting the precious time they had together on doubts and insecurities. He pressed his fingers into his eyes and kept them there until his head screamed in protest.

"Gabe?"

His heart flew into his throat. "What?" he asked, heart racing.

Ryan held an armful of snacks. "I think Zach will like these, so would you like this, or—"

"I don't fucking care about snacks, Ry!" He hadn't intended for his voice to be so loud. His throat went raw as he struggled to rein it all back in. "Sorry," he said, shooting the wide-eyed cashier a look. He hated himself for making Ryan's eyes so wide and hurt. Taking Ryan's arm, he dragged him behind a shelf. "Fuck. I'm sorry."

Ryan cleared his throat. "So... when I was a kid, my mom got sick."

Ryan's mom had a disease similar to dementia. Her wolf couldn't forge the bonds she needed to stay human, so she'd forget those she loved and go feral for brief periods. She always came out of those episodes, but it still sounded terrifying.

"The doctors told me she'd never get better." Ryan averted his gaze. "She has her good days and her bad days, but she always comes back to us, no matter how deep she falls into her wolf. Max'll be okay, man. He'll get better because he has you. He has us, his pack." Ryan blinked fast, eyes shining.

Laughter spilled from Gabe's lips. He must be going crazy. The world around him blurred through his tears and keeping it together was suddenly so much harder. An arm flew around his shoulders and he stumbled into Ryan's body. Ryan clapped Gabe on the back and squeezed tight. Ryan was shorter than Gabe, but he gave damn good hugs. "He's gonna be okay, man."

Gabe wished he'd held Max close back in the safety of the bedroom where they'd had their first kiss. He wished he hadn't been so thickheaded, so caught up in what-ifs and future possibilities. He thought he'd known how unpredictable life could be, how someone could be there one day and then gone so abruptly. There wasn't always a chance to say goodbye, to say all the things he should have said before doubt stifled him.

He shouldn't have rejected Max's feelings. He never should have put his walls up and kept Max at a distance. He should have realized what was real and right in front of him. Now he feared he'd never get the chance to kiss Max again, to tell Max how much he cared.

Izzie called him as they reached the hospital lobby. Gabe ran until all he could hear was the blood in his ears.

Please. Please. Please!

His legs trembled, and he was gasping for breath when he arrived outside the operating room. Everyone was gone. "Shit. Where are they?" he said, his voice becoming pinched. He sniffed and caught Max's mother's scent. His feet slammed against the tile as he threw open the door to a room. Kendra, Izzie, and Zach were gathered around a bed. Gabe didn't want to speak. He couldn't know. The fear made him sick to his stomach.

Then he sensed it pulsing feebly among the tense bonds of the pack. Max's thread was weak and feeble, but it was still there. Tears burned Gabe's eyes as he leaned over Kendra's shoulder.

Max lay asleep in the bed, still pallid, his lips cracked and dry, but his chest rose and fell with every slow breath. Gabe clutched Kendra's shoulder and for the first time in two and a half hours, he could breathe again.

Boots clumped behind him. "He's going to be all right, Gabe," rumbled a deep voice.

Ben stood behind Gabe, smelling of silver and death, but he was alive and unharmed. They all were. Battered and bruised, but alive.

Gabe's knees gave out and Ben caught him as he fell. Gabe buried his face in Ben's strong shoulder, and Ben held him together as Gabe wept.

KENDRA WAS GOING TO spend the night with Max. The room was only big enough for a bed and a sofa but Gabe would sleep on the damn floor if it meant he could stay near Max.

Max's doctor smiled and said, "If you'd like to shift, you can. I'll let the nurse know so no one gets surprised."

Werewolves weren't usually allowed to shift in hospitals or in public, so Gabe was grateful she was open-minded. Once the doctor was gone, he undressed and turned into a wolf. Gabe leaped onto the bed and curled up beside Max.

When he opened his eyes again, Max was still resting. Gabe held his breath until the gentle rise of Max's chest granted him peace. Across the room, Kendra smiled and whispered, "Good morning."

Gabe carried his clothes in his mouth to the bathroom where he shifted and dressed. He wasn't wasting another second. He had to tell Max how he felt before he lost the chance to. Gabe excused himself and went for a walk to a nearby deli where they were selling flowers outside. He bought a bouquet of orange roses that reminded him of Max's eyes.

Gabe's heart pounded as he approached the door to Max's room. His stomach either felt like doing a jig or flopping out through his mouth. He exhaled, trying to think of what to say. "Okay. Max, I love you. I want you to be my mate. No. Too blunt." He cleared his throat, urging himself to relax so he didn't crush the bouquet of flowers. "Max, I've been thinking... about *what*?" He buried his fingers in his hair.

The door opened and Kendra stepped out. "I thought I'd run out and get us some coffee. Want some?"

"Sure, thanks."

"Milk, no sugar, right?"

"You got it."

"Are those for Max?" She gave the orange roses a sniff. "He'll love them. He hates that hospital smell."

Before Kendra could turn away, Gabe blurted out, "Wait. There's actually something I want to ask you. I've been so thickheaded lately. It took me far too long to figure it out. But basically..."

Shit. Was he really about to ask her such an important question in the middle of a hospital hallway? "Kendra, your son is precious to me. I didn't realize until last night when I thought he might be taken from me. So, I'd like to ask permission to become part of your family. I love your son, and if he returns my feelings, I'd be blessed to have him as my mate."

Gabe didn't realize how worried he was that she would reject him until joyful tears glimmered in her eyes. "Gabriel, of all the men in the world, I couldn't ask for anyone better for my son." She smiled, pulling him into a tight, warm hug. "Of course. Of course I'd love to have you as part of our family! Goodness, I had no idea you were such an old soul. Hurry, hurry! Go talk to him."

She practically pushed Gabe through the door before he had wrangled his emotions. The breath went out of him at the sight of Max sitting up in bed. His hair was messy and there were bags under his eyes but he smiled upon seeing Gabe.

Gabe struggled to steady himself, his knees trembling as he went to the bed and sat on the edge.

"Hey, Max."

Warm fingers settled atop Gabe's hand. "Hey."

His heart in his throat, Gabe leaned over and nuzzled his cheek against Max's. Gabe let his emotions speak for him, claiming Max's lips and letting his fingertips rasp over Max's cheek.

"How are you feeling?" he asked, pulling away far enough to rest their foreheads together.

Max chuckled. "Like I got shot."

"Doc was saying you had to have a blood transfusion to repair the damage after she removed the bullet. Pure werewolf blood."

Max's eyes lit up. "Yeah, she was telling me. My wound healed. There's not even a scar. Makes me wish I had pure werewolf blood. It would be way convenient."

"Right?" Gabe laced their fingers together and squeezed. "Here. These are for you. Thought they'd brighten up this room a bit until you're ready to leave."

Max's cheeks colored and he gave the roses a sniff. He sighed. "They smell great. Thank you." He laid them on the bed between his ankles. "So, what happened to that tattooed guy? Rooks?"

A stab of anger went through him. "Ugly motherfucker's on the run. He could know where Stone and his buddies are holed up. He needs to be found." Stone was within his grasp. He exhaled as a growl expanded in his chest. Stone was close, but Max was here, alive and right in front of him.

Gabe reached out, cupping Max's freckled cheek. "I tried to call you. To warn you. It was an ambush. The Moonborn used Gemma to get to us."

"They broke her mind. She wanted them to 'cleanse' me." Max looked away, worrying at his lower lip. Tears gleamed in his eyes. "I tried. I tried to save her."

"Hey… I know. You did everything you could." Gabe's fingers wandered through Max's hair.

"They killed her. Right in front of me. I couldn't stop them." Max's voice broke.

Gabe pressed his mouth to Max's neck, lips settling over his pulse. "They hit us real hard, but Ben made it out of the ambush. Biggest mistake those fuckers made was coming at our pack and letting us survive."

Max curled his fingers in Gabe's hair, urging him close until Gabe was nestled between his thighs. Heat pooled in the pit of his stomach as Max's pulse raced beneath his lips. He could barely stifle a growl, rubbing the bridge of his nose against Max's throat. He parted his lips, suckling at milky skin as he kissed a trail up Max's neck to his chin, biting lightly.

"Max," he whispered, bringing his lips to the corner of Max's mouth. "I've been blind and stupid. But last night, almost losing you like that—it made me realize what's important. I need you. I—"

"That might not be true." The pain in Max's voice dropped a cold lump of dread into his stomach.

Confused, horrified, Gabe looked up at Max and his breath hitched at the tears swimming in his eyes. Shit. What had he done? His hands trembled as they grasped Max's shoulders. "I do. Max, you need to believe me. I…" His voice tried to crawl back down his throat. "Max, I lo—"

Max sucked in a breath and looked away, pale fingers squeezing the sheets. "Maybe you do now, but you won't one day."

Every word was like a wrecking ball through his chest. Gabe laughed, though he wanted to cry. "No way. It would take a lot for my feelings to change like that. I mean it. You'd have to kill someone in cold blood for me to—"

Max squirmed, pressing himself against the head of the bed, trying to escape Gabe's grip. Gabe's hands dropped like stones to the sheets. Max said, "I know. About you and Zach. He told me. You're destined to be together. Why didn't you tell me?"

That explained everything. Where he and Zach had disappeared to, why Max had left so suddenly. Oh Goddess. How did he make this right? "Max…" At a loss, he slumped with his elbows on his knees. "Zach believes that I will return his feelings. For a time, I thought I believed it, too. I had no reason not to. Then I met you. Max, last night I was terrified. I thought I'd lost you and it made me realize you're not someone I want to lose. No matter what the future holds or how much time we have, I don't want to waste it."

"That's what you think now, but one day—"

"No, Max. Not one day." Gabe took his hand and held tight. "Listen. I'll talk to Zach. I'll tell him how I feel about you. Once we're done, I'll come and find you. I promise."

Max looked him in the eyes and exhaled a deep breath. He was doubtful, Gabe could feel it in the trembling of his hand, and yet he said, "Okay."

Gabe looked in Max's eyes and savored the rush of tender feeling that gripped him. "I should have told you this so much sooner. Since the night I first smelled you, my wolf has been howling for you, wanting to be with you and you alone. My wolf hasn't wanted anyone else."

It all made sense now. Why he'd felt such a powerful urge to protect Max. Why he'd pulled away from Zach. He laughed, feeling like an idiot for not realizing sooner.

"It's you for me, Max. It's only ever going to be you."

Max's lips trembled, happy tears shining in his eyes. "I feel the same." Relief warmed his voice. "The moment you held me, I knew you were someone special to me. I didn't know you felt the same way all this time."

"I'm sorry it took me so long to get it together." Gabe squeezed his hand. "There you have it. Our wolves chose each other. So, can you trust this, Max? Trust us? No matter what the future holds, you're who I choose."

The sound of Max's heart fluttered in Gabe's ears. "I do. I trust in us."

Gabe leaned his forehead to Max's and sighed in bliss.

What a relief it was, to have someone his wolf could sing for.

Three months ago...

"I love you, Gabe," Zach whispered. Zach had been gone for a week in London with Ryan, and Gabe had missed the intimacy of someone who knew his body as well as Zach did.

Gabe thought for a moment that he'd misheard, his mind pleasantly fogged with the afterglow of mind-blowing sex. "You... what?" He laughed quietly, wondering if he'd misunderstood.

"I love you," Zach repeated, his fingertips warm and damp with sweat against Gabe's cheek.

Gabe swallowed, grateful he'd controlled the urge to knot him tonight so he could roll off him and onto his side of the bed, desperately needing space. Holy shit, the last thing he wanted was to be locked in him, unable to move away while they had this unbearably uncomfortable conversation. "Love. As in..."

"As in I want us to be together. I want us to have a future together. Oh shit." The lovely haze in Zach's chocolate-brown eyes disappeared. His eyes widened,

and he looked like a single word from Gabe might shatter him. "You don't feel the same."

Gabe didn't know how to answer. He'd never expected this. This wasn't the casual affair they'd agreed to. "I, uh... can I have a moment here?" He dragged himself from the bed, pacing to the bathroom. He closed the door and locked it, leaning on the sink for support. Zach loved him—and Gabe didn't return his feelings. He wished he did so he didn't have to break the heart of the man who'd been his best friend. Zach deserved love, and he deserved someone who could love him.

He emerged from the bathroom and Zach sighed. "Sorry for making things awkward."

"You love me? I had no idea. How long?"

Zach shrugged. "Since college."

Gabe felt as if the bottom of his stomach had fallen out. "Holy—I didn't know."

"I know." Zach sat up, eyes wide and imploring. "It's fine. I wasn't going to tell you but hear me out. When Ryan and I were in London—"

And so it had begun, the story of the seer foreseeing a future where they were together. Gabe hadn't been so sure. As far as he'd been concerned, that future was one of many possible outcomes. Zach had believed wholeheartedly that they would end up together, that even if Gabe didn't return his feelings now, he would someday. He was willing to wait for however long it took.

Gabe hadn't known what to believe. He didn't believe he had forever, not when his road led to John Stone. He'd promised to keep his mind open to the possibility, but in his heart, he'd been unsure. He'd turned to Zach for the comfort he offered from the pain of Gabe's past.

Naked in his arms, so protected and safe from his demons, it'd been easy to convince himself that one day he could return Zach's feelings. But then he'd found a sweet, shy red wolf whose eyes had beseeched him for safety and companionship, and before he knew it, his heart had been stolen.

Now here he stood outside Zach's door as he'd done three months ago on the last anniversary of his father's death when he'd been walking around with a hole inside him nothing could heal. Zach had gathered him into his arms like some broken thing, and they'd gotten to drinking and talking about anything other than the anniversary.

Zach had kissed him. It'd been everything Gabe had needed but it had never been love. Not even close. Now that he knew how it felt to really love, he understood his relationship with Zach for what it was—a drug numbing all the hurt when he didn't want to feel a thing, strong spirits he could take whenever he wanted to forget and be in the moment with someone he knew and trusted.

He'd used Zach, and Zach had let him because he had genuinely wanted to be the one to pull Gabe from the darkness of his father's murder. But Zach couldn't do that. Only Max had been able to penetrate the darkness wrapped around Gabe's heart, and Max understood that darkness because it was so similar to his own.

Without trying, without saying a word, Max brought a light into the darkness. Max didn't fix anything broken in Gabe, but he made Gabe feel so whole that Gabe couldn't ask for anything more.

Gabe balled his hand into a fist and knocked. The door swung inward and Zach smiled radiantly. Gabe wondered if he'd ever see that smile again or if he deserved it. "Hey, come on in."

Gabe shuffled inside. A vast living room with floor-to-ceiling windows offered a view of SoHo beyond the patio. The kitchen flowed into the living room and that was where Zach had stopped to wait for him at a marble-topped counter.

"What's up? Come, sit. I got the good stuff." Zach held up a bottle of pinot noir, Gabe's favorite wine.

"Zach, we need to talk."

Zach frowned. "Is everything okay?" He carried the wine to the mahogany dining table.

Gabe wet his lips, unsure how to answer. He approached the table and lowered himself into the chair across from Zach. Zach's knee had started doing that little bouncy thing he did when he was nervous, making the creaky floorboard underneath his feet quiver. Did he know? Why else would he be so worried if he didn't already suspect what Gabe was going to say?

Gabe looked him in the eyes, and it was the hardest thing he'd ever done. "Zach, I'm in love with Max." Zach's knee gradually stilled. He said nothing, his face totally blank. Gabe exhaled, heart pounding in his ears. "It's more than that. He's my mate."

Zach leaned back in his chair and said nothing, wetting his lips, blinking fast.

"Zach, I thought I would return your feelings. I did. I wanted to try. I—"

"How do you know?" Zach's voice quivered but there wasn't any emotion in it.

"What?"

"That he's your mate. How do you know?"

Gabe looked down at the table as if searching for words scratched into the wood. "I didn't, not for a long time. I knew I wanted to protect him, and that he had this amazing scent. The minute I met him, I wanted to keep him safe, make sure no one ever hurt him again. I think that should have been my first clue. After last night, almost losing him like that... it was a wake-up call, you know?"

When Zach didn't say anything, Gabe looked up. Zach stared across the room. His eyes were shining. "I—I had a feeling." Zach's voice was raw. "I knew Max liked you, but I didn't know you felt anything for him. You were protective, wanted to help him. But last night when he was hurt, you were so torn up—" Zach cut himself off, squeezing his eyes shut. "I knew."

Gabe stayed quiet, blinking back his own emotions as the salty smell of Zach's tears punched a hole into his chest.

Zach sucked in a gasp and quickly wiped at his eyes. "This wasn't supposed to happen." His trembling lips thinned, his eyes hardening. "We were supposed to be together. We had a child. Why would I see that if you love Max? It doesn't make any sense!"

"I don't know," Gabe admitted. "Maybe we are together in the future, Zach. As friends. As pack."

Zach shook his head. "No. I know what I saw. We were together, Gabe. We were in love, and we had a family."

Gabe had to force the words out as his throat tightened. "Zach, I can't give you that future. Max is my future. I'm sorry—"

"I know what I saw!" The table rattled as Zach slammed his fist down. "We were a family." Tears spilled down his cheeks. Zach gritted his teeth, tears clinging to his eyelashes. "I held our daughter in my arms. She loved me, Gabe. I was her father."

The sight of Zach's tears made it nearly impossible to hold back his own. "You can still have that, Zach. You deserve it. All of it. But I can't be a part of it, not in the way you want me to."

Zach's tears dotted the surface of the table, his shuddery sobs clawing at Gabe's heart. "Go, Gabe." Zach's voice was a croak. "We'll be okay. I... I need time. So please—"

The apartment door closed behind him as he left, and Gabe slumped, closing his eyes tight as grief constricted his throat. Things would never be the same between them. He'd consider it a miracle if Zach still wanted to be his friend. Wiping his eyes, he dragged himself down the stairs and lingered in the lobby to collect himself. He dialed Ryan's number and waited.

"Hey, Ry. I talked to Zach. Told him Max is my mate."

"Oh. Shit. Is Zach okay?"

"He's really upset with me. Listen, you know how Zach's always looking out for us? Well, he's gonna need someone to look out for him, and he's not gonna let me do it. Could you look after him?"

Ryan snorted. "Don't gotta tell me twice."

"You're pissed at me."

"Why shouldn't I be? You wasted his time."

His words were like a slap in the face. "I thought I would return his feelings! If I'd known I was gonna meet Max... But it's over. He can move on, and so can I." Even though he wasn't sure things would be the same between them, there was a part of him that felt unchained, like he could finally breathe. He just wished he hadn't had to break Zach's heart to finally feel free.

"Should I go over? How is he?"

"How do you think? Wait until morning. He needs space."

"You know, I'd hate your guts if you hadn't broken up with the guy I've been crazy about since I was a pup."

Gabe choked. "Wait. What?" Gabe's brain felt cracked down the middle. "You love Zach, Ryan?"

"Yes!" Ryan burst out. "Fuck. It killed me to watch him make goo-goo eyes at you all through our academy training while you couldn't even see what was right in front of you. You never saw him, not like I did. When you finally started hooking up, I seriously wanted to rip your face off." He huffed out a sigh. "I don't know if I want to punch you or kiss you for breaking his heart. You made the right call."

"Shit, man. If I'd known, I wouldn't have come between you guys." Gabe needed to sit down and took a seat on the windowsill. "Why? Why'd you let us be together?"

"Because. Zach loved you, man. What was I going to do?"

Gabe slumped, running his fingers through his hair. "Fuck, Ry. You're much better for him than I am. You should totally tell him how you feel!"

Ryan scoffed. "Yeah, no. He's gotta get over you first. I'll look after Zach. Don't worry about him. But you better make sure you didn't break Zach's heart for nothing. Got it? Go and touch Max's butt. Like, right now. You grab that bubble butt and never let it go."

Gabe laughed despite the ache in his chest. "Good talk, Ry. And don't worry. I'm not letting Max go... or his butt." Sighing, he hung up.

Ryan and Zach made a hell of a lot more sense. He hoped Zach would see it that way someday.

CHAPTER 20

TAKING A CHANCE

MAX CHECKED THE TIME. Gabe would have already met with Zach by now, but Max knew Gabe would choose him. Gabe had never been anything but sincere with Max in the short time they'd known each other, and he wore his heart upon his sleeve. Max believed him when Gabe said it was Max his wolf had chosen.

When Gabe had taken his hand and looked him in the eyes, his heart had never wavered once. Max's wolf howled to Gabe, and Gabe's wolf sang back, the harmonies resonating with each other. Gabe would choose him.

But what if Max wasn't good enough for Gabe? He was younger than Gabe, still figuring his life out while Gabe was leaps and bounds ahead of him. Max wanted to be his equal. He wanted to get a job to help pay the rent, get back into college, graduate, and go through life as Gabe's partner, not a hindrance.

Unless Richard was right, and Max was unlovable and weak and—

No. Those were lies. He mattered to Gabe, to a whole pack who'd had his back during the most difficult time of his life. Richard had lied to him because he wanted to break Max down to nothing.

Richard was the stupid one, because he'd made the mistake of abusing the trust and love of Max's mother, the most amazing woman Max knew. Richard could have had a family, and he'd destroyed it.

Max stirred the pasta boiling in the pot with more vigor than he'd meant to, splashing hot water over the sides. Gabe wasn't Richard. Gabe saw Max's worth, even if Max still struggled to see it himself. But he liked to think he was getting there. He had friends who cared for him and were rooting for him to succeed.

What he needed to focus on now was moving out of the shadow of Richard's abuse and getting back the time he'd lost. The jobs he'd lost. Max grimaced, the weight of it all crashing down on him.

His mother chopped vegetables on the island counter behind him. "So, let's pretend the Moonborn cult is destroyed, Richard is in jail, and all is well. What's the first thing you want to do when Stone and Richard are behind bars?"

"I…" Worry gnawed at him. He wanted to get another job and start submitting applications to colleges again. "I'll try and get back on the track I was on before Richard messed everything up."

She patted his shoulder and uncorked a bottle of wine on the counter. "That sounds good. Any plans?"

Max exhaled through pursed lips. "College applications. Another job. I can't be Gabe's kept man."

His mother snorted. "Max! You are not. I'm sure he understands. There's no rush."

Max stirred the pasta, watching it swirl around in a chaotic whirlpool. "I've put my life on pause long enough. If Gabe and I are going to be mates someday, I don't want to be dependent on him."

"There's an if?" She arched a blonde brow. "Seems pretty certain to me. The boy is smitten with you."

Max shrugged, hoping she didn't notice how red his face must be. "I know how I feel. How he feels. But he's got his life together, and I'm just figuring mine out. I want to have my shit together. I don't want to be a burden."

"Look at me, Max."

Sighing, Max did.

She looked him in the eye and said, "What matters is, is he good enough for you? It's not how he feels about you. It's how you feel about him. Do you want a future with him? Is he the kind of man you want? Is he enough for you?"

Yes, Max thought. *Yes. Yes.*

He nodded.

She patted his cheek. "Then I'm so happy for you, sweetheart. Gabe's a good man. He'll make a fine mate. He's sure easy on the eyes, too."

Max snorted. "Mom..."

"And if he's foolish enough to choose Zach over you, I'll be there to box his ears."

"Zach's fine. He and Ryan would be better together."

His mother went to her room with her wine. Max dumped the pasta in a colander and searched the cabinets for some pesto. He paused as a scent tickled his nose. He smelled wet fur. Dirt. Blood. Max's breath hitched. The scent was creeping in from under the front door. Max peered through the peephole and saw nothing, so he opened the door slowly.

There was no one in the hallway. A couple of plump pigeons lay on the doormat, neatly placed to avoid getting blood on the carpet. Max scented it, elm trees and springtime. The scent mingled with the birds and trailed away down the hall.

Gabe had been here. He'd left this for them. But why—

Max's breath caught.

It was a message, one without words.

Gabe was out hunting for him. Showing off his skills. Showing he could provide. Showing he was strong.

He'd talked to Zach. He'd made his choice.

Max closed his eyes tight, happiness blooming warm in his chest.

He'd chosen Max.

GABE WAS MORE TRADITIONAL than Max had initially thought. During the day, he was by Max's side constantly, whether it was bringing him coffee in the morning, cooking together at the end of the day, or going grocery shopping. At night, Gabe would go out for a hunt and leave Max freshly caught birds and squirrels.

"You don't have to do this, you know," Max said, freezing the squirrels and googling recipes using squirrel meat. There weren't very many.

Gabe smiled. "Maybe I want to."

"The neighbors will complain."

Gabe's eyes glittered. "Only if I get caught."

Max rolled his eyes, but his chest tightened with affection.

"Come on, Lobito." Gabe walked into the kitchen and cozied up behind Max. He pulled Max's back to his chest and rubbed his face in the crook of Max's neck. "Let me do this. Sure, we could exchange bites, but there's more to being mates than that. At least, to me."

Max touched Gabe's arms, running his fingers over the underside of Gabe's wrists. "Yeah? What does it mean to you?"

"Proving myself."

"How?" Max leaned his head back on Gabe's shoulder and closed his eyes, enjoying the warmth of Gabe's mouth against his neck.

"Proving that I can support you. That I can care for you the way you deserve, especially after all you've been through. You deserve that."

Max ran his fingers over the dark hair on Gabe's arm. It was overwhelming to see the depths of Gabe's devotion to him, and he would have gladly hunted for Gabe under normal circumstances.

The minute the Moonborn were gone, Max was going to bring Gabe more rabbits than he could ever hope to eat.

Until Kendra and Max could safely work again, the agency was giving Max and his mother weekly checks to tide them over. Max had expressed his desire to contribute that money to the household funds, as had Kendra, and Gabe was happy to let them.

Max's pride stung from accepting money he hadn't earned, but it was only temporary. Being able to help Gabe pay the rent made him feel less like a burden and on more equal footing with him.

Max couldn't believe it had only been a month since the agency had found them and given them a place to feel safe, a supportive space to recover in so they could move on. He was so grateful. He felt so much more like himself than he had since Richard had snaked his way into their lives.

Still, after the last attack against the agency by an unknown enemy, the agency was on high alert. No new clients were being accepted. Security had been ramped up with bag checks at the doors.

Armed guards patrolled day and night, and Ben had a bodyguard assigned to each of the high-profile members of the pack. Nowadays Max rarely saw Ben, who was holed up in his office giving orders to agents on the hunt for Rooks.

There hadn't been any sightings of Moonborn cultists, and the body count had been going down. The Moonborn were either playing it safe after their failed attempt at destroying the agency, or they were ramping up for a bigger attack.

Max didn't know how celebrities tolerated a big, hulking bodyguard shadowing them everywhere they went. Far from feeling at ease, Max just felt even more uncomfortable at the reminder of the threat they were under whenever their guard had to drive them places. Max accompanied Gabe to the agency when he had to work, spending his time wandering HQ and visiting with the pack.

Like most days, today he'd gone looking for Ryan in the library so they could eat lunch together and he'd walked right into Zach. Zach froze, and Max's skin prickled. Zach didn't look like himself. His eyes were baggy, and his smile was missing.

"Hey," Max whispered, stepping aside for him.

Zach dipped his head, averting his gaze. "Max. How are you?"

"I'm okay."

Zach made a quiet noise in his throat. "Good. That's good. We were all worried about you for a minute there."

Max laughed but it was forced. "Yeah. I'm doing a lot better."

"Cool." Zach stepped past him, then stopped, looking over his shoulder. "How's—" There was a question in Zach's voice, but he choked it off. He walked away without a word, and Max smelled the tears Zach wouldn't let him see. As if he'd sensed Zach's distress, Ryan materialized from around the corner and went to Zach's side. They walked away together.

GABE WAS TWENTY-SEVEN YEARS old, but he still had nightmares that sank their fangs and claws into him. He smiled so brightly and easily that sometimes Max forgot about the demons that lurked in his mind, waiting until he was vulnerable to strike. And strike they did.

Max slept in the living room, so he was the one who heard when Gabe kicked and thrashed, when he sobbed and whimpered. Max went to him—he couldn't stay away. Gabe had always done the same for him.

He would find Gabe covered in sweat and pale in the darkness, his pulse beating wildly and the blankets strewn all about him. He kicked and clawed, shredding the sheets under his claws. He snapped and snarled. He cried, breath hitching in his chest, whimpering for his father.

Max woke him with a touch, whispering to him, "Gabe. You're safe. I'm here. You're okay." He never woke quite the same way. Sometimes he clutched at Max, shaking so violently in his arms that Max feared he'd shatter to pieces.

Other times he woke with a vicious start, swinging at the darkness with his claws, fangs bared and eyes glowing. Those times there was a feral fury in his eyes and though Max feared in those brief seconds that Gabe was lost, he would recognize Max and Max would stay quiet while he collected himself.

Sometimes he was awake when Max went to him. He hated that the most. Max would find him completely silent and still, paralyzed. The smell of his fear was palpable. Max didn't touch him then. He would sit at the side of the bed, close but not too close, and let Gabe come to him. He knew when Gabe was ready for him by his arm wrapping around Max's waist, the touch of his clammy fingers on Max's hand.

Sometimes they whispered together in the dark. One night Gabe put his arms around Max and exhaled shakily. "It feels like he could strike at any time. Like he's just waiting for us to slip up. What we have could be gone so quickly."

Max took in a breath and tried not to show how much that thought terrified him. "We'll be ready for him and Richard."

Gabe shivered against him. "Nothing can happen to you, Max. Nothing."

Max kissed his cold fingertips. "Nothing will. I'm safe."

Max stayed with him until morning.

It wasn't long before Max migrated from the sofa bed to Gabe's bed. Not because Gabe couldn't sleep without him—many nights Gabe slept fine by himself—but because Max simply wanted to be close to him.

Gabe never asked him to go and welcomed Max to his bed with his arms around Max, his lips to Max's forehead. Then they'd fall asleep like that. Maybe they'd drift apart in the night but come morning, Max would wake with his face on Gabe's chest, their arms and legs and feet tangled beneath the sheets.

Waking up next to Gabe never failed to make Max smile. Gabe was the "picture of grace" with his cheek smooshed against the pillow, hair all askew, mouth hanging open, and drool puddling on the pillow. Max thought he must be truly smitten to find such a hilarious sight utterly endearing.

It was getting harder to imagine waking up alone.

"Hey." Gabe leaned in the bedroom doorway, hands in his pockets, head cocked, and shoulders back.

Max imitated his stance. "'Sup, bro?"

Gabe snorted, a bright smile breaking across his face. He shuffled from one foot to the other, worrying at his lower lip.

"What?" Max asked, chuckling at his nervousness.

Gabe rolled his shoulders. "Just thinking."

"About?" A smile tugged at Max's mouth.

Gabe's mouth twitched. "Stuff." He passed by Max, bumping their shoulders, and sat in the desk chair.

"What kinda stuff?"

"You and me," Gabe drawled. Max straddled him, knees on either side of Gabe's thighs. Gabe kissed his way up Max's neck, his stubble scraping Max's skin. Warm, inquisitive lips trailed up Max's jawline to his ear. Teeth took hold, nibbling gently. Max shivered, laughing quietly even as his balls tightened.

They'd been dating for about three weeks now. They hadn't had sex yet, but it had been a near thing. It was something they were building toward when they were ready. Max had been with a few guys before Gabe.

Things had never progressed farther than sloppy make outs and hand jobs. Max had kept himself too busy in school to really interact with guys that way and he couldn't remember wanting any of them this much.

Kissing Gabe, touching him... it was perfect, but Max couldn't deny he wanted more. It could wait, though. Sex sounded great, and sex with Gabe got him light-headed thinking about it. All that bare skin. His lean body. His tender, eager touches... He would be gentle and considerate. It was who Gabe was. Max knew he could trust him with his body and his heart.

"I want us to go out," Max said. He couldn't remember the last time he went on a date, if ever.

"Me, too," Gabe agreed. "Won't it be a buzzkill with a bodyguard tailing us?"

"We'll pretend he's not there." Max's mouth brushed Gabe's when he spoke, his voice a low, pleasant rumble that filled the space between them.

"I'm good at playing pretend. When do you want to go?"

"Tonight."

"What do you want to do?" Gabe wove his fingers through Max's hair.

Max dipped his head and devoted his attention to Gabe's exposed throat, kissing and licking and getting his scent thoroughly mingled with Gabe's. "Don't know. Whatever. We could see a movie. Go for a run in the park? I'm fine with anything." As long as they were together, but Max didn't say that aloud.

Gabe moaned quietly and Max furthered his efforts, pressing a deep kiss over Gabe's fluttering pulse. The scent of Gabe's arousal gave Max a thrill. *He'd* done that.

"Your ma still lives here. She's going to know exactly what you did to me."

"Shit. I didn't think of that. I might die of embarrassment." Max licked a line down Gabe's throat, stopping to nip his skin. "Guess you'll have to stop me."

Gabe chuckled, one hand curling around the nape of Max's neck. "Think I can deal with the embarrassment. I'd rather have your bite."

Max's fangs dropped before he could stop them. The wolf in him wanted to cover Gabe in his marks, claim him for all the world to see.

"Max?" The door opened. "Have you seen the—oh!" His mother averted her eyes.

Max jumped out of the chair and tripped on the carpet.

"My. I'm starting to feel like a third wheel around here." Smiling, Max's mother left them alone.

Gabe wore tight denim jeans and a plain white dress shirt for their date. He'd popped the buttons at the top to show off his collarbones, and the shirt had parted enough to tease a view of his firm chest. He'd waxed his chest, and it was smooth and probably as soft as velvet to the touch. His shoulder-length hair was put up in a bun, and his beard had been trimmed into a neat scruff.

Gabe's chest shouldn't have distracted Max nearly as much as it did, yet all he wanted to do was lick it.

Fuck.

Gabe's mouth curled into a truly sinful smile, and Max realized Gabe could smell the desire oozing from him. He must smell like a brothel.

"Ready to go?" Gabe asked, kind enough not to tease Max. Yet, anyway.

Max was. He'd dressed in jeans and his best pair of sneakers. He wore flannel over a plain white tee he'd ironed, even though he'd never ironed anything else in his life. "Yeah. Yes. Let's go." Damn it, why was he distracted by Gabe's silky-smooth chest?

Gabe took Max's hand and they walked out into the hall. Gabe had booked them reservations at an Italian restaurant, so Max bought them tickets to see an old monster movie at a theater in the Village. Max wasn't sure a crappy monster movie would hold up well to Gabe's dinner reservation, but Max's reasoning was that the plot would be so boring, they'd find much better use for their time in the back of the movie theater.

Their stoic bodyguard drove them to their destination.

"Making any plans for the future?" Gabe asked, his cheek on Max's hair. Max could see their reflection in the rearview mirror. It was surreal to see them there together, to see how dopey Max looked when he smiled. How content Gabe looked. To be reminded of the happiness Max had found. He hoped it lasted.

"Sort of," Max admitted, chin sagging to his chest. "At this rate, I might not get back into school by the fall. Which won't matter anyway if Richard and Stone aren't caught."

"They will be." Gabe squeezed his hand. "Any schools you're looking at?"

"Hunter College. Sarah Lawrence... I'm not sure. A lot. Too many." There were so many places he could go. It was overwhelming. And even if he did get in, he wasn't sure what he'd study. It was scary to be pushing forward when things were still so chaotic, but daring to dream of a future free of the cult was what Max needed right now.

Gabe squeezed his hand. "Yeah. It's crazy stressful. It'll be great when all that hard work finally pays off, though."

Max nodded, trying to imagine it but only spiraling more as he thought about what he might actually do when he finally got back into school. There were too many possibilities. He supposed he'd have to try a ton of them until he found something that fit.

The movie was predictably dull—zombies biting people, people screaming, and cheesy nineties effects. Max slid his hand over Gabe's warm thigh and smiled as a full-body shiver ran through Gabe's body. Max kept his focus fixated on the screen, the weight of Gabe's hungry eyes prickling over his skin.

As a zombie bit someone in the movie, Gabe leaned over and pretended to take a bite of Max, nipping his neck. Max laughed too loudly and slapped a hand over his mouth. Chuckling, Gabe smoothed his hand over Max's knee and cupped his inner thigh.

Gabe was much more interesting than the movie, with his tight jeans and billowy shirt, his hard chest, his hot mouth on Max's lips and neck, and his hands gripping and squeezing whatever part of Max he could find. Max was drunk off him, reckless with wanting. He thought the only reason things didn't escalate further was because a gaggle of noisy teens took up the seats in front of them.

They backed off then. Gabe's scent was spicy with arousal, but things went no further. Max's chest rose and fell quickly, his body running hot. Reaching over the armrest, Gabe took his hand, lacing their fingers together.

It was perfect.

DINNER WAS DELICIOUS. GABE ordered fettucine and Max ordered spaghetti and meatballs, and the chef turned those basic dishes into a phenomenal experience. With their guard shadowing them, they walked through Central Park together. Gabe swayed from his glass of wine, bumping into Max. Max chuckled, and Gabe hip bumped him deliberately.

Their guard gave them some privacy but stayed within earshot as they stumbled off the path. Gabe led Max into an open field and toward a shaded grove of trees. It was dark, far away from any streetlamps on the main path. It was easy to pretend they were in the wilderness.

There were a few beer bottles littering the ground that Max toed aside, the scents old and stale, and there was the unmissable odor of a used condom lying somewhere upwind.

Out of sight of prying eyes, Gabe unbuttoned his dress shirt and draped it over a tree branch. Max was mesmerized as moonlight glimmered over Gabe's fair skin. Gabe's lips quirked in a cocky smile, and he arched a brow. "Wanna go for a run?"

Max nodded, throat dry as Gabe unclasped his jeans and pulled down the zipper. Gabe paused, one thumb hooked in the waistband of his jeans as he met Max's gaze. Max's face ran hot. Before he could look away, Gabe pulled his jeans down slowly, toeing off his shoes, then kicking his jeans off. His legs were as fair and muscular as the rest of him, smattered with whorls of dark hair.

Max knew he should look away but he couldn't, and Gabe never asked him to, holding Max's gaze when he hooked his fingers in the elastic of his briefs. Max had never allowed himself to look, even though he'd seen Gabe naked before after a shift. He'd never really *seen* him. Not until tonight.

"You're gorgeous," Max said, voice breathy with longing.

"Not so bad yourself." Gabe scratched the back of his head, cheeks pink. Max took off his shirt and the warm summer breeze tickled his bare skin.

When he found the nerve to meet Gabe's amber eyes, they were dark and heavy-lidded. Heart thundering, Max looked away and noticed that Gabe's cock was showing interest in his nudity. Not that Max was any different.

Leaves crunched under Gabe's bare feet as he drew closer. Max dug his toes into the dirt, heart racing. Gabe reached for him, curling his fingers in Max's hair. Gabe's breath warmed his mouth, his lips smelling like Italian spices and red wine. Max wanted to taste him more than he wanted his next breath.

Before his eyes, Gabe shifted to his familiar black wolf. His amber eyes glowed, and he dropped into a play bow, growling happily. The wolf was in control. Grinning, Max undressed quickly and shifted too, his animal instincts filling him with the desire to run and chase his mate.

They ran through the trees together, pouncing on each other, nipping at heels, chasing squirrels, and howling together until Max's throat was sore.

Finally, when they were too exhausted to go on, they returned to their belongings. Locking away his animal mind and instincts was hard for a moment, but then he felt the warm pulse of Gabe's bond in his chest and found his way back to his human form.

When Max stumbled to his feet and looked up, Gabe was human before him. His skin was bare and beautiful under the moonlight. Max ached to touch him and took a step toward him.

But Gabe came no closer. His scent soured. Max's heart sank and he looked up, confused.

Gabe's expression was unreadable, but his scent was dark. He reached out to Max, gently pulling a leaf from Max's hair.

"You're perfect, you know?" Gabe murmured, a smile on his face. It was fragile and sad.

Max couldn't find the words to say how much he felt the same way about Gabe.

Gabe clasped Max's hand and tugged, urging him to sit as Gabe unfurled a blanket from his bag. He'd packed it in case the theater was too cold as they usually were in the summertime.

Max lay beside him, and they gazed at the moon together, hands touching in the space between their bodies. The moon glowed. In only a day or so, it would be a full moon.

Gabe gazed up at the stars. His scent soured with anxiety.

"Is everything okay?" Max asked.

"I'm just worried about everything stacked up against us. Stone. His cult." He exhaled, rough and shaky. "It's the prophecy. Max... I don't want to leave you alone."

Max shivered, suddenly unbearably cold.

"I saw what happened to my mother. After my father... How she grieved. How she broke into pieces. She was in so much pain, Max. No one could make it any better. She mourned him for a long, long time. She still does." Gabe's eyes glistened with tears. "How can I do the same to you?"

Max didn't know how to answer.

"Gabe," Max tried to say. He cleared his throat, fumbling for words. "No one's future is clear. Not even yours. You could still live."

"But there's a chance I might not. I couldn't mate with you and then leave you, Max." Gabe squeezed his hand tight. "I couldn't do that to you."

"And what if I left you first? If something happened to me? Do you see? Nothing's certain." Max swallowed the ache in his throat, weaving his fingers with Gabe's. "Whether we say goodbye when we're both old or weeks from now... I think what matters isn't how much time we have together, but what we do with it."

Gabe's eyes were dry now, and he gazed at Max like he was seeing a sunrise for the first time.

"You make me happy, Gabe. Right now, that's what I know."

"You, too," Gabe whispered, like a prayer.

Max smiled. "So, what do you want?" Max knew. Even in this storm of uncertainty, he knew.

Gabe inched closer, cradling Max's face in his hands. "You," Gabe said. "I want you, Max. For a night. A year. Forever." His breath tickled Max's lips.

"Okay," Max whispered. "That sounds... It sounds perfect."

Gabe leaned in and sealed their promise with a kiss.

The clouds glided over the moon, choking out the light, and to Max it seemed an omen of things to come.

CHAPTER 21

BLOOD MOON

BEN SAID, "WE FOUND the bastard. We found Rooks."

Gabe squeezed his phone so hard, he thought it would crack. "How?" he said through gritted teeth. His fangs were sharp in his mouth, his claws cutting into the desk.

"Someone recognized him from the wanted posters. Ugly mug like his is hard to forget. The creep was hiding out in Inwood Park."

Gabe lurched to his feet and paced, his hands balling into fists at his sides. His claws cut deep into his palms, the sharp stab of pain distracting him from his fury. The wolf wanted to hunt, wanted to shred flesh and crunch bone, lay his prey broken and bloody at his mate's feet and prove that no one would ever hurt him again.

"Wanna come and have a chat with him?" Ben asked.

"On my way," Gabe said. He hung up. His phone's screen was cracked down the middle from how hard he'd gripped it.

The door closed in the front hall. Gabe's heart stuttered.

"Gabe?" Max's voice was tense. He could sense Gabe's fury.

Gabe sucked in a deep breath, willing his heart to settle, the fury to evaporate. He couldn't worry Max. "Gabe?" Max poked his head into the office. The scent of cinnamon and chilis settled Gabe's nerves and he managed to smile.

"Everything okay?" Max asked, handsome face wrinkled in concern.

"They found Rooks." Gabe went to him, folding Max into his arms and parting his lips against Max's neck.

"Finally." Max shivered, angling his head so Gabe could suck and nip. His skin smelled so sweet today. It was the full moon's influence, and Gabe's wolf sang a song of *want* and *mate* and *mine, mine, mine*. A song Max answered, claiming Gabe's mouth with his.

The rage quieted. His wolf settled, content and happy.

"What's the plan?" Max asked.

"We'll interrogate him. Figure out where Stone is. Once we know, we'll shut his cult down for good." Vengeance was so close, Gabe could taste it. "It could all be over as soon as tonight."

"Does it have to be tonight?" Max's brow furrowed in worry. "There's a supermoon." Max wet his lips, his scent soured by anxiety. "It's more than that, Gabe."

"I know. I always keep track of the cycles." Gabe's stomach writhed. Tonight was a blood moon, just like the one in the prophecy predicting his death. "Tonight could be the night where Stone finally dies. Or... or where I..."

"You won't." Max gripped Gabe's face between his hands. "You'll be fine. You just need to be careful."

Gabe made himself smile. "I will, Max. You don't need to worry about me."

Max exhaled shakily. "How can I not? You could—"

"I won't." Gabe kissed him firmly. "Let's talk about something else."

Max nodded, but worry still furrowed his brow. "Okay. So, we'll kick Stone's ass and destroy the cult. If it's still dark out, we can go to the supermoon festival together," Max said, his tone light and eager. He curled his fingers in Gabe's hair, stroking slowly. Gabe closed his eyes, breathing in Max's scent.

"Sounds fun," Gabe said, sliding his fingers into the back pockets of Max's jeans and squeezing. Max exhaled, hot and pleasant against his neck. "How about we meet there tonight? We can slip away from the crowd.

Then, when we're still naked from our shift, I can get your back up against a tree. Bite you. Claim you till the whole forest hears you howling for me."

The spicy notes of Max's arousal left Gabe aching for him. He was hard against Gabe's thigh, and Gabe thought about how he'd looked beneath the moonlight last week when they'd lain in the park. His fair, freckled skin, those beautiful copper curls, his lean and slender body, his cock hanging between his milky thighs amidst whorls of ginger hair.

He was so looking forward to their mating, to exploring Max's body, worshiping every inch of him the way he deserved, but it was more than that. He wanted to wake up every day with Max. He wanted to watch Max find his dream job and go to his dream school, watch him graduate and see what he did with his life. He wanted to go on that journey with him, build their lives together.

Unless the prophecy came true. By the goddess, he hoped he didn't break Max's heart. He couldn't leave Max like his father had left his mother. Max had been through so much hurt, and Gabe wanted only happiness for him.

"If you're ready," Gabe added. The last thing he wanted was to rush their mating.

Max brushed his knuckles over Gabe's cheek. "I am. I'm so ready for you."

Gabe kissed him, a thousand *I love yous* rising to his lips.

He would tell Max tonight when they met beneath the supermoon. Not if. When.

John Stone wouldn't ruin this for them.

If anyone deserved to know he was loved, it was Maxwell Gallagher.

"Gabriel, I'm so happy for you."

Gabe's face warmed, his mother's voice light and happy in his ear through the phone.

"I must meet this Max!"

"You will, you will." Gabe would have loved to introduce them sooner. His mother was visiting family in Madrid.

"When is your mating ceremony?"

Gabe's face warmed. "We haven't decided yet. Soon, though." More traditional werewolves waited until after the ceremony to claim each other, but it wasn't unusual for the ceremony to be held after the mating.

"Are you nervous, mi sol?"

Gabe's stomach fluttered. "No. Yes. Maybe a little? I don't know. I keep wondering when he's going to open his eyes and realize I'm all kinds of wrong for him."

A roar of pain made him jump. Ben was having a "chat" with Rooks down in the agency's basement. It sounded quite productive if Gabe could hear it all the way up here.

"Ah, this reminds me of when your father proposed." His mother's voice was all dreamy through the speaker. "He wanted everything to be right, so he did all this research about how to propose to a human. He was so scared he'd chase me off."

Gabe checked the time on his phone. The moon would be rising now. "I thought I blew my chance, to be honest. I'm amazed he still wants anything to do with me."

"Do you love him?"

He tried to imagine never waking up next to Max, never kissing him or embracing him, living alone again. That sort of future was bleak and meaningless to him now. He couldn't fathom being alone again after knowing Max. "I do, Mamá."

"Then that's all that matters. Have a good time with him, Gabriel. Cherish him. And bring him over for dinner sometime. Tell me his favorite recipe."

Gabe laughed. "He loves filet mignon. I hope we can see you soon."

There came a growl from downstairs. Gabe tensed, his own snarl building in his throat.

"Is everything all right?"

Gabe hesitated. "Ma... You know I love you, right?"

She laughed softly. "Yes, of course, mi sol. I love you, too."

His eyes stung. If he was going to his death tonight, he needed her to know. He hadn't been able to tell his father. He cleared his throat. "Max and I will see you soon for dinner. Goodnight, Ma." He hung up and dried his eyes.

Izzie jogged out from around the corner. "Ready to kick this guy's ass?"

Gabe exhaled. "Yeah." He was feeling calmer after talking to his mother. It was why he'd called.

Izzie folded her arms before the basement door in a way that reminded Gabe of their mother right before a lecture. "You have to let me get at least one kick in."

Gabe cracked his knuckles in preparation. "Sure."

"Oh!" She clapped her hands. "How about I sit on him and hold him down while you kick him in the balls?"

Gabe widened his eyes at her. "Anyone ever tell you you're scary, Izzie?"

She flipped a lock of hair behind her shoulder. "Dad's death left me with a lot of unresolved anger. That's what my therapist said, anyway."

Gabe squeezed around her and the guard opened the door for them. He hesitated at the top of the stairs. Behind him, Izzie raised her brows expectantly. "We gonna kick his ass or what?"

Gabe wet his lips. Chained or not, Rooks was still a werewolf, and a fanatic at that. "How about you let me do most of the swinging? I need you here to keep me levelheaded." He needed to be in control if they were confronting Stone tonight.

Izzie glared. "So I'm supposed to stand by and look pretty while you do the dirty work? Because I'm a woman, or because I'm your baby sister?"

"Uh—"

"Fuck that, Gabriel." Izzie shoved him aside with her shoulder. "Gabe, don't make me sit this out. He hurt my friend, and he's working for the man who abducted you and killed our father." Izzie looked him square in the eye. In her anticipation, her claws were sharp, her facial features distorting as her wolf neared the surface. She stuck out a hand. "Suprema-cist-smashing siblings?"

Gabe sighed and tried not to smile. "Lose the dumb name." He clasped her hand and shook, and they descended the stairs. In their cells, feral wolves barked and snarled.

Ben panted, slamming the door to Rooks's cell. He eyed them narrowly. "He won't talk. You two wanna give it a try?"

Rooks's nostrils flared, and Gabe imagined he'd curse them out if not for the washcloth crammed in his mouth. Aside from the wolfish eyes, Rooks was still in his human form, tied to a chair with his arms bound in silver cuffs behind his back. His wolf was suppressed, and he was weak in this state.

"Hey, jerk," Izzie said, smiling as Rooks growled. "How are those bonds fitting? Good?"

Rooks growled, narrowing his eyes at her. The coppery scent of dried blood made Gabe's gums itch. An image burst in his mind—high school after hours, blood on the floor of the history classroom. The coppery taste in his mouth from where he'd bitten his lip. The smug grins of the werewolf boys surrounding him. They'd thought a hybrid couldn't fight worth shit, that hybrids were victims they could shove and insult in the hallways or at lunch. Gabe had proven them wrong.

How his mother had cried when she saw his bruises and cuts. How he'd scared her with his reckless antics, making her terrified she'd lose her only son on top of her husband. Guilt clenched like a fist in his stomach at the thought of what his mother might say to see him now. To see how little he'd changed from the hotheaded punk constantly getting into scrapes with hybrid-hating wolves. Gabe gritted his teeth and shook his head.

No. She'd understand, though she'd bristle knowing he'd brought Izzie into the same room as a hateful supremacist. It was the world that hadn't changed since his high school days. The world was full of bullies but not all of them grew out of their hateful ways. Sometimes they became like Rooks and Stone. Sometimes they stopped shoving and name-calling, and took lives.

This, this was justified. This wasn't for him. It was for hybrids everywhere. After tonight, after Rooks talked—because he would—the terror hanging over hybrids, hanging over *Max*, would be lifted. Gabe would finally find closure for his father's murder.

Ben opened the cell door for them. "Keep him alive until we get the information we need."

Gabe knelt, the tile cool against his knee. He ripped the gag from Rooks's mouth. "Where's Stone?"

Rooks curled his lip. "I didn't kill that friend of yours, did I?" Gabe thought he sensed apprehension in Rooks's gravelly voice.

"No," Gabe growled, curling his fingers. "You didn't. But Stone sure isn't gonna be happy with you when he finds out you almost killed his target."

Rooks's eyes widened as he looked away. Gabe lengthened his claws. "Hey. Eyes on me. I'm your problem right now. Not Stone."

Rooks sneered. "You're a hybrid. Weak. You can't hurt me."

Gabe yanked up his sleeve, baring his scars. "I think I know a thing or two about pain. You know what's good for you, you'll talk. Stone's not coming for you."

"You don't know—"

Izzie rammed her foot into Rooks's stomach. "Start talking."

"Tell me where Stone is or else."

Rooks sneered, coughing. He'd vomited on the pristine tile. "No, I'll never—"

Gabe raked his claws across Rooks's face. He howled, blood running in rivers from the gashes. Rooks's eyes widened when the wounds kept flowing, the silver negating his ability to heal.

The smell of blood burned Gabe's nose. His fangs lengthened, cutting into his lower lip. He willed the wolf back even as the sight of Rooks, bound and weak like prey, compelled him to rend flesh. No. He was better than this. "Tell me where he is, what he's planning," Gabe said through gritted teeth, a warning edge to his voice. He hoped that if he kept talking, he'd stay human.

"No! I'll never betray Stone. He ever finds out, he'll fucking kill me!"

Nose wrinkled in disgust, Izzie threw a hit at Rooks's face. His nose shattered with a crack and more blood pooled on the tile. The contrast with the white tile only made the crimson blood stand out in sharp relief. A growl curdled in Gabe's throat. Rooks coughed, choking on blood. He spat a mouthful onto the tile.

"Gonna have to do better," Rooks croaked, blood staining his teeth when he sneered. "Won't... won't break to some mutt. When I get outta here, I'll rip your throat out, hybrid bitch."

Gabe plunged his claws deep into Rooks's belly, sinking past soft flesh and hard muscle. Blood poured hot over his fingers. Rooks hunched into himself, spasming in agony.

"You won't hurt anyone again!" He'd had enough of these people, had enough of their vitriol and hatred. The world would be so much better if they died. He rocked the chair back and slammed Rooks's head against the wall, reveling in the crunch of his skull.

"Tell me!" Before he lost all reason, before he was beyond comprehending words.

Rooks clenched his teeth, seething through bloody nostrils. "When I get outta here, I'll make that redhead hybrid squeal. All of you will suffer at Stone's hands!"

The threat to Max, to his fucking *mate*, brought Gabe's wolf to the surface. Gabe snared Rooks's throat between his teeth. Rooks's pulse raced beneath Gabe's tongue. Fur grew thick on his arms and face. His clothes ripped and strained as his body tried to shift.

Ben grabbed Gabe's shoulder. "That's too far, Gabe! You're shifting!"

"North Brother!" Rooks shrieked. "The island! An old sanatorium! Stone is there!"

Izzie asked, "What's he planning? Talk!"

"A-An attack! He wants to... He wants to leave the island and round up more hybrids tonight!"

"When?" Izzie growled.

"Midnight! Midnight! Please, let go!"

Ben touched Gabe's shoulder. "Enough. We got our info."

Gabe growled around the flesh in his mouth, the taste so sweet he could hardly bear to relinquish his prize. His prey.

"Gabriel," Izzie said. "That's enough!"

Gabe panted hard through his nose, closing his eyes tight as he fought for control. The wolf wanted to kill. He had to stop.

Izzie grabbed the back of Gabe's neck and hauled him away from Rooks. She shoved him toward the door, away from the stench of blood.

"Gabe," Ben began, eyes wide in worry.

Gabe turned away and slammed a fist into the wall. Everything was falling apart. In five hours, it would be midnight. The big heart-to-heart with Max, their mating beneath the supermoon that he'd fantasized about—it would have to wait for another night.

Will there be another night? whispered a voice inside him. Dread clamped around Gabe's heart. Tonight he would face John Stone for the first time in fifteen years. One would rise while the other fell. Gabe swallowed with difficulty.

"It's happening." He panted. "The blood moon. The confrontation with Stone."

Ben shook his head. "You can't come, Gabe."

"No," Gabe snarled. "Don't you do this, Viejo. Don't you tell me to sit this one out."

"You could fucking die!" Ben slammed a fist against the wall. "I'm just supposed to let you go to your death?"

Gabe squeezed his hands into fists. Fuck, he was scared. Scared of dying. Scared of leaving Max, his friends, and his family. "I have to do this. No matter how it may end, I have got to see this through. Just..." A lump rose in his throat. "If anything happens to me—"

"Gabriel." Izzie gripped his shoulders. "You are not dying tonight. I swear to the goddess, if you break Max's heart like that, if you break our mother's heart—I'll kill you myself." Blinking hard, she turned on her heel.

BEN HAD INVITED EVERYONE to the agency headquarters to celebrate the supermoon and to prepare for the assault on North Brother Island. In a short while, they would leave for the docks and take boats to the island. Gabe, Zach, Ryan, and Izzie had been training in the courtyard, getting their bodies ready to fight. They met Max inside the dining hall where he and a few others listened to Ben give a rousing speech.

"Tonight," Ben declared from the staircase, "we end the Moonborn's reign of terror over New York. We will never get back the lives the Moonborn cut so short, but we can make sure no hybrids are ever hurt again."

Cheers and howls filled the room. Gabe stayed silent, feeling sick with anticipation.

The supermoon hung low in the sky, staining the ocean blood red. Gabe had a good view from the dining hall window. It would have looked better in Central Park's Sheep Meadow, where the supermoon festival was usually held. The agency was doing their part to celebrate, with supermoon-themed drinks at the bar. It was hard to be festive when he wasn't sure he'd be alive in a few hours.

Ben walked by and patted his shoulder. "Quit sulking around, kid." Ben led him to the bar selling vodka martinis with coconut cream and sangrias made with Blue Moon Belgian ales. Gabe chose a martini, enjoying the coconut piece carved to look like a moon decorating the rim of the glass. Normally he wouldn't drink, but what the hell? He might die tonight. Ben ordered a sangria and they sat side by side on the barstools.

"Ready to face Stone tonight?" Ben asked.

"You gonna let me?" Gabe arched a brow, challenging him.

Ben sighed. "I keep forgetting you and Izzie are grown-ups. I remember when she was a pup. When you were traumatized after your father's death."

Gabe took a swallow of his drink. "I stopped being a kid after he died, Ben. I've been ready for a long time." He didn't sound so convincing, his mind torn between Max and Stone.

"All right, you gotta tell me what's got you lookin' so pathetic," Ben said.

Gabe took a sip of his martini. Coconut danced across his tongue, softening the burn of the vodka.

A smile tilted Ben's mustache and he glanced in Max's direction where he sat talking to Ryan over a mocktail. "Your angst wouldn't have anything to do with a certain redhead, would it?"

His cheeks warmed. "He's got everything to do with it."

Ben chuckled and took a drink. "Congrats. If he can make your cheeks turn the color of a smacked bottom, he's good for you."

Gabe choked on his drink and coughed as the vodka hit him. "Fucking hell, Ben." Ben thumped him on the back. Once he recovered, Gabe sputtered, "You're not even surprised, are you?"

"I had a feeling, that day you told me how happy his scent made you."

Gabe gaped. How had Ben figured out his own feelings before Gabe had?

Ben chuckled. "When their scent makes you forget everything bad that's happened to you, that's when you know."

Gabe's face warmed. "He smells... damn, like so much. All good. It brings back good memories." He should have known the very first day he'd caught that scent. The feeling of joy Max's scent stirred in him was more powerful than anything he'd ever felt. "He has chosen me. He's told me. But... I can't wrap my head around it. Why me of all people? I keep thinking there's gotta be someone better."

Ben drained the last of his sangria. "I'll tell you a story, kid. A bit of a lesson in here for you. I was mated to a woman named Heather. We split." Ben took a long drink.

"We're still close, and I care for her, but she was never my fated mate. Anyone can be your mate, but only one person will be your fated mate. You'll know the minute you find the one you're fated for. It's like... Hell, I don't know, it's instantaneous. If you share a special scent, it's a sign from the goddess that no matter the obstacles, you two were made for each other."

"Yeah. I think I know what you mean," Gabe said with a smile. "So, who was your fated mate?"

Ben stiffened. He stared into his drink, his gray eyes stormy. Setting his drink aside, he grabbed a crumpled pack of Marlboros from his pocket. Ben lit up the cigarette and took a deep drag, exhaling smoke. "A human. His name was Isaac."

Gabe gaped. "Wait, you're gay? Viejo, why didn't you tell me?"

Ben's mouth twitched beneath his brown-and-silver mustache. "You know bisexuals are a thing, right?"

Gabe winced. "Right! Of course, I—never mind. What happened to him?"

Ben dragged on his cigarette, eyes closed tight as if trying to lose himself in the smoke. Gabe wondered if he knew how much sorrow showed in his face when he mentioned this human man. Sighing out a cloud of smoke, Ben said, "Hell if I know. I don't even know if he's still alive. He disappeared... oh, years ago."

"Where'd he go?" Gabe had never seen this side of him before.

"I still don't know," Ben said, his voice clipped, his eyes hard around the edges, "and I've stopped trying to figure us out. Point is, no one else has come close, and none of my relationships have lasted. I'm done with mates. It's not for me. So here's some advice from a lonely old fool: if you think Max is it for you, don't let him go. Otherwise, you're gonna find yourself alone at forty-seven years old, wishing you'd chased after him."

Gabe's throat tightened. He'd had no idea about Ben's past relationships. "What did your mate smell like? Isaac, I mean."

Ben's gruff mask slipped, a sliver of pain leaving his eyes bright. "Like the pavement after a rainstorm…" He blinked, jaw tightening. "Doesn't matter. He's gone, and that's fine by me. I've got enough on my plate. You, my sons, the LPA… I've got all I want."

Gabe didn't believe him. He wished he could say something to take away the hurt. "That's rough. I'm sorry."

Ben curled his lip around his cigarette. "The only thing you should be sorry for is that you're still sitting here."

He was right, and Ben's story had helped steel his resolve. If Gabe met his end tonight at Stone's claws, then at least he would die knowing he'd had a shot at happiness with Max no matter how long it lasted. He squeezed Ben's shoulder. "Thanks, Ben."

"No problem." He grabbed Gabe's shoulder before he could go. "Do yourself a favor, Gabe. When Max tells you he loves you, believe him." There was a look in Ben's eyes that reached into Gabe's soul. "I don't know what that… beast told you, what parasitic thoughts he infected you with. But he was wrong, on all counts."

Gabe swallowed, suddenly at a loss for words. He clasped Ben's shoulder and held tight. It was hard to tell himself Ben was right in the same way it was hard to trust that he and Max would get their happy ending.

But tonight he'd try and tell himself the scars on his skin were just that, scars and nothing more. Not a death sentence or a definition of who he was or a presage of the kind of life he was destined to lead. He was more than his scars. Max seemed to think so; he'd chosen Gabe for who he was. Gabe would have to believe him.

Breathing in deep, Gabe motioned for Max to follow him away from the crowd. They stepped outside and sat on the steps.

"Where's Kendra?" Gabe asked.

"She heard Luke was short-staffed in the clinic. She wants to assist in any way she can in case people come back injured."

"That's nice of her," Gabe said.

Max turned his face toward the moonlight. He smiled, but it didn't reach his eyes. "I feel so at home here."

"Yeah?" Gabe nestled close, hoping Max didn't feel his arm tremble as he slipped it over his shoulders.

Max nodded. "You guys are the family I never thought I'd find." He swallowed, blinking fast. "I can't lose you, any of you..."

Gabe's throat tightened. "Max, no matter what happens to me tonight, I..."

Max shook his head, lips thin. "Don't. This isn't how it's supposed to be. So don't you dare." Gabe held his breath, transfixed by the fire in those honey orange eyes. Max bumped their foreheads together, eyes fixed on Gabe's. He kissed Gabe hard on the mouth, clutching Gabe's face between his hands. "You're coming back from this. And then we'll talk. Okay?"

Gabe's lips trembled when he smiled. "Yeah. Okay."

CHAPTER 22

TO HUNT A MOONBORN BEAST

"I'M COMING, TOO," MAX said, following Gabe and Ben to the car. Their other packmates were climbing into their vehicles. Several other agency wolves were preparing to leave as well, armed with silver weapons.

Gabe's heart sank at the thought. "No! It's too dangerous."

Anger hardened Max's eyes. "Richard's with them. I'm stronger than I used to be. I want to face him."

Gabe gripped Max's shoulders. "Absolutely not! The cult wants you dead, Max! I can't let you walk into there!"

"And I don't want to stay here while you guys get hurt because of a mess I dragged you into!"

"Enough!" Ben's booming voice silenced Gabe's retort. "The cult needs to be stopped. The LPA will handle this, Max. Go home."

Max's eyes went wide with disbelief. Gabe felt guilty, but it was for the best. "Max, the minute it's over, I'll come and find you."

Max's lips trembled. He fisted Gabe's shirt and pulled him into a kiss fueled by urgency. Gabe's arms flew around his slender shoulders, bringing Max as close as he could. His fangs came out, nibbling at Max's lower lip.

A shiver ran through him as Max clasped the back of his neck. Gabe's body burned for him as their lips parted, tingling from Max's kiss.

271

"Promise me." Max's eyes gleamed with unshed tears.

Throat tight, Gabe nuzzled into Max's neck, his lips seeking that spot between his neck and shoulder. "If you're waiting for me, mi amor, I will always come back." He couldn't die, not when there was a future awaiting them.

Ben coughed loudly behind them. "Wrap it up, kids."

Gabe brought his lips to Max's once more, tracing his jawline with his thumb, trying to memorize every detail of Max's face through touch alone. Words pressed into his throat, words he was so afraid to say aloud in case it was the last time. He swallowed them, turned away, and took a step toward the car. Then he stopped, Max's eyes burning into his back.

No. He wouldn't walk away from the truth. So much was already spiraling out of control. He wouldn't let John Stone steal tonight from them.

Gabe turned around and before Max could say a word, Gabe took Max's face in his hands and kissed his lips. Gabe caught his breath, unable to wipe the smile from his face as he gazed into the honey orange of Max's eyes.

"What did you call me?" Max whispered, voice hoarse and low.

Face warming, Gabe pressed his lips to Max's and smiled. "Mi amor. My love."

Max's breath hitched and despite the tears in his eyes, a quavering smile bloomed across his face.

Gabe ran his thumbs over Max's cheekbones, his jawline, and his lower lip, memorizing the shape of Max's face down to his very bones. "I love you, Max." Gabe had worried for hours, agonized over those three words—How to say it? When to say it?—and all his worries had amounted to nothing.

"I love you, and I'm coming back." Gabe pressed their foreheads together, squeezing the nape of Max's neck.

Ben cleared his throat, suddenly interested in his toes. "Gabe, we gotta go," he said gently.

Gabe managed a smile, even though he wanted to break apart as he released Max from his arms. He didn't let himself look back as he followed Ben to the car and leaped into the passenger seat.

"Gabe!" Max's voice echoed behind him and he ran after the car as Ben raced up the street. Gabe whirled around, craning his neck to stare out the rear window as the distance swallowed Max up. Tears nipped at his eyes, and he quickly looked away from the window.

"Damn. Think you guys gave me a toothache," Ben muttered. "Chin up, kid. We're not going there to die."

Gabe's heart raced with anticipation. Every minute, every second since his father's death had led to this very moment. He felt each and every scar across his body more keenly than ever before. The wounds burned, reminding him of the knife against his skin and that hateful, sunken face and long, stringy hair, those animal eyes with their irises blazing yellow against sclera black as tar.

Mommy and Daddy aren't coming for you, Gabriel. They left you here with me. We're going to have fun together, you and me.

But Gabriel Reyes wasn't a scared little boy anymore, defenseless against his tormentor. His lips pulled back, fangs puncturing his lower lip in his fury. Tonight John Stone would taste the wrath of the very monster he'd created the moment he'd torn Gabe's father out of his world. He'd die before Stone hurt anyone he loved ever again.

They drove through island greenery and arrived at the waterfront. The agency wolves departed their vehicles and marched for the piers where the agency moored boats for water rescue scenarios. Ryan sounded the horn on his boat as Ben and Gabe made their way to the docks. Ben boarded the boat and Gabe followed, swaying on his feet as the boat rocked.

"Hey, guys! Good night for a boat trip, huh?" Ryan called from the cabin. Izzie huddled under a blanket, clutching her stomach. She was too queasy to greet Gabe.

"Looks like Zach's here," Ben said, looking back toward the dock.

Zach pulled up in his car and stepped out. The back door closed, and Max and a few other agents walked out from around the side of the car.

"Max!" Gabe exclaimed. "You can't be here!"

"Well, I am. You aren't facing this threat without me." Max boarded the boat with Zach.

"Zach, what the hell, man?" Ben rounded on him. "It's too dangerous for Max to be here."

Zach raised both hands. "Ben, come on. He's pack, too, isn't he? It isn't fair to make him wait back at HQ worried about us."

Ben sighed. "Too late to send him back now. Just stay close to us, okay?"

Max took Gabe's hand. "This is my fight, too. I need to face Richard. I need to know he's gone."

Gabe squeezed Max's hand tight. If anything happened to him...

Ben clapped Max's shoulder as he passed. "Ryan, full speed ahead!"

It was a long ride to the island but eventually North Brother materialized through the fog. Smokestacks peered from above a forest of untamed trees, and a dilapidated pier awaited them, covered in slimy moss and bird droppings. A few boats rocked in the harbor, no doubt used by the Moonborn in their comings and goings from the island.

They pulled up to the dock and one by one they climbed out. More agency boats docked, and soon the shore was full of wolves hungry for Moonborn blood.

Gabe sniffed the air and the hairs on the back of his neck stood up. The stench of old sour urine stained the air. Wolves had prowled this pier and recently, judging by the fresh smell of piss and scat. Old blood had seeped into the wood over time, but Gabe couldn't tell what it was from. Gulls cried overhead as they ventured into the forest, where the treetops were so overgrown they blocked out the sky.

The agency wolves surrounded Ben. He addressed them in a low rumble. "Spread out. Turn this island upside down. If you see any Moonborn, kill them. We're not here for chitchat. Let's end their reign of terror here and now!"

The hunt began.

Gabe's heart thundered, and he squeezed Max's hand. "Stay close to me."

"I won't leave your side," Max murmured, touching their shoulders together.

Gabe squared his jaw. "Let's do this."

Ryan punched the air. "Let's kick their asses!"

Zach chuckled at his enthusiasm.

Ben led the way into the forest. Gabe, Izzie, Max, Zach, and Ryan followed. The other wolves formed small groups and split off. Gabe jumped as Izzie flew forward, colliding into his back. "You okay?"

"The ground is so uneven," she stammered.

Roots snapped and cracked under their feet, waiting to trip anyone who wasn't watching their footing, and Ben stumbled a couple of times as they neared the crumbling ruins of the sanatorium. The brickwork was stained with moss, and part of the wall had collapsed, flooding the entranceway with wood and bricks.

Gabe sniffed, disappointed when he realized the scent of wolves was old here. "No one lives in this dump. Not worth the hassle of moving in."

Zach motioned ahead. "What about over there?"

A crumbling smokestack reached above the trees. Ben led the way forward, sniffing as he went. "Smells are stronger this way," he declared. Gabe and the others followed him.

The roots sprawling across the ground gave way to concrete, as if telling them they were on the right path. The scents of wolves congregated around a building with crumbling smokestacks devoured by ivy. The shattered windows revealed only darkness. Unlike the previous ruin, the scents of other wolves dominated the area along with fresh urine and shit, warning away any who might trespass.

Something crunched under Gabe's boots. The empty eye sockets of a bird skull stared up at him. This condemned ruin was the wolves' lair.

"We found them," he murmured through his fangs.

Ben shouldered forward, the whites of his eyes turned black, and his eyes blazed. "Let's go."

Gabe stalked Ben's heels, following him through the doorway. Old floorboards creaked precariously. A stairwell led up to the second floor. More bones cracked under his feet and as his eyes adjusted, he counted wing bones, skulls, and rib cages. Feathers scattered the floor, flying up and away from their feet. The smell of wolf was so potent here, Gabe felt as if Stone were standing in this very room with them.

Izzie gasped as above their heads there came the scraping of what sounded like claws on the floor. The ceiling creaked, dust scattering as if something were moving upstairs. Gabe peered up into a hole in the ceiling where jagged bits of wood emerged like ribs bursting from a grisly wound.

Something growled, and as Gabe looked around, he realized it wasn't any of his companions. Yellow eyes glimmered in the darkness above like embers in a fire. Fangs gleamed as a black wolf emerged from the shadows, snarling down at them. A growl rumbled from their left and the stairs creaked as another wolf materialized from the dark, then another, gliding easily through a hole in the wall from the outside.

Gabe gripped Max's arm and held tight, baring his fangs as the wolves advanced on them. One by one, Gabe and his friends pressed in close, forming a tight circle as the wolves drew closer. The ground shuddered under their feet, the floorboards bowing. Gabe dropped to the floor, all the wind knocked out of him as one of his legs plunged through the boards. His fall made the other floorboards creak and shudder.

Then he was falling, dust rising around him in a cloud as he landed. He sucked in air and only breathed in dust, coughing and blinking harshly as he stood, surrounded by total darkness.

"Gabe!" Max cried.

There came snarling and snapping from above. Upstairs, a wolf howled and from afar more howls answered as the Moonborn readied themselves for a fight.

"Max!" He had to find a way out. The pack was fighting without him. He blinked, eyes adjusting to the dark. A single rolling bed stood in a corner, straps dangling down to the floor. Rusty surgical tools lay where they'd been left long ago, perfectly in place beside the operating table as if waiting to be used any day now.

A bone snapped behind him. Gabe whirled around and a blur tore from the shadows toward him, clutching a syringe. A sharp stab of pain cut into his neck, and his flesh burned. *Silver! Oh fuck!* He stumbled, and the ground came rushing toward him.

Stay awake. Stay awake. You'll die, you can't—

Gabe's vision blurred as a figure loomed over him, eyes glowing in the dark. A cold hand that smelled of dust and plaster gripped his chin. Pointed teeth gleamed, and hot breath that smelled of rotting meat blasted his face. Long strands of hair tickled him.

Then a hand gripped his leg and pulled. Gabe's eyes rolled back as his head struck a brick. He was lifted over a hard, bony shoulder and carried. Dread erupted through his stomach as he was laid down on something hard. The bed?

Oh fuck. No, no, no, move! Do something!

His arms were pinned at his sides, and something stretched tight across his chest. The straps. He could hardly draw in a breath in this seemingly airless room, but with the straps across his body, it felt like his chest was caving in. Someone was humming.

The dizziness subsided slowly.

"Hello, Gabriel."

The voice—deceptively soft and pleasant—reached a cold hand deep in his chest. All the fight went out of him. It was the voice of a monster. Suddenly, he was a boy again, trapped in a dark room where no one could find him. Where nothing existed except pain and fear. But he wasn't alone. The monster visited him. He brought knives, but sometimes he used his bare hands to hurt, those cold hands that always smelled of dirt and blood.

Sometimes he called Gabe's parents. He'd tell them, "This is for bringing hybrid scum into this world." Then he let them listen as Gabe screamed until his throat was raw, begged them to come and find him, to help him. He didn't believe they would. He thought he would stay in the darkness forever, at the mercy of Stone's cruelty.

But his father had come, and to this day, Gabe wished he hadn't. He'd carried Gabe from that dark, painful room into the forest above. They'd crossed a river swollen with rainfall. There was the crack of gunfire and his father had disappeared beneath the river's roaring currents.

Then there'd been an empty seat at their table. His mother had cried when she'd thought they were still asleep. His father had never walked through the door again, arms wide open and waiting, never come in before bed to kiss him goodnight.

He was gone. A monster had taken him away, and Gabe had been powerless to stop it.

But Gabriel Reyes wasn't a helpless boy, not anymore. He was bigger, stronger, and he'd kept himself alive for this day when all he'd wanted to do after his father's death was die.

John Stone stepped from the shadows, his unnaturally wide and baggy eyes gleaming in the dark. The years hadn't been kind to him; shadows pooled in his gaunt face, which was consumed by an overgrown beard, and tendrils of long greasy hair swayed with each step he took. He came closer, overgrown toenails scraping against the floor, the whites of his eyes consumed in black. He was lost to his inner animal, kept human only by his hate.

No, it was an insult to compare Stone to an animal. An animal could be taught loyalty, kindness, and respect. The most rabid of wolves had more decency in a single claw than Stone.

"Did you miss me, Gabriel?" Stone's dirt-encrusted fingernails screeched over the metal tray, fingers settling on a rusty knife. "I missed you. I was so lonely when you left. There was so much more I wanted to teach you."

Stone held the knife up. It was sharp, like he'd been tending to it, anticipating its use. Dread left him in a cold sweat as the tip of the blade ran across his shirt, prickling against the bare skin of his collarbone and gliding cold over his throat.

"Do you know why hybrids are inferior to pure-blooded wolves?"

He'd asked that very question the day Gabe had awoken in a strange room, away from his bedroom, away from his family. Gabe gritted his teeth, his breath coming in short quick puffs as the blade settled below his chin. He hated that he knew the answer.

"They bleed," Stone said and with a swift jerk of his hand, burning pain sliced into Gabe's cheek. His own blood ran hot down his skin.

Gabe gnashed his teeth as with each word, more shallow cuts opened across his skin, one across his chest, the other across the bridge of his nose. He seethed through clenched teeth, his heart hammering to escape his chest, yet he was paralyzed.

Upstairs, pained howls and snarls echoed. Ben and the others were distracted. Gabe was on his own.

The cold blade of the knife scratched across the corner of his mouth. Stone's wide eyes kept him rooted in place, like a rabbit under the crazed eyes of a hunter. "Your blood is impure. You've been tainted by a human. You dare defile this gift given to us by the goddess. You are unworthy of her blessing. You should die like the mutt you are, but to be honest, this is a good look for you, Gabriel."

He leaned over, greasy strands of hair tickling Gabe's face like the legs of a spider. Stone took in one long, deep sniff and exhaled in a gratified sigh. "The smell of your fear is so lovely. You're still such a good, obedient boy. How much more can I break you, I wonder? There's so much we can explore together."

A wave of horror washed over him and brought him to life. Gabe thrashed, trying to free himself. "You always did have some fight in you. So stubborn, the way you refuse to acknowledge your inferiority." He pressed his knife down against Gabe's throat. "By the time I'm done with you, you will beg. You will scream. You will bend to me. And only then will I kill you."

Something slammed into a door somewhere in the room. The ceiling rattled, and dust cascaded from above. With another slam, the door hurtled open, and Max stumbled into the room.

Gabe lunged, straining at the bonds. "Max! No! Get out of here!"

Max's eyes blazed in fury. "Get the hell away from him!"

A grin split Stone's face in two. "My special little red wolf. I was hoping you'd show up." He snapped his fingers.

From the shadows behind Max, two clawed hands pierced the darkness.

"Max!" The scream tore at Gabe's throat.

Max flew backward, razor claws leaving dimples in his throat. Richard was even more wolflike than when Gabe had last fought him, his face covered in dark fur, his fangs long and sharp.

"Good." Stone reached a clawed hand behind his back, lifting the back of his shirt to reveal the hilt of a dagger, the runes upon the hilt pulsing like dying stars. "Hold him steady."

A snarl rumbled in Gabe's chest. He ripped into the leather straps with his claws, freeing himself. Stone had already taken his father and destroyed his family—he wasn't taking Max. Gabe locked eyes with him, and something quelled the fear in Max's eyes.

For a moment, Gabe swore Max's eyes went from a fiery honey orange to the silver of pale moonlight. The wooden beams in the walls groaned, and the bricks rattled. Gabe lurched off the table and struggled to breathe as sudden pressure held him down. Stone grunted, knees buckling. He dropped the dagger to the ground. Richard stumbled and collapsed on top of Max.

A deafening crash came from above. The wolves fighting upstairs yelped in alarm.

"Get out!" Ben roared. "The building's coming down!"

Stone bolted, thundering up the stairs. Max tried to stand but stumbled and fell against the wall. His face was paler than usual and shiny with sweat, as if he was ill. As another shudder racked the building, Max collapsed, appearing too weak to even hold himself up.

"Richard!" Stone roared over the groaning and creaking of the building. "Grab him!"

"No way!" Richard shoved Max aside and tore up the stairs. "Not dying for some hybrid!"

The building shuddered again, debris raining down in a corner of the room. Max ran to his side and grabbed his hand, yanking him to his feet. Gabe tore up the stairs with Max as the ceiling crashed down and filled the basement behind them. Stone's wolves yelped in pain and fear as they fell through the ceiling and into the basement.

Ben and the others waited for them up above. The front doorway was flooded with debris. Stone and Richard had already fled the building.

Ben pushed himself up. "We need to find a way out before they escape!"

They tore through the remains of a cafeteria. The walls shuddered and the roof came crashing in behind them as they entered the room, sealing them in. Gabe leaped over a fallen table and landed beside Izzie, taking her hand in his as he led her farther into the room.

"The hell?" Ryan yelped, eyes wide as he looked left and right. "Where's the way out?" There was a single window, high up but accessible.

Ben knelt, hands open. "Go, I'll boost you!"

Ryan ran toward Ben and stepped into his hand. Ben boosted him up and Ryan grabbed the windowpane and clawed his way outside. One by one, they climbed out the window. Zach helped Gabe stand and they took in their surroundings.

Wolves howled in fear within the ruined sanitorium, trapped and soon to be dead. Gabe might have felt bad for them, meeting such a terrible death, if they weren't all supremacist assholes. Gabe sniffed the air, scenting Richard and Stone. "They're heading for the water."

Ben grimaced. "They must have a boat. We've gotta get to ours and see if we can catch up."

Gabe growled, "We will catch up!" He wasn't letting Stone go. He didn't care what happened to himself. They ran as the sanitorium collapsed behind them with a deafening crash, shaking the earth and filling the air with the smell of dust. They returned to the docks and boarded their boat. It listed from side to side as the pack piled in.

"Look!" Izzie pointed east. The lights of a small boat glimmered on the water as it departed from the island.

Ryan howled. "Grab on, ladies and gents!" He unmoored them from the dock and the motor roared as they took off after Stone and Richard, skipping over the small waves. The boat ahead of them sprayed them with river water as Ryan steered their boat right up behind them.

There was enough lighting on board to make out Richard, who was steering the boat, a handful of Stone's pack who'd managed to get out in time, and Stone, the runes on his dagger glowing in the dark.

"On my count," Ben began, but Gabe wasn't waiting. He charged, leaping from Ryan's boat toward Richard's. He hung suspended for a moment, river spray cold on his face and waves rolling by beneath his feet, then flew toward Stone, his claws lengthening and fangs sharp.

Gabe's claws fastened in Stone's back, tearing through flesh to the bone beneath. Stone yowled as they rolled over. Stone's claws tore at the boat's flooring, blood dripping as he rose. He'd always looked so big, so indestructible.

But as Gabe found his feet, he towered over Stone. He'd made the monster bleed. He was nothing but a gangly sack of bone and flesh hiding behind fangs and claws. The wolves crammed into the boat howled in delight as Stone and Gabe circled.

With a crash, Max and the rest of the pack landed in the boat beside him. Ryan remained at the helm of his boat and sounded the horn.

Gabe whirled toward Max, shouting, "Go back!"

Max snarled in Richard's direction. "This is my fight, too!" He came to stand beside Gabe and took his hand, Max's steady in his.

Stone brandished the dagger. "You can't stop what's coming, Gabriel!"

A roar echoed over the open water. Richard had shifted, his enormous black wolf prowling toward Max while another of Stone's people took the helm. Stone's pack surrounded the agency wolves. Gabe released Max's hand and Max turned until his back pressed against Gabe's. The pounding of Max's heart fell into sync with his own.

With a howl, Ben led the charge. The change came over Gabe and he shook off the tattered remains of his clothes. He flew forward as a wolf, claws tearing at the floor. Stone sprang toward him in a blur of black fur. His fangs tore into Gabe's side, ripping away fur and flesh. Gabe pinned Stone beneath him, driving his fangs into Stone's neck.

Stone plowed his paws into Gabe's ribs, claws shredding his skin. Gabe tumbled over, paws slipping on the slick deck. Richard advanced on him, lips pulled back from his gleaming fangs. Max charged, leaping atop Richard's back and driving his fangs into the back of his neck.

The pair thrashed, entangled, until Richard was on top, but then Max threw Richard off him. Max snarled, and waves crashed against the boat, spilling in over the sides and soaking the floor. Richard shook himself free of the water and tackled Max. Gabe ran to assist him, but Stone hurtled into Gabe's path, his fur bristling.

Stone and Gabe collided. Stone's paw caught Gabe across the snout, scraping away the thin skin across his nose. His claws slashed across Stone's face, ripping out a clump of fur and strips of skin. Blood welled in Stone's eye, spattering across the ground as he stumbled away, yelping and pawing at his face.

Stone's people shouted in alarm. Stone turned, ears flattening. Gabe looked where Stone was staring and his heart sank. An enormous wave towered over the boat. Gabe didn't know how it was possible, but it sure looked real enough.

Stone shifted into a man and lunged, wrenching one of his own men away so he could grab onto the boat's mast.

"Gabe, Max!" Ben's voice echoed as Ryan pulled up beside Stone's boat. "Hurry up and get over here!"

Max yelped as Richard crushed him to the ground, pinning him. Stone grinned at the horror that must be plastered on Gabe's face. Croaky laughter crawled from Stone's throat. "Seems you have a choice, Gabriel. Who will it be? Me, revenge for your poor, poor daddy? Or the boy?"

Gabe didn't have time. He could only drag one of them off the boat and as the wave cast its shadow over them, he didn't have time to think—but he didn't have to. He rammed into Richard and bowled him off Max. Gripping Max's scruff in his teeth, he hoisted Max to his paws and nudged him toward Ryan's boat.

Max shifted and jumped across but barely made it, grabbing onto the railing and struggling to pull himself aboard. Ryan grabbed Max's arms, and Izzie reached out for Gabe. "Jump!"

Gabe hesitated for a second too long, water sloshing over his paws. He'd promised his father he would catch John Stone, that he wouldn't allow him to hurt anyone else. But he'd promised Max he'd come back alive.

Stone flew past Gabe, feet leaving the boat as he sprang, soaring toward Max. The dagger gleamed in the moonlight, clutched in Stone's fist and raised high over Max's back.

No. Never again would this man hurt someone he loved. Gabe charged. Gabe's paws left the ground, waves roaring beneath his claws. Gabe's fangs found the back of John Stone's neck and fastened in. Then the wave broke over Gabe's back, crashing over him and Stone. Stone grabbed onto Gabe, clinging as Gabe was sucked down into the depths of the river.

Gabe shifted beneath the water, weightless in the deep blue depths. The cold numbed him, the water pressing into his ears and muting all sounds except his own grunts as he struggled to hold his breath. He kicked and clawed but the pressure from the passing wave was too strong to fight.

Stone's eyes glowed in the darkness. Gabe dragged his claws across Stone's face, and beads of blood drifted up into the water around them. Stone struggled to break free, and his foot rammed into Gabe's stomach. Gabe grunted as the air was pushed from his lungs, and water rushed in.

He thrashed, choking, and Stone let him go. The other man swam for the surface, slipping beyond Gabe's reach.

So this was how it ended. This was how he died. He'd promised Max. He'd promised his father. The moon glowed big and bright.

A shape drifted in front of the moon, the water rippling around him. Someone swam toward him silhouetted by the supermoon, hair drifting around their head. The moonlight glimmered on a freckled face and twinkled in fiery locks. Max seized Gabe's arms and hauled him in close, and then they rose toward the surface.

Halfway there, Gabe's vision narrowed, going black at the corners. Then his head broke the surface of the water. Gabe tried to suck in air and choked on the water in his lungs.

"Gabe." Max panted, coughing. "Gabe, hang on. You self-sacrificing ass, don't you dare die!" Max's voice shook, and he coughed as a small wave crashed over his head.

More waves lapped at them, and they paddled toward their boat. The wave had overturned it, but the rest of the pack was clambering on top. Arms went around Gabe and hauled him from the icy depths of the river. Gabe collapsed on the solid surface, still trying to suck in air. The ache in his head receded and he concentrated on breathing.

"You're all right, Gabe. We're here." Max knelt beside him, pale flesh riddled with goosebumps, hands shaking as he rubbed Gabe's shoulders. Max's teeth chattered through his clenched jaw, lips quaking as he glared out over the water. He was pissed. Gabe followed his stare.

Richard's boat rocked from side to side, but it was still afloat. The bodies of a few of Stone's men floated on the surface of the water. What had become of Stone and Richard? Were they dead? Gabe had to know and tried to sit up but Max yanked him back against his body.

"Would you quit it? You look like a drowned rat! We have to get you home."

To Gabe's horror, Richard surfaced and swam for the boat, dragging Stone's limp form through the water.

"No," Gabe snarled, fighting to pursue, but Max tightened his arms around Gabe's middle.

Richard hurled Stone into the boat, then started the engine. The boat put on a burst of speed and churned up waves as it sped away.

Fury made Gabe gnash his teeth and he slammed his fist down. "Fuck!"

Max gripped him tight. "Next time, Gabe. Next time, we'll win."

Gabe slumped, his head to Max's chest, and watched the moonlight sparkle like scattered gems over the waves.

CHAPTER 23

LOVE

THE REST OF THE agency wolves met up with them nearly thirty minutes later and followed them back to Manhattan. According to them, no other wolves had escaped the island.

The Moonborn cult was officially down to two members, but Gabe didn't feel like celebrating. Not while Stone still drew breath. The pack prepared to part ways and said their farewells at the docks.

Ben patted Gabe's shoulder. "We gave it our all."

Gabe wished he could believe that. "Lobito, let's get home." He touched Max's shoulder and Max bucked out of his hold and walked past him.

Ryan winced. "Someone's in hot water."

Gabe scowled. "Why? What did I do?"

Izzie shrugged. "Aside from being your noble, self-sacrificing self? Who knows?"

Gabe ran a hand through his wet hair, hoping Max would at least want to talk to him when they got home.

The sun was rising by the time Gabe and Max arrived home. Gabe swayed on his feet, grateful his building had an elevator. "Home sweet home."

Max grunted beside him, the most noise he'd made since they'd left Ryan's boat. They took the elevator up to a quiet apartment. Gabe entered

287

his bedroom and flicked on the light. The familiar smells of his home brought him some comfort.

Golden rays of dawn spilled through the slit in the curtain, pooling on the bed. Gabe kicked off his clothes and changed into a robe. He collapsed onto the mattress with a groan as the aches and tension eased. His head felt too heavy to lift, and his body seemed to sink into the mattress. Goddess, he ached to sleep.

He closed his eyes and remembered Stone's blazing eyes beneath the water. They'd come so close to stopping Stone tonight, and Gabe cursed to think he'd let Stone escape his grasp.

He heaved himself onto his elbows as the bathroom door opened. Max walked in, a towel around his red hair. "I told you I'm fine, Mom. I had to go. I needed to be there for the pack. No, you may *not* ground me. Yes, Gabe's fine. Yes, everyone else is fine." He sighed and tossed the towel in the hamper. "Get some rest, okay? Sleep over at HQ. You've earned it. Love you, too." Max hung up and set his phone on the dresser. He stripped out of his damp clothes and into drier ones.

Gabe frowned. "You ever gonna talk to me?"

Max shrugged into a T-shirt. "Sure, when I'm not pissed about what a self-sacrificing, impulsive, reckless—"

"Me? You wanna talk reckless and impulsive? You followed us to the boats after Ben told you to stay!" Gabe gaped, astonished to see Max bristling with anger, so much so Max's face and ears reddened.

Max's shoulders rose up to his ears, fists clenched at his sides. "Why did you have to be a superhero and pull Stone into the water with you!"

"To protect you!" Gabe said. Hadn't he done a good thing? He'd saved Max from Stone's clutches.

"I never asked you to!"

Gabe rolled his eyes so hard he thought they'd get stuck in the back of his head. "You didn't have to! If it ever comes down to my life or yours, I will always protect you, Max."

Max looked ready to explode. "Cut it with the heroic machismo crap! I thought you were gonna die right in front of me, like the seer predicted!" Max blinked hard, furious tears in his eyes. "Now—now I want to kill you myself for being so, so—" Max strangled a growl and Gabe's body reacted, cock twitching to spite Gabe's own frustration. "If you ever do that again, we're done!"

Gabe's heart sank. He lurched to his feet. "That's it? No asking me if that's what I want?"

Max stuck out his chin, arms tight across his chest. He was still cold from their dip in the river, arms rippled with gooseflesh and nipples hard through his thin cotton shirt. "No. I don't give a damn if that's what you want. You're not putting me through that again. Not ever."

"Too bad." Gabe crossed his arms, mirroring Max's stance. "'Cause I'd do it again."

"Yeah, so would I."

Gabe wanted to rip his own hair out. Or kiss Max. He couldn't decide. "You know, I wouldn't have almost drowned if you'd stayed like I suggested!"

Max barked a laugh, fangs sharp. "We both know you'd be dead if I wasn't there to save your ass. But no, you wanted me to stay behind, like I'm weak, like I'm this burden holding you back!"

Gabe gnashed his teeth. "That's not why I asked you to stay, and you know it!"

"It sure seems like it!" Max's eyes blazed.

"It's not!" Gabe's voice filled the room like the snarl of an animal with its back in a corner.

"Then why—"

Gabe latched onto his shoulders. How could Max be so sensitive and observant, yet so oblivious when it came to recognizing his own worth? "Because I couldn't lose someone I love, okay?"

"Neither could I!" Max's eyes widened. Gabe's heart stopped and restarted, warmth blooming in his cheeks. He blinked fast, feeling naked without his anger as the revelation of Max's confession left his throat raw and his eyes hot and wet. Gabe ducked his head, trying to hide his emotions as his hands shook on Max's shoulders.

Max clutched at Gabe's robe. "When you—when you went under, I thought..."

Gabe hugged Max's head to his chest, swallowing around the ache in his throat. "Me, too. I thought I was done for." Max's shoulders trembled. He hit Gabe's chest weakly. "I'm here. Max, I'm here." Gabe laughed, weak-kneed with relief. "I'm alive. The prophecy didn't come true."

"I... I don't think the prophecy was referencing tonight." Max squeezed Gabe's knee. "Think about it—the prophecy alluded to a lunar eclipse. There wasn't one. And no wargs showed up either, whoever they are. Besides, Stone's still alive."

Gabe held on fast to his hope before it could run away. "Let's... let's not talk about this tonight, huh? I'd much rather talk about that confession of yours."

Max *loved* him. No matter what came to pass, in this moment, Gabe had never been happier.

"You—" Gabe faltered, voice cracking. "You love me, Max?"

Max swallowed, the sound loud in the quiet between them. Max's lips thinned, and he blinked fast. "I'm still pissed at you."

Laughter bubbled to Gabe's lips. "I mean, if you wanna break up, I'll honor your wishes, but I may have a thing or two to say in objection—*oomph*."

Max pushed his mouth against Gabe's, and he raised his trembling hands from Gabe's shoulders to frame his face. Gabe parted his lips, moaning his approval as Max's taste danced across his tongue. His hand trembled as he raised it high enough to twirl his fingers in Max's wavy locks.

Max pulled away, eyes dancing with joy as he gazed into Gabe's eyes. He smiled radiantly and claimed Gabe's mouth in a series of quick, hungry pecks. Gabe's blood simmered as he moved away, lips still tingling delightfully from Max's affectionate assault.

Max hummed, contented, and asked, "How are you feeling?" Max rasped his fingertips over the stubble on Gabe's jaw.

Gabe turned his head to place his lips to Max's palm. "Tired," he mumbled.

Max grinned, laughing quietly. Gabe imagined his beard must tickle his skin. "Yeah. Me, too. Hungry, though."

"Starved. Escaping certain death works up an appetite." Gabe's stomach growled longingly.

"Be right back." Max swept from the room. Gabe lay down on the bed and slumped against the pillows, smiling widely when he recalled Max's heated confession. Max *loooved* him! That was hands down the best moment of his life.

Max returned shortly, armed with two microwave meals of meat loaf and mashed potatoes. Gabe managed to prop himself up, wincing at the pain in his side. Their injuries had been bandaged during the boat ride home, but Gabe suspected he'd be sore for a while. Max set the tray in his lap. They ate in comfortable silence.

Max smiled when he met Gabe's eye. "What?"

Gabe cleared his throat, mashing his potatoes with his fork. "So. You love me, huh?" He'd wanted it to be all smooth and casual. Instead, he grinned like the biggest idiot in the world, voice radiating smugness.

A grin bloomed over Max's face, which was flushed bright pink. His shoulders shook with laughter and he put his plate on the nightstand. Gabe almost dropped his food as Max tackled him, arms around his shoulders. Gabe set his food on the comforter and clung to Max's back.

Clearing his throat, voice husky, Max said, "Yeah, I... Of course, Gabe. I... I love you. Like, a lot."

Gabe could have died a happy man then. Max pulled back, their noses inches apart, his breath warm against Gabe's mouth. Max blinked, eyes widening. "What? Was that not good enough?"

Gabe laughed, warmth blooming in his chest. "It was more than enough."

Gabe claimed Max's mouth in a firm kiss, fingers curling in his hair. Max surrendered with a sigh, arms encircling Gabe's shoulders. Their chests touched with every breath; their hearts raced, each beat so perfectly in sync it was hard for Gabe to believe for one second their bodies had been built for anyone but each other.

"Feel it, Max?" His lips caressed Max's with every word. "The way we fit together like this... It's flawless. We're mates, Max; we were fated for each other."

"I know." Max's voice trembled. His breath warmed Gabe's mouth, tempting him closer. "But what about the prophecy? The one where you die or Stone does." Max looked away, exhaling shakily. "Doesn't that still bother you?"

Gabe's stomach churned at the reminder of the shrouded future ahead of them. "It does," he admitted, but nearly losing Max had slotted something into perspective. "I... I don't know what's in store for us. And yes, that freaks me out, but..." He made himself look Max in the eyes and stuck his chin out defiantly. "But turns out I'm more afraid of wasting the time we have than anything Stone could throw at us."

Max looked away fast, biting his lip as if to try and force back the radiant smile that lit up his face. "Me, too." Max resumed eating. "Why did you sound so surprised when I told you that I... you know?" Max's face flushed. "I thought you knew how I felt?"

Gabe poured some more gravy over his own potatoes. "I knew... I guess a part of me was waiting for you to change your mind. To realize you deserved better than the bloody future I'm offering."

"You do know the future can go many ways, right?" Max took a bite of meatloaf. "You could survive. You will. Then there's the vision the seer showed Zach with the little girl. Did he tell you that part?"

Gabe nodded, chewing.

"Well, maybe she was ours."

Gabe almost dropped his fork, a hundred different emotions whirling through him. Could that be true? Was there a possibility he and Max could have a family in the future? That Stone would be out of the picture? He put his empty plate on the nightstand.

Max set aside his food. He gripped Gabe's shoulders and urged him down to the mattress. He leaned over Gabe's chest. "I don't want better. I want you. All of you."

Gabe's cock twitched, his mouth going dry when Max's gaze dropped to Gabe's mouth. Max's breath stuttered as he rocked their hips together. His eyes rolling back, Gabe gripped Max's hips tight.

"So tell that voice in your head to shut up."

Gabe nuzzled his forehead to Max's, arm winding around Max's waist. His fingertips were inches away from Max's round ass, and Max wasn't pushing him away. "Sure. When you realize you're worth every risk I've ever taken for you. For this. Us." Max sighed when Gabe squeezed his buttocks, breath puffing hot against Gabe's neck. Max nipped and sucked at Gabe's neck, fangs sharp and dimpling Gabe's skin.

"Fuck." Gabe breathed, woozy and breathless. "I want you, Max."

Max rocked his hips, his hardness tenting his sweatpants. "You have me."

Gabe curled his fingers in Max's hair. Max's throat bobbed beneath Gabe's lips as he kissed his way up Max's pale throat. He darted his tongue out to lick a stripe from Max's throat to his chin, tasting sweat. Max's chest rose and fell fast against Gabe's body, and Gabe tugged his hair and angled Max's neck for better access, enjoying the little whimpers spilling from his lips.

Gabe's cock swelled beneath his robe, and they hadn't even kissed yet. The musky scent of Max's arousal went straight to his cock. "Gabe," Max said, panting, and Gabe's name vibrated through the thin skin of Max's throat.

Breathing fast, Gabe grabbed fistfuls of his ass, squeezing hard enough to bruise. Max rutted against Gabe's thigh in response.

Gabe attacked Max's neck, kissing a wet trail up to his ear and nibbling the flushed lobe.

"Gabe." If Max said his name one more time... "How far are we—I mean, how do we—uh..."

Gabe nipped his chin, kneading the supple globes of his ass. "Whatever you want. However much you want. Tell me what you want."

Max's throat bobbed when he swallowed. "I want to... I want everything. I want all of you." His face was the color of a tomato.

Gabe touched his lips to the freckle at the tip of Max's nose. "I'm down for that."

Gabe closed his eyes, kissing the cupid's bow of Max's upper lip, the freckle at the side of his mouth. Max's lips quivered when their mouths finally met. Max fisted the fabric of his robe and squeezed tight as Gabe sighed, leaning into Max's body, pleasantly surprised by the firmness of his chest and stomach. He was growing stronger, changing each day in only the best of ways.

He wasn't the little lost wolf they'd found shivering in the bushes, the young man who'd grown weak and fearful in the dark. In this moment, he was stronger than all his demons. Powerful, confident—beautiful, from his freckled face to the depths of his soul. Longing throbbed deep in Gabe's chest and heated his blood.

If Max could rise above all the pain and hurt and still press forward, then it gave Gabe hope that one day his own scars would cease to ache and the memory of his father would no longer be tainted by blood and sorrow.

Fuck. I love you, Max Gallagher.

And he wanted Max, needed him in ways he'd needed no one else.

Needed to claim him, body and soul.

Gabe allowed his hands to wander, gliding beneath Max's T-shirt. He sighed, skimming his fingertips over warm, firm muscle. Max's low moan set Gabe's blood aflame, and Max captured Gabe's lower lip between his teeth. Gabe rasped his fingers through the fuzz on Max's chest, feeling his heart racing as if Gabe held his heart in the palm of his hand. Gabe pinched his perky nipples between his fingers and squeezed tight, pulling a gasp from Max's lips.

Gabe scooted back toward the headboard. He motioned Max over. "Lie down next to me."

Max froze, wetting his lips. He seemed at a loss.

"Nervous?" Gabe's fingers encircled Max's wrist. "Don't be. I won't bite."

"N-no," Max stammered. "I haven't done this before. I mean, I've done some stuff. But nothing like this."

"I had a feeling." Affection tightened Gabe's chest. "If you're nervous, we can stop."

Max shook his head emphatically. "No. I want this. I was just warning you. In case I suck." Max quickly looked away, Adam's apple rising and falling as he swallowed.

Gabe opened his arms. "Come here."

Max obeyed, eyes wide in anticipation. Gabe leaned in, licking Max's plump lower lip, drawing it between his teeth. Max's breath quickened and Gabe's lips wandered, tongue darting out to taste the soft skin of his throat, enjoying the moan that vibrated beneath his tongue. Gabe clasped Max's hand and guided it past his hips. Max sighed softly, squeezing Gabe's hardness through his robe.

"All you've done is kiss me, and I'm hard as hell for you. You're a natural."

Max snorted, ears reddening. He rocked his hips, driving the swell of his heavy cock against Gabe's thigh.

Gabe chuckled. "Not too patient, are you?"

Max shook his head. His warm hands wandered through the opening of Gabe's robe. "I've wanted you for so long."

Gabe's mouth twitched. "How long?" He reached down, squeezing the bulge straining Max's sweatpants.

Max gasped, pushing his hips into Gabe's hand. "I don't know!"

"So, you probably have a few ideas of what you'd like me to do to you, huh?"

"N-not really." Max's red face contradicted him. "I mean, you could do anything, and I'd probably like it."

Gabe raised the hem of Max's T-shirt, sucking a hickey onto the sharp jut of his collarbone. "Giving me free rein?" Oh, he could have a lot of fun with this. "Relax, mi amor. Let me take care of you."

He nudged Max's hips, rolling Max onto his back so Gabe could settle atop him. He gave Max's drawstring a tug, eyes lingering on Max's to gauge his reaction. Max's eyes were wide and the pupils blown, darkening his eyes. Lower lip between his teeth, he arched his hips, urging Gabe on without saying a word.

Fuck.

Drawing Max's pants down to his knees, Gabe swallowed at the sight of tight black briefs teasing the outline of his long cock curling beautifully toward his stomach. Gabe brought his mouth to the fabric of his briefs, tracing the swell of him with his lips. Max was unable to quiet a moan, writhing when Gabe squeezed the bulge of the knot at the base of Max's cock.

He'd never bottomed before, but he'd be lying if he said the thought of Max locked inside him, their naked bodies tied together as they writhed in the throes of pleasure, didn't get him as hard as iron. He'd love for Max to claim him, to show him who Gabe belonged to—if Max didn't die from embarrassment first. He parted his lips, making sure Max felt the heat of his breath, a taste of what was to follow.

Max fisted the sheets with a gasp. "Fuck, Gabe."

"More?" Gabe hooked a finger in the elastic band of his briefs.

Biting his lip, Max nodded. "Yeah."

Max's briefs pooled around his thighs. His cock was beautiful, long and thick, flushed and begging for his hands, his mouth. Then there was the patch of curly ginger hair between his thighs—fuck. Gabe couldn't stifle a growl. He hungered for Max like nothing else. He reached out and Max's whole body shuddered, head falling back against the pillows as Gabe wrapped his fingers around his hot, taut flesh. His foreskin was soft as velvet in Gabe's hand.

Max gasped, his eyes falling shut as Gabe worked him in long, slow pulls. His chest rose and fell, gasps spilling from his lips. Gabe shifted closer, letting his breath puff against Max's shaft. He breathed in and the salty, earthy smell of Max's arousal made his dick twitch. He needed to taste him, feel him hot and heavy in his mouth, hear the sounds Max made when he let his shy side go and lost himself in lust.

Gabe licked from the base to the tip in one long motion. Max grasped his hair in a trembling grip and squeezed. Gabe grunted as Max tore out a few strands. It stung but in the kind of way that sent a heady pulse straight past his hips.

"S-sorry!" Max stammered, loosening his grip.

Gabe pulled off him, running his tongue along the underside of Max's shaft. Panting, Max curled his toes against the sheets. Gabe said, "Be as rough as you want. I can take it."

Max nodded, red right up to his ears, and wove his fingers through Gabe's hair. Gabe drew him into his mouth and Max's fingers curled in his hair, tugging him forward faster. Gabe obliged, bobbing his head to take him in more quickly.

Max's breaths quickened, brows puckering, and he bit his lower lip to stifle the whimpers rising in his throat. Gabe thought it was likely he could get off on Max's reactions; the sight of Max wrestling to contain his pleasure, knowing he was the one to make Max look so damn sexy, was euphoric.

Max's hips jerked and Gabe pulled back so he didn't choke. Max's face was bright red. "Sorry, I didn't mean—"

Gabe smiled, tracing the head of Max's cock with his lips. "Wanna fuck my mouth?"

Max's eyes went wide, breath quickening. A shallow gasp pulled from his lips as Gabe swallowed his cockhead, lapping at the bitter precum. Max's hips arched, pushing himself deeper in. He was close. He wanted to get off, but he was too shy to tell Gabe.

"Go on," Gabe said, and he licked from Max's hole up over his balls to the tip of his dick. "Choke me with your dick."

Max looked away, face red as his hair. He raised his hips, fucking into Gabe's mouth with increasing urgency. Gabe moved with him, his cock painfully hard as Max glided in and out between his lips.

That was all well and good, but Gabe wanted to step things up. He pulled off Max and left him breathless and shuddery, his hips thrusting into empty air. He glowered, eyes wide and desperate while Gabe opened the nightstand.

He found the lube and coated his fingers. Max's breath hitched as Gabe ran a finger from the tip of his shaft down past his swollen knot, pressing against the tender skin between his heavy balls and his entrance. He circled Max's hole, thumb rasping over the little curls of fine copper hair around his asshole. "Want my fingers inside you?"

Max swallowed and slowly opened his thighs. "Yeah."

"If it hurts, tell me. It might be a little uncomfortable at first." Gabe found himself holding his breath as he pressed the tip of his pointer finger slowly in. Max's breath caught and he made a face but when Gabe looked to him for permission, Max raised his hips. Gabe bit his lip, practically swooning as Max's heat sucked him in. Fuck, if he was this tight around his finger...

He brought his lips to Max's cock, parting his mouth around the swollen head that was leaking for him. Max squeezed the sheets but he wasn't as vocal as before, and his face pinched when Gabe's finger shifted inside him. Gabe curled his finger, and Max's whole body stiffened, a low groan tumbling from his lips. Gabe grinned. He'd struck gold.

"Holy—"

Gabe smirked and moved his finger in a beckoning motion inside him.

Max's claws came out, piercing the sheets as he whimpered. "Fuck! What *is* that?"

Gabe grinned, enjoying his breathless confusion. "It's what's gonna have you howling for me."

"I will not— Oh, oh, *fuuuck...*"

Gabe lapped at Max's cock. Arching beneath him, Max thrust his hips faster into Gabe's mouth. The muscles in his legs tensed, his hips rolling to meet Gabe's every lick and suck. Gabe added a second finger, opening Max up to him, his hole making slick little sounds when Gabe pumped his fingers in and out.

"Oh fuck. That's so good, Gabe. More. Please, please, *please.*" Max tilted his head back, his lip between his teeth as he whined and panted, tightening his asshole around Gabe's fingers. Max flattened his feet against the bed and raised his hips up and down, each time taking Gabe's fingers in deeper and faster. Max whined, his eyes rolling and the muscles in his stomach clenching as Gabe curled his fingers. He was close, had to be.

"Like this?" Gabe thrust his fingers in and out, and Max thrashed beneath him.

"Yes! Oh my Goddess... Yes..."

Gabe lunged to kiss Max, swallowing those needy, desperate moans. He pulled back to lick at the sweat on Max's salty lips. "Fuck. I wanna be inside you so bad, Max." He grasped Max's cock and shuttled his fist up and down the length of him, matching his strokes to every thrust of his fingers.

"Want you inside me, too." Max grunted, and a shiver ran through Gabe when Max wrapped his fingers around Gabe's length.

Gabe's chest heaved. Every stroke of Max's hand was like an electric current up and down his shaft, which was hard as iron in Max's fist. He gave Max's ass a slap, nearly blowing his load when Max groaned. "Gonna fuck you hard. Knot you, tie you to me, make you mine. Want that?"

"Yes! Fuck, yes!" Max bucked his hips to meet every stroke, his voice rising. "So good. So fucking good. Please, Gabe!"

Gabe reached down and swirled his fingers into Max's slick heat, curling them against his prostate in time to every tug on Max's cock. Max's pretty little face pinched in desperation, and he shouted Gabe's name amidst a flurry of breathless curses, his hole tightening around Gabe's fingers. Max's hips shot off the mattress, face twisted in blissful agony as he came all over himself, strings of cum matting in the ginger hair on his stomach.

Gabe pumped Max's cock through his release, squeezing out one last spurt of cum. Max collapsed, one hand over his mouth to stifle his gasps and pants. Gabe groaned, loving the way Max looked covered in sweat and cum. Gabe hoped every tenant on the floor had heard Max scream his name.

Max tightened his fist around Gabe's cock, but Gabe batted his hand away. A primal urge had come over him. He wanted to mark Max, cover him in spunk until he looked totally ruined. Gabe jerked his cock until he threw back his head and snarled, fangs piercing his lower lip when he spilled across Max's chest and stomach, leaving his mark. Max groaned, his torso drenched and flushed from head to toe.

Thoroughly fucked out, Gabe collapsed into Max's arms, gasping and shaking, his heartbeat a roar in his ears. Max's chest cushioned his head, rising and falling rapidly as he caught his breath.

Every muscle in his legs ached, his loins throbbing and tingling. The smell of their combined sweat and sex left him reeling. A contented growl rumbled in Gabe's throat. They would smell like each other, even though they hadn't mated or exchanged bites. Everyone would know Max belonged to him and that he belonged to Max.

Max laughed quietly as Gabe's tongue darted out, licking at the sweat beading on his chest. His arm dropped over Gabe's shoulders, his fingers curling in the hair at the back of Gabe's neck. Gabe propped his chin on Max's chest, content to pass the early morning admiring the dewy glow brightening his face. Max's cheeks colored when he returned Gabe's stare, and he smiled wordlessly. Gabe shimmied forward and tucked his arms underneath Max's shoulders, nuzzling his face into his neck.

"Best birthday present ever," Max said, laughing quietly.

Gabe's eyes snapped open, and he did his best to feign surprise. "What?"

Max's cheeks flushed and he shrugged. "It's my birthday. Don't worry about it. We just started dating. I didn't want to make a big deal over it."

Gabe knew, of course. The thirty-first of July was Max's birthday. They had Max's paperwork, but he'd wanted to surprise Max later. "When were you gonna tell me?"

Max cringed. "We've had so much going on! Birthdays were the last thing on my mind."

Gabe leaned in, pressing his mouth to Max's. He lingered, wanting to communicate every tender feeling he was too flustered to put into words. His hand settled on Max's cheek, thumb running along his cheekbone. He pulled away far enough to be able to look into his eyes. "Happy birthday, Max."

Pink blossomed in Max's cheeks, and his lips trembled as he smiled. "Thanks."

Gabe felt like some kind of sex addict for still wanting Max. He'd never felt so greedy, so insatiable, but to his great delight, Max proved to be quite insatiable himself, and Gabe lost track of how long they stayed in bed. Gabe would never get tired of the way Max fucked into his mouth. It was enthralling to watch him let go, thoroughly red-faced and ravished. The sound Max made, hoarse and desperate, when he came down Gabe's throat would inspire his hottest dreams.

Max's enthusiasm took Gabe by surprise. He swallowed Gabe's cock hungrily, so eager to please as he learned his way around Gabe's body with each stroke and lick. Max sucked on him like he wanted to draw Gabe's soul out through his dick, and Gabe's ears rang so hard when he came, he thought for a moment Max had been successful.

Max was laughing at him. Gabe laughed too, delirious in the aftermath. He hoped Max felt proud of himself—Gabe couldn't remember the last time he'd been so vocal or come so hard. Still laughing, he put his arms around Max's shoulders when he nuzzled into Gabe's neck. Max laced their fingers together against Gabe's chest, sighing dreamily. Gabe's chest tightened and he laid his cheek against Max's damp hair, glad he was here and that they were together.

They hadn't even gone all the way yet, and Max was still the best he'd ever had. Golden rays of afternoon sunlight pooled on the bed, haloing Max's hair and lighting hues of red, gold, and copper aflame. Gabe smiled, realizing he'd never stayed up so late with another guy before.

"Can you die from this?" Max panted, breath warm and moist against Gabe's neck.

Gabe raised his brows, the thought humorously morbid. He planted a hearty kiss on Max's damp forehead. "Probably. What a way to go." He squeezed a plump pink buttock.

Max's little giggle made Gabe's face hurt from smiling. "Sounds embarrassing."

"Maybe for the poor people that find us. Me, I could die right now, and I'd die happy, Max."

"Please don't." A warm hand, damp with sweat, clasped his, squeezing tight.

Gabe rolled over and angled himself so he could kiss his way down Max's neck to his chest, his teeth coming out to nip at Max's pectoral. "And leave you? No way."

Max's breathing slowed and he stared up at the ceiling, seeming not to feel Gabe's attentions to his body. His hand wandered idly through Gabe's hair. "Is this normal?"

The sight of Max's frown unsettled Gabe. "What?"

"This... thing between us?"

Gabe's heart sank. What other poisonous things had Richard planted in his poor head? "Max." He clasped Max's face in his hands and looked him in the eyes. "Two guys together is perfectly normal."

Max's eyes widened. "No, I know that. I meant, am I some kind of... sex fiend or something?"

Gabe grinned and caressed Max's milky thigh. "That's fine by me if you are. What's wrong?"

Max shrugged his shoulders, his face bright red. "We did it twice, and I still... want you. Is that normal?"

Gabe laid his chin on Max's chest, studying the damp hair that clung to his forehead, and then his eyes wandered from freckle to freckle. Max's lips were flushed and swollen from Gabe's attention, and the sight set the blood afire in his veins.

"In my experience, no," he admitted. "I don't know, Max. Aside from a mutual acquaintance of ours, I've never been with anyone more than once. I've never wanted anyone the way I want you." Gabe's heart wanted to burst as Max's eyes went wide. Gabe crawled up to lie face-to-face with him, wanting to memorize every detail of those honey orange eyes. "And I never will. You and me, Max. It's always going to be you and me."

Max's hands were unsteady as they settled on Gabe's jawline, drawing him close. Gabe closed his eyes tight, breathing in deep the smells of their sweat and sex. He was greedy. He never wanted anyone else to know the way Max smelled when he was sweaty and spent, never wanted those sweet eyes to look at anyone the way Max looked at him. The thought made his wolf growl low in his chest.

"You and me," Max whispered, and all Gabe could do was hold him tight as their lips met, his heart pounding hard enough to burst in his chest. He had nothing left to give to anyone else. From the moment they'd met, he'd given every piece of his heart to Max Gallagher.

CHAPTER 24

ONE OF US

Later that evening, Max and Gabe had just returned to the apartment from a run in the park when Max opened the door to a chorus of "Surprise!"

Max laughed, delighted by the sight of Ben, Kendra, Ryan, and Izzie, all wearing party hats. Ryan blew on a noisemaker. "Happy birthday!"

"You guys!" Max bounded over and hugged his mom, then crushed Izzie and Ryan in a group hug. Ben grunted when Max squeezed him too hard.

"Think you popped my back on that one, kid," Ben said, chuckling and patting Max's arm.

Gabe squeezed Max's shoulder. "Guess I fooled you."

Max took his hand. "You mean you knew?"

"Of course! It's all in your paperwork. I just wanted to surprise you."

Max loved him too much for words, so he stood on his toes and kissed him. "Thank you."

"Kendra, come here!" Izzie called, skipping into the kitchen. "I'll show you how to make a tres leches cake."

While Gabe and Max had been out, Ben and the others had stocked the table full of drinks ranging from alcohol to various sodas, and plates of cheese and meat, vegetables and dips. Ryan grilled up some elk burgers on the stove while Izzie and Kendra prepared the batter and got the cake in the pan.

Glancing around as if to make sure no one was watching, though unaware Max had his eyes on him, Gabe stuck his finger in the leftover batter in the bowl and crept out of the kitchen with an approving smack of his lips. He caught Max staring and gave his finger one long, slow suck, throwing him a wink.

Max sighed, his heart rate quickening as a surge of delicious heat swept past his hips. He was having fun, but what he wouldn't give to steal a few minutes with Gabe, feel his large warm hands across his body and that hungry, talented mouth around his cock. Recalling their time together made his body tingle with heat as he tried to stifle a grin.

He never wanted anyone else in his bed. Gabe knew his body as well as Max did, knew where to lick, suck, and touch to make his toes curl. Ever since the day they'd met, Gabe made opening up his body and soul so easy. He brought out a confidence in Max he hadn't known he had within him.

A sly chuckle made his ears burn. "I don't even need to guess what you two have been doing. Man, did you guys even shower?" Ryan had the biggest smirk on his face. "Couple of animals."

Max threw a pillow at him, but he couldn't deny it. He didn't want to deny it.

"Look, I'm happy for you guys. It's been way too long since I've seen Gabe so carefree."

Max bit back the urge to inquire about Zach. He was the only one who hadn't shown up. Despite everything, though, Zach had been there last night when the pack had needed it. Despite Gabe choosing Max over him, Zach had seen how worried Max was and helped him join the pack in the fight. Max appreciated him immensely. Maybe once Zach overcame his heartache, they could be friends.

"I guess Zach's not coming."

Ryan shook his head. "He and Gabe need space. He says it's not personal, but..." Ryan squirmed in his seat. "It'll be a while before he's himself again. But he wanted me to tell you happy birthday for him."

"Oh. Tell him thank you for me." Max was pleasantly surprised.

"Sure thing."

"Ryan, get your butt back in here. The burgers will burn!" Izzie shouted.

Ryan jumped. "Hey, in another year you'll be able to drink with us!" He clapped Max on the back and hurried to the kitchen.

Across the room, Ben and Gabe chatted over whiskey on the rocks. Max approached Ben, who raised his glass in greeting. Gabe went into the kitchen to make a salad. "Birthday boy! How's twenty feel?"

"Pretty good," Max admitted, dropping into the armchair beside him.

Ben glanced at Kendra, then splashed a little of his whiskey in Max's empty glass. "Don't tell."

Max sniffed and winced. The scent had surely burned off a few of his nose hairs.

"I didn't see any of those wolves with the tree tattoo during our raid on North Brother."

"I know. It's concerning that they're still out there." A shiver ran through Ben and he took a drink.

"You didn't think they were Moonborn. Did you ever find out who they are?"

"I looked up that symbol on their fur. Only one group uses it: the Wargs of the Apocalypse."

"Wargs? What's that?"

"Wargs of the Apocalypse. A terrorist group. No, they're not actually wargs from Norse mythology, just your run-of-the-mill werewolf supremacists. They're the same kind of crazy as Stone. They kill anyone they perceive is perpetuating the oppression of werewolves—humans, werewolves who ally with humans, and of course hybrids are on their shit list since they represent human-werewolf couplings."

"Makes sense they'd ally with Stone."

Ben grimaced. "This is a new development. Moonborn have been around for years. I think we'd have heard sooner if Stone was working with a terrorist group. Shit, saying that aloud makes my hair stand on end. The Wargs and the Moonborn combined could make one hell of a nasty cocktail. Hopefully, with the cult destroyed, the Wargs will go back into the shadows."

Max gulped down the whiskey. "Whoa!" He coughed, alarmed by how it burned his throat and settled like fire in his gut.

Ben pulled out his phone. "There's something I wanted to talk to you about. I have an old friend who works as a historian on the Council of Lycanthrope Affairs."

"Wow. You have friends in high places."

The Council had been founded back in the sixties after the Lupine Riots. Max vaguely recalled learning about the Lupine Riots in school. Werewolves all over the country had demanded equal treatment from humans after years of everything from don't-ask-don't-tell tolerance to downright hostility from humans, and the protests had turned bloody.

The Council was the reason shifters could coexist with the non-paranormal. Each councilmember represented one of the fifty states, and they worked alongside a human governor to make sure shifters and humans weren't stepping on each other's toes.

"His name's Greg. I reached out to him, asking about why the cult might be interested in a red wolf specifically. He wanted to talk to you directly. Wanna talk to him now?"

Max's heart lurched. He could finally get an answer to the question that had been nagging him since the cult first abducted him. "Sure."

Ben motioned for Max to follow him somewhere quieter, and they went and sat in the guest bedroom. Ben video called and put his friend on speakerphone.

"Hey, Ben! How's it going?" Greg's face filled the screen. He was bald and had a thin face with high cheekbones.

Ben's face softened when he smiled. "Good, good. I got my friend Max here."

"Ooh, the red wolf you mentioned! Hey, Max!"

"Hi," Max chimed in, waving. He elbowed Ben and murmured, "Are you and he part of some bald men's club or something?"

Ben glared at him but without heat.

Greg chuckled. "Wow... Your hair paired with your orange eyes... I can see the red wolf in you, even in your human form. How incredible."

Max squirmed, his face warming.

"Sure, he's pretty," Ben agreed, making Max sputter. "But Stone doesn't want him because he's a handsome fella."

"No, probably not." Greg stroked his chin thoughtfully. "But I have an idea why they might."

Max's heart raced. "Why?"

"Because historically, red wolves have had a connection to the She-Wolf."

Max frowned. "Huh?"

"The first and only red wolves in recorded history were Romulus and Remus from ancient Rome. They were human babies, abandoned in the wild, and the goddess nursed them. It's her only known interaction with humans. Many scholars believe she wished to spread the gift of lycanthropy to humans. From her milk, they gained the ability to turn into wolves. Red wolves, specifically. Their unique appearance suggests the goddess was a red wolf herself."

Max's head was spinning. "So, the cult wants me because of some hypothetical connection to the goddess? How can I even be connected to her?"

Greg shrugged. "Who knows? Perhaps she blessed you for reasons we aren't aware of. Maybe you are very distantly related to the twins and, like ginger hair, your red fur is a recessive trait. But if that were the case, why haven't we seen more red wolves pop up over the centuries?"

Max slumped, rubbing his temples. "Doesn't make any sense..."

Greg hummed thoughtfully. "I hate to confuse you even more, but I have to ask. Have you noticed anything... odd about yourself lately?"

Max laughed. "Everything about me is odd right now."

"I can imagine! I only meant... Hmm. Does anything weird happen when you're around water? Or perhaps, do you feel stronger when the moon is out? Does the moon... speak to you?"

Max shook his head. "No. Why do you ask?"

"Oh." He sounded disappointed. "Well. That would have explained quite a bit, but if you're sure…"

Ben wrinkled his brow. "The hell are you talking about?"

"Nothing, nothing. Just the ramblings of a geeky historian. Back when Stone served on the Council, the story of the twins was one of his favorites. You wouldn't think it, but he was one hell of a geek before he went off the deep end. Anyway, stay safe, the both of you." Greg waved. "I'm going to reread the story of the twins once more. If I come up with any more theories, I'll be in touch. Ta-ta!" He hung up.

Ben snorted. "What a geek."

"Why did he ask about the moon?"

Ben stood and grabbed his whiskey from the end table. "Hell if I know. But he's a smart guy. Maybe he'll brainstorm and get back to us." They returned to the living room and sat on the sofa together. "Anyway, happy birthday, Little Red." Ben drank his own drink with ease and gave a satisfied sigh. "The twenties suck. Not gonna sugarcoat it, kid."

Max laughed. He hadn't been expecting him to.

"They're confusing and overwhelming. There's so much you could do, so many possibilities, and it's hard to decide on one thing."

Max knew what he meant. Thanks to the LPA, a whole world was opening up to him. "I know. It's paralyzing."

"Shit. Didn't mean to make you spiral. You don't have to know any answers. Get out there and get your feet wet. Do you wanna go to any colleges?"

"I got expelled before my second year of college."

Ben's lips twisted as he took a gulp of whiskey. "Wanna go back and finish?"

"I do, but I'm not sure what I'd study."

He'd been so indecisive about what he wanted to do with his life. He'd thought for a time he might be a lawyer but now that he'd stepped back for a while and gotten perspective, he knew the law wasn't for him. As for what degrees he might aspire to or even jobs after college—the thought made his head spin.

"What did you do, Ben?"

Ben cast his gaze to the ceiling, stroking his bushy beard in reflection. "Me? Always knew I'd follow in my father's footsteps and lead the LPA. Generations of my family had done similar work to help werewolves, but my grandad founded the LPA, made it all official. My dad grew up in the business, so he trained me to take over. That's what I worked toward for years. I grew up in Ohio in a small pack town where everyone knew each other. I shocked the hell outta my folks when I told them I wanted to move to the big city and work in the new agency office opening there."

"A pack town? No humans at all?"

"Yeah. Some werewolves prefer to live among their own kind. The Council manages each town. Tensions between wolves and humans were so bad in New York, my parents were scared to death when I told them I wanted to leave, but life in that small town wasn't for me. Many choose to stay on pack lands out of fear of humans. Pretty understandable, but I didn't wanna live my life in fear of a world bigger than my own."

"Weren't you scared?" Max couldn't imagine making such a huge life change.

Ben scoffed and shot him an incredulous look. "Kid, I didn't even know what a McDonald's was, and I sure as hell had never ridden the subway before. Shit-myself scared. But I wanted more than what the town could offer, so I left and managed the brand-new branch of the LPA in NYC, the second location to open in the whole country."

"Wow. That's really cool."

Max was quiet, his mind spinning. A thought burst into his head—what if he joined the LPA? He could give back to those who'd supported him, help others who'd been abused and mistreated. "Could I join the LPA?"

Ben's eyes lit up and he smiled. "Sure, but you'd need to go to the Lycanthrope Academy. It's a school specifically for aspiring agents. There are many roles within the agency. We have skilled trackers like Gabe who get ferals off the streets, counselors who specialize in restoring humanity. We look for missing persons, do search and rescue. Oh, and you gotta brush up on your knowledge of shifter law, understand the dos and don'ts of—"

Max blinked fast, his brain struggling to keep pace with all the requirements.

Ben chuckled and clapped him on the shoulder. He squeezed tight. "Kid, you'd be a natural."

Max flushed, warm to the depths of his soul. "So you think I should try?"

"What're you asking me for? That's up to you!"

Max liked the idea. He'd love to help others like him recover from the scars of their past.

Color rose to Ben's cheeks. "Actually, I've been hoping you'd ask for a while now. I think you'd be a great fit for the agency. So..." He reached into his pocket and pulled out a rectangular box wrapped in blue paper. "I had something made for you."

Max smiled, his own face heating up. "You didn't have to."

Ben rolled his eyes. "It's your birthday. 'Course I did."

Max took the box, surprised by the weight of it. Kendra and Izzie sat in the armchairs across from the sofa. Ryan leaned over the back of the couch. "Open it!"

Ben rekindled his interest in his whiskey while Max admired the silky blue ribbon tied with care. His heart pounded. Max removed the wrapping paper and opened the box. His breath caught.

Inside was a pewter badge in the shape of a wolf's paw print. The Lycanthrope Protection Agency was inscribed on it. Below that, in the center of the paw, was a name: Maxwell Gallagher. Max ran his fingers over the indentations of his name, at a loss for words.

"It's still your choice, of course." Ben's face was hideously red as he went on sipping his whiskey. "Know that whenever you're ready, the door's open, kid. And even if this life isn't for you, you'll always have a place. Here. With us."

Max's heart swelled with emotion, and he pressed the badge to his chest. It was so precious to him already.

"You can't really wear it yet, not in public," Ben was saying, but his voice was far away. "I guess that's silly in retrospect, givin' you a gift you can't even wear."

Max shook his head, blinking hard. It wasn't silly, not at all. It was potential. It was a future. A bright light in a life that had been so dark for so long. It was belonging to something bigger than himself, belonging to a pack.

"Oh Max..." Kendra whispered, wiping her eyes.

Max swallowed hard. "You guys really want me to be part of your pack?"

Ryan grinned and clapped Max on the shoulder. "You have been, man. For a long time. You too, Ms. G." He gave Kendra a silly thumbs-up.

Izzie sat on Max's left and hugged him. "You're pack, Max!"

"One of us, one of us!" Ryan chanted.

Max couldn't wipe away his tears fast enough. He wanted to spend the rest of his life making sure his friends, these people who'd become his family, never regretted making space for him in their hearts.

Max leaned over and put his arms around Ben's soft middle and held on tight, burying his face in his chest so no one could see his tears. Ben grunted, and some of his whiskey spilled on Max's back.

"Thank you," Max croaked.

It wasn't enough, not nearly, but there weren't enough words in the universe to describe what this meant to him. What it meant to know that he was loved, despite his baggage and his shortcomings, for all he was and wasn't—unconditionally.

"Shit, you guys, I'm gonna cry now!" Ryan ran around to the front of the couch and joined the group hug.

The awkward tension left Ben's body, and his big warm hand ran over Max's shoulder. "Happy birthday, kid." He patted Max on the back and let Max hold on tight while he composed himself.

Wrapped in the arms of his friends, his *pack,* Max knew he was one of them. Even if he wasn't an agency wolf yet, that didn't matter. He belonged to them, and they to him.

Kendra hugged Ben, smiling a joyful, watery smile. "Thank you, Mr. Stroud."

"Just Ben." If Ben's face got any redder, it would turn into a tomato.

"We love you both," Izzie assured Kendra, squeezing her tight. "Anyone messes with you two, they mess with us."

Wiping his eyes again, Max left Ben's arms and sniffled, sure he looked like a mess. Across the room, Gabe watched him from the far side of the counter. Gabe's bond blazed like the summer sun in Max's chest, flooding him with warmth. He gave Max a wavering smile so special and tender, and Max's heart felt so full of love. Max went to him and laid his head on Gabe's strong shoulder, sighing as Gabe's arms went around him.

"That wasn't your idea, was it?"

Gabe's chest shook when he laughed, his warm hands running up and down Max's back. "I wish. Ben's way more thoughtful than people give him credit for. He doesn't want people to take advantage of that. Don't worry, I'll think of something equally good to give you."

Max stood on his toes to kiss him, wishing he could find the words to tell Gabe that what he'd given Max was worth a thousand birthday presents.

"Dinner's ready!" Kendra cried, motioning everyone to the kitchen to plate up the salmon salad and elk burgers.

Max joined them all at the table. Looking around, such a feeling of love swept over Max. He wasn't a scared little wolf anymore, broken and bleeding. He was so much stronger now, thanks to this pack who'd made him whole. There wasn't anything he wouldn't do for them.

Izzie's phone rang halfway through the meal. "Ooh, look, Ryan! Zach's calling *me* for a change. Don't I feel special?" She answered, laughing when Ryan threw a piece of tomato at her. "Hey, Zach! We're having tons of fun. You should totally be here. What's that?" Her smile fell off her face. "Hang on. Slow down. Where are you?" She stood up and paced away from the table. "Okay. Pier Six. Got it. Be there soon." She hung up.

"What's going on?" Ryan asked, worry creasing his brow.

"Zach was out jogging and ran into some feral kids who need help."

Ryan pouted. "Why'd he ask you and not me?"

"Because I am awesome." Izzie poked her tongue out at him and they both laughed. She grabbed her purse. Her bodyguard followed her to the door. "Sorry to run out like this, Max. I promise I'll be back soon."

Max waved her onward. "No, no, go! The kids are way more important. Hope you and Zach can help them."

"Be careful," Gabe said around a mouthful of burger.

"We will! Who knows, maybe someday you'll be the one I call when I need help on a job, huh?" She winked and Max's heart warmed. He would like that. Izzie smiled over her shoulder at him, then walked out the door with her guard.

The next hour flew by. Kendra cut the cake, setting aside a piece for Izzie. The cake was so good Max had two pieces. Gabe kept his hand on Max's thigh beneath the table, the weight warm and comforting. Ryan regaled them with stories about his, Gabe's, and Zach's days at the Lycanthrope Academy. Ben watched them all with a fond smile, glass of whiskey in hand. His mother laughed and smiled like the scars Richard's abuse had inflicted were nothing but a distant memory. Max never thought he'd see her so happy and carefree again. Meeting Gabe and the pack had changed their lives for the better.

Max's phone rang. Izzie's name popped up on his screen. Max excused himself and went into the bedroom where it was quieter. "Hey, Izzie. Did you rescue the kids?"

Shaky breathing answered him.

Unease crawled down Max's spine. "Izzie?"

A shivery gasp. "Max... I'm so sorry." Izzie was crying.

Icy dread flooded Max's veins, raising the hairs on his arms.

"Max?" Gabe's voice rippled through his mind. He could sense Max's fear.

"I'm fine. It's nothing." Max thought back. He had to stay calm or else the pack would pick up on his anxiety. He felt for each of the bonds and muted them. He still felt them, but all the emotions were muffled, both theirs and his. He needed the privacy right now.

"He hurt Zach," Izzie croaked. "There were no feral kids. It was a lie. He's here, Max. Made me call you. He's here, and he wants you to come to the piers, or he's going to kill both of us."

"Wait." Max panted, closing his eyes tight. "Izzie, hang on..." His heart was racing, thoughts scrambling as he tried to figure out what the hell he was supposed to do. He made himself breathe.

"Max," Izzie whimpered. "Don't come. Please, you have to stay away. You—" She yelped and fell quiet.

"Izzie?" Max hissed, squeezing the phone. *"Izzie?"* Oh Goddess. No. She couldn't be—

A voice said, "That's quite enough from you, darling."

Fear and fury had Max's jaw clenching. "Stone." The name fell in a growl from his lips.

"Maxwell," Stone crooned. "Do I have your attention?"

Max's fangs dropped, his claws lengthening. "What the fuck have you done?"

"What have *I* done? Your friend Zach's the one who made all of this possible. He's the one who called Gabriel's sweet baby sister. Lured her right into my clutches. I'll give credit where it's due. I had to work hard to... persuade him. Broke his fingers every time they tried to heal. Carved into his flesh. Snapped his leg. How he screamed!"

Max swallowed the acid in his throat. "You're fucking vile."

"Tell me, Maxwell," Stone went on, his voice light and carefree, "Who else do I need to hurt before you show yourself? How about Gabriel's pretty sister? A hybrid who can't heal their own wounds. I could bleed her dry." Fury twisted Stone's words.

Izzie's agonized scream pierced Max's ears.

"Stop it!" Max snarled, his knees shaking so badly he thought he'd fall down. "Stop! What do you want? Tell me, I'll fucking do it!"

"Come to the warehouse on Pier Six within the hour. I'll be as patient as I can, but the smell of blood and fear has always rankled my wolf. I can't promise I'll be able to control myself before you arrive." His voice was wet with saliva. "Come alone. I get even a whiff of your packmates, and your friends will be dead. Am I clear?"

"Okay," Max croaked. "Okay, I'll do it. I'll come, but you let them go. You take me, and you let them all go."

Stone clicked his tongue. "Maxwell, Maxwell... Who do you think you are? The gall of you, setting conditions with me. But very well. I'm a man of my word. Pier Six. You have an hour."

The call ended, and Max's ears began to ring. A wave of dizziness washed over him, and his heart beat so loud and out of control, he thought it would explode. His knees gave out, and Max clutched the dresser for support.

Stone had Izzie and Zach. They would both die unless... unless Max took their place. But it didn't have to be that way. He could open the door and run to Gabe and the others. The pack would spring into action. Stone and Richard would be easily outnumbered.

But the seer's prophecy haunted him. He'd almost lost Gabe the night of the supermoon. If Gabe knew Stone had Izzie, he would hunt Stone down without a second thought. The moon might not be a blood moon tonight, but that didn't matter.

If Stone and Gabe clashed, Max didn't know who would walk away alive, and that wasn't a risk he would ever be willing to take. He couldn't lose Gabe and he couldn't let Zach and Izzie be hurt because of him.

From the day Gabe and Zach had found him, scared and alone beneath the bushes in Central Park, the pack had saved his and his mother's lives. And now... now it was time to save theirs. He'd never given much thought to how he would die.

For a time, he'd thought he'd die alone in Richard's pantry, but then he'd found Gabe and the others. The family he and his mother had always been looking for. If he had to die, then he would gladly die for them, for the pack who had made him whole.

Wiping his eyes, Max turned the knob and opened the door. The voices of Gabe, his mother, and his friends washed over him. They were gathered around the table, laughing and talking. They hadn't noticed him. Max ached to go and join them. His heart longed to say goodbye, to hold Gabe in his arms one last time and see his mother smile.

He turned to the front door, grasping the knob.

Ben called, "Where're you going, Max?"

His heart jumped. Easy. He had to be calm. Forcing a smile, Max turned to face the pack. "I think I overindulged in Izzie's cake. I'm gonna run to the drug store." It wasn't a lie—his stomach really was a mess right now—so his heart didn't betray him.

The pack made noises of sympathy.

Gabe frowned. "I can go for you if you'd like to lie down."

Goddess. His mate was so sweet. Max blinked away the tears. "No. That's okay. But thank you."

Gabe stood. "I'll make you some ginger tea to wash the meds down." He went into the kitchen.

Throat tight, Max turned his back on the pack.

Goodbye, Gabe, he thought, wishing Gabe could hear him. *Thank you.*

Max opened the front door and closed it softly behind him.

Thank you for giving me someone I would die for.

CHAPTER 25

MAKE YOUR CHOICE

HELICOPTERS ROARED OVER MAX'S head as he ran, the breath tearing from his lungs. He'd raced from the apartment to the train and ditched his bodyguard in the subway, but he'd made it on time. At the end of a long stretch of piers was a warehouse. The sun was setting over the Hudson, staining the sky a blood red. The moon was faintly visible in the darkening sky.

Max shouldered open the door and a shiver ran through him at the wall of darkness ahead. Balling his hands into quivering fists, Max took a step into the darkness. He blinked, his eyes adjusting to the dark. The windows were boarded up so no light could get in. The scent of sawdust clotted the air, obscuring all other smells and threatening to make Max sneeze.

John Stone bared his fangs in a grin, one clawed hand curled around Izzie's neck. Izzie's blouse was ripped and bloody. "Oh, this is too perfect!" Stone began to laugh, eyes dancing with delight. "Not only do I have Gabriel's pretty little sister but his boyfriend, too!"

Izzie shook her head, tears glimmering in her lashes. "No... Max, no!"

Max raised both hands, trying to smile. "It's going to be okay, Izzie. I'm here now." That was when he spotted Izzie's guard dead in a pool of blood a few feet away. Dread coiled like snakes around Max's heart. "Where's Zach?"

"Here, Max," Zach croaked. He was behind Max. Richard had him by the scruff. Zach was barely recognizable. Blood soaked his clothes and matted his hair. They'd tortured him. "I'm sorry." Tears mixed with the blood on Zach's face. "Max, Izzie, I'm so sorry..."

"It's not your fault..." Max looked him in the eyes, needing him to know. He and Zach hadn't been the best of friends, but he knew Zach well enough to know he was loyal to the agency.

"Sons of bitches," Izzie snarled, wincing when Stone's claws cut into her neck. "You made him do this!"

Stone laughed. "Let's make this interesting, why don't we? Come with us, Max, and you'll be given a choice. That's right—you get to choose who walks away tonight. Gabe's sweet little sister or his best friend."

"No," Max whispered. "No. Don't do this. I'll go with you. I'll go, okay? Just let them both go."

Stone scoffed. "*Both* of them? No, no, no. That's not how this little game works! Clock's ticking, Maxwell. Start... now."

Zach panted on the ground, squinting at Max through blood-rimmed eyes. Gabe's friend since college. The man Ryan loved.

Izzie shook her head, lips trembling. Gabe's little sister. His family. Max's friend. Gabe had already lost his father to this horrible man. Losing his sister would kill him.

"I can't do this." Max gasped, shaking so badly he thought he'd fall over. "I can't. Stop. Don't make me."

Zach croaked, "Save Izzie. Stone, you can have me, please—"

Stone snarled. Richard kicked Zach in the head.

"I don't give a damn about you!" Stone sneered. "You're nothing to Gabriel. Losing you would hurt, maybe. But his sweet baby sister. His beloved mate. Now, that would just rip him apart. Might even drive him feral. I could finally break him the way I've always dreamed of. Or... or he might not go feral at all. He might simply roll over and give up. Won't even put up a fight when I bend him over and stuff him full of my—"

"Shut up," Max snarled, claws and fangs dropping. "Let them go! I'll go with you. You can kill me, hurt me, I don't care. Let them fucking go!"

Stone set his blazing gaze on Max, spit frothing on his lips. "Make your choice! Gabe's filthy sister or his best friend."

Zach. Izzie. Oh Goddess. He couldn't do this.

Stone made a buzzer sound that cut through Max's thoughts. "Time's up." His smile sent a chill down Max's spine.

Izzie closed her eyes tight. "Max," she began. "Don't go. Don't—"

Her words died in a choked gurgle. Stone's claws cut through her flesh like it was butter. Blood flowed over her white blouse. Izzie's knees hit the dusty floor. Her eyes rolled back. She fell, skull cracking against the floor.

"Izzie!" Zach wailed.

"No!" The scream tore Max's throat.

Max ran and Stone lunged, his arms flying around Max in a mockery of an embrace, claws slicing like daggers into Max's back. Max kicked and clawed, screaming Izzie's name.

"Walk!" Stone roared, shoving Max back. Richard pointed a gun at Zach. "Walk or he dies here!"

It was like he'd walked into a bad dream. He wanted to wake up. He had to wake up, because this couldn't be real. It wasn't. Izzie couldn't be dead. Her bond still pulsed, but it was feeble like a dying heart. Was there a chance she'd be saved? If they left now, if Zach was still alive, he could get her the help she needed to live.

Stone grabbed Max's throat and forced him back. Max went, taking long strides backward until his back slammed against the exit door.

"Open it," Stone rasped.

Max fumbled blindly for the handle and forced the door open. He stepped out into the darkening piers.

"Max!" Zach called, his voice hoarse. "I'll find you! I promise!"

Over Stone's shoulder, Max had a view of Richard towering over Zach. Richard pulled the trigger. The gunshot drowned out Max's scream as blood burst from the side of Zach's head. He collapsed and didn't move.

The fight went out of Max. He didn't care what happened to him. His friends had just died right in front of him. A wave of numbness washed over him and when Stone grabbed the back of his neck and hauled him along, Max didn't try to fight.

The tears misting Max's eyes blinded him. All he could do was follow Richard and Stone. The roar of helicopters got louder. They were nearing the heliport. Max remembered this place. Richard had a home in the east Hamptons. They'd come to the heliport on occasion to take a ride to his beach house.

"Go get your chopper ready," Stone growled to Richard. "Let me know if the coast is clear."

Richard walked around the chain-link fence and went into the yard full of helicopters. A few moments later, a helicopter's blades began to whir. Richard howled, signaling them. Stone shoved Max ahead into the yard full of choppers. Richard's familiar black helicopter awaited them, but Max doubted they were going to his beach house.

"Drop your phone," Stone ordered. Max pulled it from his pocket and dropped it. Stone crushed it under his boot.

Goddess... he was going to die. He wished he'd held Gabe tighter. Wished he'd told his mother he loved her. Wished he'd had more time to spend with his pack.

"Get inside, Maxwell." Stone leered. "You're going for a ride. The last ride of your life."

Swallowing a sob, Max climbed into the helicopter's dark interior, and the door slammed behind him. Stone climbed up front with Richard.

The helicopter left the ground and soared over the Hudson.

Zach... Izzie... I'm so sorry.

Tears fell down his face, and Max dropped his head against the window.

Goodbye, Gabe. I love you.

Max had been gone a long time. Almost an hour had passed. Max was out of range of their telepathic bonds, so wherever he was, he sure as hell wasn't at the pharmacy. Max's bodyguard had followed Max a few seconds after he left. According to him, Max had suddenly detoured to the subway. Just before the doors had closed, Max had shoved his bodyguard onto the platform. Neither Izzie nor Max were answering their phones.

The fear made Gabe feel feverish. Why would Max have lied to his face about where he was going?

Ben paced, the phone to his ear. "No one's seen them? Are you sure?" He was calling the agency. Hanging up, he glared at the cluster of bodyguards. "Why can't anyone get in touch with Xavier? He went with Izzie!"

Gabe curled his fingers in his hair and panted, heart slamming against his chest. "I'm going out again." He'd found Max's scent when he went looking earlier, but the trail had vanished. He pulled on his shoes and his phone suddenly rang. It was from a number he didn't recognize.

"Hello?"

"Is this Gabe Reyes?" It was a woman's voice.

"Y-yes," Gabe stammered, confused and disappointed. "Who is this?"

"This is Lisa Kim. I'm a doctor at... your sister Isabella is in very serious condition..."

Gabe's ears were ringing. The ground was breaking apart under his feet.

"Gabe." Ben's hand fell upon his shoulder. Gabe barely felt his touch. "What happened?"

His hand shook so badly, Gabe dropped the phone. "Izzie. She's hurt."

The pack sprang into action around him. Kendra's arm went around his shoulders and she escorted him downstairs. Ryan started his car. Ben called Gabe's mother. Gabe was too numb to speak. His sister was in "very serious condition." What the hell did that mean? Was she dying? Panic closed an icy fist around his lungs. Not his sister. Goddess, he couldn't lose another family member.

The car stopped outside the hospital. His knees buckled when he jumped out, and he would have fallen if Ryan and Ben hadn't grabbed his arms. They practically carried him inside. Gabe felt as if he were underwater, choking on the terror drowning him. Then he felt it—Izzie's bond, beating feebly. He came alive, wiggling free of Ben and Ryan. He ran through the halls, following her scent. He crashed through the doors to her room.

Gabe's stomach bottomed out. "Izzie!"

His sister lay in bed. Blood crusted the stitches in her neck.

"Goddess, no," Ben said, voice choked with despair.

"Izzie..." Gabe croaked, collapsing at her bedside. He took her hand. Her ashen face became a blur through his tears. "What happened to you?"

"She's alive." The familiarity of that voice made his heart lurch. Zach stood in the doorway behind him. He wore a hospital gown, and dried blood stained his skin.

"Zach!" Ryan ran from Izzie's bedside and threw his arms around him, nearly bowling him over.

"Healed her." Zach gasped. "Gave her my blood, then rushed her here." There was an especially bloody gash along the side of his head, cutting through his hair.

"What the hell happened to you two?" Ben asked, lips trembling and eyes wide.

Izzie's lashes fluttered. Her brown eyes filled with tears. "Gabriel... they... they took..."

"Shh," Gabe whispered, brushing back her hair to kiss her forehead. "You're okay now. Ma's coming. She'll be here soon, okay?" Fury burned inside him. Whoever had harmed his friend and his sister was—

"Where's Max?" Kendra whispered, echoing Gabe's own question. Her face was white.

Ice fell into Gabe's stomach.

Zach blinked fast, lips trembling. "Stone. Richard. They tortured me. Made me call Izzie. They killed her guard when she showed up. Richard... he shot me. Damn fool's hand was shaking too much, so the bullet only grazed me. Otherwise, I'd be dead. Played dead, waited until he was gone, and healed Izzie. But I couldn't... I couldn't stop them from taking Max." His voice broke. "I'm sorry. I'm so, so sorry!" Tears spilled down his face.

Gabe closed his eyes and told himself to breathe but could only manage a pinch of air as panic froze his lungs.

All the blood drained from Kendra's face.

Ben spoke first. "Where is Max now, do you know?"

Zach whimpered and shook his head.

Gabe's hands shook, breath quickening as he began to piece things together. "Zach," he managed to say, lips numb. "Do you know where Max is?"

Zach's body shuddered with sobs. "Heliport. Pier Six. They... took him away. Don't know where."

Kendra stumbled, eyes rolling back. Ryan caught her before she fainted. Words failed Gabe.

The man who'd killed his father had Max.

Ben whipped out his phone, fingers flying over the screen. "I'm calling HQ. I'll have every agent searching the piers. I'll get them in helicopters to pursue the bastards. We will find him."

Gabe's ears rang, eclipsing all sound. Terror and despair dragged him back down to the basement where Stone had imprisoned him all those years ago.

The monster from his childhood had ripped his heart straight from his chest. John Stone had won. And there in that dark, cold basement where no light could ever touch him again, he screamed in agony and despair as he shattered to pieces.

CHAPTER 26

BLOOD UNDER THE MOON

IF THIS WAS THE last time he would see New York, Max couldn't think of a more perfect view.

The city sprawled out below them, a vista of twinkling lights from the Chrysler Building to the Empire State. In the river below, Lady Liberty's beacon glowed, casting light across the water. Central Park sprawled out below them, a patch of emerald green among the gray jungle of concrete. Gabe's apartment was down there somewhere.

By now, they would have realized something was wrong. They'd be worried sick. Gabe would be terrified for him.

I've caused you so much trouble, and now I'm causing you pain, too. I'm sorry, Gabe. I hope you can forgive me.

Tears burned in his eyes when he thought of Zach and Izzie, dead because of him. If there was an afterlife, maybe he would see them again.

Gray clouds choked out the light of the Empire State Building. On the horizon, bursts of lightning illuminated the clouds. Rain lashed at the windows as they hurtled over the Hudson. Storm clouds swallowed the view of NYC as they left the city behind.

They flew over lakes and rivers and rolling hills, soaring over mountain peaks. Max's stomach churned as they neared the ground. He had no idea where they were, or if they were even in the state anymore.

They landed with a bump atop a mountain, with nothing but dark, rugged wilderness every way he looked. A single radio tower loomed over the trees. Max hoped someone was up there, but he doubted it. The lights were out.

He was going to die out here, alone and far away from home.

"Move, brat," Richard growled, and he slammed a hand into Max's back. Max stumbled forward and Stone's cold hand grasped his arm. His nails dug into Max's skin as he led him into the darkness of the trees. Richard's phone cast a light ahead of them, but Max's feet still caught on sprawling roots.

"Get up!" Stone snarled, wrenching on his arm and cutting off Max's circulation as he threw him back to his feet. Max stumbled into a tree, the rough bark scraping his face. He allowed himself to be corralled through the woods, rain soaking through his clothes and blurring his vision. They stopped suddenly, and an eruption of lightning illuminated a strange stone structure in front of a mirrored lake.

It was an altar, stained green with moss, with roots crawling in through the cracks in the stone like maggots into an open wound. The air smelled of old blood, spattered across the trees, and something else, like lightning slumbering beneath the earth.

"The hell is this place?" Max asked.

Stone sniffed the air. "A sacred grove. Only a few of them in the state. The druids performed sacrifices beneath an oak that once grew here." A cruel smile twisted his face. "The oak's long gone, but we don't need it."

Laughter crawled from Stone's lips, and he squeezed Max's arm. "When Richard brought you to me, I thought you were a filthy hybrid like any other. He kept claiming you were special. That your red fur gave you a cosmic connection to the goddess. I didn't believe him, not until the moon came out. A mutt like you can't even comprehend the gift you've been given. A filthy hybrid is unworthy of such a blessing."

Anger overran Max's fear. "What blessing? I don't get it!"

"You are blessed, boy. Touched by the She-Wolf. Your wolf is special, unique. It's only right that a pure-blood werewolf should harvest it."

He was crazy, he had to be. Max almost laughed. "There's nothing special about me! Richard could tell you."

"Precisely," Richard growled. "You have no idea of the potential you wield. Such a powerful soul is wasted on you."

"It should be mine," Stone growled.

"Ours!" Richard snapped. "You wouldn't have got this far if it weren't for me! I deserve a share, too!"

"Shut up, dog." Stone thrust Max at Richard. He opened his backpack and put on some gloves. "Bind him," he commanded, tossing Richard some chains from his bag.

Richard kicked the back of Max's knee and he crumpled onto the altar. Richard rolled him over onto his back and chained him tight across the altar, saying, "I knew you were special, brat. I knew the moment I saw you. To think, a hybrid of all things would be the key to the salvation of our species."

Max strained against the chains across his chest, but they were tight and made of silver. The strength to struggle seeped from his body as if he were sinking into a bog. His arms were too heavy to lift. He couldn't continue to fight. He had to conserve what little of his strength remained.

The clouds parted to reveal a sliver of the moon. Stone loomed behind Richard, and rays of moonlight gleamed against the dagger in Stone's fist. Richard grunted and staggered forward. His mouth twisted in agony, and he collapsed, cracking his head against the altar as he fell and revealed the dagger buried to the hilt in his back.

Of all the ways Max had imagined his tormentor would finally get what he deserved, this wasn't one of them.

Strange runes upon the dagger's hilt began to glow as Stone ripped the dagger from Richard's ribs. A shuddery gasp made Max jump. Richard was still alive, his mouth twitching, wide eyes fixating on Stone.

Richard gasped in pain as Stone's clawed fingers fisted in his hair. Richard choked, eyes burning with rage. "Why? Stone, you... son of a bitch... After everything..."

Stone smirked. "You had your uses, Richie. Played your part like a good, faithful dog. But only one of us is worthy of the She-Wolf's throne."

Richard's pleas died in a gurgle as the blade flew across his throat. His throat opened as easily as if the flesh were paper. Max closed his eyes tight, stomach churning as Richard gurgled and choked on his own blood. When Max opened his eyes, he wished he hadn't.

Richard's jaw gaped, widening until with a crack, his jawbone split in two. A snout emerged from what had been his mouth. Richard's skull cracked and shattered into a million bloody pieces as, like a snake from its skin, a wolf crawled from Richard's lifeless body, covered in blood and gore. Richard's wolf collapsed, dead, and its body crumbled to ashes that were blown away in the wind.

Max swallowed, realizing this same fate awaited him.

The runes on the dagger pulsed like a heartbeat. "Like it?" Stone's gravelly voice made Max shiver. Stone twirled the dagger in his grip. "It's an ancient thing, made of silver. It was created to rip the wolf from within us, an especially cruel kind of punishment crafted by the druids themselves. But they were all burned or driven into hiding before they had the chance to use it. It never forgot its purpose. And now it exists to serve our kind in the betterment of our future."

Lightning flashed as Stone raised the dagger high, poised to strike deep.

"With your gift at my command, I will invade the She-Wolf's hunting grounds. When she lies broken and bloody with her throat between my teeth, I will claim her powers for myself and be a god! And it will all be thanks to you!" Stone ran the tip of the blade along his bony finger. "It's always bothered me that the She-Wolf could allow humans and hybrids to taint our species. I could never justify that, not even in the depths of my piety. Knowing she'd gift someone so unworthy with her blessing, though... That was the breaking point. The She-Wolf is no longer worthy of the status of godhood. It's time someone more deserving took her place."

"And how exactly will you do that if I'm dead?" Max snapped.

Stone grinned. "Every soul before yours was weak. Yours is strong, as strong as a hybrid's can be. Your soul will survive, I'm sure of it, and I will make it my bitch."

Max closed his eyes. The afternoon he and Gabe had spent together seemed a lifetime ago. He didn't want to die. He wanted to be in Gabe's arms again. He wanted to hold his mother tight.

Goddess. Please. I know I've never prayed but I need you now. Give me one more day with them. I don't want to die.

A light swelled behind his shuttered lids, growing brighter and brighter. Max opened his eyes and the moon seemed so much closer than before, as if he could reach out and touch it. His body felt lighter than before, as if the silver chains were relinquishing their grip on his inner wolf.

The tip of the dagger hurtled toward him. Max closed his eyes tight, trying to brace himself for the end. An explosion pierced his ears, almost drowning out Stone's howl of pain. Something sharp flew across his cheek. Max's eyes flew open. Stone cradled his hand as it smoked, dripping blood. The hilt of the dagger lay in the dirt, the shards of the blade smoking like a fallen meteorite and glittering like stars in the grass.

Max caught his breath, unable to believe it. He was still alive, but for how long? If he couldn't get out of these chains, then he was as good as dead.

"How—how could this happen?" Stone seethed. His lips pulled back from his fangs, eyes blazing feral yellow in his fury. The whites of his eyes turned inky black as he snarled. "Of course... your soul is far too powerful for this simple blade. Of course it didn't fucking work!" Max's heart sank as those furious eyes bore into him. "You ruined it. You fucking ruined everything!"

Clawed hands squeezed his throat, nails cutting into his skin. Max thrashed against his chains, panicking as he struggled to suck in even a pinch of air. It was no good. He'd never break free. He would die on this altar, and no one would ever find him.

No! Gabe. His mother. The LPA. He had to see them again. He couldn't die. He could not die!

His claws came out and slashed to the side, nails piercing Stone's ribs. Hot blood dampened his fingertips. Stone howled and tumbled off him onto the grass. Hope brought back his fighting spirit. For some reason, the silver wasn't working; his wolf was still there, snarling below the surface. Using his feet, he pulled himself toward the end of the altar until the chain pressed uncomfortably close to his neck. He grasped it in his clawed hands and pulled.

The links ripped apart in his grasp and he lurched off the altar as Stone pounced, claws scratching the stonework. Max kicked and thrashed to free his feet and once he was free, he jumped to his feet and whirled around to face Stone. Stone's ears were sharp points, his clothes ripping and straining as his body changed, fur thick upon his face.

The moon called to him as it never had before. He had to answer, and he did so in the only way he could. He raised his head to the sky and sang. The song poured from somewhere deep inside him, through a door deep in his soul that had been locked with doubt and fear. There could be no doubting tonight, and fear would not hold him back.

He was going home.

The earth trembled beneath his paws, the trees shuddering. He became hyperaware of each and every drop of rain against his skin and this strange sensation of lightness about him, as if he were both here and not.

The fury burning in Stone's eyes had been extinguished. A growl rumbled in Max's chest. The rain fell harder, and Stone blinked as it spattered in his eyes. Max felt oddly dry and became aware the rain wasn't hitting him anymore. It flew right over him, hurtling toward Stone.

Stone stumbled backward, squinting at Max as the downpour left him drenched. Thunder rumbled to the growl in Max's throat. Whatever was happening now, the storm was in his favor.

Max charged, spraying water behind him. He leaped over the altar and weightlessness overcame him, as if he were nothing more than a feather in the wind. He flew toward Stone, fur floating around him, the wind silent in his ears. He found the fur around Stone's neck but Stone's claw caught Max across the snout. He stumbled, shaking blood out of his eyes, and Stone pounced. He slammed his paws into Max's ribs and bowled him over into the mud. Fangs fastened around his neck. Max struggled, paws flailing, but he couldn't throw him off and thrashing only made blood seep into his fur.

As unconsciousness came for him, he shifted back to a human. The moonlight glowed, reflecting over the still surface of the lake beyond the altar. As he recalled the rain, how it had flowed in the direction he needed it to, an impossible desire swept over him. He reached out a hand and moonlight glowed at his fingertips.

The waters churned, sloshing restlessly at the shore. The ripples became small waves, churning from the center of the lake. Stone's jaws loosened around his neck, and a frightened whine spilled from his bloody maw.

Max lunged, leaping for high ground as the lake surged forth in a furious tide, consuming boulders, curling around trees. Stone turned to run but the water swallowed him, pulling him beneath the surface. Max shifted atop a boulder, gasping, his hands shaking.

What in the hell had come over him? Had he always been able to manipulate water like this? The moon winked down at him, and then the clouds hid her from sight. The floodwaters flowed back to the lake and gradually stilled. Max slid from the boulder, feet squelching in the mud. He parsed through his memories.

That night when he'd confronted the memories of his painful past, the pond had overflowed. The wave that crashed over Stone and Richard's boat during the pursuit from North Brother Island. He hadn't been in control those times, drowning in anger or fear, but tonight determination had fueled Max with purpose. Whatever these powers were, he could use them to survive.

Lightning flashed on the horizon, illuminating the fire tower. If the tower was still in use, could he use it to get home somehow? He had to try. He turned but saw something move out of the corner of his eye. The lake stirred, ripples spiraling outward from the center.

A head curtained in black hair broke the surface of the lake, clawed hands flailing. Burning eyes set their sights on him. Waves lapped at Stone as he strode from the lake, his eyes intent upon Max. Max curled his fingers.

Hurry, do it again!

But no matter how hard he willed it, the water wouldn't obey. The moon's reflection had gone dark. There was a connection between these abilities and moonlight—and the weather wasn't in his favor. Stone tore from the lake, feet becoming clawed paws as he ran, fangs gleaming.

Get to the tower!

Max turned and ran. The ground shuddered as Stone gained ground, and fangs snapped at his heels. The path twisted and turned, the ground hiking upward, and the fire tower loomed above the hill.

Jaws snapped shut around his heel, fangs driving like a knife under his skin. Stone's weight came crashing down on him, pinning him into the mud. Max landed on his back in cold mud.

Max choked and thrashed but Stone shifted atop him and crushed him into the mud. He was too heavy, too strong. Max tried to breathe and only sucked in water and dirt. He lunged, hands slamming into Stone's bony chest.

Stone cried out in terror, his weight flying away from Max's body. Max gaped, stunned by what he saw. Stone was suspended in midair, flailing and screaming. Surprise stole away Max's fear and a smile tickled the corner of his mouth.

All right. Let's try something else.

If he could suspend things, then maybe he could even do the opposite. Max swung his hands down toward the earth and Stone came crashing down into the mud. He cried out in dismay, hands clawing at the mud, but he seemed unable to move.

"What the hell are you doing to me? Hybrid freak!" He grunted, voice strained as if an immense weight were holding him down.

A grin tugged at Max's lips. "I am a hybrid, but I'm the hybrid that kicked your ass!"

As if to mock him, clouds obscured the moon. On trembling arms, Stone hoisted himself from the mud. A grin tore his face in two. Max turned and ran, slipping on the metal steps of the fire tower. He jumped the stairs and hurled himself at the door. It flew open and Max stumbled inside.

Only cobwebs and a leaking ceiling greeted him. The tower was nothing more than a viewpoint. There was no radio equipment or anything. Despair crawled up his throat. How would he get home now?

Stone hurtled inside the tower. He narrowed his eyes, his fangs bared in a snarl. "End of the line, crossbred bitch." The wind lashed at the windows, making the tower sway.

A terrible idea possessed Max, but he had no other option as Stone came toward him, blocking his only way out. Max closed his eyes and focused on the subtle rocking of the tower. It was old, had probably been here for many years. He tightened his fist and felt the warm glow of moonlight.

The walls groaned, the metal creaking and straining as gravity pushed the tower down. The ceiling shuddered; wood snapped. Max hurled himself flush against the wall as the roof came crashing in, trapping Stone on the other side. Something screeched and Max felt it in his bones, the shuddering of old metal beams as they caved.

Stone flew into the window and Max toppled to the floor as the tower lurched to the side. Max took one step toward the door and a floorboard bent and snapped inches from his feet, falling far below. He got closer to the door with each careful step. If he was quick enough, he could make a run for it and be out of there before the whole thing came crashing down.

"This isn't over, mutt!" Stone screamed, huddling against the wall. "I'll find you! I'll tear you to pieces!"

Max grasped the doorframe as the tower slanted, metal screeching and screaming far below. "No! You'll never hurt anyone again!"

Max threw himself through the door as the cabin caved in, flooding the insides with wood and debris. Max bolted down the stairs as chunks of wood and metal rained down on him from above. The tower lurched forward, and Max flew out into nothingness, latching onto the railing to avoid falling to his death. His feet dangled over empty air, the ground far below him. Rocks hurtled into the trees below as the cliffside crumbled under the weight of the falling tower.

Metal creaked and strained. Any second now it would come crashing down, and Max would go with it. His eyes burned. He'd never see Gabe again.

The tower shuddered and Max lost his grip. His cry echoed into the night air as he fell. He closed his eyes tight, waiting for his bones to break upon the ground, for his skull to shatter. Waited to die in the mud.

But the collision never came. Max's eyes opened to a starry sky, rain spattering cold upon his face. His hair drifted around him as if he were underwater. He looked down to the ground below him, his feet swaying over empty air. Max's arms left his sides, reaching out and feeling the wind curling gently through his fingers. He was... floating?

Before his eyes, the tower fell with an earthshaking crash into the earth below, but Max didn't fall with it. Incredulous laughter spilled from his lips. He kicked out, like he would if he were swimming, and drifted through the air. He did a little spin and found himself stuck upside down. He reached out, kicking and clawing, until his fingertips settled on sol-id ground. Clouds concealed the moon, and gravity came rushing back, crushing him to the ground.

He lay facedown in the grass, struggling to even lift a finger. His body was overly heavy. The sense of weakness gradually faded, and his knees wobbled as he approached the edge of the cliff. The tower lay in ruins below. Wood cracked and snapped and to Max's horror, a clawed hand erupted from within the ruins.

John Stone crawled his way to the top of the rubble, the smell of his blood carrying all the way up to the cliffside where Max stood. Stone ripped a piece of wood from his leg, the blood ceasing to flow as the flesh knitted itself together.

Fangs gleamed in the dark as Stone's lips curled around a malicious smile. Then he was gone, pelting off into the woods. Max was too far away, and he could barely continue to stand. There was nothing he could do, but he was alive. He'd done what he could. It was time to find a way home, back to his mother and the pack, back to Gabe.

The distant stink of exhaust fumes made Max's heart soar. There was a road nearby. Shifting to a wolf so he could move faster, he limped through the trees. As he walked, his wounds ached less, and the blood stopped flowing. The moonlight caressed his fur and to Max's amazement, his wounds healed right before his eyes.

The trees parted to reveal an asphalt road, empty this late in the night except for a tanker truck rolling up the path toward him. Max shifted into a man. They'd freak out at his nakedness, probably speed on by, but he had to try. He grabbed a large leaf to cover himself and ran out, waving his arm wildly.

The tanker slowed to a stop, the window rolled down, and the wide eyes of the driver surveyed him. He pushed up his baseball cap to get a closer look. "Holy shit. What happened to you, kid?"

"I was… camping with my friends. They robbed me. Some friends, huh?"

The driver snorted. "Yeah, I'll say!"

"Can you help? I need to get home!"

"Where are you going?"

"I need to get to Manhattan."

The driver scratched at his untrimmed scruff. "I don't go all the way, but my route is close enough. I'll take you, but first, you ain't sitting your naked ass on my seat. Here!" He tossed Max an oversized hoodie. Way oversized—it went down past his hips. Climbing in, he realized the driver was a big guy with a robust gut and several chins. He took a slurp of soda and stamped on the gas.

"Thanks, man."

"Sure. Just don't tell anyone."

They sped over the highway. Max tried to see through the heavy clouds on the horizon, wishing he could catch at least a glimpse of New York. He'd never felt so far from home.

"Where are we?" he asked.

The trucker quirked a bushy eyebrow. "You went camping, didn't you?"

"Yeah, uh, I was kinda wandering in the woods for a while."

"Jesus. Well, Bald Mountain's that way." He jerked a thumb behind them. Max supposed that was where Richard and Stone had taken him. "Manhattan's about five hours from here, so we've got a ways to go. Shit. Where are my manners, man, you gotta be hungry. Here." He tossed Max a package of chips. "I got more. Just ask."

Max took a grateful, crunchy bite. "Thanks. Hey, do you have a phone I can use?"

He handed Max a phone with a cracked screen. Max's heart raced as he tapped in his mother's number, cradling the phone to his ear while he waited to hear her voice.

"Hello?" Her voice was breathless and wobbly, like she was close to tears. "Who is this?"

For a moment, he struggled to speak as tears burned his eyes.

"Mom, it's me."

"Max?" Her voice trembled. A gasp spilled from her lips, and she started to cry. "Max! Are you all right?"

"Yeah, Mom." He choked through his tears. "I'm okay, I'm fine—"

"By the goddess... We've been looking all over for you!" She broke down in joyful tears.

"Mom, listen, Izzie and Zach were hurt. They're at Pier Six. You and the pack need to get to them, right now!"

"Max, honey, it's all right. Breathe. Zach survived. He brought Izzie to the hospital. She's all right. They're both recovering right now. They'll be okay."

Max couldn't believe what he was hearing. He was scared to hope. He'd watched them die right in front of him. "They're... they're alive? Really?"

"Yes, honey. I promise."

The relief brought a fresh wave of tears to his eyes, and he laughed. "Thank the goddess..."

"Gabe, it's Max! He's alive! Come quickly!"

"Max?" Gabe's voice undid him. He'd never heard Gabe so close to tears before. Max turned away so the driver wouldn't see the tears coursing down his cheeks.

"Gabe. I thought I'd never..."

Sobs tore from Gabe's throat. "Max." He choked. "Max. Max. I thought—"

A smile burst across Max's face, and he wiped at his eyes. "I know. Me, too."

Gabe's laughter made Max laugh, too. Gabe's laugh was hysterical and so unlike him, unhinged and joyous. Gabe caught his breath and asked, "Where are you? Are you okay?"

"I will be. I'm coming home, Gabe. I love you so much, and I'm coming home!"

CHAPTER 27

THE PROMISE

THE DRIVER STOPPED AT a gas station along the highway. "Well, kid, this is about as close to the city as my route takes me. Look, I know you're in a pinch, so I've got no problem taking a detour."

Max smiled. "Thanks so much, but that's okay. My boyfriend is coming to get me."

"He on his way?"

"Yeah, I gotta text him the location." Max thanked him for his help and asked him for directions, which he texted to Gabe. He returned the trucker's phone and thanked him once more, and the trucker left him with some water and more snacks and hit the road.

Max sat outside on a bench, crossing his legs so he didn't flash anyone. He watched as cars came and went, stopping to fill up on gas while drivers ducked inside for coffee or food. His heart raced; he couldn't wait to see Gabe.

The hours dragged by. Bored, he took a walk around the station. Dogs tugged their owners to the grass for a quick pit stop while young children let loose all their pent-up energy and ran around in the grass, their parents following close behind. A few people glanced at Max's bare legs, and his skin prickled uncomfortably.

Max had circled around to the back of the building when the rumble of an approaching motorcycle kicked his heart into gear. He ran for the front of the gas station, heart pounding as a sleek black Harley pulled up. The driver wore a helmet concealing their face.

Max sniffed the air. The breeze carried the smell of leather and exhaust fumes to his nose but buried below that was a familiar smell that brought tears to his eyes. The driver swung a long leg over his bike and closed the distance in swift strides. Gloved hands swept the helmet from his head, and as it clattered to the ground, Gabe Reyes stood before him.

Gabe opened his arms wide, smiling and blinking back tears. And Max ran to him.

Max threw himself into Gabe's arms, clinging to his broad shoulders and holding on tight. Gabe stumbled but caught him, his arms looping around Max's waist. His powerful shoulders quivered when he laughed, and his tears were damp against Max's neck.

Warm, eager lips cascaded kisses across his neck and Max turned his head so their lips could meet. Their noses bumped together in their haste, their lips colliding in a kiss that was all teeth and tongue. Max moaned softly, clasping Gabe's sweaty hair between his fingers as a hungry tongue plundered his mouth, and he struggled to catch his breath between the urgent collisions of their mouths.

Tears leaked out of his eyes as their desperation melted away, and Max traced the shape of Gabe's angular jaw, his thumbs brushing over Gabe's cheekbones. His chest tightened as he wiped away Gabe's tears, and Gabe put his arms tight around his shoulders. A hand clasped the back of his neck and held tight, guiding Max's face to his shoulder.

Gabe's shoulders shuddered, and he gasped against Max's ear, sucking in a quivering breath as his lips sipped at the shell of his ear. "We all thought you were…"

"I know," Max croaked. "I'm so happy to see you." He couldn't believe Gabe was here in his arms. A part of him was afraid Gabe might vanish, as if it were all a cruel dream. How could it be that he was fortunate enough to see him again? "How's Izzie? Zach?"

"Izzie will be okay. She healed so quickly, the doctors may let her leave tomorrow. Zach's in good shape, too. Ryan's never going to let him out of his sight, though. What about you? Are you hurt?"

"No," Max assured him, "Just exhausted."

Gabe drew Max's head to his chest and held him tight, his chest swelling against Max's body to the rhythm of a deep breath in. "You're practically naked, mi corazón. We should get you some clothes." Gabe went to the storage compartment atop the back of the bike and handed him a change of clothes. "Your legs are lovely to look at, but you'll get sunburnt."

Max accepted gratefully. "Thanks." He yawned.

Gabe frowned. "Bet you haven't slept in hours. I passed a few motels, so if you're tired, we can spend the night. But hey, if you're up for the drive—"

Max stood on his toes to cover Gabe's mouth with his. Desire formed a tight knot in his stomach. Gabe's hands wandered, cupping and squeezing Max's ass, and Max moaned his approval as Gabe's fangs nipped his lower lip. He couldn't wait until they were back in the city to share a bed with him, and if the swell of Gabe's cock jutting against his thigh was any indication, Gabe didn't want to wait either.

"Motel it is," Gabe murmured, his breath hot against Max's mouth. "Go get dressed. I need to fill up." He sent Max on his way with a slap across his bottom. Max laughed, his whole face warm as he hurried inside to the restroom. He changed into the jeans and flannel shirt Gabe had brought. Gabe had forgotten to pack him underwear, or chosen not to, which was fine by Max.

Max laced up the sneakers Gabe packed him and rejoined Gabe outside. He was waiting with a spare helmet and helped Max put it on.

"I never knew you rode a motorbike," Max said.

Gabe cracked a grin. "I've had this sexy beast since I was twenty-one. Ever ridden one?"

Max quirked a brow as if to say "really?" "Never. I always thought they were cool. Aren't they dangerous, though?"

"Sure. Same as driving a car can be dangerous." He squeezed Max's shoulder. "Don't worry, I've got precious cargo. I'll drive safely." Gabe threw one long leg across the bike, squeezing the handlebars. Max swallowed, thinking he looked unbearably hot straddling a bike. Gabe popped his helmet on. "Sit behind me and hold on tight."

Max slid onto the leather and wrapped his arms around Gabe's waist—tightly.

"Don't be scared, Lobito. I got this."

The engine roared to life, the vibrations thrumming between Max's thighs pleasantly. He put his face in Gabe's neck, squeezing him tight. A growl rumbled in Gabe's throat, and his shoulders tensed. Max smiled, liking that he got to him. The highway sped by in a blur of lights.

Gabe wove the bike in and out of traffic, gliding ahead of cars. Max hung on tight but found himself relaxing during the ride. Gabe was a competent and confident driver. Max closed his eyes, leaning his head against the leather of Gabe's jacket.

They pulled up outside a motel twenty minutes from the gas station. The motel parking lot was vacant, which relieved Max for some reason. He couldn't look at motels the same way after *Psycho,* Richard's favorite movie, which Max supposed was telling in its own way.

Gabe parked the bike and Max followed him to the front door. A sleepy lobby awaited them, offering coffee, places to sit, and a receptionist's desk. The receptionist gave them a room and handed Gabe the key. They went back outside and took the stairs up to the balcony above.

Gabe let them into their quaint room with a double bed and a cramped bathroom. Max sniffed the air, and though it smelled stale and like carpet cleaner, he didn't smell anything unusual. To be sure, he checked under the bed.

Gabe flashed him a grin. "Looking for where they hide the bodies?"

Max smiled sheepishly and checked behind the curtains, too, which were only hiding a view of the highway stretching off into the distance. Without the faint buzz of traffic, the room would have been totally silent. Max was grateful. He was so accustomed to the noise of the city he couldn't sleep with total silence buzzing in his ears.

"Hungry?" Gabe asked.

"Starved." Last night's dinner seemed so long ago.

Gabe looked out the window and pointed to a pizzeria across the road. "Pepperoni pizza sounds fuckin' beautiful right now."

Max's stomach practically moaned at the thought.

Gabe went to get them a pizza. Max showered and changed into a fluffy white robe. He only had to wait a few minutes before Gabe returned carrying a box that smelled of sausages, pepperoni, bacon, and melted cheese. Max helped himself to a slice while Gabe ducked into the bathroom for a quick shower and emerged in a white robe that was parted to show off his collarbone. Max hungrily eyed his long legs.

Gabe joined him at the end of the bed and grabbed a greasy slice of pizza. They devoured two pieces each and put the rest away to save for dinner. Max lay back against the soft pillows and Gabe sighed as he joined him.

His heart raced as Gabe locked their fingers together and squeezed tight. Gabe met his gaze and Max frowned when he saw the pain knitting Gabe's brows. "Can you tell me what happened after they took you?"

Max took in a breath, trying to compose his thoughts. "I thought it was over for me," Max admitted. He felt sick remembering, but he pushed through it, squeezing Gabe's hand tight. He wanted to get all of this out of his system. Maybe then, he'd sleep tonight.

"They took me to Bald Mountain where there was an altar. Stone killed Richard with this ritual blade. He died, but his wolf didn't. Gabe, I saw it. His wolf burst from his skin! It was so..."

Gabe rubbed Max's arm.

Max gulped, feeling sick. "He wanted to use this weird ritual dagger to carve out my wolf and possess it for himself. But the dagger shattered when he tried. He said something about how he'd use the power of my soul to enter the She-Wolf's realm and kill her. Gabe, the guy wants to be a freaking god."

Gabe's eyes went wide. "Shit. I knew he was cray-cray, but aspiring-to-godhood kind of crazy? Color me surprised."

Max's heart raced. He didn't know how to describe what happened next. "He tried to kill me. I was fucking terrified. I wanted to see you and the pack so badly. Then... something changed in me. Woke up. Gabe, I could control water. I could fly, or make others fly, like gravity was at my fingertips. The moonlight even healed my wounds—" Max felt dismayed when he saw how wide Gabe's eyes were. "I know it sounds so crazy, but you need to believe me. I brought a whole tower down. I—"

Gabe blinked fast, brows furrowed. "No, I believe you. Shit. That explains what happened that night in Central Park. You were suspended, like you were floating. The duck pond was overflowing." Gabe exhaled, scrubbing a hand over his eyes. "It makes sense now, why Stone would want you. Holy shit, Max, this is huge." He pinched the spot between his eyes, closing them tight. "I guess the stories of red wolves having a connection to the She-Wolf were true."

Ben's friend Greg had been right. "I don't understand why or how, but the She-Wolf protected me. And she protected me the night Richard sent me to the cult, I just couldn't remember. Have you ever heard of something like this?"

Gabe shrugged his shoulders helplessly. "Well, I can agree on one thing—you are special, Max, but you didn't need some weird powers from the She-Wolf to tell me that. What happened to Stone?"

Max hesitated to speak. He knew Gabe would be disappointed. "I brought the fire tower down with him in it. He should have died, but he didn't. He got away."

Gabe's face darkened. He said nothing and stared up at the ceiling.

"I tried, Gabe, I really did." Guilt tightened Max's throat. If he'd been able to kill Stone then and there, Gabe's life wouldn't still be in danger. Everything the prophecy foretold could have ended tonight.

"I know. Who knows where he is now, what his next move is? That's good." He smiled darkly. "That means I can still find him. Kill him myself."

Max didn't want to worry about that tonight. He leaned in and touched his mouth to Gabe's. Gabe's lips were still against his, his eyes dark and distant when Max pulled away. "Gabe, there's nothing we can do. What matters is that we're both alive." He framed Gabe's face in his hands. "We're together."

Gabe swallowed hard. "When I realized he had you—I've never been so fucking scared." Tears spilled down his face, dampening Max's hands. It broke Max to see Gabe crying, and it made him whole again to know that he was loved. So deeply loved. He turned his head and kissed Gabe's palm, his knuckles, the tips of his fingers.

Gabe kissed the tip of Max's nose. His eyes found Max's and a quiet sigh slipped from his lips. "You're not someone I wanna lose, Max. You're it for me. I knew the moment I held you."

"Did not."

Gabe rolled his eyes and Max laughed. "Okay, it took me a while. But my wolf knew you were the one. My mate."

Max's chest tightened. He kissed the space between Gabe's brows. "You, too."

A teasing smile tugged at Gabe's lips. "You sure you wanna tie yourself down to me so early? What if you go to college, meet some cute guys?"

A growl rumbled in the back of Max's throat. He gripped Gabe's shoulders, swinging a leg across his hips to pin him to the mattress. "I don't want some frat boy who doesn't have a damn clue what he wants to do with his life. I chose you. Remember?"

Gabe bared his teeth in a smile and bit Max's chin. "Hell yeah, you did. Don't you ever forget that, even if you meet some sexy jock in college."

Max glared him down. "I'm serious, Gabe. Wherever my life takes me, I want you there with me. I want to come home to you. I want to hunt in the park with you every night. I want to eat with you. I want to wake up next to you. I want you."

Gabe looked away, a flush coloring his ears. Damn, it felt good to make him blush for a change. Desire ignited Max's blood and he shifted his hips, rubbing his stiffening member against Gabe's bare thigh. Max pressed his mouth to Gabe's neck, smiling when Gabe sighed.

Max said, "I wanna be tied to you. Tonight. I know it's not a full moon anymore. I know we missed our shot." They could have been mates the night of the supermoon. "But I still want you." He parted Gabe's robe, let his fingers wander across Gabe's warm chest. "I want us to be mated. If not tonight, then someday. Soon."

Gabe's eyes were dark, his pupils huge as he swallowed. Gabe swept aside Max's robe to grab a handful of his ass, squeezing and kneading. Warm lips traced the corner of Max's mouth, then lower, fluttering over his pulse, which raced faster with every hot press of Gabe's mouth. Gabe's low voice vibrated against his throat. "Then get on your back, mi amor."

GABE HAD NEVER BEEN so hard, and all they'd done once their robes were off was kiss. Skin to skin, his hands wandering Max's body, smoothing over his ribs, his fingertips tracing the delicious jut of his hips, slipping underneath his warm thighs to cup and squeeze the globes of his buttocks. He tongued Max's soft lower lip, cock twitching when Max let him in. He fought back the urge to plunder Max's mouth and instead let their tongues caress, savoring the taste of him and the zesty Italian spices that still clung to his lips.

He wanted to take things slow and savor every second. This wasn't some hookup—this was Max. Max, who was beautiful in body and in soul, who was precious to him in a way he never knew anyone could be.

Fuck, I don't deserve this sweet, beautiful man.

Gabe followed the graceful slope of Max's neck to that spot between his neck and collarbone. Closing his eyes, he kissed over warm, freckled skin, feeling his way around Max's body with his mouth. Max sighed, chest rising and falling faster as Gabe suckled a nipple, which was hard and tight under his teeth and tongue. He nipped and worried at it, enjoying the way Max's heart raced beneath his lips.

Max sucked in a gasp, arching his back, and encouraged by his heavy breathing, Gabe ventured lower. He dragged his mouth across the inside of Max's thigh, his teeth coming out to nip at his skin.

Max curled his fingers in Gabe's hair, squeezing when Gabe's mouth neared his cock. The earthy smell of him invaded Gabe's senses. The glistening slit of his cock had Gabe lunging forward, drawing him into his mouth. Max's whole body shuddered, and his hips lurched off the bed. A strangled sound was pulled from his throat as Gabe lapped at the head of his cock.

Max's little whimpers and moans made him want to cut the foreplay short and bury himself deep inside Max. He sucked in a breath through his nose, urging himself to be patient. They had forever to learn each other's bodies as well as they knew their own. Wanting a taste of what awaited him, Gabe flicked his tongue over Max's entrance, and it tightened at his touch.

Gabe fumbled for the lube he'd bought from a vending machine in the lobby. He coated his fingers and pressed one in, his breath hitching as he sank into Max's heat. His tightness urged Gabe in deeper, and he curled his finger, pulling out ever so slightly until he struck the spot that left Max's toes curling. Sweat glimmered on Max's heaving chest as he squinted at Gabe through dark eyes, lower lip between his teeth.

"Good?" Gabe asked, lips twitching in smug satisfaction because he knew the answer.

Max flushed, embarrassed laughter dying in a groan as Gabe thrust against that spot. "So good. Fuck me, Gabe. Come on." Gabe couldn't stifle a groan as Max's hips rocked to every curl of his fingertip.

"Gabe." Max panted, one hand on his cock. "I need you. Please. Now."

His breath caught in his chest, Gabe slicked himself with lube, growling low as the pleasure ran through him. "I know, mi amor. I'm gonna fuck you real good. Make you feel amazing." He draped himself over Max, their faces inches apart. Max drew his knees to his chest. Gabe rocked his hips, biting his lip to hold himself together as he pushed slowly into Max. He was tight and hot, squeezing so perfectly around him, sucking him in deep.

He hadn't realized he'd closed his eyes until he was opening them to check on Max. "Good?"

Max nodded, his chest rising and falling quickly. "Yeah. I think so."

Worried, Gabe leaned down and pressed his lips to Max's. Max gasped, his hips rising as Gabe squeezed the tight knot at the base of his cock. With a gentle roll of his hips, Gabe settled into a slow pace. Max's breath puffed against his ear, hot and wet, and his voice grew louder, more encouraging.

His mouth parted against Max's neck, fangs extending as he nipped at his skin. Trembling fingers squeezed his hair, and nails became claws, driving into his shoulder. It stung, but knowing he was bringing out Max's inner wolf got him more worked up. He drove his hips forward, pelvis slamming against Max's ass. Max's eyes rolled back as he raised his hips up and down to meet Gabe's thrusts.

"Good, Max. That's real good. You're fucking perfect, mi amor." Gabe praised him, breathless and jubilant as he lunged down to kiss Max. The way they moved together... as in sync as only two souls could be when they'd found their perfect match.

The mattress creaked and the sheets rustled, harmonizing with the slick, wet sounds of skin against skin. Gabe worried at Max's lips, sinking his fingers into tousled red hair damp with sweat. Gabe lost track of which tongue was his as they licked into each other's mouths.

Their bodies were so intertwined it was hard to differentiate which hands were whose, which leg was his, whose voice was crying out in a way he didn't recognize as his own. It was as if Max's voice were Gabe's, Max's arms and legs, hands and feet extensions of Gabe's own body. Gabe found unity with Max that he'd never found anywhere else.

Gabe leaned back and pumped his hips, enraptured as he watched his dick slide in and out of Max's body. It was primal, the joy he took in knowing he was fucking Max, that Max was letting him, that they would never do this with anyone else. That he was Max's. That Gabe was his. It unraveled within him, powerful and devastating, ready to ruin him. His cock twitched, his knot already expanding.

Max gasped. "Fuck! Gabe, is that—"

"Want it?" He could hold his knot back. He didn't want to, but if Max felt uncomfortable—

Max clasped the back of his neck, urging Gabe closer. "Knot me. Wanna be tied to you so bad."

"I got you, mi amor. I'm gonna take care of you, give you everything you need." Gabe rocked his hips and Max cried out as Gabe swelled inside him, tying them together.

Max put his arms around Gabe and held him tight, bringing Gabe's face to his neck. "I know. I trust you. I love you. Only you," Max whispered, voice breaking as their bodies came together in slow, powerful movements. "Gabe," he grunted, his cum hitting Gabe's chest and stomach in hot bursts.

Those sweet words, the tightness of him clamping down around Gabe's knot so perfectly—it undid him. Nothing mattered. Not the future or the past. Gabe was home. Wherever Max was, was home.

He collapsed, gasping for breath as his body shuddered. Even the slightest movement throbbed blissfully. They were tied, he realized, and he was unable to pull out of Max's warmth. Fine by him. He could have stayed like this forever and died a happy man, buried to the root inside the man he would someday call his mate.

Max ran his fingers gently through Gabe's hair as his freckled shoulders quivered beneath Gabe. "I'm so happy we're here. Together."

He raised his heavy head from Max's shoulder to check on him. He smiled up at Gabe, skin soft and dewy with sweat, tears glittering in his eyelashes. The sight robbed Gabe of breath.

Gabe's mouth quirked into a smile, and despite the uncertain future ahead of them, his heart was full. "Me, too."

Max shuddered, arching his hips. "Fuck. That feels so..."

Gabe frowned, heart sinking. "Does it hurt? Are you comfortable?"

Max bit his lip. "I feel so full of you. It feels right. Like we were made to fit together like this. Like we're one."

Max's lips were salty with sweat when Gabe leaned down to kiss him. "We are, Max."

Max sighed softly, breath warm against Gabe's mouth. "Don't worry. Okay? Not about Stone and that prophecy. Not about what comes next. This moment's for us."

Gabe swallowed hard, a bitter taste in his throat. "We could have been mated a few days ago, Max. And Stone's still out there. Who knows when he'll come for us?"

Max cupped Gabe's face between his hands. "We'll face him together."

Gabe's throat tightened. "It's going to be dangerous, Max. He took everything from me before. If he takes you, too—" The thought ached too much to continue.

Max pressed his lips to Gabe's forehead. "I chose you, Gabe. The good. The bad. All of it. I'm with you all the way."

Gabe couldn't speak. All he could do was lean in and touch his lips to Max's, clasping the back of his neck to keep him right there in this moment with him. No matter what tomorrow held, Max was in his arms, kissing him as if they had an eternity together.

When they pulled away, Max leaned their foreheads together. Honey orange eyes burned with a strength Gabe had never seen. A promise, come what may. "Okay?"

Gabe captured Max's face between his hands and closed his eyes tight as the fire in those eyes burned bright within him, consuming him with their promise.

"Okay."

CHAPTER 28

WARGS OF WAR

The oil plant went up in smoke, and wolves howled their victory to the night sky. The human workers dragged from the flaming ruins screamed and pleaded for mercy. The firelight illuminated the wolves, each marked with a tattoo of a wolf howling at the base of a tree.

A worker trembled, pale-faced and bug-eyed in terror. "Oh God. Please. Destroy the factory, but let us go! We just work here. We don't condone any of the drilling in werewolf territory!"

Oh, how the humans infuriated him. He curled his fingers and barely refrained from gouging her face open. "And yet you contribute to the destruction of the forests and lands that my people call home." A smile curled his lips. "There will be no mercy. Your kind defiles the land that by all rights should belong to wolves."

"Please," a woman wailed. "I have a family!"

He turned his back on her pleas. "Kill them all."

His wargs snarled and the screams began among the crescendo of ripping flesh and snapping bones. Music to his ears. In destroying this plant and ending their assault on nature, the wargs were one step closer to cleansing the world of human filth.

In his pocket, his phone vibrated. Scowling, he checked the number. It was from an unknown caller with a New York area code. He smiled. About time he got some news out of New York. He winced as a shrill scream blasted his ear. He strode into the woods beyond the oil plant where things were considerably quieter and answered his phone before it could stop ringing.

"Stone. About time. Sorry to hear about your little cult falling apart."

A growl answered him. "Not in the mood for your shit, Councilman."

"Chatty as always. Where are you now, hmm? Expecting me to bail you out of jail?"

"Almost out of New York. Got myself a lift. Lay down in the road, waited for someone to drive past."

"And?"

"A man. He had little children with sweet flesh. I killed them all, ate their innards. Saved the boy for last and made him scream. Then I stole their car."

The councilman made a face. Always so grisly with the details. "Where are you now?"

"Driving without a clue where the fuck I'm going. I need a new plan."

The councilman's brow twitched. He pushed off from the tree he was leaning on. "Tell me you didn't fail."

A growl. "Max Gallagher was so much more than I thought he could be." There was fury and awe in Stone's gravelly voice.

The councilman balled his hands into fists. "What does that mean exactly? Stone, did you siphon his wolf or not?" He gritted his teeth while he awaited Stone's reply, the distant screams starting to wear on him. It really was too much to ask for the humans to die quietly, wasn't it?

"No," Stone finally answered. "The blade... it wasn't enough. It shattered before I could pierce his flesh."

Then the She-Wolf's power was well out of their grasp, and the Wargs would only be measly environmental terrorists. They were meant to rule over humans, and this was how their reign ended? With a whimper! His claws came out, and he swiped at the bark of a tree.

"Do you realize what your incompetence has cost me? My pack? With the She-Wolf's soul, the humans would have been at our mercy! This world would have belonged to apex predators once more. And you fucked it up!"

He paced, ready to hang up. "To think I covered for you all these years. Hiding you from the Council at the risk of my reputation, my career! I sacrificed some of my most devoted wolves in that fucking ambush because you told me the LPA was a threat that needed to be extinguished! My wolves gave their lives because we believed in your goals! And this is how you repay me, with failure and mediocrity!"

"The mutt is still alive. There's still a chance—"

A bark of laughter tore from the councilman's throat. "Like he matters at all! Without a means to siphon his soul, he's useless to me. I ought to tell the Council I've learned of your location, have you hunted like prey, and watch as the Council rips you to pieces. Our cooperation is concluded, Stone."

"Councilman—"

"Your cult is gone. You really think you'll be able to cleanse this world of hybrid filth on your own? I've already risked enough by associating with you, and the risks outweigh the reward, I'm afraid. I refuse to lend any more of my wolves to your cause. You're of no further use to me. Goodnight."

"There's another way! Another weapon."

The councilman paused, his finger poised to end the call with a single swipe.

There was a grin in Stone's voice. "Still there, Councilman?"

"Talk fast." He was growing tired of this conversation. "Tell me what you mean."

Stone tutted. "Don't you know our own history, Councilman? Someone wanted the She-Wolf dead before and almost succeeded. Think."

The councilman racked his brains, parsing through what little lycanthrope history he knew. He laughed as he understood. "Really, Stone? You're going to chase after a legend now?"

"The story of Remus the Betrayer is as real as all our other myths. As real as Maxwell Gallagher and his connection to the She-Wolf. You know the story. You know how close Remus came to ending the She-Wolf's reign. The key to godhood is still within our reach; we just need to find it. What do you want, Councilman? To bend the world to the will of wolves, or continue blowing up oil plants for the rest of your life?"

Gritting his teeth, the councilman turned his face to the moon and reached out his hand. It was far away enough that his palm completely covered it, as if he held it in his hand. Everything he'd ever wanted was within his grasp. If John Stone made him regret trusting him again...

"There's a historian in Alabama," he told Stone. "He's renowned for his knowledge on our myths and legends. I'll send you the coordinates but finding him is up to you. I can't risk exposing myself. He may know the location of the weapon. Don't call me again until you have the information we need."

The call disconnected. The councilman tossed his phone in the air and caught it with a smack in his palm. Face upturned to the sky, he reached out and closed his fist around the distant moon.

"Maxwell Gallagher, huh?" A smile curled his lips as he warred with his disgust. "Who'd have ever thought a hybrid would finally prove useful?"

The hunt, it seemed, was still on.

He howled and his wargs answered him, their voices echoing as they sang their song of war to the moonlit sky.

What's next for the LPA wolves? Don't miss the next installment in the series!

The Lycanthrope Protection Agency #2 – Child Of The Moon

THANK YOU!

Thank you for reading! If you enjoyed, please consider leaving a review on your preferred platform of choice. Indie authors like me depend on word of mouth reviews like yours. Additionally, please consider recommending this series if you enjoyed it! Thank you again!

WANT A FREE EBOOK?

Curious about Jin and Marcus, Max's former classmates who ran into him during his lunch with Gabe? Sign up to my newsletter to receive a free prequel to The Lycanthrope Protection Agency series, Before Moonrise. This novella features forbidden love, friends to lovers, possessive werewolves who adore their mates, and sexy times on a beach, in a barn, and a broom closet just to name a few locations. Additionally, you'll receive bonus content, cover reveals, and news about new releases. What are you waiting for? Sign up at CJRavenna.com!

ABOUT CJ

CJ Ravenna loves to tell stories where the ordinary meets the extraordinary. Her books often feature an explosion or two, possessive and protective werewolves who adore their mates, steamy and swoony romance, and of course a happy ending. Connect with me on:

My website: cjravenna.com
My Facebook group: Ravenna's Ravens
Instagram: @cjravenna
TikTok: @cjravenna
Goodreads: goodreads.com/cjravenna
Bookbub: bookbub.com/authors/cj-ravenna